William Augustine Leahy

The Incendiary

William Augustine Leahy

The Incendiary

ISBN/EAN: 9783337126025

Printed in Europe, USA, Canada, Australia, Japan

Cover: Foto ©Andreas Hilbeck / pixelio.de

More available books at **www.hansebooks.com**

THE INCENDIARY.

THE INCENDIARY

A Story of Mystery.

BY ,

W. A. LEAHY.

CHICAGO AND NEW YORK:
RAND, McNALLY & COMPANY,
MDCCCXCVII.

A PRIZE STORY

In THE CHICAGO RECORD series of "Stories of Mystery."

THE INCENDIARY

BY

W. A. LEAHY.

(This story—out of 816 competing—was awarded the fourth prize in th(
CHICAGO RECORD'S "$30,000 to Authors" competition.)

THE INCENDIARY.

CHAPTER I.

FANFARE: THE PLAY BEGINS.

It was about half-past three in the afternoon when Bertha, the housemaid, came running down the steps, with a shrill cry of "Fire!" and fell plump into the arms of the bake-shop girl, who had seen the smoke curling from Prof. Arnold's window and was hastening across to warn the occupants of his house. The deep bark of a dog was heard within and presently Sire, the professor's old St. Bernard, rushed by the two young women and darted hither and thither, accosting the bystanders distractedly, as if burdened with a message he could not communicate.

"Ring the alarm!" cried Bertha and the bake-shop girl in a breath, as soon as they had recovered from the shock of their collision. Their cry was taken up by a knot of three boys, who, as usual, were the first on the spot; passed along till it reached some loungers on the corner, whose inertia was more gradually overcome; and presently half the neighborhood, as if by a spontaneous impulse, came thronging into Cazenove street, each following his leader, like a flock of startled ewes. Bertha, caught in the middle of this ring of sight-seers, stood paralyzed a moment; then singling out the one man of action, she broke through the crowd and stopped him midway in his advance.

"For the love of heaven, will you ring the alarm?"

The postman turned and scudded to the box. There was an interval of suspense that seemed an age.

"Is there any one in the house?" was the first question of Patrolman Chandler, when he galloped up to the scene. He had been attracted at once by the barking of Sire.

"Mr. Robert," cried Bertha, wringing her hands. "Mr. Robert was in the study." The crowd looked up and measured the swift gains of the destructive element.

"Young Floyd?" said Chandler. Then he rushed into the house and up the first flight of winding stairs, the dog, as he did so, following him with a great fusillade of delighted barks.

"There's some one inside," said the crowd, and the rumor passed from mouth to mouth.

"Fire! Fire!" called Chandler from the corridor window above. "Yell, you fellows, as you never yelled before!"

In response a cry of "Fire!" went up from man, woman and child, bass and treble intermingling, loud enough to have waked the seven sleepers from their trance. But no one stirred inside. Just at this moment the tardy bells rang out the number of the box, and almost immediately, as an engine came rounding a distant corner and the great gray horses bounded up the grade, the uproar began to subside. On, on, past the doomed house, now enveloped in flames, to the nearest hydrant, the driver lashed his pair. The hydrant cover had been thrown off and the first block of coal flung into the engine's furnace before Patrolman Chandler reissued from the door which he had entered.

"There is no one there," he gasped, as if choking with the smoke. But the dog continued to leap about, accosting the bystanders appealingly, until his barks and pawing became a nuisance to several and they spurned him pettishly away.

Now engines from many directions came clattering by and the air was full of clangor. Lines of hose were unraveled, ladders hoisted against the walls, and finally, amid hoarse shouts that pierced the deep sighing of the flames within, a rubber-clad, helmeted fellow, with a nozzle strapped to his body, slowly led a line up to the second-story window, where the fire had apparently started. There was another interval of suspense, orders to and fro, and then a helpless pause. Something refused to work.

But the fire met no such impediment. Suddenly an explosion of uncertain origin shook the air, and the onlookers retreated in terror, as if the ground were yawning beneath them. Of a sudden one, two, three slack, snaky hose lines rounded out, and a burst of foam, battering in window-panes and sashes, inaugurated the great combat of elements—one angry, vindictive, as if ravening to sunder the bonds of control cast about it by the pigmy, its master, the other docile and benignant, but in the end the more puissant of the two.

"Exactly nine minutes from the start before a drop of water fell on that fire," said the bake-shop girl, who was noted for her accurate observation of time. By the "start" she meant the moment when Bertha and she collided on the doorsteps, but the fire must have gained a strong headway before that. For every timber in the house was flaming now. The heat scorched the firemen's cheeks and made frightened children in the windows opposite turn away. All the neighbors were packing up their valuables, preparing for the worst. Singed and blinded, the firemen had been driven back down their ladders and compelled to fight from the street. At 3:40 the district chief ordered a second alarm rung in, and, as this was followed by another explosion, a third alarm immediately after. Amid a great clanging of bells, engine after engine, with drivers standing at the reins and firemen riding backward, drove up and sought out positions of vantage.

With the arrival of Chief Federhen their plan of attack seemed to assume a definite shape at once. The ding, ding, ding, of his light carriage, riding over distended and bedraggled hose, told the impatience of the man on the seat. A tall, gaunt figure, wrapped in a cloak, which he threw off as the excitement grew on him, he first turned his attention to the police and the crowd.

"We want room to do this work in," he cried in a loud voice, and the bluecoats began vigorously routing the onlookers back until the fire was to them like something seen through an inverted opera glass, and the sagging ropes nearly broke under the black weight of humanity which they fended off.

Federhen's practiced eye saw the doom of the dwelling-house. So he called off his engines and threw up ladders against the great mercantile buildings to leeward and in the rear. It was from one of these, presumably the fireworks-room of Schnitzler Bros., that the second explosion, scattered and prolonged like an enfilading volley of musketry, had come, and already a thatch of flame had run around under the projecting roof of the structure. Against this the fire tower was slowly brought into position and sloped over, its tip just topping the eaves, but the axes of the squad sent up failed to make any impression on the solid sheathing of the roof. When the tower ladder itself began to take fire, and a stream had to be played on it constantly, the order was given, none too early, "Come down!" and the firemen's first ambition, to get above the enemy, had to be abandoned for less efficacious measures. Fountain jets, rising from the street, and level streams from the roofs of the dwelling-houses opposite, did their ineffectual best to quench the red thirst of the triumphing element.

"This is glorious!"

"Tristram!"

The girl pulled a dolman over her shoulders, fear simulating cold, before the savage dance of the flames. Their carriage had passed through Broad street, in the rear of Cazenove, a few minutes before, and when the alarm sounded Tristram had ordered the coachman to turn and drive them back.

"Glorious, Rosalie!" he repeated, looking up at the red streamers and the swirling smoke.

"It was just here we met your friend, Harry Arnold," murmured Rosalie. "Did you notice he had only one glove on?"

"Glorious!" echoed her enraptured brother, as a section of the wall fell in, disclosing an oven view like the interior of a Bessemer blast furnace.

"See the horses pawing. The sparks will fall on them. Let us drive away."

"My palette!" was Tristram's answer. "Brush! Easel! Canvas! Oh, the lost chance of a lifetime!"

"Doesn't it make you shudder?"

"Certainly, my dear. That is the very deliciousness of it."

"But the danger!"

"Ah, you know I'm a perfect Bluebeard in the taste for horrors. I really envy Parrhasius his enjoyment in flaying the old slave—or did he flog him? But it's of no consequence which. He tortured him somehow, you remember, and chained him to a stake in his studio, so that he might paint Prometheus' writhings to the life."

But just here something happened which cut short his tirade of irony.

It was on the Broad street side of the Harmon building (such the great six-story structure was called), just where the Marches' coachman had halted their span, that the most pitiful incident of this memorable fire took place. By 4 o'clock everybody conceded that the Harmon building was lost. Occupied principally by dry-goods firms, whose light wares, spread over the counters, were like so much hay to the flames, it needed scarcely more than the touch of a match to convert it into smoke. At the sound of the second explosion hundreds of salesgirls and male employes had rushed to the exits, barely outstripping the fire. It was supposed that all had been warned and escaped, and only a signal shriek from the top story in the rear notified the beholders that human lives were in peril. Looking up, they saw at the windows a dozen girls and half as many youths huddling together with the blanched faces of deadly fear. Thick smoke was already curling up and enveloping them and reflections of the flames, like an aurora rising in the north, were visible behind. The cries they made could not be understood, but their gestures were dumbly eloquent.

"Jump!" came the cry from a hundred throats below.

A teamster pulled the rubber covers off the Protective company's wagon. Firemen and policemen improvised nets of canvas, which they tore from the awnings near by and spread under the shrinking group. Two or three of the girls, who leaped for a telegraph pole on the outer edge of the sidewalk, almost miraculously succeeded in scrambling down. Others climbed out on the ledge and made as if to jump, but drew back from the awful plunge. The fire was upon them now, and one could weep to see the men, brave fellows, coaxing their timid companions to take the leap. One woman of coarser build ran along the dizzy ledge, which scarcely yielded footing for a sparrow, and sprang into the branches of a tree on the corner, her dress saving her at the cost of fearful laceration. Then a form came crashing down into the outspread nets, another and another, without pause, without certainty of aim. Two struck the sidewalk and were carried off shapeless and silent. One young girl's fall was broken by a policeman's brawny arms—no other than Patrolman Chandler. She picked herself up laughing, only to faint away, while her rescuer was borne off groaning. It was all over soon—a tragedy of five minutes— but those who witnessed it felt as if their hearts had been standing still for a century.

"Let us drive away," said Rosalie, a sickness seizing her.

"Yes," answered Tristram; "the people are beginning to stare at you." His sensitive lips were pale and he shut his eyes lest their film of pity should be seen. It was true, some of the bystanders had pointed out his companion to one another as Rosalie March. The face of this beautiful girl had become familiar since Manager Mapletree the season before had persuaded her to come out from the privacy of her home and assume two or three roles in his revival of Shakespeare's comedies. Perhaps they wondered who the gentleman beside her might be. Brother and sister bore each other little specific resemblance.

"What's that carriage halting here for? Do you think this is a procession? Pass on!" cried Federhen to the coachman, who whipped up his horses in a hurry. The police had not yet got around to this side of the block, but the fire chief seemed at all times to be where the crisis was. At a word from him ambulances arose from the very ground and the dead and injured were carried off to the hospital. His straggly gray beard confronted the fire-fighters everywhere, goading on the laggards, cheering the valiant. Indomitable, tireless, he sent them again and again at the ruined shell, drowning the neighboring dwelling-houses meanwhile in a flood of water. The calm air favored him. People said "him," for somehow the forces of salvation seemed to be embodied and centralized in one implacable form. But the wind created by the fire was carrying sparks and brands to a distance of half a mile. The awed spectators winced and scattered at these hot showers. It was still a speculation where the holocaust would end.

If the Southern depot caught, then the whole Bay quarter, a warren of tinder-box tenements, swarming densely with poor tenants, was in peril. To save the depot was to win the day. But special editions of the newspapers, appearing at 5 o'clock, were only able to announce, under half-column scare-heads, that the result was still in doubt; and when twilight came it was not the sunset glow (for a storm was gathering in the overcast sky) which burnished the factory windows across the harbor till they shone like plates of gold.

CHAPTER II.

MIDNIGHT—ALL'S WELL.

"Accident is out of the question, John Davidson." The hands of the clock were moving toward midnight in Klein's restaurant, but mugs were still clinking, dishes rattling and waiters hurriedly cleansing soiled tables with their towels. The freedom of the saloon had been extended to the victorious fire-fighters, who, after supping with Duke Humphrey, were not at all reluctant to lunch with Commoner Klein.

"A health to Carl Klein," shouted one, tossing a tumblerful high in air.

"Your health!" the place echoed, as the whole group stood up and shouted a rousing toast. They were tough, middle-sized fellows, all of them, of the true fireman's build, which is just a shade taller and broader than a sailor's. The smiling old German hovered near and bowed and rubbed his hands in appreciation. To judge from the girth under his apron, he was himself a worshiper of the worthy trinity, breakfast, dinner and supper, which he served. The two men chattering in low tones at a side table had not stood up or noticed the interruption.

"I can't believe it, McCausland," answered John Davidson, the fire marshal. "There is no motive. It's devilish. It's beneath flesh and blood. Four lives already and heaven knows how many more. It isn't in human kind to do that without a reason."

"Mankind is my kind, too," answered McCausland, pleasantly, but in such a manner as to convey the idea that he was a diver of some experience into the deep-sea depths of human turpitude. "But suppose we look at the status quo. Everybody—Wotherspoon, Chandler and all the others—agreed that the fire must have been going some time when the servant-girl ran out of the house. If her story is to be believed, and she never turned a hair under cross-questioning, you'll allow?"

"The girl's fair spoken, I admit that," answered the marshal.

"Then the blaze started in a room two flights above the only fire which was going in the house, and that one a low coal fire in the cook stove. The cook stove and the study-hearth get their drafts from different chimneys. No possible connection there?"

"No," answered the marshal, for McCausland's last inflection had been slightly interrogative.

"The cast-away cigar doesn't fit," continued his companion, telling off the thumb on his chubby left hand.

"There was no tobacco allowed in the house. Mungovan, their last coachman, was discharged for smoking on the sly. The professor was eccentric, you know, and this was the stanchest of his dogmas."

"Well?"

"No boys with firecrackers playing around. It's the lull between the 17th of June and the Fourth."

"No."

"No phosphorescent rat-bane on the premises," went on McCausland, telling off finger after finger. "You heard what the domestic said?"

"Yes; she was positive about that."

"Because they were not troubled with mice. Another accidental cause removed. But if rodents were swarming like flies in a meat shop, I don't see what substance more combustible than the pasted bindings of old books they could have found in that library to nibble. The lucifers were all kept in a safe downstairs, excepting a few for the sleeping-rooms."

"That's true, but——"

"Number six," interrupted McCausland. "What shall it be? Cotton waste taking fire spontaneously? Benzine? Naphtha varnish? Celluloid? None of them about, according to Bertha. I'm at my rope's end. Where are you?"

"Do you suppose they have been as careful since the professor died?" asked the marshal.

"That was only four days ago and the study has been locked ever since. Only opened fifteen minutes before the fire."

"Aren't you done guzzling yet?" broke in a strident tone of command from the open door. Chief Federhen's face was haggard and sooty, and his voice, naturally harsh, had a ragged edge from shouting that grated on the ear like the squawking of a peacock. But the firemen leaped immediately to attention. They did not resent their gray chief's reprimand, for they knew that he himself had gone without any supper at all and that he stood ready at that moment to lead wherever he ordered them to follow. In personal courage, as well as generalship, he was believed to be the foremost chief in the country, and, though not exactly popular personally, he was professionally adored. Only the insurance companies had ever ventured to criticise his bold methods, and they, as everybody knows, are simple-minded idealists, who expect an immunity from fire such as even the arctic regions can hardlly enjoy.

"Take your machine alongside of fourteen, Tyrrell, and keep two lines on the Harmon building all night."

"All right, chief," answered Capt. Tyrrell, and his men followed him out through the curious crowd that stood peeking in on their collation.

"Impossible!" exclaimed the marshal, raising his voice, now that they were nearly alone.

"Impossible, that's what I say," smiled McCausland; "we're not living in fairyland. This is earth, where effects have causes."

"But who would have the heart to set it?"

McCausland shrugged his shoulders.

"If that's your impossible," he replied, "in the case of my own son, I'd rather his defense were a concrete alibi."

Inspector McCausland was a detective of the good old school, renowned in many states and not unknown to Scotland Yard and the keen Parisians. Nature had favored him with an exterior of deceptive smoothness. No vulpine contraction of the muzzle, such as would have suggested the sleuth and invited suspicion. Round, florid, pleasant-faced, a little sloping in the shoulders, decidedly suave of voice and genial in manner, he did not look the figure to be feared. Yet some, not easily frightened, would depart in haste from the neighborhood of Richard McCausland.

"The only living occupants of the room," he continued, unfolding his chain of reasoning to the still skeptical marshal, "at the time when Bertha went in, were the St. Bernard, Sire, whose barking had attracted her attention upstairs, and the canary bird, whose life she tried to save."

"Probably the delicate creature was dead when she opened the door," said the marshal.

"At any rate, it is impossible that an old dog, sleeping on the mat, or a golden-feathered songster, whistling in his cage, could be the author of this fire——"

"And loss of life."

"If the housemaid is telling the truth there was some other cause; and if she is lying," he concluded, arising to go, "it must be to cover up carelessness or guilt, either on her own part or on the part of some one in whom she takes an interest."

Intimate associates found McCausland a rollicking companion; but, in the pursuit of crime, he was a practical believer in the doctrine of total depravity, or, rather, to be just, he knew the potential evil which is harbored in every human heart until some life-or-death temptation effects, perhaps, the wreck of honor and humanity.

"Well, this is another feather in Federhen's cap," said the marshal, cheerily, at the door.

"He must share it with Jupiter Pluvius," answered McCausland.

As dark came on there had been a heavy fall of rain, which dampened the roofs and stifled many a darting tongue and incipient blaze in the vicinity, though it appeared to have no more effect on the body of the fire than so much fuel thrown into its maw. But it had enabled Federhen to concentrate his streams, which before this had necessarily been scattered about, protecting exposed points of danger. In fact, one or two serious subsidiary fires had only been checked with the utmost difficulty. If either of them had extended, and the Bay quarter once fairly caught, 500 poor families might have been ruined and two hotels and one depot would have been included in the loss.

At 6:45 Federhen had issued an order to blow up the Columbia shoe store building. Against the frantic protest of the owners his oracular answer was "Necessity!" and a high-handed jostle of the remonstrants to one side. The magazines were promptly laid and a wide space cleared. Precision and dispatch followed, like two leashed hounds, in the footsteps of the chief. At 7 o'clock, with a mammoth concussion, the middle of the building seemed lifted bodily into midair. Its walls caved in, and at once twenty lines of hose were wetting down the debris, while pickax men began widening still further the breach on the side toward the van of the approaching fire. This corner building laid low, the flames were sixty yards away from the depot, and all their surging and leaping failed to clear the gap. Confined at last, assaulted from every side, drenched, smothered and confounded, they spent their rage in a blind, internal fuming.

Those who returned to visit the fire in the evening, attracted, perhaps, by the noise of the last concussion, witnessed a miraculous transformation. The black night made a spacious and harmonious background for the flames, now a spectacle of sinister beauty, charging heavenward solidly to great heights only to flutter back and writhe at their manifest impotence. The streets below, flushed with rain, were glistening in the lamplight and the awestruck wonder of the crowd had subsided to a mere vulgar curiosity about details. Already the event was old to many, its solemn lesson and the revelation of underlying forces making only a shallow impress on shallow minds. Gangs of rowdies swung to and fro, elbowing respectable sight-seers into the puddles and rendering night hideous with their ill-timed pranks and depredations, like prowlers stripping the slain after battle.

The police were occupied guarding the ropes and ejecting without ceremony all intruders whose credentials were imperfect. Lines of hose lay about in inextricable confusion, half-buried in an amalgam of lake water, litter and mud, while at every corner the engines still sent up showers of sparks, the rhythm of their dull pumping resounding through the city like the labored beatings of some giant heart. Comments on the losses, the injuries, the probable hour when the flames would be conquered, beguiled the ranks of spectators who lined the ropes, those behind crushing forward as the front file yielded place, and drinking in all they could (not much at that distance), until the exhaustion of their interest in turn became evident by their repeated yawns. It was Saturday night, the late night in America, but by 11 o'clock there were gaps in the solid phalanxes and the homeward-bound stream far outnumbered that flowing toward the still vigorous but dull-red and smoke-colored sheet of fire.

Eleven was just ringing when a young man rushed up to the lines stretched across Cazenove street at its junction with Meridian, and half by force, half by entreaty, breasted his way to the rope.

"I wish to pass, officer; my property is among those burned," he said.

"Your property?" echoed the policeman, a phlegmatic-looking fellow. The youth was not over 21 and Higgins had heard this story at least a dozen times within an hour. His orders were to throw the burden of proof in every case upon the petitioner.

"Yes; that is to say, not mine, but my uncle's. I am a nephew of Prof. Arnold and lived with him."

The slight correction which the young man made in his explanation evidently prejudiced his cause in the policeman's eyes—as if confusion were a mark peculiar to the glib kinsmen of Ananias. The youth had slipped under the rope and the crowd craned near, expecting an altercation.

"Get back there!" came the sharp rebuke, and a heavy hand was laid on the young man's breast, gathering up the lapels of his coat and half his vest bosom.

"But my uncle's house is burned, I tell you," he protested.

"Outside!"

"I am also a member of the press."

"Outside the ropes!"

"You're a bully," cried the young citizen, pushing sturdily on his own side and fairly holding his own. "Sergeant!"

The sergeant in charge had come over when he saw trouble brewing and stepped closer at this personal appeal.

"I think you must know me. My name is Floyd. I am a

nephew of Prof. Arnold, in whose house the fire is said to have started.   Am I refused permission to pass the ropes?"

"I'm afraid there's little to be seen of your uncle's house, Mr. Floyd," quietly answered the sergeant, who knew him.   "This gentleman is all right, Higgins."

Higgins nonchalantly moved a few steps off, doubtless reflecting that he had only erred on the side of vigilance.

"But the servants—do you know where they may be found?"

"Try opposite.   They're still at home.   The wind was the other way, you see."

The young man sped up to the site of his former home. One look at the black ruin sickened though it fascinated him.   In that old-fashioned house on the hill he had lived since infancy.   Indeed, he had known no other home, no other parent save the eccentric old professor, his uncle.   On Thursday, the body of Prof. Arnold had been carried away and laid in another resting-place.   Tonight the old home smoldered before him, a heap of blackening embers, wearing no vestige of resemblance to its beloved familiar contours.   But little time was given him for meditation now.

"Oh, Mr. Robert!"

He felt his hands seized in a warm, strong grasp, which did not quickly loosen.

"Oh, Mr. Robert!" repeated Bertha, drawing him into the doorway of the bake-shop and beginning to cry.   "I thought you were burned in the fire.   Where have you been all the time?"

"Only at Miss Barlow's.   How did it happen?"

"It was soon after you left.   The library took fire.   I heard Sire barking and ran down to find out what was the matter, when what should I see but the room full of smoke."

"Ellen is safe, I hope?"

"Ellen went out.   We haven't seen her yet.   But if it hadn't been for Sire——"

They had gone inside the shop and the great St. Bernard jumped up and fondled his young master joyfully, but again with that strange undertone in his barking, as of one who had a tale to tell, if only stupid men folk could understand it.

"What ails you, Sire? Poor fellow! Old master gone; house burned down; getting old yourself. Yes, it's too bad. Good dog."

Sire whined at the sympathy in Robert Floyd's voice.

"Nothing was saved?" asked the youth.

"Not a stitch. But I don't mind if I was only sure Ellen——"

"Are you really anxious about Ellen? I thought she went out?"

"Oh, yes. It was her day out. But when she came back to supper she ought to have looked for me."

"Perhaps she did hunt for you and missed you, or went to her sister's in the confusion. You haven't found a lodging yet yourself for the night?"

"I suppose I'll have to go to my aunt's."

"Mrs. Christenson's. That's the place for you; and take good care of Sire until I call for him."

"Go with Bertha, Sire," he commanded, but the dog had to be dragged away, the tall Swedish maiden laying her hand on his collar.

"Well, your house, as the little girl said in the story, presents a remarkable disappearance."

Robert turned toward the stranger who was so facetious out of season. Inspector McCausland had just parted company with the fire marshal and was sauntering carelessly about.

"How did it happen? Do they know yet?" asked Robert, anxiously.

"I don't," answered McCausland. "Possibly so"— he filliped off the lighted end of his cigar, but it fell into a black moat alongside of the curbstone and went out with a gentle hiss.

"But none of us smoked."

"Perhaps it was of incendiary origin," said the detective. "There have been some strange fires lately."

"It is a mystery," answered Robert Floyd.

CHAPTER III.

SEQUELAE.

"You don't care for 'The Headless Horseman'?" said Robert to little Elsie Barlow, who was sitting on his knee in Emily's parlor. "Which of the stories do you like best of all?"

Elsie shut up her book of fairy tales, trying to think.

"You ask mamma which she likes best, Bessie or me?"

"Oh, Elsie, that's dodging," laughed Robert.

"No, 'tisn't dodging," protested Elsie. " 'Cause mamma don't like either of us best; and I like 'The House of Clocks' and 'The Ball of Gold' just the same as each other."

" 'The Ball of Gold'—what a charming title! Tell me that. It can't help being pretty."

"Well, you see there was a great, tall giant," began Elsie, hunting diligently for his picture in the wonder-book, "and this giant had a ball of gold that rested on a saucer in his castle, just like an egg in its cup. It was round-shaped like a crystal and weighed, oh, ever so many tons. See, there he is."

"Ugh!" Robert shuddered realistically. "What a monster!"

"And oh, so cruel! Every knight that rode by he would challenge him to battle, and the giant would cut off his head and hang them around his belt, and the bodies he would throw to three great, savage dogs. That was all they had to eat."

"What cannibals!"

"Here comes Emily," said Mrs. Barlow, who had been rocking in her chair. The young lady wore a water lily at her bosom and was reading from the Sunday Beacon.

"Six lives lost, Robert," she cried, "and the Beacon has started a subscription for their families."

"But I haven't finished my story," pouted forgotten little Elsie.

"Put it away, dear," said her mother, riding roughshod over the child's wishes, as the best of mothers do. Perhaps these crosses are educational.

The following list printed in heavy capitals was the first paragraph Emily read:

KILLED.

MARY LACY, salesgirl.
FLORENCE F. LACY, bookkeeper.
ALEXANDER WHITLOVE, elevator boy (colored).
OSCAR SCHUBERT, ladder man.
An unknown girl.

"At midnight," she continued, reading aloud, "Rosanna Moxom, a lace-worker, was reported dying, and the injuries of nearly a dozen others are serious enough to excite alarm."

"Did you say the Beacon has started a relief fund for their families?" asked Robert.

"Yes, and headed it with $1,000."

Robert inwardly resolved to make the total $1,025.

"Most of those dead or likely to die," continued Emily, while Robert held Elsie and Mrs. Barlow rocked in her easy-chair, "belonged to the hapless group that had been penned in the top story of the Harmon building. They were employes of the firm of Carter & Hallowell, lace dealers. Shut off by a solid wall from the Cazenove street side of the building, they had not heard the shouts of fire until too late. A broad sheet of flame barred their exit to the stairs, which were midway along the corridor. Over fifteen of the girls, however, had come down safely in the elevator, and Alexander, the colored elevator boy, had promised to make a return trip for the others. He was true to his word and was seen remounting as high as the fifth story. But here the heated iron cables refused to work, and the poor fellow, stuck fast between two floors, unable to escape from his wooden box, must have suffered a martyr's death."

"Poor boy!" murmured Mrs. Barlow. Perhaps she was thinking of her own 17-year-old son, whose death within a twelvemonth had deprived her home of its only masculine presence.

"Heroism!" cried Robert. "It is all around us in homespun, and yet we run back to search for it under togas or coats of mail."

"Oscar Schubert's death was equally mysterious," continued Emily, turning the Beacon inside out. "He was a hook-and-ladder man, attached to company 3, a German, and in every way a valuable servant. The poor fellow left a wife and two flaxen-haired children, whose lamentations at the hospital when the body proved to be that of their father brought tears to the eyes even of the stoical attendants, accustomed as they are to the surroundings of death."

Here Emily was interrupted by a glee of laughter from a romping group downstairs. It was the children coming home from Sunday school. A tiptoe peep at the visitor magically hushed their merriment, but Robert persuaded the youngest to intrust herself to his unoccupied knee, where he held her as a counterpoise to Elsie, inwardly resolving to increase his subscription to $50 for the sake of Oscar Schubert's two little ones.

"But the tenderest sympathy," read Emily, "is reserved for the Lacy girls, sole supports of a large family, the cares of which, however, did not seem to weigh upon their amiable dispositions. They had embraced each other on the ledge before jumping, and leaped together, arm in arm, missing the extended net by taking too strong a horizontal impulse, which threw them almost to the curbstone. In the case of Mary, the elder sister, death was instantaneous, but the features were not marred in the least. The face of Florence, the younger, had been crushed in beyond recognition, yet she lingered on and it was nearly two hours before her heart finally ceased to beat. A feeble mother, an irresponsible brother and several small sisters are left to mourn these truly estimable young women."

During this paragraph Robert's promissory subscription had silently risen to $100. If it continued mounting he would soon have little ready cash to meet his current expenses with. Little Elsie and Bessie, the midget of all, listened wonderingly on his knee; and it is not surprising if during the paragraph that followed, all about money losses and insurance policies and proprietors' histories, his thoughts, startled by a casual mention of Prof. Arnold's name in the reading, roamed away to his own teens, when he used to sit on his Uncle Benjamin's knee, as the little girls were sitting on his.

He called up a picture of the Yorkshire youth who had been brought over to the new world, with a younger brother and sister, by parents richer in virtue than in coin of the world. Both the sons had won wealth and Benjamin fame. Beginning as a gardener, he soon wrung recognition for his botanical learning from a world which he affronted from beginning to end by an independence passing far over the line into the region of eccentricity. He belonged to the rare class of self-made scholars, and a popular herb-balsam of his compounding had laid the corner-stone of a fortune which sixty years of prudent addition had reared even higher than that of his brother Henry, the banker. An Englishman by birth, he had refused to change his allegiance. "Salute the flag you're born under," was the motto he preached; and, consistently inconsistent in this regard, he applauded the equally strong American loyalty of his sister's son, Robert Floyd.

How upright, how unimpeachable, he had been, thought Robert, in his old-school fixity of principle! Overbearing to those he distrusted, irritable among shams, he was charity itself to real merit and to the poor. His pet aversions made a long and amusing list—lawyers, electric lights, theaters, agnostics, cats; but each was only the reverse side of a medal whose obverse was passionate love. If, for instance, he was known to have stoned stray kittens from his garden, he made up for his cruelty by treating dogs almost as human beings.

"You and I have the canine temperament," he would say to Robert, a touch of self-sufficiency mingling with

his character, as is not unusual in really benevolent men.
"You and I have the canine temperament. Thank the
heaven that blessed us, and beware of cats. Two-foot
and four-foot, it's all the same. Feline! Catty!" The
last word was pronounced with all the explosive scorn
which features as incapable of sneering as a hound's
could manage to express. Robert saw the great smooth
face rise before him now, tinged by time and weather to
a pure cherry-wood red, and crowned with luxuriant silver hair fringing out from under the skull-cap. Sometimes, indeed, in the drawn corners of the mouth and the
limpid brown eyes, he had read a true affinity to the noble
St. Bernard who used to lie stretched upon the mat between them.

"Three o'clock, latest. Here's something special."
Emily's rise of tone recalled the young man out of his
dream. Elsie was once more deep in her wonder-book
and Bessie had slipped down from his knee and run to
the window.

"At 2:49 Rosanna Moxom passed away at the hospital,
making the sixth victim of the fire. An employe of John
Kalinovitch, the furrier, who occupied rooms on the same
floor with Carter & Hallowell, has identified the unknown
girl as Katie Galuby, a young Polish maiden——"

"Katie Galuby?" cried Mrs. Barlow. "Can that be the
girl we know?"

"What about Katie Galuby, mamma?" asked Elsie,
looking up.

"She's dead," said mamma, and Elsie's lip quivered at
the awful word.

"A young Polish maiden, who stitched pelts in their
musky establishment. She had probably run the wrong
way," Emily read, "as children will—for Katie was no
more than a child, though a workwoman these two years
—and so, finding herself with the Carter & Hallowell
group, had followed them in their random flight and
shared their unhappy fate. This was the girl Patrolman
Chandler caught in his arms, who laughed and then
fainted away. The smile was still on her lips in death,

and her face looked sweet in its expression of happy innocence, though old, prematurely old and wan."

"Perhaps the poor girl is more blessed out of this
world," said Mrs. Barlow, whose eyes showed that she
herself had not had a fair-weather voyage through life.
The Galubys lived in the next block, where there was a
colony of poor Poles, and she had often spoken to Katie.

"Listen," cried Emily, reading another paragraph:
"Up to 2:30 o'clock no news has been received of Ellen
Greeley, the cook in Prof. Arnold's house. Inquiries
made at her sister's failed to throw any light on the question of her whereabouts. Dark rumors afloat, however,
at a late hour, emanating from an authoritative source
and rapidly taking shape, seemed to put her disappearance in close connection with other mysterious facts, to
the detriment of a well-known young man's reputation."

"I wonder who that can be?" asked Mrs. Barlow, but
before any one could answer a loud murmur in the street
interrupted the quiet party.

"Look, mamma, see all the people coming!" cried Bessie, pulling Mrs. Barlow nearer to the window. Oaths
and imprecations in some unknown tongue thrilled the
little group of listeners.

"It's a riot among the Poles," said Mrs. Barlow. Emily
and Robert at once joined the group in the bay window.

"There he is!" shouted some one in the crowd, pointing, and immediately the covered heads became a sea of
upturned faces—for the parlor was one flight up—foreign
faces, inflamed with passion. A hatless father, brandishing a hatchet, led them on. But whither?

"They are breaking in our door!" shrieked Mrs. Barlow. "And Mr. Galuby at their head."

Almost instantly a volley of stones crashed against the
side of the house and the windows were riddled. Emily
and her mother drew back, with the whimpering little
ones, but Robert stood his ground, watching old Galuby
hacking at the door like a madman.

"What are you doing?" he called down, raising the
sash.

There was a furious ring at the bell, followed by a snap,

as if the cord were pulled out. A small pebble sailed through the open window and struck Robert in the cheek. At sight of the blood, though it was no more than a strawberry splash, Emily seized his arm.

"I must go down and stop this, Emily."

"No, Robert; they are savages when they get excited."

"What do they want?"

"Heaven knows! We have never quarreled with them!"

By this time the mob was augmented by swarms of gamins and roughs of the neighborhood, but a change of tone in the uproar indicated that there was some opposition to their mischief-making.

"It is the police who have come," said Mrs. Barlow, but Emily clung to Robert, so that he could neither approach the window nor go downstairs to the door without violence to the fragile girl he loved. For many minutes she held him there, till the murmurs below were mingled with shrieks of pain, and their dispersion and diminution told of the scattering of the crowd. Mrs. Barlow cautiously peeped out.

"They are arresting Mr. Galuby. He is covered with blood," she cried. Just then came a loud knocking at the front door. Robert tore himself free and ran down to open it. A police sergeant stepped inside.

"What is it all about?" asked Floyd.

"We'll give you safe escort to the cars. Hurry up!"

"Why should I be escorted?"

"Galuby's girl was killed in the fire and the Poles learned you were here."

"What of that?"

"Why, it's all over town that you set it."

CHAPTER IV.

THE INDEX FINGER POINTS.

John Davidson, the marshal, was officially supposed to be endowed with insight into the origin of fires. In fact, he drew a comfortable salary for pursuing no other occupation than this. A swift horse and a buggy enabled him to be among the first to arrive and a uniform of dark blue cloth, such as old sailors cling to, but with brass buttons for insignia in place of the little woven anchor that serves to remind the old salt of his element, entitled him to salutes from fire captains as well as from the rank and file. His written reports were read by insurance underwriters, and his wise shake of the head went a great way with those who knew little about fires and less about John Davidson.

For "old John Davidson," as he was generally known, had one failing which sadly impaired his official usefulness. He was an innate and inveterate optimist. The mild-blue eyes which beamed from behind his spectacles —old eyes, too, that no longer saw things as vividly as they used to—were meant to train fatherly glances on winsome children or dart gleams of approval at heroic hosemen whose sacrifices were rewarded by medal or purse. Indeed, he was very popular in both these functions, for old John Davidson had himself served his country and was comrade John of Sherman post, No. 5. But these kindly orbs were not those of the hawk, the lynx or the ferret, like Inspector McCausland's, of whose small gray pair, eyelets rather than eyes, rumor said that the off one contained a microscopic lens and its nigh fellow never went to sleep.

"John Davidson will never set the world on fire himself," Inspector McCausland had said when the veteran's nomination was first reported. Yet "old John" went his way cheerfully poohpoohing suspicion and really diffusing a globe of good feeling by his presence such as no fox in the police ranks could pretend to radiate.

However, the wisdom of the serpent is called for at times, as well as the meekness of the dove. When Marshal Davidson, against all proof and persuasion, gave out his intention to report the Arnold fire as accidental, originating in some unknown manner, or by spontaneous combustion, owing to the extreme heat of the day (the thermometer having registered 97), it was felt by his best friends that he allowed his optimism to blind him too far.

He had made the same report in the Low street fire, the authors of which, an organized gang of blackmailers, trapped on another charge by McCausland, had just confessed their crime. Such laxity could only embolden the firebugs and encourage an epidemic of burnings. Something must be done, the police department thought, and when they selected Inspector McCausland to work up the case there was a general faith that something would be done.

By Sunday noon the inspector had gathered an array of data, sufficient to give a start to his active faculty of divination. Critics said that his one failing was a slight impatience in feeling his way to a conclusion, or, as his brother detectives expressed it, a tendency to "get away before the pistol shot."

"Going to hang some one, Dick?" asked Smith, whose specialty was counterfeiters.

"Well, we are sowing the hemp," answered McCausland, always ready with a jovial answer.

The first person upon whom suspicion rested was the Swedish housemaid, Bertha Lund. But it did not linger long, or with more than a moth-like pressure, on that robust and straightforward individual. Her story, thrice repeated in response to questions by the marshal, Chief Federhen, Inspector McCausland and the district attorney, had not varied a hair, although each time new details were added, as the questions of the different examiners opened new aspects of the affair.

"Prime proof of her honesty," said McCausland. "The rote story shrinks and varies, but never expands."

So the only fruit yielded by the ordeal which Bertha underwent was a thorough description of the house and household, pieced together from her replies, and McCausland had soon left her far behind in his search for a tenable theory.

The cook, Ellen Greeley, had not yet made her appearance. Bertha professed to have seen her dressing herself in her chamber and gave a clear description of her clothing, for the benefit of McCausland's note-book—green plaid skirt, brown waist, straw hat with red, purple and yellow pompons. Ellen was dressing "uncommonly rich" of late, they said. Bertha had talked with her upstairs and had heard the back door slam about the time when Ellen might be supposed to be departing. It had been the cook's holiday afternoon, and she was going to run over to her sister's, as she generally did, and return for supper, leaving Bertha to keep house.

But her sister had not seen her and she had not returned. A slow, heavy girl, rather apt to take the color of her mood from those around her, she seemed a creature who might be influenced to wrongdoing, but hardly the one to instigate it. So far as could be learned, the plain truth was romantic enough for Ellen Greeley, and she was not accustomed to embellish it with flowers of her own imagination. Nevertheless, after exhausting this subject, McCausland checked her name with the mental note "an accomplice, if anything," and the woman's prolonged absence, together with those "uncommonly rich" dresses she wore of late, the more he dwelt on them, prompted him the more to erase the modifying clause and let his mental comment stand "an accomplice."

But of whom? Ellen's sister and Bertha had both mentioned one Dennis Mungovan, the cook's sweetheart, who, until three weeks ago, had been coachman at the Arnold's. Some repartee, or insolence, when reprimanded for smoking (he was described as a tonguey lout) had provoked his discharge and he had been heard to threaten vengeance behind the professor's back, though at the time his words were muttered they were ignored as a braggart's empty vaporing. Twice he had called to see Ellen at the house, but he had not shown his face since the week before the professor died; and even at his favorite haunt, a certain Charles street stable, all trace of him had been lost. As he was a resident of this country for less than a year he may have crossed the water again to his home, but if this were so Bertha felt sure Ellen would have manifested her lonesomeness. "She had a great heart to the man," said the Swedish housemaid.

"Well, what have you collected against him?" said the
district attorney, to whom McCausland had just been
exhibiting these results of his investigation. They were
alone, save for a bloodhound, in the inspector's office at
police headquarters.

"Opportunity, motive and circumstances. I don't rule
out the other two as accessories, you understand." The
"other two" were Mungovan and Ellen Greeley, who
with Robert had been arranged in a triangle by the detective.

"That remains to be fitted into the developments, I
presume?"

"First, as to circumstances. The young man turns
up about 11 o'clock at a fire which started at 3:30, which
destroyed his own home, and which was advertised all
over the country within a radius of thirty miles before
sunset."

"In itself not a very damaging circumstance. It might
be explained. You have questioned him on his movements?"

"In two interviews," replied the inspector, puffing his
cigar leisurely and watching the smoke curl as though
it were the most fascinating study in the world just then.

"Account not satisfactory?"

"He has none to give." (Puff.)

"What does he mean by that?"

"Memory a blank between 3:30 and 7:30." (Puff.)

"Up to some mischief, then."

"A curiously opportune lapse," said the inspector, his
eye twinkling humorously. "So much for circumstances
after the fact. And now for opportunity."

"Of course the evidence for opportunity will depend
upon the inmates of the house. You are convinced of
Bertha's candor?"

"On my reputation as an adept in mendacity. You
have not found me overcredulous, as a rule?"

"Quite the contrary."

"Bertha was upstairs, Floyd in the study, Ellen, the
cook, had just gone out. After awhile the barking of the
St. Bernard in the study aroused the girl. Something

was wrong. She ran down, opened the study door and fell back before a live crater of smoke and flame. Accident, we agree, is out of the question. The front door was locked. There was no approach to the study (up one flight, remember) from the street, unless you raised a ladder to the window, and half the neighborhood would have seen this. At least I'm sure the bake-shop girl, Senda Wesner, would have seen it. The previous actions of Floyd were those of a criminal meditating crime; his subsequent course until 7:30 he refuses to explain."

"But the motive, McCausland?" said the district attorney gravely. McCausland contracted his beady eyelets till they shone like two pin punctures in a lighted jack-o'-lantern. But a knock at the door delayed his answer. The bloodhound promptly arose, grasped the knob in his forepaws, and turning it skillfully, admitted a mulatto attendant in fatigue uniform, the bloodhound's master patting him approvingly for the performance.

"Officer Costa to see the inspector," said the attendant.

"Send him in," answered McCausland. "One of my fetch-and-carry dogs—willing enough, but no hawk."

"I've looked the matter up," said Officer Costa, saluting, and glancing from McCausland to the district attorney.

"With what result?"

"Dennis Mungovan and Ellen Greeley were privately married on June 18, before Justice of the Peace Gustavus Schwab, at 126 Harlow street," said Costa, as if proud of his morsel of information and its precision of detail.

"Is this our Mungovan?" asked the district attorney, evincing keen interest.

"What was his description, Costa?" said McCausland.

"Native of Ireland, aged 29; a coachman by occupation. The bride a cook, born in New Brunswick."

"Very well done. Will you look over the steerage list of the European steamers for a fortnight back and ahead? We want that couple, if possible."

"I will," answered Costa, in a manner which showed that the compliment was not wasted. Once more McCausland rose and looked out before shutting the door.

Evidently this was another of his mannerisms, and perhaps not the least useful, since one never knows what interlopers may be harking about.

"We have connected numbers two and three of the triangle," he resumed at soon as he was fairly seated, "the interests of Mr. and Mrs. Mungovan being presumably identical."

"I cannot; seriously I cannot credit the charge against Floyd," said the district attorney, "in face of the tender relations known to have subsisted between the young man and his uncle."

"Tender"—McCausland's fat face creased all over into dimples of merriment. "Do young men elope with their grandmothers?"

"Not often," answered the district attorney.

"Neither do they dote madly on their crotchety uncles in the slippers and dressing-gowns of 78."

"Even at 78 I should expect consideration from a nephew whom I had taken in as an orphan and raised to wealth and position."

"Wealth and position! Perhaps that's the rub."

"Just what do you mean?"

"I mean that all was not smooth in the Arnold household; that nephew and uncle were cut too near together from the same block of granite to match; that they wrangled constantly and that one of their wrangles led to this very crisis of the will."

"A will?" echoed the district attorney.

"A will" (puff), smiled McCausland, relapsing into silence.

"Prof. Arnold left a will?" repeated the district attorney, slowly, but McCausland only nodded mysteriously and puffed.

"And—and disinherited the nephew?"

"Exactly—cut him down to $20,000."

"Where is this will?"

"This will was burned. It was the cause of the burning." McCausland had lowered his voice, if anything, but the district attorney stood up in horror.

"More wealth changed hands by the destruction of that

document," continued the inspector, "than was converted into smoke and ashes by the fire."

"You mean that young Floyd planned to burn up the will which left him a pauper, so that he might obtain his interest as heir-at-law?"

"That's the motive you were asking for when Costa interrupted us. It was clumsily done, wasn't it? But not so clumsily, when you look at it further. The professor kept his valuables in an iron lock-box which he called a safe. To blow it open was dangerous, unless"—McCausland paused to drive his meaning home—"unless the sound of the explosion could be smothered in the general confusion of a fire."

"You attribute the explosions to——"

"Placed the charge himself in a wooden box under the safe. Told Bertha a plausible story to provide against discovery."

"Six human lives to pay for a few paltry dollars."

"Five million dollars! The professor must have left nearly ten and Floyd would have shared them equally with the other nephew. Hardly a paltry figure, $5,000,-000! I've seen murder committed for a 10-cent piece."

"But that was manslaughter in the heat of a quarrel."

"To be sure; and by expert Sicilian carvers, with magnifying-glass eyes and tempers formed between Etna and Vesuvius. But $5,000,000 is a fortune, Bigelow."

The district attorney paced up and down, meditating. At last he turned and brought his fist down on the table so hard that the bloodhound bayed.

"This is murder as well as arson. I want that understood."

"I understood it," smiled the inspector.

"Who saw this will?"

"There's no secret there. Its contents are common property, I should say. It was Mrs. Arnold, the sister-in-law, who dropped me the first hint; and Floyd himself has owned that his uncle made a will three weeks ago, cutting him down to $20,000."

"How did the professor come to postpone his will-making so long?"

"Satisfied, I suppose, with the laws of intestate descent."

"The other heir gets it all?"

"Harry Arnold? No. I believe some goes to charity, the servants and so on. A $10,000,000 cake will cut up into several neat slices, you know." But the thoughts of the district attorney seemed to move habitually on a higher plane.

"Floyd was a sister's son. Perhaps that is why the professor preferred him to his cousin," he said.

"A life-long preference which does not appear in his testament, however."

"But why did he cast him off at the eleventh hour?"

"The boy didn't know enough to groom and currycomb the old gentleman properly. Only 21, you know, and self-willed. That's in the Arnold blood. Besides, he's a socialist or anarchist, I'm told, and keeps company with a photographic retoucher as poor as Job. Something of the sort. Who knows? A straw will turn a man's mind at fourscore."

"And how about Mungovan and the Greeley woman?"

"Accomplices," said McCausland, but added more cautiously, "from present appearances, at least."

There was a knock on the door and the bloodhound again performed the duties of sentinel, receiving his master's praise with such marks of dignified gratification as became his enormous size.

"Miss Wesner," announced the mulatto.

"Presently," answered the inspector. "Well, action or inaction?" he said, presenting an alternative of two fingers to the district attorney.

"I must go over this evidence in detail. Will you send the Swedish girl to my office again to-morrow?"

"I think I can lay my hands on her."

At that very moment, in another part of the city Robert Floyd was walking down to the electric car between a squad of policemen, followed by a motley crowd that profaned the Sabbath with its clamor. Once aboard the swift vehicle, he was safe from pursuit, but his liberty was short-lived. For, as a result of Noah Bigelow's second inter-

view with Bertha and his review of McCausland's reasoning, a warrant was made out and he was arrested Monday noon on the charge of arson and homicide.

CHAPTER V.

HE IS TRIED IN THE BALANCE.

There was a pause in the little court-room when the
formal proclamations of the crier and clerk were ended.

"Are you guilty or not guilty, Robert Floyd?"

He bore the scrutiny of many hundred eyes calmly.
Earnestness must have been the usual expression of his
face, but today its flashing eyes and curled upper lip con-
trolled the aquiline features and made their dominant
aspect one of defiance.

He was olive-skinned, as his uncle may have been in
his youth. His hair was dark. Spots of dark red were
burning in his cheek, and his voice, when he spoke, of a
rich contralto quality, had some subtle affiliation with
darkness, too. Altogether a Roman soul, the unpreju-
diced observer would have said, but somewhat lacking in
the blitheness which is proper to youth.

"Not guilty," the answer was recorded.

The spectators listened in a strained and oppressive
silence. Within the bar sat old John Davidson, looking
very sympathetic and not a little perplexed as he reared
his chair back against the railing. Through the open
door of an ante-room peeped the chubby form of Inspector McCausland, cordially shaking hands with
acquaintances and answering to the sobriquet of "Dick."
For professional reasons the inspector avoided making
his person known to the multitude, but once or twice
he sent in messages to the district attorney, and finally
stepping to the door, caught his eye and beckoned him
outside. Noah Bigelow had been sitting silently at the

prosecutor's desk, his prodigious black beard sweeping
his breast and his tufted eyebrows leveled steadily at the
prisoner, as if to read his soul. When he rose at McCausland's signal the entire court-room followed his broad
back receding through the door of the chamber.

"The prisoner," said the judge, "declines the advice
of counsel and offers himself for examination unaided.
He is hereby warned of his right under the law to challenge any question which may incriminate or tend to
incriminate him. The court will see that this right is
protected. We are ready for the evidence."

"Miss Bertha Lund," called Badger. She arose, the
same tidy, buxom maiden as ever, but pale and with
traces of tears. An oath was administered and the young
woman motioned to the witness-box.

"How long have you been a servant in the Arnold
house, Miss Lund?" asked Badger, who was conducting
the case for the government.

"Going on six years."

"And you have known the prisoner all this time?"

"Of course."

"You were in at the time of the fire, on Saturday?"

"I was."

"And gave the alarm, did you not?"

"I did."

Bertha's rising inflection had hardly varied in the last
three answers, and her blue eyes were riveted on the
lawyer's.

"Won't you tell the court how you were occupied prior
to your discovery of the fire?"

Thus directed, Bertha half-inclined her person toward
the judge.

"Part of the time I was dusting the study and part of
the time I was upstairs."

"What were you doing upstairs?"

"Nothing, except looking out of the window into the
street."

"What window?"

"Mr. Robert's."

"And what street?"

"Cazenove street."

"Was any one else in the house at that time?"

"Not after Ellen went out."

"You are sure Ellen had gone out?"

"Well, what do you mean by sure?"

"What made you think she had gone out?"

"She told me she was going out. She was dressed in her street dress and I heard the door slam. That's three reasons."

"You heard the door slam? The front door, I suppose? There is only one door?"

"No, there's the back door, leading into the passageway."

"And where does the passageway lead?"

"Why, it runs alongside the house from Cazenove street to Broad."

The district attorney diverted attention for a moment by making his way to his seat through the crowd. He was the opposite of Badger in everything; the one burly and slack, but with the stamp of moral energy in his bearing; the other immaculate from cravat to cuff borders and athletic if slight in build.

"Was it the back door or the front door you heard slam, Miss Lund?" resumed Badger, continuing to confer in an undertone with the district attorney.

"It was the back door, sir, I suppose."

"Aren't you sure?"

"Pretty sure."

"Wasn't it probably the front door?"

"No, it was the back door, I'm positive."

"Then Ellen went out of the back door and left you and Floyd alone in the house?"

"Yes, sir, Mr. Robert and I were the only ones in."

"Just when was this slamming of the door, at what time? With reference, I mean, to your own movements and the movements of others in the house?"

"Well, I was up stairs and down, in and out, and Mr. Robert was in the study. I couldn't tell you just when."

"Very well——"

"And, if it's not improper, I wish to say that I am not

here of my own choosing, for as sure as my name is
Bertha Lund, Robert Floyd never set that fire."

This sally was received in silence by the spectators.
They looked expectantly toward the judge and the attorneys. Floyd's look was as spirited and firm as ever,
as he scanned the faces packed around him, nodding
to a lady in the front bench, but letting his eyes dwell
oftenest, with a kind of interrogative look, followed by
an expression of soft satisfaction, on a younger face. It
was golden-haired Emily Barlow, transfixed with interest
in the proceedings. Not even the dark visage of the
negro in the corner stood out so cameo-like from the
multitude as hers, partly by its sweetness of beauty, but
more by the parted lips and eager gaze.

"The witness is not to volunteer opinions, but simply
to give the facts she is requested to give, clearly and
truthfully, as her oath requires." This reproof was not
harshly spoken by the judge. "You may continue, Mr.
Badger."

"Mr. Floyd was in the study, then?"

"Yes, sir, he was."

"Where the fire started?"

"It started in the study."

"Will you describe to the court, without any omissions,
everything you did and everything you saw Mr. Floyd
do from the time he opened the study door until you
descended the stairway and discovered the room afire?"

"Well, sir, when Mr. Robert unlocked the door——"

"Which door?"

"The study."

"It had been locked, then?"

"Yes, sir; Mr. Robert had locked it after the professor
died."

"Which was on Tuesday?"

"Yes, sir."

"Go on with your story."

"After Mr. Robert opened the study door he was
acting lonesome. I went in and said, 'Shall I dust the
room, Mr. Robert? It needs it.' 'Yes, do, Bertha,' said
he. 'I'm expecting a lawyer. Is Ellen in?' 'She was

going out,' I answered, 'but I think I heard her run up-stairs to her room.' Well, I went for the duster, and when I came back Mr. Robert was standing over the hearth. 'Is that you, Ellen?' he said, dazed-like and absent-minded. But when he saw it was me he only laughed."

"What was Mr. Floyd doing when you startled him?" interposed the deep bass of the district attorney, cutting short the progress of the girl's high treble.

"Why, sir, he was stooping over."

"Over the hearth, you said?"

"Yes, sir."

"Did you see anything in his hands at the time?"

"Why, he was picking up little bits of paper, as though he had just torn a letter to pieces."

"Go on," said Badger, making a note of this fact.

"While I was dusting the furniture Mr. Robert went out into the professor's chamber and brought in the canary. The poor thing hadn't sung since the professor died. It was he who used to feed it and talk to it. But when Mr. Robert brought it into its old room and I pulled up the curtains to let in the sunshine it set up such a trilling and chirping I could hardly help crying."

"On which floor is this study?"

"The front room, one flight up."

"How high above the street? You couldn't reach it from the sidewalk?"

"Not without a ladder."

"And you didn't keep a ladder resting against the front of your house, usually?"

"No more usually than other folks do."

"There was no tree," asked the district attorney, "whose branches hung near the window?"

"No, sir; there was none," answered Bertha, respect-fully.

"Now, the rest of your story, Miss Lund," said Badger; "the canary bird had been brought in. Did it perch on Floyd's finger?"

"Canary birds will use their wings like other folks if

they are let. No, it was brought in in the cage and the cage hung on the hook, just as it used to be."

"Why had it been removed?"

"So as to feed it," answered Bertha, triumphantly.

"Was there any other living thing in the room at this time?"

"Is a dog a living thing?" Being human, Bertha resented catechising. The temptation to answer one question by another is strong, even when one isn't a New-Englander by birth.

"Previous to its death, it may be considered alive," answered Badger, dryly.

"Well, Sire was there."

"A dog, I presume, from your last response. Continue from the point when the cage was brought in."

"I went upstairs, as I told you before, when I had finished my dusting. Then I sat down in Mr. Robert's room."

"Was that all you did?—to sit down?"

"Yes."

Bertha's replies had gradually come down to monosyllabic length and it looked as if the next step might be silence. But the district attorney interposed with a nod and a smile, which worked like magic in loosening her tongue.

"Well," she continued, "I was sitting at Mr. Robert's window when I noticed Sire's barking. I thought it was odd if he was playing with Mr. Robert, they both took on so at the professor's death. But it kept up and kept up, so I slipped down to see and the first thing I smelled was smoke. It was leaking out through the study keyhole and I could hear Sire barking and pawing at the knob inside. Of course I opened the door and rushed in to save the canary, but the fire stung me so I thought I was suffocated. Sire began running around and I called for Mr. Robert, thinking he was in the room, for the smoke was hiding everything. Oh, I tell you my heart stopped when my voice came back to me all hollow in that empty house. It was then I ran down to the street."

"One moment, Miss Lund. Did you or did you not observe anything new or unusual in the room when you were engaged in dusting the chairs?"

"No, sir; I don't remember anything unusual."

"How long were you upstairs?"

"I couldn't say. I'm not good at guessing time. There are some folks, like Senda Wesner, seem to have a clock going in their heads, but I'm not one of them. Perhaps it was ten minutes."

"Miss Lund," the district attorney stroked his great beard, as he was apt to do in driving home a crucial question. "Can you now fix more precisely the moment of the door slam, which you say convinced you of Ellen's departure?"

"No, sir; the door slam," Bertha touched her forehead, trying to remember, "the door slam is all mixed up with the barking and fire, so I can't untangle it at all."

"It seems to be a part of this chain of events you have just narrated so clearly for us? You think, you thought at the time, it was Ellen leaving the house?"

"Yes, sir. It was the back door. Who else could it be? Besides, Mr. Robert was quiet. He never slammed the door."

"I simply wanted the girl's best evidence to the fact that they were alone in the house at this time," said the district attorney.

"But the girl, Ellen, seems to have been about until the fire was set," answered the judge.

CHAPTER VI.

AND IS FOUND WANTING.

After the noon recess Bertha was called to finish her testimony, with the promise that she would not be detained long.

"A description of the study, Miss Lund, when you were dusting."

"Everything was left just as it was when the professor fell dead on the threshold Tuesday evening."

"Did you notice any foreign substance—any accumulation of what might afford fuel for a fire?"

"No, sir."

"Any odor?"

"Only that the room was close from being shut up."

"Describe the contents of the room."

"Well, it was full of books, on shelves that ran all around."

"Yes?"

"Two windows; a cage before one, the nearest to the door, and a writing desk before the one in the farthest corner."

"Well?"

"A safe partly built in the wall beside the door."

"How high from the ground?"

"About up to my waist."

"Did you notice anything underneath it?"

"Yes, there was the gunpowder box Mr. Robert put there."

"A box full of gunpowder placed there by Floyd?"

"Yes, sir."

This statement made a profound impression, but Badger did not push the subject further. The prisoner almost smiled.

"Well?" Badger said.

"Oh, everything else was just as the professor left it. His slippers under his chair, his dressing-gown over the back of it, his spectacles on the desk, his bible laid down open. He was going to meet a caller, you know, when he was taken with the stitch."

"Very well. Perhaps we have had enough of the professor," said Badger. But the accused did not find these minutiae trivial. For the first time his proud face broke and he hid the tears with his hand. The mention of the bible, slippers and the other personal mementos had called up the dearest picture he ever knew.

All the grand life, equally compounded of whims and

principles, passed before him at Bertha's mention of the empty chair.

But the sympathy of the spectators was short-lived. While Robert wept a strain of sad music stole into the court-room. Faint at first, it rose in volume as the players approached, but still with a muted sound, as if their instruments were muffled. The drum-beats were rare and unobtrusive, and the burden of the melody, if melody it were, was borne by proud bugles and quivering oboes. Its cadences were old and mysterious, like some Gregorian chant intoned in cloisters before organ and orchestra had trained our ears to the chords of harmony. No wonder the court-room was hushed until it died away in the distance.

It was the Masonic dead march, for on this day the funerals of the dead whom Robert Floyd was accused of murdering were being held. Oscar Schubert, as a member of the mystic order, was buried with all the pomp of its ceremonies, and it was his cortege, proceeding to the sepulcher, whose passage occasioned this pause in the trial.

The revulsion of sympathy was instant. Every man in the court-room saw the wife and two children, sitting behind drawn curtains in the carriage of the chief mourners, and beyond this picture the bodies of six victims, four of them young girls, done to death at the prompting of avarice. The prisoner himself seemed to understand, for he shut his teeth, though his bold eyes still dared the multitude. But they rested more and more upon the lovely face which was his one point of consolation in that unfriendly assemblage. Badger's indifferent voice showed no quiver when he asked Miss Lund to step down and called for Robert Floyd. It was a brusque opening.

"What was contained in the safe in your uncle's study?"

"I never opened it."

"You knew, however?"

"What he had told me."

"Was his will there?"

"I have reason to believe so."

"Did you believe so on Saturday, while you were in the room with Miss Lund?"

"I did not give the matter any thought at that time." Floyd spoke as though the spirit burned hot within him. "And I will add——"

"Nothing," said Badger. But the judge looked up.

"This is a court, not a court-martial," he said, quietly, a pale, studious man. "The witness has a right to modify his answers."

"I have only this to say," continued Floyd, "to hasten as much as possible this preposterous trial, that I indorse every word of Miss Lund's testimony, and accept it and proffer it as my own upon the points which it covers."

"We prefer——" But the district attorney interrupted his assistant. "Are you aware, Mr. Floyd, of the gravity of the position in which Miss Lund's testimony involves you? Sole opportunity is almost the major head among those which the government is required to prove."

"I accept it in toto, subject to the privilege of volunteering a statement if my examination is incomplete or misleading."

"We shall endeavor to make it both adequate and fair," said the district attorney.

"Leaving the safe for a moment," resumed the examiner, "will you kindly relate your movements, Mr. Floyd, subsequent to the time when Bertha left you to go upstairs?"

The young man hesitated. The pause was so long as to be embarrassing. Old John Davidson coughed loudly to relieve his agitation. When the witness spoke at last he seemed to be remembering with difficulty.

"I remember leaving the house and walking about among the fields, in the park, I think. Yes, I took a car for the park. In the evening I called upon Miss Barlow."

He looked up at the aureoled face and faintly smiled. The sight appeared to revive him. "From that point my recollections become as distinct as usual. But——" He hesitated once more and Badger left him unaided in his distress. "The truth is, this was my first visit since his death to my uncle's study. The executor had telegraphed and afterward written me to close and lock it. This I did. But that afternoon I was expecting a visit from him——"

"Who is this executor?"

"Mr. Hodgkins Hodgkins."

"Of the firm of Hodgkins, Hodgkins & Hodgkins?"

"I believe so. My aunt, Mrs. Arnold, had called at 3 o'clock to say that he had arrived from New York and would take possession of the papers that afternoon. So I unlocked the room and let the servant dust it. The whole meaning of my loss seemed to come over me then, when I saw the empty chair. Before that I had been calm enough. But the sight dazed and staggered me. I went out, fled, taking no note of time or place. I believe, I know, I was in the park, but until I arrived at Miss Barlow's, outward occurrences made little memorable impression upon me."

"I presume you saw or were seen by persons on the way?"

"I do not remember any one in particular."

"Are we to understand," said the district attorney, listening intently, "that you passed this long period in a species of reverie or trance?"

"An intense fit of abstraction," answered Robert; but the district attorney looked puzzled, as if an utterly new and virgin problem had been put before him to solve.

"Without food until you returned at 11 o'clock to the fire?" asked Badger.

"Excepting a light lunch at Miss Barlow's. Her mother noticed some fatigue in me and pressed me to take refreshment."

"Was there no mention of the fire there—a fire which was destroying your home?"

"We spoke of it casually, but I did not know until later that it was destroying my home."

"Was it not described in the evening papers?"

"Not in the early editions, Badger," put in the district attorney. "Only in the later specials."

"Very well. Now let us get back to the safe. Your uncle had made a will, I believe?"

"He made a will several weeks ago."

"What were the terms of that document?"

"I do not know them in full."

"As to your share?"

"My legacy was $20,000."

"Out of an estate valued at?"

"I have heard $10,000,000."

"You are an anarchist, Mr. Floyd?"

"No, sir."

"But a radical of some sort?"

"I am a socialist; a developer, not a destroyer."

"Ah!" said Badger. His exclamation was icy cold. "And you differed from your uncle on other points, did you not?"

"We took the liberty of honest men to differ."

"In religion?"

"Yes. He was a high churchman. I am—simply a Christian."

This avowal of a creed brought titters among the spectators, who apparently were accustomed to definitions narrower if more precise.

"And as a result of these quarrels your uncle disinherited you?"

"Sir?"

For a moment the prisoner's outburst of indignation checked the current of opinion which had been flowing swiftly against him.

"In one sentence you have managed to outrage the dead as well as the living—and to convey two impressions distinctly false. My uncle and I never quarreled, never! He was a father and more than a father to me. Neither did he disinherit me. It was his wish to assign me the whole property. I begged him to omit me without more than a memento or keepsake, that I might enter life as he had done, as every man should, untrammeled— but with the advantage, I feel sure, of an example and an inspiration given to few to enjoy. The sum left me was far in excess of my desires."

There was another long silence after this statement, but it expressed only incredulity.

"When was this very extraordinary will drawn up?"

"Three weeks ago."

"The witnesses are living, then? It is to be presumed that they, too, were not carried off by the holocaust which so reduced our population last Saturday." Badger's sarcasm was brutal, but it told.

"The witnesses were three neighbors, called in. The servants could not act, as they were remembered in the document."

"No lawyer was present?"

"My uncle seldom employed a lawyer."

Such a statement, relating to a man of Prof. Arnold's wealth, might have excited doubt if his eccentricity on this point had not been noised about beforehand.

"He drew up the will himself, then? Has any one seen it except you?"

"Not so far as I know. I myself never saw it."

"But you knew it was in the safe?"

"I supposed so."

"One moment," said the district attorney, interrupting. "Once more, why did you reopen the study on this particular day?"

"Because I had been informed that Mr. Hodgkins was coming to remove the will."

"By whom were you so informed?"

"Mrs. Arnold drove up about 3 o'clock and mentioned the fact. Indeed, she had expected to find him at the house. He was an old acquaintance of hers, as well as of my uncle—her legal adviser, in fact."

A stylish woman, still fair in spite of her 50 years, was sitting in front of Robert as he testified. She was the widow of Benjamin Arnold's brother, Henry, and her son, Henry, or Harry, had just offered a reward of $5,000 for the incendiary—a sum which McCausland might well have hopes of securing. The inspector was still hovering about the threshold of his ante-room, and now that Floyd's examination was concluded he called the district attorney to one side, apparently urging him to reserve the remainder of his evidence, which would naturally consist of rebuttal of Floyd and corroboration of Bertha. At any rate, Mr. Badger arose, and, announcing that the case was closed, offered a summary of the evidence, rapid, methodical, but unimpressive, like himself. Then the prisoner was asked if he desired to speak in his own behalf.

"Your honor," he said, "this monstrous charge of having set on foot a fire in the most populous section of our noble city overwhelms me so that I am impotent to express the indignation I feel. I leave it to your own sense of justice, your own discrimination, whether I am to be dishonored with the suspicion of an infamous crime, on evidence so flimsy that the bare denial of a veracious man should be sufficient to upset it. I read in many faces around me the hunger for blood; the unthinking call for a victim. Heed that, and my good name is taken from me. I am irreparably wronged. Resist it, and you will prove yourself worthy of the honorable title which you bear."

Not a few were swayed toward the youth by his manifest emotion. But the judge waited fully a minute before he arose and his eyeglasses were trembling in his hand.

"You have elected, against good counsel," he began, "to be your own advocate. I cannot and do not adjudge you unsuccessful, in the sense of having demonstrated your guilt rather than your innocence. But that you have failed to break the government's chain of evidence in its most damaging links—sole opportunity, motive and suspicious conduct, especially after the act—is plain to me, and would be plain to any mind accustomed to weighing such evidence calmly.

"It is true the evidence is wholly circumstantial. No eye but God's saw this foul deed done. But since William Rufus was found dead in the New Forest, with Walter Tyrrell's arrow in his breast, men have been convicted of murder on circumstantial evidence, and will continue to be so convicted as long as probability remains the guide of life.

"I am obliged, therefore, to remand you for trial, not

only on the charge of arson, but upon the graver charge of homicide involved in it under the peculiar circumstances of the case. This is not a final verdict. Far be it from me, one erring man, to say that the government has fastened this crime upon you beyond reasonable doubt. But in the face of the evidence which has been brought forward I could not order your release. It becomes my unhappy duty, as the examining magistrate, to commit you to custody, to await the approaching session of the grand jury."

When Emily Barlow awoke from her swoon she found herself in the arms of old John Davidson. Perhaps it was as well she did not hear the jeer of execration which greeted the prisoner outside when he passed over the sidewalk, ironed between two stalwart officers, into the jail van. McCausland's identification with the case had affected public opinion profoundly, for he was said never to have failed to convict a criminal whom he had once brought into court. But possibly the outburst was due to the circumstance that this was the neighborhood in which the Lacy girls lived and that their funeral had taken place that very morning.

CHAPTER VII.

THE CLOUDS THICKEN.

"Shagarach is the man to defend him, Miss Barlow," said old John Davidson. She was lying back against the cushions of the cab, with cheeks as white as the handkerchief she held to her lips. For the marshal had kindly offered to accompany her home and she had told him part of her story.

She was, as McCausland had said to the district attorney, a photographic retoucher. You must know that a negative when it leaves the camera is no more fit for display than milk fresh from the cow is drinkable. All the minor blemishes which you and I, not being made in

the stamp of bluff old Oliver, dislike to see perpetuated in
our counterfeit presentments, must be carefully stippled
out. The work is not without its irksomeness, requiring
long hours of labor as well as firmness of touch. The
strain upon the young lady's eyes was evident, and her
face, for all its beauty, was as delicate as thinnest porce-
lain. One felt that her fingers, if she held them toward
the sun, would show the red suffusion of a child's. But
her earnings supported a family of five, and her character had won the love of Robert Floyd.

"Who is Shagarach?" she asked, as if struck by the
name.

"Shagarach! Why, Shagarach's the coming man, the
greatest criminal lawyer in the state and the greatest
cross-examiner in the world—a mind reader, black art
in it. Never lost a case."

"This is my number, Mr. Davidson."

"Ho, there! John! Cabby!" The marshal rapped at
the window.

"What was the number, miss?"

"Four hundred and twelve."

"Stop at 412."

"You have been very kind to interest yourself in one
who is not known to you, Mr. Davidson. I should have
been badly off without your assistance."

"Didn't do half enough," answered the marshal. "Glad
to be of service. Call on me again. Here's Shagarach's
address. Take my advice and look him up."

He had been writing on the back of a card while the
cab-driver was slowing his team around in front of Miss
Barlow's door. It read in a scrawl, rendered half-illeg-
ible by the jolting: "Meyer Shagarach, 31 Putnam
street."

Emily looked twice at the singular name. McCausland never failed to convict his prisoners. Shagarach's
clients invariably escaped. What would happen if the
two were pitted against each other? This was her
thought when she mounted the dear steps of home and fell
weeping into the arms of her mother.

The following morning a remarkable discovery was

made on the site of Prof. Arnold's house. The burned district had been roped off and was guarded by policemen, owing to the danger from the standing walls and still smoking debris. But tip-carts had begun to remove what was removable of the wreck, and the work of clearing away the ground was already well under way. Sightseers in great numbers went out of their course to pass the ruins, for the Harmon building was of recent erection and had been styled a model of business architecture.

But "Toot" Watts, "Turkey" Fenton and "The Whistler" were not indulging in reminiscences of departed architectural glories that morning. They averaged 14 years and 110 pounds, a combination hostile to sentiment in any but its most robust forms. "That nutty duffer gives me a pain," was their unanimous criticism from the gallery of the "Grand Dime," upon the garden rhapsodies of their co-mate and brother in adolescence, Romeo. But in the evenings, if that long fence, which is the gamin's delight, happened to be under surveillance from the "cop," they would march up street and down, Turkey mouthing his harmonica, Toot opening and shutting a wheezy accordion, the Whistler fifing away with that thrush-like note to which he owed his nickname, and all three beating time by their own quick footsteps to the melody of some sweet, familiar song. Amid such surroundings even the ditties sung by our mothers many seasons ago can bring up wholesome sentiments in which the boyish musicians who evoke them are surely sharers.

On the day before Toot had surreptitiously conveyed a fresh egg to school and rolled it playfully down the aisle, whereupon Turkey, as he was walking out at 4, had set the stamp of approval on his friend's property. All three had decided to take a day off until the affair should blow over, and no better pastime suggested itself than a visit to the fire, in which they took a sort of proprietary interest, since they had been the first after the bake-shop girl, to arrive on the spot. The passageway beside the house was still left open and unguarded. So our urchins, approaching from the Broad street side, coolly entered the forbidden precincts thereby, thus eluding the blue-coated watchers by a flank movement as simple as it was effective.

"I'm goin' to pick up junk and sell it to Bagley," said Turkey, filling his pocket with bolts, nuts and other fragments which he deemed of value. The others followed his example and began rummaging about with insecure footing among the heaps.

"Whew!" the Whistler emitted a long-drawn note no flute could possibly rival. He had been brushing away the ashes from a heavy object, when his eye was attracted by a fragment of cloth, which clung about it. His whistle drew the attention of his companions, but it also invited a less welcome arrival, no other than one of the patrolmen doing guard duty, who swooped down and seized Turkey and the Whistler by their collars, while Toot scrambled off with unseemly haste and escaped down the alleyway.

"What are you doing here?" said the officer, shaking the boys till their teeth chattered, and several pieces of iron, dropping out of Turkey's pockets, disclosed the object of their visit. "Stealing junk, 'eh?"

"Say, look," said the Whistler, who was cool and inventive; "it's a woman." He was pointing to the object he had laid bare. The officer slackened his grip.

"My God!" he cried; then stooped and by a full exertion of his strength lifted the thing out of the ashes and half-burned timbers which overlay it. It was, indeed, the body of a woman, short and stout. The boys did not run. They looked on, spellbound, in open-mouthed wonder.

"Run and call the sergeant," said the policeman to his quondam captives.

The news spread like wildfire. Hundreds swarmed to the scene, but none among them who had the key to the woman's identity. Her charred face and burned body rendered identification difficult. It was Inspector McCausland who, after consulting his notebook, recognized the garment and the form which it clad as Ellen Greeley's. An ambulance was called and the corpse of the poor woman carried away to the morgue, to await her sister's instructions.

Senda Wesner, the bake-shop girl, had described this discovery for the eleventh time to her customers, and was standing on the steps of her store alone—a condition to which she was by nature averse—when the golden-haired lady "flashed in upon her," as she afterward said, "like a Baltimore oriole." It was Emily Barlow, who had run down during her lunch hour to the scene of the tragedy. At the first mention of her name, Miss Wesner knew her.

"Oh, you're the young lady he kept company with," she said. "Isn't it too bad? I don't believe he ever did it. No man in his senses would set his own house afire and then walk out in broad daylight, as I saw Mr. Floyd do."

"You saw Mr. Floyd coming out, then? Pardon my curiosity, but I am so deeply interested——"

"I shouldn't think much of you if you were not," said Senda Wesner. "I'm glad to tell all I know about it, and I can't see for the life of me why they didn't call me to the stand."

Emily saw that no apology was needed for questioning the bake-shop girl. She was easy to make free with and fond of running on. Being a little reticent herself, Emily was glad to be relieved of the necessity of putting inquiries. So she simply guided the little gossip's talk.

"You did see Mr. Floyd leave the house? Was it long before the fire broke out?"

"Four or five minutes. I'd noticed Bertha raising the curtains—two Washington pies? yes'm—I'd seen Bertha up in the study, I say, but then Joe Tyke, Joey, we call him, the cripple newsboy, though he is quite a man now, but he never grew, deformed, you know—Joey was trundling himself along on his little cart, and I couldn't take my eyes off of him—20 cents, yes'm." The bake-shop girl continued to spread jam, ladle milk and wrap warm loaves in fresh brown paper, all the while, but her interruptions only formed tiny ripples on her flowing stream of prattle. "Then Mr. Robert came out and walked down to the corner slowly. But do you know what puzzled me? What was he stooping over the hearth for and picking up those pieces of paper?"

"People often do that. Perhaps he had torn up a letter and some of it had scattered outside the fireplace."

"Well, I didn't see another thing, not one thing, against him," said Miss Wesner, decidedly. Her ideas on the value of evidence were certainly of the most feminine order. "I'm sure he's a young man of the highest reputation. Never smoked or drank or——"

"You didn't see any other person coming out of the house?"

"No, I didn't. Yes, Gertrude, and how's your mamma? That's a sweet thing, only 10 years old, but does all the errands and half the housework for her mother, that's sick, and never slaps the baby."

"Or any stranger about?" edged in Emily again, when the spigot was finally turned off and the waters of gossip had ceased to run.

"Do you know——" The bake-shop girl dimpled her cheek with her forefinger. It was a healthy cheek, but not beautiful. "Do you know, there has been the oddest peddler around here for the last three weeks?"

"Do tell me about him. What did he look like? A stranger?"

"Never passed this street before as long as I know and that's a good many years. He was a sunburnt sort of man, like all the peddlers (only I'd say homelier, if I wasn't a fright myself), and with crazy blue eyes. Always came in a green cart and sold vegetables, no, once potted plants. But how he would yodel. Why, he'd make you deaf. Ellen used to buy of him sometimes. Nobody else ever did, and it's my opinion when he left the Arnolds he used to whip up his horse and hurry right round the corner."

"Was this peddler here lately?"

"Not since Friday, the day before the fire; I'm positive."

"He wasn't here Saturday?"

"No, he wasn't. But I must say, peddler or no peddler, I don't believe Robert Floyd ever set that fire."

There was more that Senda Wesner believed and disbelieved—so much, indeed, that when Emily left her she had asked herself twice what a room full of Senda Wesners would be like. But she checked this uncharitable thought. The girl was good-hearted and her information about the peddler might prove a clew. After making a half-circuit of the house which was so familiar to her, for she had visited it often, she returned to her stippling pencil in the photograph gallery, pondering now upon the identity of the strange peddler, now upon the sad fate of Ellen Greeley, and oftenest of all on the lover who was spending his first day in the solitude of a felon's cell.

CHAPTER VIII.

ENTER SHAGARACH.

"Meyer Shagarach, Attorney-at-Law."

The shingle could not have been more commonplace, the office stairs more dingy. A Jewish boy opened the door at Emily's knock and a young man of the same persuasion arose from his desk and bustled forward to inquire her business.

"Meester Shagarach is in. Did you wish to see him?"

After a moment a second door was opened and Emily was motioned into the inner office.

"This way, madam."

The man writing at the table barely glanced up at first, but, seeing who his visitor was, he rose and placed a seat for her. There was courtesy but no geniality in the gesture. Shagarach did not smile. It was said that he never smiled.

From the beginning Emily felt that she was in the presence of a man of destiny. Before sitting down her intuitions had determined her to enlist this force on Robert's side at any cost. Shagarach's body was small, his clothing mean and crinkled all over, as if its owner spent many hours daily crouched in a chair. But the face drew one's gaze and absorbed it. With care it might have been handsome, though the dead-black beard grew wild and the hair, tossed carelessly to one side, fell back at intervals, requiring to be brushed in place by the owner's hand. Under the smooth, bony brow that marks the Hebrew shone two eyes of extraordinary splendor, the largest, Emily thought, she had ever seen, and set the widest apart—brown and melting as a dog's, but glowing, as no dog's ever did, with profundities of human intelligence. Wide open at all times, they cast penetrating glances, never sidelong, always full—the eyes of a soul-searcher, a student of those characters, legible but elusive; which the spirit writes upon its outer garment. Their physical dimensions lent a large power to the face, as if more of the visible world could be comprehended within those magnificent organs than the glances of ordinary men compass. But the mouth below seemed rigid as granite, even during the play of speech.

"My name is Miss Barlow," said Emily.

"Come to engage my services for Floyd?" he inquired. It was his habit to cut into the heart of a problem at the first stroke and Emily felt grateful on the whole that the preliminaries were shortened.

"Mr. Floyd is innocent and I want you to save him."

"Why did he not employ an advocate?"

"The judge——"

"Pursued the only course open to him. The evidence was damaging. What have you learned since yesterday?"

"Ellen Greeley——"

"Is dead. The dog's instincts were right then. There was some one inside. Aronson."

The young man answered this peremptory call.

"My Evening Beacon."

It was brought at once.

"The newspapers are correct in their surmise. Ellen Greeley went upstairs, as Bertha testified. The day was hot. She lay upon the bed in her own room, and fell asleep. The barking of Sire did not wake her. Her room was in the rear, two flights up. The shouting of the crowd did not wake her. The fire may have waked her too late and her shrieks escaped notice in the uproar; or she may have been suffocated during her nap."

Shagarach spoke in a clear, loud voice that expressed and carried conviction. Emily wondered at his familiarity, far surpassing her own, with the details of the case.

"You see the improvement in our cause at once?"

Emily tried hard to think.

"Of course it proved Ellen could not have been a confederate," she suggested, modestly.

"Ellen Greeley sleeping in the attic chamber, who slammed the door?"

Shagarach's eyes shone like carbuncles. "It was not Floyd. He was not in the habit of slamming doors. And no man seeking to escape does that which will attract attention—unless"—he dwelt on the word significantly—"unless he is fleeing in haste."

"Then you believe, Mr. Shagarach——"

"It was the back door which slammed. They failed to confuse Bertha on that. It slammed after Floyd had gone out. Did Floyd go out the back door?"

"Miss Wesner, the young lady who lives opposite, saw him coming down the front steps."

"When?"

"Four or five minutes before the fire."

"Ellen did not go out the back door. Floyd did not go out the back door. Some one else did."

"And you will take the case, Mr. Shagarach?" Emily awaited his answer as breathlessly as if Robert's life or death hung in a trembling balance which Shagarach's finger could tip to one side or the other.

"It interests me. Have you a photograph of the accused with you?"

"No," answered Emily, thinking the request somewhat strange.

Shagarach began gazing at her with extraordinary intensity. The great will inclosed in his little body seemed to bear down hard upon her so as really to hurt. But

she felt no resentment, only a kind of satisfied acquies-
cence, as if all were for the best. Yet, among ordinary
people Emily was an individuality rare and fragrant, as-
serting herself forcefully, without being in the least self-
assertive.

"Have you anything else?" asked the lawyer. Emily
did not know how long the interim was.

"There is the strange peddler," she ventured to say.
This time his answer was an interrogative look.

"Miss Wesner spoke of him today—a vegetable vender, who has been coming to the Arnold's for the last
few weeks——"

"How many?"

"Three or four, I think."

"Since the will was made, then?"

"And dealing with Ellen. About the will——"

"Let us finish with the peddler."

"He had blue eyes and drove a cart painted green. Nobody had ever seen him in the neighborhood before, till
he came selling vegetables and potted plants. His last
visit was made on Friday."

"Not Saturday, the day of the fire?"

"Miss Wesner, who is very observing, has not seen
him since Friday."

"Not as a peddler," said Shagarach, sotto voce. "Now
as to the will. You wish to say that Floyd has told you
of his uncle's desire to make him sole heir and his own
aversion to the responsibilities of so large a property."

"Does he practice clairvoyance?" asked Emily of herself.

"Robert is no lover of money," she said. "To allege
avarice against him as a motive is monstrous."

"Avarice, Miss Barlow? To love money is not avarice.
Men grow to their opportunities. Without opportunities
they wither and without money today there is no opportunity."

"The artist—does his genius gain or lose when it is
gilded?" replied Emily, who felt a match even for Shagarach in the defense of her lover.

"The artist—ah, he is not of the world! Gold might

well be to him an incumbrance. But to the worker among men it is the key to a thousand coffers."

There was deep feeling in these words of the criminal lawyer. Emily wondered if there might not have been a past of poverty, perhaps of spiritual aspiration and disappointment in his life, all subdued to the present indomitable aim at fortune and reputation.

"The refusal was a folly, a stripling's fatal blunder—yet a blunder of which not three men in our city are capable. Let us leave the will. It may reappear in its proper sequence. No suspicious character was seen loitering about or leaving the house on Saturday?"

"My inquiries have been limited to Miss Wesner."

"Aronson!"

The young man reappeared as before.

"Make thorough inquiry this evening in the neighborhood of the Arnold house, rear and front, for a stranger seen loitering about the premises or issuing from them on Saturday afternoon."

"Yes, Miss Barlow, I have a theory," resumed Shagarach, turning to Emily again. He folded his arms and looked at her steadfastly, yet as though his gaze were fixed on something beyond.

"I see your lover's photograph in your eyes—mild blue eyes, but touchstones of integrity, hard to deceive. He impresses me well. His story, moreover, bears a somewhat uncommon voucher. It is true because of its improbability. How improbable that any man would refuse a gift of $10,000,000! How improbable that any man, not a sleep-walker, would wander through the streets of a city without any record of his sensuous impressions!"

"But——"

"The improbability of the story demonstrates its truth. Men lie, women lie, children lie. Have you watched a band of girls playing at the imitation of school? How cunningly the teacher feigns anger, the pupils naughtiness and sad repentance. Have you observed the plausibility in the inventions of toddling babes to escape imminent chastisement? Falsehood is a normal faculty and equipped with its protective armor, plausibility. Your friend's story is too preposterous to be untrue."

Emily was bewildered by these rapid paradoxes.

"I congratulate you upon your friendship with so unusual a specimen of our kind, the man who cannot or will not lie. But I should not like to present his defense on such grounds to twelve of his fellow-creatures, normal in that respect. Fortunately we are not driven to that extreme refuge.

"The material for a theory is meager; the chain shows many gaps. But I find no evidence that Floyd attempted to get rid of the servant, Bertha. A child, meditating this crime, would not have neglected so obvious a precaution. Her continued absence was only an opportune accident. Her re-entrance would have resulted in his discovery. The point is pivotal.

"I find that a favorite house dog was left in the room to be sacrificed—a needless cruelty if the incendiary were his master, a necessary precaution if he were a stranger whose actions the animal would have understood and whom he would have followed to the street."

"But would Sire have allowed a stranger even to enter the study?"

"True; but between strangers and friends there is a middle category consisting of persons whom we may call acquaintances. Into these three degrees we are divided by dogkind. It was not a stranger or he would have been attacked. He had no friends left but Bertha, Ellen and Floyd. The dog was drowsing on the mat. The man who entered was an acquaintance.

"Who was this man? We have a few items of his description. Some one known to the dog, familiar with the premises and interested in the destruction of the document of which that house, that room and that safe were the triple-barred shrine. An expert criminal could have destroyed the safe without detection, but the incendiary was an amateur, and such an act would require time. There was no time, not an instant. The executor was to arrive that afternoon. McCausland started right. The Harmon building was destroyed and seven lives sacrificed in order that Benjamin Arnold's will might be irrevocably canceled. Who benefited by its destruction? "The professor had desired to make Robert Floyd his sole heir, in other words, to disinherit Harry Arnold!"

Shagarach's monologue had reached its climax. The name of the other cousin came out like the ring of a hammer. He waited, as if yielding Emily an opportunity to object, but as she sat passive and expectant, he went on, his arms still folded, and his glowing eyes evincing deep absorption in the problem he was elucidating.

"Harry Arnold was in disfavor, then. The drafting of the will must have been communicated to him, but probably not its items. The mere fact, however, was ominous. It might mean the loss of a fortune. One of the servants was dressing 'uncommonly rich' of late. The wherewithal came to her as payment for conveying to Harry Arnold all she could pick up about the will. It may not have been pleasant news.

"It was from Mrs. Arnold McCausland first learned of the will. It was Harry Arnold who hastened to advertise a reward of $5,000—McCausland's fee if——"

"As to the fee," said Emily.

"I understand; the legacy of $20,000 amply protects me."

Emily was uncertain whether or not Shagarach meant to demand the whole $20,000 for his services.

"I find that the flies were about the honey pot. Mrs. Arnold's carriage drove up about 3 o'clock. The executor was to call that afternoon. Revelation could not be long delayed. The plot was desperately formed, favored by circumstance and executed by Harry Arnold and his accomplices."

"But Harry Arnold has been ill, Mr. Shagarach."

"The name of his physician?"

"I believe, Dr. Whipple, the pathologist. You suspect Harry, then, of the crime?"

"I have not studied him yet. This is only an alternative theory. You see how easily it could have been constructed in your friend's behalf.

"Mungovan, the discharged coachman, has not yet

been found. The strange peddler may prove a confederate. You will send Bertha to me. She is the central witness. Is Floyd in jail?"

"Yes," said Emily, sadly; "but a permit———"

"I shall not need one. I am his counsel."

Emily descended the creaking stairway and rode home
with a certain new elation, such as we sometimes feel
after contact with some electric character, some grand
reservoir of human vitality. Meyer Shagarach meanwhile began pacing up and down, occasionally speaking
to himself sotto voce.

A criminal lawyer, but with the head of an imperial
chancellor.

What was known of this rare man's history? About
thirty years before he was born in a small town on the
upper Nile, a descendant of those mighty Jewish families
whose expulsion impoverished Spain, while spreading her
tongue throughout the orient, even beyond the Turco-
man deserts to the unvisited cities of. Khiva and Merv.
Languages were his birthright, as naturally and almost
as numerously as the digits on his hands. In his youth
his father had wandered to America—refuge of all wild,
strange spirits of the earth—and died, leaving a widow
and a son. The boy had been visionary, unpractical—a
white blackbird among his tribe. For years he had struggled to support his mother, first as an attorney's drudge,
then as a scribbler. There was no market for his wares.
Then by a sudden wrench, showing the vise-like strength
of his will, he had burst the bubble of his early hopes and
chosen for his profession that of all professions which requires the most thorough subjection of the sentiments.
It was six years since he had first rented the obscure
quarters he now occupied, the same where, as a lad, he
had sighed away many hours of distasteful toil.

For the first two years Shagarach's face showed the
desperation of his fortunes. His own people shunned
him as a seceder from the synagogue. To the public he
was still unknown. But one day a trivial case had
matched him against a certain eminent pleader, a Goliath
in stature and in skill. The end of the day's tourney wit-

nessed his bulk prostrated before the undersized scion of the house of David. From that hour the dimensions of his fame had grown apace. Critics noticed an occasional simplicity in everyday matters, just as a gifted foreigner who has become eloquent in our tongue may have to ask some commonplace native for a word now and then. Rivals questioned his technical learning, who had little else to boast. Yet Shagarach's knowledge, practical or legal, was always found adequate to his cause. Whether he was pedantically profound in the law or not might be an open question. But all who knew him at all knew him for a Titan.

The man appeared to be lonely by nature. Excepting the young assistant, Aronson, he associated no colleague with him, carrying all the details of his growing volume of business in his own capacious mind. Other men made memoranda. Shagarach remembered. What he might be in himself none knew; yet "all things to all men" was a motto he spurned. Shagarach was Shagarach to judge or scullion, everywhere masterful, unruffled, mysterious. Were it not for the luminous eyes he might be taken for an abstract thinker. These orbs supplied the magnetism to rivet crowds and suggested a seer of deep soul-secrets (unknown even to their possessor), dormant, perhaps subdued, but not annihilated, under the exterior equipment of the criminal lawyer.

Shagarach often colloqued with himself as he was doing now. In his trials, though he neither badgered witnesses nor wrangled with opponents, he was noted for sotto-voce comments, sometimes ironical, that seemed scarcely conscious. These mannerisms might be relics of a solitary pre-existence, in which the habit of thinking aloud had been formed.

"Was it Arnold or Mungovan who touched the match?" He continued his pacing in silence. "Both knew the premises, Mungovan the better of the two."

The electric street lamp shone into his room and the footfalls of the last tenant, receding on the stairs, had long since died to silence.

"I will study Arnold," he said, finally, buttoning his coat, as if the problem were as good as solved.

CHAPTER IX.

THE ROYSTERERS.

"Get the mail, Indigo."

The letters made a goodly heap on the salver, but Harry Arnold sifted them over with an air of dissatisfaction. One cream-colored envelope, superscribed in a dainty hand, he laid apart. The rest he tore open and tossed into Indigo's lap, as if they were duns, invitations and other such formal matters.

"Drop a line apiece to these bores," he said to his valet, with a yawn. Like the whole tribe of the unoccupied, he was too busy to answer letters.

"Where's Aladdin?"

"Grazing in the paddock."

"Did you get the roses for Miss March?"

"Two dozen Marechal Neils."

"I want some paper for a note to go with them. Mother's prompt," he added, opening the letter he had reserved, while Indigo went on his errand. It was headed "Hillsborough," and ran as follows:

"Dear Harry: It is a pleasure to be in our old summer home again, especially after the trying day I spent in that court-room. The orchards are no longer in bloom, and the pear tree in the angle (your favorite), which was just a great pyramid of snowy blossoms when we arrived last year, is now budding with fruit. These things remind me how late the season has begun this year. Do not prolong it too far, Harry, dear. I am sure, after your illness, the mere sight of the open fields would do you good. Woodlawn is suburban, but it is not real country. Besides, we are only twenty miles out and you could ride in town in an hour whenever you liked.

"Be assured you shall have the money for your club expenses as soon as I can collect it. But property has its embarrassments, you know; and we may be rich in bonds and indentures, yet lack ready pennies at times, strange as it may

seem to your inexperience. Do not worry, dear. In your present delicate state of health it may injure you more than I care to think. The very next time I come to town you shall have what you desire. But I make my own terms. You must be a good boy and come to Hillsborough for it. Forgive my writing so soon. I have been thinking of you, and it surely cannot displease you to hear once more how dearly you are remembered, wherever she goes, by your loving mother,
"ALICE BREWSTER ARNOLD."

"Once more! No, nor a thousand times more!" cried Harry. "But I wish she'd come down sooner with the cash," he added. "What's this? Postscript?"

"Your friends, the Marches, have taken their cottage in Lenox. Possibly this may hasten your coming more than my entreaties."

"Jealous of Rosalie, already," laughed Harry. "Poor mother! What, another?"

"P. S. (Private)—It would be wise, Harry, if you should call upon your cousin. A visit from you would look well at this time."

"A call on Rob? Gad, I never thought of that. Give me the stationery, Indigo."

For five minutes Harry Arnold was alone, writing his prettiest note of compliment to accompany the gift of flowers to Miss Rosalie March. He had just moistened the mucilage when there came a ring at the bell.

"See if that's the fellows, Indigo. Look through the shutters."

"It's Kennedy," said Indigo, twisting his neck and eyes so as to get a slanting view of the callers.

"Who else?"

"Idler and Sunburst."

"Let them up."

"Well, Harry," cried the first of the three bloods, extending a hand, "what's the tempo of your song this morning?"

"Allegro, vivace, vivacissimo, Idler. Convalescing; doctor says I may go out; mother agreeable; medicine chest thrown to the dogs. Have a pill; only a few more left."

"Hello!" cried the fragile youth who had entered last. "Miss Rosalie March!" He picked up the envelope which Harry had laid down. "Sits the wind in that quarter still, Horatio?"'

"The actress, Harry?" cried a second of the trio.

"What actress, you booby? Miss March isn't an actress."

"Nevertheless, she occasionally acts," retorted Sunburst. His yellow beard entitled him to this alias.

"Just the opposite, then, of her brother, Tristram," said the tall, sallow youth addressed as Idler. "He is a sculptor, but he never sculps. Did you see his alto-relievo of a Druid's head in the Art club? Capital study. Why in the deuce doesn't he work?"

"If he did he might get his goods on the market," said Kennedy.

"Out on you for a Philistine, a dunderhead!" cried Harry. "Do you confound genius with salability? Idler could correct you on that point. You remember his satire on 'The Religious Significance of Umbrellas in China?' Was anything ever more daringly conceived, more wittily executed, more—but I spare the shades of Addison and Lamb. And how much did it fetch him? A paltry $15."

Idler was the only one of these well-born good-for-naughts who ever turned his gifts to use. Sketches over the sobriquet by which he was known to his friends occasionally appeared in the lighter magazines.

"But my 'New Broom' made a clean sweep, Harry," he protested.

"Murder," groaned Harry. "He had that in for us. A prepared joke is detestable. It's like bottled spring water."

"Hang spring water!" said Idler. "Hang water anyway!"

"Indigo," cried Harry, jumping at the hint, "fetch us some very weak whey from the spa. Let's have a real old high jinks of a slambang bust to celebrate my convalescence. Hello! What's that?"

The wild wail of a bagpipe smote the air and the four boon companions rushed to the window.

"Have him in!"

"Yoho!"

"Here, Sawnie!"

"He's coming."

Indigo and the piper entered from opposite doors at about the same time, the former fetching the "whey," which had a suspiciously reddish hue and was served in narrow bottles, the latter arrayed in all the bravery of his plaids, with a little boy by his side in similar costume.

"Hit her up, Sawnie," cried Kennedy.

"Let him wet his whistle first," said the Sunburst.

"And here's a handsel to cross his palm," added Harry, passing the piper something invisible. The minstrel pocketed it with an awkward bow and drank down the proffered "whey" at one gulp.

"I'll be reminding you, gentlemen," he said in "braid Scots," "lest ye labor under a misapprehension of my cognomen, that my name is not Sawnie, but Duncan Mc-Kenzie Logan, and this is my wee bairn, Archibald Campbell of that ilk. We're half-lowland, as ye doubtless know, the Logans being a border clan."

"Why don't you make the youngster blow the bellows?" cried Idler. "The organ-player never does the pumping."

"I'm no organ-player, if you please. 'Tis the hieland pipes I play, and there's no blowing the bellows except with my ain mouth. But the laddie dances prettily. Show your steps, Archie. Show the gentlemen a fling. Ainblins they've never seen the like of it before."

Archie was as highland as his father in rig, from his jaunty feathered bonnet to the kilt just reaching below his bare, brown knees. His firm boyish face had a Scotch prettiness in it, nothing effeminate, yet sweet to look at, and he went through the steps of the highland fling gracefully, one hand on hip, the other over his head, reversing them now and then, and occasionally spinning around, while the piper struck up "Roy's Wife." The conclusion was greeted with a burst of applause.

"Can't we dance to that tune, boys?" shouted Harry, seizing Kennedy around the waist. "Choose your partners. Give us a Tarantella."

"There's nae such tune in the hielands," said the piper, gravely.

"Well, the skirt dance will do. Hit her up and I'll make you a present big enough to buy all your aunts and cousins porridge for a fortnight."

"There's nae skeert dance known to my pipes," said the highlander, shaking his head. "Dinna ye mean the sword dance?"

"Try 'Highland Laddie,'" suggested Idler, hitting up a lively jig on the piano. The piper fell in and soon was pacing up and down the room, red in the face from his exertions, while the four merrymakers capered, kicked and skipped, with all sorts of offhand juvenilities. Harry, though the tallest present, was graceful as a girl.

"Hold up, fellows," cried the Sunburst, at last, puffing audibly. But the piper continued pacing up and down, forgetting everything in the furore of his enthusiasm except the moaning and shrieking of his instrument.

"Hold up, I say. Shut off your infernal drone. We can't hear ourselves think."

"'Tis the wind wailing on Craig-Ellachie I hear," said he of the Caledonian names.

"I think it's delirium tremens. Take a nip of the whey. That'll cure you. Here, Indigo, tap the geyser again for Sawnie."

Logan was not the man to set up frivolous punctilios against such an order as Idler's.

"There's medicine for the inner mon," he said, smacking his lips with gusto.

"Medicinal, eh? If you happen to take an overdose it's a medicinal spree, I suppose."

"I say, isn't tomorrow the Fourth?" cried Sunburst. "Play something patriotic, Sawnie, 'Hull's Victory,' or 'Lady Washington's Reel.'"

"There's nane o' them known to me or my instrument," said the minstrel. "It's a Scotch pipe and will play nane but the auld tunes of Scotland."

"Scotland! What's Scotland?" asked Idler.

"Wha—can it be ye never heard tell o' bonnie Scotland?" gasped the highlander, who was nearing the condition which Idler had described as a "medicinal spree."

"What is it, a man or a place? Did you ever meet the name before, fellows?"

All three solemnly shook their heads, whereat the Caledonian's jaw dropped in amazement.

"Wull, wull, I knew 'twas a most barbarous country I entered, but I'd thought the least enlightened peoples of the airth had heard of the glory and the celebrity of bonnie Scotland."

"Bonnie Scotland? Is Bonnie his first name?"

"Why, 'tis the country o' Scotland, I mean."

"Oh, I know," interposed Harry; "that little, barren, outlying province somewhere to the north of England."

"Oh, that!" cried the others, in contemptuous chorus.

"Where the coast line gets ragged, like an old beggar's coat," said Idler.

"And the people live on haggis and finnan haddie," added Kennedy.

"They are mostly exiles of Erin that have drifted back into barbarism," cried the Sunburst.

"Yes, that's the place," said Harry. "I've heard travelers tell of it. I believe it's put down in the latest gazetteer."

Poor Logan looked like a stifling man, but before he could launch his reply the long-drawn tones of a rival troubadour invaded the apartment. Once more the four roysterers rushed to the window.

"It's a dago!"

"Ahoy!" they signaled, waving their hands.

"Open the door for him, Indigo," cried Harry.

"Did you ever hear tell o' such savages, Archie?" whispered the piper to his son; "that had no enlightenment on the name o' bonnie Scotland, which is famous wherever valor and minstrelsy are honored."

"They maun be jestin', daddy."

"Jestin'? Tut, tut! Whaur's the jest?"

"Presto bellisimo, Paganini," cried the four youths, each rushing to the door and welcoming the organ-grinder, with a warm shake-hands. The Italian smiled profusely and doffed his cap, his monkey climbing to the organ top and imitating him in every gesture.

"Tune up your bagpipes, Sawnie," cried Harry. "We are going to have a tournament. Take a smell, Paganini?"

"Noa," answered the Italian, shaking his head, "noa drink—a."

"Then you're a bigger fool than you look," cried Idler, stumbling tipsily. "(Hic) I'm losing control of my curves."

"What tunes have you got in that box?" asked Harry of the organ-grinder, while Logan eyed him grimly with a look of scorn.

"What-a sing-a? 'Anni Runi.'"

"That will do. Grind away. Hold on. Get a full breath, Sawnie. Now for a medley."

The organ-grinder began turning his crank, but the Scotchman sulked in the corner.

"Stop there, Paganini. False start. Try again."

"I'll accompany nae uncivilized barrel-box, that's only fit to dandle idiot bairns wi'."

"What are you talking about?" cried Idler. "Uncivilized! You wildman of the hills! A red outlaw in his war paint couldn't look and act more outlandish than you do."

"Smooth him down, Harry," cried Sunburst. "Here, Sawnie, how much will you take for your pipes?"

"Enough to buy me them back again," answered the Scotchman, cannily, "and a bonus for the time o' their privation."

"You'll do," said Idler.

"Have another nip of the whey and let's hear you drown the dago," whispered Harry, confidentially, patting Logan on the back.

"Drown him? 'Twad na tak' a big puddle to do that."

"Of course not. But he's vain enough to think just the opposite. A good swig! Start her up now."

Idler drummed on the piano a few bars of "Scots Wha Ha'e," which set the piper marching and stamping again. At a nod from Harry the bowing Italian resumed his tune, and when the four carousers took hands in a circle and began chanting "Should Auld Acquaintance Be Forgot," the air was infernal with discord.

"Faster! Faster!" cried Harry. The Scotchman pranced in his industrious ecstasy, while the Italian put both hands to the organ-crank and turned for all that was in him.

"Oh, a smile for my Rosalie!" shouted Kennedy, maliciously, changing the air.

"None of that!" cried Harry, barely making his voice heard above the din. The little boy sitting in one corner had clapped both palms over his ears, and the monkey, watching his gesture, gravely climbed up and perched beside him, doing likewise.

"A kiss for my Rosalie," roared Kennedy, tantalizing his host. Half-angry, Harry caught up a wine bottle from the tray and pointed it at his tormentor.

"Pop!" the cork flew out and Kennedy put his hand to his eye with an exclamation of pain.

"Hello! What have I done?" cried Harry.

"Didn't know it was loaded," jeered Idler. But the concert had stopped, and when Kennedy uncovered his eye there was a blue swelling already under the lid.

"A surgeon!" cried Sunburst. "Amputate his head. It is the only hope of saving the eye."

"What's good for a black eye?" asked Harry, less unfeelingly than the others.

"Black the other for symmetry," cried Sunburst.

"Get some beefsteak, Indigo," said Harry.

"Kill the Jersey cow, Indigo, and cut off a sirloin," mocked Idler, who was half-seas over now. Meanwhile the Scotchman and the Italian, counting their emoluments, had folded their instruments and silently stolen away; while Sunburst, apparently as porous as a sponge, calmly and steadily put the bottle Harry had popped to his lips and drained it to the dregs.

CHAPTER X.

APPEARANCES AND DISAPPEARANCES.

"Now for Sir Galahad in jail!" said Harry, touching the bay with the point of his whip.

"He was an awfully virtuous cad!" laughed Kennedy. Sunburst had offered to convey Idler safely home, while Kennedy, the black-eyed, accompanied Harry, himself none the better for his morning bottle-bout, to the club-house in town. On the way they would make the visit to Robert.

There was evidently a strong dash of the Arnold blood in Harry. He showed more resemblance to his cousin than to the proud, thin-lipped woman who had sat through Floyd's preliminary trial. A stranger might even confuse them at the first glance, though Harry was five years the older of the two. It could not be gainsaid that he bore his age well. His movements were leopard-like in their swiftness and ease and his eyes shone with mesmeric power. The little darkness under their lids might be a peculiarity of complexion, but occasionally, in moments of repose, a shadow, no more, seemed to cross the cheek and make it look worn. His companions had noticed that the cue-point wavered a trifle in his hands of late and that his masse shots sometimes failed to draw the balls. But he was still facile princeps among gentlemen boxers of the city; and his long, brown arms were a delight to watch on the river, crossing and recrossing in the graceful rhythm of the practiced oars-man.

Arnold's true nature was hard to judge, for circumstances had conspired to spoil him from the cradle. A comely child, he had been allowed to carry the knicker-bocker period of tossing curls and gratified whims far into his teens, and the discovery that her darling was a man, and no longer a painted picture to be gazed at and displayed, had come upon his mother suddenly, like an unforeseen catastrophe. It had cost her many a pang to realize that she, who aspired to be sole mistress of his heart, shared now only a divided affection with a score of alien interests. Still she continued to indulge and anticipate his desires. They were rich and social station was her birthright. But it was with a jealous gnawing in her heart that she would sign the check for his new pleasure yacht or watch him pat the neck of his steeple-chaser Aladdin.

The dislike she bore to Robert Floyd was a natural consequence of his uncle's partiality. The families were outwardly upon good terms. If early influence counts, there could not well be much similarity of taste between the youth whose steps had been guided by the virile head of Benjamin Arnold and the idol of that indulgent, world-ly mother who never forgot that she belonged to the Brewsters of Lynn.

"Hold her ten minutes," said Harry, giving the reins to Kennedy at the outer gate of the jail. His name was a sufficient passport to the officer who guarded the outer turnstile, and he was directed across a bricked yard to the jail building proper. Here a more detailed explana-tion was exacted. Harry answered the questions suavely but not without some suppressed impatience. A few moments of delay, which he beguiled with an incessant finger-tattoo, and he was conducted to murderers' row.

"This isn't much like home, Rob," was his greeting, fortified by a hand extended through the cell bars. Floyd pressed it somewhat coldly.

"I'm grateful for the visit, Harry," he said.

"I was deucedly down with malaria when uncle died, you know."

"I was sorry to hear that from your mother."

"Yes, might have come around to the trial, I suppose; but mother wouldn't have it. You understand how she feels. Besides, what good could I do?" ·

"You are better now?"

"Awoke this morning as fresh as a new-born babe.

Going down to play with the foils awhile. Can't stop long."

Was it the glow of convalescence or of wine that shone in Harry's face? He made one or two imaginary passes with his cane, regardless of the feelings of the prisoner, to whom such a picture of prospective enjoyment could hardly be soothing.

"But I say, Rob," he cried, apparently remembering himself, "this is hard on you. What do you think of it all?"

Floyd eyed his cousin, as if the appropriate answer were not easy to find.

"It is hard," he replied.

"What would Uncle Ben say if he were alive?"

"Uncle Benjamin would be the first to proclaim my innocence," said Robert, his voice vibrant with emotion.

"To tell the truth, Rob, I don't know whether to be sorry his old scrawl's canceled or not. I had my doubts how I fared at Uncle Ben's hands. Mother said my half was hunky, but you know uncle hadn't that respect for my precious person she has." Harry's laugh showed that he was well aware of his mother's weakness in that regard. "How was it? Do you know? Did the old gentleman forget me?"

"I believe we were treated nearly alike," answered Robert.

"Gad, then I owe you $5,000,000——"

"Did you come here to insult me?"

At this outburst of indignation the sheriff's deputy drew near.

"That was nothing, Rob," said Harry, sobering up. "Only my cursed thoughtlessness. I'm sorry, on my word, you've got into the fix."

"Carry your condolences somewhere else."

"Oh, well——"

"I was always literal and I mean now what I say. Your apology only makes the matter worse."

There is nothing more subversive of dignity than an unpremeditated sneeze. Not that Saul Aronson had much dignity to spare. On the contrary, he was an ex-

tremely modest young man, with apparently one great
passion in his life, the service of Shagarach. On this occasion his resounding ker-choo proclaimed from afar the
arrival of that personage and threw a ridiculous damper
on the rising temper of the cousins. Seeing the two
strangers approach, Harry fumbled out a farewell and
withdrew with an air of languid bravado. Shagarach
watched him as he passed.

"Follow that young man for a few hours," he said to
Aronson. "I should like to know his afternoon programme."

Aronson hung on his master's lips and trotted off to
obey his command.

"I am Shagarach, come to defend you," he said to the
prisoner, still flushed with the remembrance of the quarrel.

"Who sent you to defend me?" was the curt reply.

"Your friend, Miss Barlow."

"Emily?"

Robert's voice grew softer.

"I have some questions to ask you."

"What have I done to be questioned as if I were a cut-
throat? What have I done to be jailed here like some
wild beast, before whom life would not be safe if he were
let at large?"

"I know you are innocent, Floyd."

Only the falsely accused can tell how the first assurance of trust from another revives hope and faith in their
kind. Robert Floyd was no man to lean on strangers,
yet Shagarach's words were as soothing to him as a gentle hand laid on a feverish forehead.

"Your cousin Harry came here to verify his knowledge
of the will, which disinherited him, did he not?"

"Harry was disinherited, that is true."

"How came you to give up the profession of botanist,
in which your uncle trained you?"

"Men interest me more than vegetables."

"But you refused your uncle's wealth, that would have
given you power among men."

"It was not mine. I had not earned it. I feared the temptation."

"You are a journalist, I believe?"

"Six months ago I happened to report a conference of charities for the Beacon. Today I am eking out my income by occasional work for that paper."

Shagarach thought of his own first brief. A youth, imperfectly acquainted with English, was charged with the larceny of an overcoat from his fellow-lodger. Something about him enlisted the sympathy of a kind-hearted lady who drew Shagarach into the case because of his knowledge of the Hebrew jargon which the prisoner spoke. The youth was acquitted and was now a student of law, being no other than Shagarach's assistant and idolator, Aronson. That was years ago. Today hundreds flocked to hear his pleading of a cause, judges leaned over alertly, as if learning their duty from him, and the very hangers-on of the courtroom acquired a larger view of the moral law when Shagarach expounded it.

"My own beginnings were as humble," he said.

"You are a criminal lawyer by choice, people say."

"The moral alternative of innocence or guilt, of liberty or imprisonment—sometimes, as now, of life or death—exalts a cause in my eyes far above any elevation to which mere financial litigation can attain."

Robert looked his visitor over thoughtfully. The criminal lawyer was not reputed the highest grade of the guild. But there was a sneer, too, in many quarters for the journalist. He, too, must mingle in the reek of cities, share Lazarus' crust and drink from the same cup with the children of the slums.

"And you have risen to the defense of murderers," he said.

"Men accused of murder," answered Shagarach.

"You are reputed to be uniformly successful."

"That is no miracle. My clients are uniformly innocent. My first step is to satisfy myself of that."

"When were you first satisfied of my innocence?"

"When I saw you here."

"I am to be removed to the state prison while the jail is repaired," said Robert, who had indulged dreams of some powerful intervention which should procure his release. "How long before a final hearing will be given me?"

"Two months at most. The evidence against your cousin is growing rapidly under my hands."

"It was 'evidence' that brought me here. Is your 'evidence' against Harry no more valuable?"

"I am not prosecuting Harry Arnold, but every item that points to his guilt guides the finger of suspicion away from you."

Shagarach was satisfied with his interview. He had elicited proof to his own mind of Robert's innocence and legal evidence of Harry's disinheritance under the will. To fasten knowledge of the fact upon the cousin would now be an easier task.

"Miss Barlow will be permitted to see you," was his parting assurance to the prisoner before he hurriedly returned to his office, to find an unexpected client awaiting him.

John Davidson, the marshal, had a friendly habit, the legacy of a country bringing-up, which his acquaintances found both useful and agreeable. Our tired Emily, trudging to Shagarach's with the heavy message of a day's failure, must have agreed with them heartily. At least, she did not decline his invitation when the kindly old gentleman drove up behind her and urged her to share his seat in the carriage.

"I am bringing him some evidence now," said Emily in answer to the marshal's first question, after he had settled her according to his liberal ideas of comfort and clucked his horse to a gentle trot.

"Evidence—no need of evidence, miss. If Shagarach has your case, that will be prima-facie evidence in itself of your sweetheart's innocence."

"He is a wonderful man. But do people like him?"

"Like him? Well, 'like' is a medium word, you see, used for medium people. He's a good deal of a sphinx to us all, my dear. But aren't you a brave girl to be tramping the streets for your sweetheart? Don't mind being called sweethearts, I hope? That was the old-country word when I courted Elizabeth. But I believe young folks now call it fiancee, inamorata—French words and Italian, as though they were ashamed to speak it out in good old English."

"Oh, we prefer sweethearts a hundred times. But I see Mr. Shagarach's sign."

The marshal handed her out with old-fashioned gallantry, threw his horse's head-weight on the curbstone and accompanied her upstairs. Neither Aronson, nor Jacob, the office boy, answered his knock, but a throaty falsetto, somewhat the worse for wear, was intoning an evangelical hymn within. Strange quavers ad libitum and a constant beating of the foot, occasionally heightened to a break-down stamp, intermingled with the air. It was only by giving a rap with his whole clenched hand that the marshal was able to arouse the attention of this musical inmate.

"Evenin', Mr. Davidson. Keepin' house, you see."

"Good evening, Jupiter." Then to Emily: "This is Pineapple Jupiter."

"Cullud gospel-preacher, missus. Belong to the mission upstairs. Buy a mission paper, missus?"

His complexion was as black as a coal shovel, but everything artificial about him made the antithesis of the swan to the raven. His suit was of bleached linen, his shirt bosom, choker and spotless cravat, all the color of snow. Even his wool was wintry and the rolling eyes and brilliant teeth gave his ensemble the effect of a pen-and-ink sketch, or one of those black-and-white grotesques that recently captured a passing vogue.

"When will Shagarach return?" asked Davidson, but a light step on the stairs, which Emily knew to be his, rendered an answer needless. The lawyer bowed with his usual stateliness and ushered them in.

"Remain outside till Jacob comes, Jupiter," he said. The negro salaamed deferentially.

"As a result of today's inquiries," Shagarach folded his arms, "two desirable witnesses are missing. The peddler, as I surmised, is not a peddler; and the incendiary, who could assist us materially in our researches, still remains in the Arnold mansion."

Emily's face was puzzled at this enigmatic opening.

"That is to say, he was not seen by any one coming out. I believe, however, that he succeeded in getting away unobserved, as I think I had the pleasure of meeting him this afternoon."

"The incendiary?" cried Emily, and the marshal echoed her.

"At the county jail."

Emily's heart fluttered. Had Shagarach become a convert to the belief in Robert's guilt? And if so?

"You know Harry Arnold?" he asked.

"I have never met him." She colored a little, for she was not descended from the Brewsters of Lynn. "But it seems to me your argument against him is inferential, Mr. Shagarach." Twenty times she had gone over it on her pillow the night before.

"Were the a priori case against Mr. Floyd as strong, you would have more reason than you have to be apprehensive, Miss Barlow," said Shagarach, in that ringing tone of his, from which all the sap of emotion seemed purposely wrung out, leaving only a residuum of dry logic.

Immediately he began writing a letter, as if to terminate the interview, and John Davidson reached for his hat, casting a glance down at his carriage in the street. Then with an effort Emily unburdened herself of the portentous message which she had come to deliver.

"I have done my best," she said. "But Bertha Lund is not to be found."

CHAPTER XI.

A KISS IN THE DARK.

Bertha Lund's aunt, Mrs. Christenson, kept a boarding house for Swedes, on a street near the water front. By virtue of an intelligence-office license she was also empowered to obtain places in domestic service for newly imported Frederikas and Katherinkas. But the Swedish housemaid is one of those rare commodities in which the demand exceeds the supply. So there had been no crowded gallery of sodden faces around the waiting-room when Emily called Thursday morning before going to work, but only two or three laughing maidens who chatted with the boarders. All had the bloom of a winter apple in their cheeks and their blue eyes sparkled with reflections of the sea. Mrs. Christenson was making terms with a lady in an inner room.

"You wish for a servant?" she said, coming forward pleasantly.

"My business is with Miss Bertha Lund, your niece. I believe she is lodging here."

"My niece is gone," answered the landlady, unceremoniously turning her back and shutting the door with that emphasis which is feminine for profanity. Then her voice was heard, pitched a little higher, as she interpreted the silvery Swedish of the girl within, for the benefit of her future mistress.

"Something must be wrong," thought Emily. But there was nothing for her to do but retreat, somewhat hurt and a great deal troubled. She had reached the head of the stairs when one of the domestics in the waiting-room came forward sympathetically and in her pretty, broken English explained Mrs. Christenson's conduct. Bertha, it seems, had not returned home since the night of the trial. Search had been made for her, but without result. From what the girl said, though this was put guardedly and in an almost inaudible whisper, Emily inferred that Bertha, who was naturally quick-tempered, had chafed under her aunt's imperious discipline and had probably gone to board with some friend, registering herself for employment meanwhile in one of the other intelligence offices. Once before she had manifested the same impatience of restraint and had disappeared into the country for an entire summer.

It was still possible, even probable, that she could be found if search were instituted at once. Bertha had only a day's start of her pursuer, and it was not likely that she had secured a situation to her taste so soon. Emily formed the heroic resolve to scour the intelligence offices herself. Finding the list in the directory incomplete, she boldly visited police headquarters, from which licenses are issued, and copied the name and address of every keeper in the city.

With a letter from one of the police commissioners and a minute description of Bertha at her tongue's end, Emily had passed from office to office, braving discourtesy and even insult. As this was the busy season her truancy from the studio would have to be made up by lamplight work, which meant ache to her weary eyes, and the unwonted climbing of stairs and trudging about for hours soon exhausted her small stock of strength. But Emily was less concerned over her personal sacrifice than over the failure of her inquiries. By 4 o'clock her task was still uncompleted. The rounds of the offices had not been half-made. Still no Bertha could be found, no girl answering her description or dressed as Bertha had been dressed at the trial having applied for work on the previous day. With a cloud of despondency forming over her heart, only lightened by a dim hope of consolation from Shagarach, she had turned her steps in the direction of his office when John Davidson overtook her.

"Not to be found!" echoed the marshal.

"When was she seen last?" inquired Shagarach, calmly.

"The evening of the trial," answered Emily. "She hasn't returned to her aunt's, where she was lodging, since then."

"Why, I saw the girl talking with McCausland," said Davidson.

"When?" asked the lawyer.

"Tuesday evening. Everybody else had gone and Miss Barlow and I were alone in the ante-chamber. McCausland put his head in, as if he wanted the room, and I noticed two women behind him. One was the housemaid and the other was——"

"Mrs. Arnold?"

"True enough. 'Twa'nt no need to tell you, was it?"

The marshal's eyes grew big with admiration.

"Merely a guess. Bertha Lund is a government witness, and McCausland has a habit of keeping his witnesses under cover, especially when they are poor and he is fighting wealth or influence. However, we have a right to know all Bertha knows. Could you find out if she is living with the Arnolds?" he said, turning to Emily.

"They are out of town, but I'll make inquiries," answered the resolute girl.

"This may be of use." Shagarach handed her the note he had rapidly written. It was unsealed and addressed to the warden of the state prison. When the young girl was settled again to John Davidson's satisfaction in the seat of his buggy, she opened the envelope and read its contents aloud:

"My Dear Sir: The bearer, Miss Emily Barlow, is assigned to important duties for the defense in the cause of Commonwealth vs. Floyd. I shall esteem it a favor if you will grant her admission to the defendant as my personal representative at all times when she may apply to you. Respectfully yours,

"MEYER SHAGARACH,
"Counsel for the Accused."

"Well, that was clever, wasn't it?" said old John Davidson, and for the rest of the ride he entertained her with anecdotes of Shagarach's most memorable victories, as well as other fascinating relations. For the marshal, among his many virtues, was a famous traveler, being one of the handful who can boast of having set foot in every state of our union. He may not have been a marvel of detective cunning, as McCausland had intimated, but Emily had forgotten all about her fatigue and was in an agreeably hopeful frame of mind when he set her down before her house door in the plain side street.

That night Robert Floyd slept in a state prison cell. The atmosphere of the place oppressed him. Everything, down to the very keys and padlocks, was more massive than at the county jail. Led along a narrow corridor by tenanted cells, whose inmates came to the bars and greeted him, or crouched in the inmost recesses, he was reminded of a menagerie of dangerous beasts. At the door of his own cell the revulsion had seized him like an epileptic fit and he had wrenched himself loose from the jailer. In an instant four vise-like hands were tightened on him and he was flung bodily into the apartment. The iron door swung to with a clang and he heard the jailer's footsteps receding.

"Coo-ee! Ducky, don't ee like ee c'adle?"

"He's a lifer, sure!"

"Don't cry, Johnnie. You'll never get out any more."

"I move a resolution of sympathy for our newly elected associate. All in favor, curse Longlegs!"

There is a passage in Bach's "Passion" music where the infuriated Jews, being offered the choice of pardon for Barabbas or the Savior, shriek out the name of the robber. Robert remembered thinking that up to then he had never heard anything more devilish than the roar of rage with which the multitude express their preference for "Barabbas!" But the chorus of curses from the convict pack that greeted the sobriquet of "Longlegs" was like an uproar from still lower deeps, where spirits more hideous than the deicides may be confined.

This is not the normal temper of prisons, by any means. But the Georgetown prison had been for months in a state of incipient mutiny and the brewing storm was now threatening to break. Among the grounds of complaint alleged against the present warden was his retention of the obnoxious turnkey, "Longlegs," who was loathed as a "squealer," because he could not be bought. It was further alleged that the men's tobacco rations had been unjustly diminished one-half, such a thing as gratitude for the allowance of this luxury at all not entering their minds. The teams that carted goods from the workshops had recently been put in charge of prison employes, and a useful means of communication with outer friends thus cruelly cut off. In the eyes of the "solitaries" and "hard-labor" men their bill of rights had been monstrously trampled upon, and there was ample cause for the deposing of Warden Tapp and the establishment of anarchy in the institution. Only the "lifers" were for peace.

"Half a plug is better than no smoke, boys," said John Bryant, who had killed his wife, humorously. But he had served fourteen years already and lived in hopes of a pardon some Thanksgiving day for his good behavior.

After exhibiting so clearly their position "against the government," Robert's fellow-lodgers began to put inquiries to himself.

"Say, freshy, what's your name?"

Robert was too exasperated, too disgusted, to answer.

"He's tongue-tied."

"Wants his supper."

"Look out for a spy, fellers. That ain't true blue."

"Mum's the word."

It was evident that Floyd's refusal to make free had branded him at once with the stamp of unpopularity. But the young man had other thoughts to occupy his mind. He was pondering upon his own terrible plight and upon Shagarach's visit. Fully an hour must have passed in these reflections, for it was very dark, when they were disturbed by a low remark from his left-hand neighbor.

"Say, chummy, I hain't one of these 'ere bloomin' mutineers."

It was a wheezy voice and Floyd remembered to have heard at intervals from that quarter one of those racking coughs which distress the listener almost as much as the sufferer. The man seemed to be in the rear of his cell and to have his mouth to the wall. Robert said nothing, but his interest was languidly aroused.

"Say, get into the hospital, Dobbs," remarked a voice that was beginning to be familiar to Robert.

"I 'ave been in the 'ospital, you unfeelin', bloomin' coves," replied the asthmatic prisoner.

"Ho, ee's Henglish, ee his," said some one, whereupon there was a faint storm of laughter. Robert's sympathy was enlisted on the side of the man called Dobbs. His uncle had been an Englishman and the national feeling was strong in the nephew. Speaking as low as possible, so that the others might not hear, he said to Dobbs:

"You are an Englishman? This is bad company you've got into."

"Lord, me boy, Hi know that—a scurvy job lot o' bloomin' ordinary coves as I'd cut dead if Hi was a

gentleman of fortune. But you see Hi hain't. Being
only Bill Dobbs, Hi can't afford to preach hinnocence,
and choose me hown 'ouse-mates, like a juke."

The cough choked his utterance for awhile and evoked
further remonstrance from the yawning crew around him.

"What is your sentence?" asked Robert.

"Height years for burglary—if they can 'old me," and
Bill Dobbs chuckled knowingly, like one who had tested
the fragility of prison walls before. "W'ich, bein' a slippery fish, is a question Hi 'ave been considerin' seriously."

"Why did you leave England?" asked Robert.

"The climate is gettin' so warm," answered the
cockney. "W'y, the gulf stream is comin' so near us there
it would almost boil a turkey. Hawfully bloomin' 'ot, you
know, chummy. I'm a-winkin' at you."

"Especially about Scotland Yard, I suppose. You're
a professional burglar?"

"Not always, young man. Hi 'ad a Henglish mother
once, w'ich I shall never forget 'ow she 'eard my prayers.
And hevery day Hi dressed myself up in my blue blouse
and breeches, and my dinner pail (w'ich wasn't hempty)
under my harm, and hevery bloomin' bobby I met says
Hi to him, says Hi: 'Hi'm Martin Thimblethorpe, from
the west country, and can you tell me w'ere's Regent
row?' Blarst me if they wouldn't point their fingers this
way and that way and follow my departing footsteps with
a look of pride, as much as to say: 'There goes a honest
Hinglish workingman; see 'is hindependent hair."

"But you never worked very hard, I fancy, with your
blouse and your dinner-pail?"

"'Ard? Hi fancy Hi did."

"What did you do?"

"Jeweler's 'elp."

"That is, you sold your plunder to a fence?"

"Fence? Wot fence? Hi 'ad an accommodatin' friend
in the business, who asked no impertinent questions and
paid me 'alf price for my contributions—w'ich was bloomin' low figures, considering Hi never accepted hanything
cheap. If there's one class Hi 'ate, positively 'ate, young

man, it's them bloomin' shoddy gaffers wot sport a genteel reputation on plated spoons and paste."

"You always discriminated against such people?"

"Halways! Ho, it used to do my 'eart good," continued Dobbs, chuckling at the reminiscence, "w'en they
wrote up one of my nocturnal visits (Hi halways make
my collections in the quiet hours of the hevenin') as 'ow
the leavin' of the plated ware and the abandonin' of a
temptin' case of hartificial diamonds shows the 'and of the
solitary cracksman. There's appreciation, Hi used to say!
There's fame! You 'it it 'appily, young man. Hi always
discriminated."

"Martin Thimblethorpe, then, was the solitary cracksman, and your real name is Dobbs?"

"Bill Dobbs. Wot's your line, chummy? Fashionable
embezzlement? Hi admire that line. It's genteel and
the perquisites is liberal accordingly."

Floyd was getting interested in spite of himself. These
first-hand experiences of a professional burglar were life,
and in spite of the fellow's utter villainy and vulgarity (he
could almost see his cunning leer through the walls) they
had a spice of romance that held him. But their colloquy
was interrupted just here by a sound of footsteps and the
approach of a light, which set the whole ward raving
again.

"Shut up your screeching," came a voice of command,
at which the mutinous crew subsided, and Robert heard
apologetic remarks.

"It's Gradger."

"It isn't Longlegs."

"We thought it was Longlegs."

Gradger, for some reason, was a favorite with the men.
He went straight to Floyd's cell and pointed him out to
Emily Barlow.

"Emily!"

"Robert!"

That was all they could say for awhile.

"My darling," cried Robert, who was the first to recover command of himself. He was indignant to think

that she, too, should be forced into these surroundings.
"Why have you come here?"

"Only to be with you for a few moments, Robert. I
thought of you all friendless and lonesome."

"God bless you, dear. But you must not remain. Go
away quickly and do not come here again."

It was the old, natural instinct to screen the purer half
of our race from degrading contact with things we ourselves must meet.

"But why should I not visit you, Robert?"

"Because this is hell and you are an angel."

He drew her to him and kissed her through the bars.
Instantly the sound was re-echoed a hundred times, dis-
torted and vulgarized, throughout the ward. In the silence which followed Emily's first words, the sweethearts
had forgotten their audience of thieves and cutthroats,
to whom every syllable was audible. Hierarchs of sin,
virtuosos in infamy, all the demon in their souls seemed
roused by this innocent pledge of mutual faith between
youth and maiden, and even the stern threats of Gradger
could not silence their outbreak of hideous derision.

Emily started back as red as fire.

"Go, darling," cried Robert, between his set teeth,
while shouts of "Ta, ta, Robert," "Kiss me, Emily," intermingled with the foul ribaldry generated in minds shut
away from all purifying touch of womanhood, taunted the
fleeing girl and roused her imprisoned lover's passion to
frenzy. He could have strangled three of them single-
handed.

"Better call daytimes, miss, when the men are working in the shops," said Gradger. He had not taken Emily
for a girl who had herself to work daytimes in a shop.

Meanwhile the storm raged louder and louder, and
several turnkeys were called to quell the disturbance and
carry the ringleaders away to the "block." But the more
it volleyed around him the cooler grew young Floyd.
His resentment gradually hardened to a kind of pitying
scorn, and when the last oath had died away it was with
sweeter thoughts than he had indulged for three bitter
nights that he laid his head on the pallet and drowsed

into oblivion. His pillow lay close to the point of the wall where Dobbs liked to do his talking, and while the midnight bell was ringing he thought he heard the cracksman whisper:

"The young lady stretched it, chummy. You 'ave one friend 'ere. Let 'em screech their bloomin' lungs off."

But this may have been a dream.

CHAPTER XII.

SIMPLE SIMON.

"The appointment you heard them make. I missed the rendezvous."

"Harry Arnold said Wednesday was his locky day——"

"Lucky day," corrected Shagarach.

"His lucky day," said Aronson, "and if the old lady put up he would break the bank."

"That I understand. A gambling tryst. The old lady is his mother. Put up means to pay his money. But the place—what was the name of the place?"

"When they left each other Arnold said: 'Wednesday at the Tough-Coat,' and Kennedy said: 'All right, Harry.'"

"Repeat that word."

"Tough-Coat."

"Repeat it again."

"Tough-Coat."

Still Shagarach looked nonplused. The syllables conveyed no meaning whatever. Yet Aronson felt sure of the substantial accuracy of his version.

"Very well." The lawyer dismissed the subject, sent Aronson off on irrelevant business and gave a few hours of attention to his other clients. The law's delay had not infected Shagarach. Whatever the matter he undertook, he was punctual as the clock in its performances, though not, in the ordinary sense of the word, a methodical man.

Early in the afternoon an unlooked-for visitor took his

place among those waiting in the outer room. Jacob hastened to give him the chair of precedence, and announced his name to Shagarach, then in closet conference with an honest-appearing bookkeeper, whose acquittal on a charge of forgery he had just procured.

"I will see Mr. Rabofsky next," said the lawyer to Jacob.

The man so called was a short, bulky Hebrew, of 60-odd winters (one would prefer reckoning his years by the more rigorous season). His nose was like an owl's beak and his beard spread itself luxuriantly over his face, plainly undefiled of the scissors. The hair was indeterminately reddish and gray and his eyes were the color of steel. Shagarach bowed him into his private room, the caller strutting like one accustomed to homage.

Although the door was closed behind him as usual, Rabofsky glanced suspiciously around and spoke in the Hebrew jargon—that grafting of foreign idioms on a German patois which his tribe has carried all over eastern Europe, and latterly, via Hamburg, into the cities of America.

"It is a long time since we have met, kinsman Shagarach," he said.

"A long time since I have had that honor," replied the lawyer, bowing with the Hebrew's respect for age.

"Not since your respected father's funeral, I believe. He was one of my friends, whose memory always remains to uplift me—a glory to our race and religion."

"My respected father's friends are my friends to the end of my days."

Shagarach's father had been a rabbin or expounder of the sacred books. Great was the scandal when Rabbi Moses' son abandoned daily attendance at the synagogue and gave himself over to the ways, though not to the society, of the gentiles. His mother, with whom he lived, still kept up the observances of the law, baking·the unleavened bread at the paschal season and purchasing the flesh only of the lawfully butchered ox. Her son neither praised nor blamed, but she knew he was no longer of Israel's sects; not even of the mystical Essenes, among

whom his father might be counted, and whose study is the
unpronounceable name of God. Others of his people
who lacked a mother's indulgence knew this, and it was
rarely that one of the orthodox children of Israel brought
his worldly troubles to Shagarach.

"Your health is strong under Jehovah, I trust," continued Simon Rabofsky.

"Have you come to inquire about my health?" asked
Shagarach. The old man's prelude, beginning so fitfully
and far away, threatened to prolong itself interminably.

"Nay, a small affair of consultation which it shall be
richly worth your while to advise upon," answered the
other, craftily.

"State the facts with brevity and clearness."

"Speedily, kinsman Shagarach, speedily." Again he
looked cautiously around. "You are aware that out of
the savings of my days of hard labor I occasionally permit the use of small sums to my friends."

"You are a money-lender? That I know. One of my
clients desires a loan of you. Which is it?"

"Not one of your clients, kinsman Shagarach."

"Who?"

"Mrs. Arnold."

Not a muscle of Shagarach's well-schooled countenance
quivered, though the old Jew's eyes almost pierced him
as he uttered the name. Opposite as the two men were
in every trait, a substratum of affinity came out in this
deadlock of their glances. On both sides the same set
lip, the same immobile forehead, trained by centuries of
traffic to conceal the fermentation of the powerful brain
within.

"I am not acquainted with the lady," said Shagarach.

"But you are acquainted with her estate under the
will of her brother-in-law."

Thoroughly aroused now to his subject, Rabofsky had
abandoned his roundabout manner and pushed his words
rapidly forth in an indistinct growl.

"Slightly so. State the facts."

"I will. Yesterday there came to my office a lady, all
veiled, and asked me for $10,000. 'That is a large sum,'

said I. 'You have it,' said she, 'and I want it. I will pay for it.' 'Yes, indeed, you shall pay for it,' I said to myself, but aloud I only asked her: 'What security could you give me if I should go about among my friends and trouble them and trouble myself for your service?' 'The security of my name,' she answered, proudly, like a queen commanding her scullion. 'I am Mrs. Arnold, widow of the banker, Henry Arnold, and a daughter of Ezra Brewster of Lynn.' 'Oh, madam,' said I, 'I am Simon Rabofsky, husband of Rebecca Rabofsky, and a son of the high priest Levi, who is twice mentioned in the talmud; but I could not borrow $10,000 without pledging something more substantial than my great ancestor's name.' Then she sneered a little under her veil, the proud unbeliever, and took out her rubies and diamonds and watch —a glittering heap. 'Keep these until I return you the money,' she said. 'This is not enough,' said I, examining the stones. 'Have you nothing more?' 'My son's interest in the estate of the late Prof. Arnold will cover your paltry loan 500 times over.' 'I will reflect upon the subject,' said I. 'Call again in two days.' So I came to consult kinsman Shagarach."

"Well?"

"Has her son any interest in Prof. Arnold's estate?"

The question had come point-blank at last and Shagarach found himself less prepared to answer it than he could have wished.

The Arnolds were financially embarrassed, possibly ruined, by Harry's infatuation for the gaming-table. This was to be inferred from the conversation with Kennedy over-heard by Aronson. Their real estate must be mortgaged to the limit, perhaps beyond its shrunken value, or Mrs. Arnold would not be begging a loan at a money-lender's shop. Family jewels were invariably the last resort of declining fortunes unwilling to abandon cherished appearances. Should he advise the loan and let Harry cast it away, as he seemed likely to do, in his ambition to "break the bank?" Such a step might place the young man in his power.

For the standing of the will was still uncertain. Evidence might be in existence sufficient to uphold the destroyed document. In that event Mrs. Arnold's promissory note to Rabofsky would be worth no more than the value of the securities he held. Robert's statement was positive that Harry was disinherited. This opened up a new view to Shagarach.

It would be fatal to the interests of Floyd if the will should be ignored and half the estate allowed him as heir-at-law. Such a parade of the profits of the incendiary's crime could not fail to rearouse a burst of public indignation which would work its way into the jury-box. Shagarach determined then and there to strive for the upholding of the will, though it should mean the ruin of the Arnold fortune and the loss to Robert Floyd of $5,000,000.

"I do not know," he answered. Something was due to Rabofsky.

"You have waited a long time. You have been thinking. What do you think?"

"It is a difficult part of a difficult problem. My advice——"

"You will not charge your respected father's friend unreasonably?" put in the Jew.

Shagarach knew that Rabofsky was a pharisee of the strictest sect and had not been his father's friend. He knew also that reasonableness of charge was not one of his own eccentricities, and probably would not be exemplified in the loan to Mrs. Arnold. But he replied:

"Certainly not. I shall consider that when the work is done."

"Now, kinsman Shagarach."

"Not now. I cannot foresee the amount of labor, the number of consultations, involved," said Shagarach, resolutely. "Do you wish my advice?"

"I shall not pay the charge if it is unreasonable," growled Rabofsky.

"For the present I advise you to lend only what you can with safety on the pledges. I will see Mrs. Arnold about the estate and confer with you further after our interview."

At that moment Aronson opened the door, his eyes dancing with excitement. He panted, as if he had just run upstairs.

"Meester Shagarach," he broke in, but stood awed in the presence of Rabofsky, who was a potent man in the Ghetto.

"Escort Mr. Rabofsky to the stairs," said Shagarach, approaching Aronson, so that the latter might have an opportunity to whisper his message. He was none too soon, for a young man had already entered the door of the outer room.

"Kennedy," whispered Aronson.

It was Harry Arnold's friend.

CHAPTER XIII.

BROWBEATING EXTRAORDINARY.

"Will you take in my card? I'm in a deuce of a rush," said Kennedy to Aronson when the latter had dismissed Simon Rabofsky. Shagarach read his name, daintily engraved in the form to which the weather-vane of fashion had at that moment veered and was imperatively pointing. It introduced "Mr. Arthur K. Foxhall."

"I will see the gentleman in a few minutes," said he. Shagarach must have transacted an almost incredible amount of business in the interim, for his waiting-room was cleared of clients when "Mr. Arthur K. Foxhall" was at length admitted.

"I received this communication from you. My lawyer informs me that it contains matter defamatory per se." He tossed a letter down on the table at which Shagarach was sitting, with his arms folded as usual. "But before taking action on the matter I thought I would give you an opportunity to explain."

"The note is in English, is it not?" said Shagarach.

"It might pass for such," replied young man supercilious.

"Then it needs no further explanation. The sooner you and your lawyer begin your action the better pleased I shall be." Shagarach began writing a letter coolly, as if the matter were at an end, but his visitor, either in nervousness or anger, tapped the polished tip of his shoe with his cane. It was certainly a most aggressive-looking weapon, with its knob carved into a scowling bulldog's head.

"Gentlemen"—he emphasized the word—"men of honor," he paused again, " do not use language of others which they cannot defend, either before the courts of law or by giving personal satisfaction."

"Gentlemen and men of honor do not fabricate lies after taking a solemn oath to tell nothing but the truth," answered Shagarach, without glancing up from the note he was scribbling.

"The third person protects you. You use the coward's refuge, innuendo, because you dare not address the charge to me directly."

Shagarach picked up his letter, which the visitor had thrown down.

"I have taken particular pains to be direct as well as explicit over my own signature. I find that I have accused you, Arthur Kennedy Foxhall," he emphasized the middle name, though it was only initialed in the address, "of deliberate perjury in the case of Commonwealth vs. Bail. My letters do not as a rule require marginal annotations or parol addition to make their meaning clear, and I am credited with sufficient prudence to foresee their consequences before writing them."

Shagarach folded his arms again and his great eyes pierced Foxhall—or Kennedy as he was generally called. It was the family name of a rich relative who had adopted and supported him.

"No," he added, slowly, "this is hardly a case for prosecution or for personal satisfaction. The duello is out of date."

"My valet might object to the opponent I assigned him," said the self-styled gentleman and man of honor. Shagarach's retort was swift, yet uttered without the twitch of an eyelash, as though he were simply recalling his visitor to the original business.

"His master lied in order to prove an alibi for Charles Munroe——"

Kennedy's chalky face flushed faintly.

"If the sword is out of fashion the cane is not," he cried, lifting his formidable bulldog.

"The principal witness against my client in the Bail case," continued Shagarach, raising his voice and controlling Kennedy with his eyes, "and himself the beneficiary of the check which my client was accused of forging."

"You got him off. That was enough. Are you trying to blackmail us for a heavier fee?"

"The case was a conspiracy instigated by Charles Munroe and abetted by his friends, among whom Arthur Kennedy Foxhall was the most conspicuous for his zeal."

"You scum of a shyster! Do you think you can jew me into a dicker?"

Shagarach arose and walked to the window. He was not an equestrian, but natural perception taught him the useful rule to turn his horse's head when he starts to run away. Facing suddenly about, he said:

"I am a Jew, true. Perhaps that is why I do not poison myself with opium."

The young man's cheek grew pale again. The cane dropped and he sunk in his chair.

"Am I to be prosecuted for that also?" The anger in his tones had flickered away to a feeble peevishness. "How do you know?"

"Because you are wearing a light overcoat with the mercury at 80," answered Shagarach, who had glanced at the thermometer in his window. "Because you have the glazed eye of a man in fever, and because you lie like an oriental!"

This time Kennedy made no protest against the insult. He was succumbing to the strain placed upon his shattered nerves by the remorseless man across the table.

"There is your cause of action," said Shagarach, tossing back his letter. Again he dipped his pen in the ink preparing to write.

"What do you want of me?" asked Kennedy.

"Nothing," Shagarach had half-filled the sheet. He was stamping the envelope when the next question slowly came.

"Why do you follow up the matter? Your client is safe?"

"But the community is no longer safe when perjurers strut about, masquerading as the sole guardians of honor."

He folded his arms once more and looked straight at his man. In another the gesture might seen theatrical, but it was Shagarach's natural attitude in thought, like the bowed head and lowered eyes of the philosopher burrowing into the depths of things, or the uplifted gaze of the poet leaving earth for the stars and sunset. The lawyer's interests lay in the horizontal plane, and the faces of fellow-men were his study.

"Yes, I am reputed inexorable to perjurers. It is true. They rarely escape me unpunished. As a consequence, witnesses prefer to tell me the truth, which is an advantage to my clients, of whose interests I am the devoted servitor."

"And you will ruin me to gratify this—this——"

"I will procure your indictment for perjury and conspiracy in the case of Commonwealth vs. Bail."

Kennedy trembled like one with an ague. But stronger men than he had yielded as abjectly to Shagarach. He was a blood of high standing, with a fortune as well as a reputation to lose. The chances of a felon's succeeding to the property of old Angus Kennedy, the millionaire, who had adopted him, were relatively slight.

"What is the penalty for perjury?" he asked, in a random way, as if at a loss what to say or do.

"Imprisonment at hard labor."

"It is not punishable by fine?"

"Never."

There was a pause, broken only by the rustling of

Aronson's papers in the outer room. Then Shagarach spoke.

"You have an appointment with Harry Arnold for next Wednesday evening."

Kennedy started up. His smooth face grew cadaverous and the helpless look of a kneeling suppliant came into his eyes, which were riveted on the great, wide orbs of his tormentor.

"At a gambling resort," continued Shagarach.

"I am not a gambler," Kennedy's voice was hollow, his expression piteous. Shagarach studied him a moment. Probably he was speaking the truth. The evil passions are jealous and absolute monarchs. Seldom does more than one of them reign at a time.

"But Harry Arnold is."

"Harry is plunging heavily."

Shagarach was satisfied at last. An adequate motive for Harry's deed was clearly in view. It was not the most heinous crime which had been committed to gratify the gamester's passion.

"I wish to be with you on that occasion."

"It will be hard," answered Kennedy, his face clouded with consternation and a torrid flush of something like shame sweeping over it. "The Dove-Cote is too well guarded."

"The Dove-Cote!" Shagarach was betrayed into an ejaculation of surprise. This was the "Tough-Coat" which Aronson's imperfect articulation had disguised.

"It may be hard, but it is not impossible."

"Not impossible, no."

"Well-known men are seen there at times?"

"Oh, yes."

Kennedy smiles.

"And your escape from prison depends upon my obtaining entrance."

The smile had faded away.

"Why do you wish to be there?"

"My reasons are my own. However, I will make a limited confidant of you. I am at work upon a cause which logical study does not perfectly elucidate. That frequently happens. I must see my man off his guard, when he is most himself. My visit to the Dove-Cote will be a psychological study."

"They will compel me to vouch for your good faith."

"You may do so. Nothing seen or heard by me there will ever be revealed. I go, as I have told you, to study a soul, not to gather facts. The facts are already mine."

"Where shall I call for you?"

"Here."

"At 8 o'clock?"

"Very well. There is one condition attached to our bargain. You shall not reveal this appointment to Harry Arnold."

"He will be there——"

"But he does not know me. We probably shall not meet. Other—gentlemen, as you call them—will be there."

"Miss Barlow," said Aronson, at this moment opening the door.

Kennedy had arisen to go, but turned curiously when he heard the sweet voice from without.

"Only a moment, Mr. Shagarach."

The lawyer stepped out and conferred with her. She had run down in her lunch hour, full of a new project which she burned to carry out, but like everything else, she had thought it best first to submit it to Shagarach. His approval was given coolly, she thought.

"Some one of the park policemen may have seen him."

"Possibly."

"If not, how can you explain those four hours of for-getfulness—I mean, of course, to the satisfaction of a jury?"

"It is not unprecedented. I have an explanation, or the germ of one. However, pursue your inquiries. They may prove of value. And, when you visit Floyd, occa-sionally wear a water lily."

"Why?"

"It was the flower he brought you that evening."

Emily caught the impertinent stare of the manikin within just as she was turning to leave.

"Understand, Kennedy," said Shagarach, "if Arnold is informed of this agreement, directly or indirectly, our contract is broken and I will spare no pains to lodge you where you belong."

His tone made the weakling shudder.

"Why do you desire to conceal it from Harry?" he asked, obstinately.

"Draw what inference you choose."

Shagarach returned to his desk and Emily was uneasily aware that the youth whom she had seen in his office passed her twice in the crowd while she was making her way back to the studio. But Arthur Kennedy Foxhall was too perturbed that day to practice with success even the easy arts of the professional lady-killer. His pursuit of Emily only registered on his memory a face which was to haunt him in his drug-fed dreams.

CHAPTER XIV.

GNAWING OF THE RAT'S TOOTH.

"Hello, Bobbs," called the solitary cracksman. "Put your hear to the chink and let's 'ave a palaver."

The "chink" was that hollow spot in the rear of the cell, where by pressing his ear against the wall Floyd could hear communications from Dobbs, inaudible to the rest of the prisoners.

Robert wondered not a little at the persistent friendliness of the fellow. He felt conscious of lacking the touch of comradeship. He might even be called ascetic, were not the stigma precluded by his passion for music and his love of landscape. Long botanical tramps with his uncle had given him an acute feeling for the moods of nature, and in his violin playing a deep sensibility found outlet through the practiced and sensitive fingertips. But in general he had little palate for the bouquet and effervescence of life, and was credited, therefore, with less readiness of sympathy than his cousin, who responded quickly to all fleeting impressions of pleasure.

While Harry, as adjutant of his crack cadets, was seen prancing on parade in all the bravery of gold lace, his sword hilt resting on his saddle, his mustaches twisted to the curl of an ostrich feather, a masterpiece of poise and splendor, Robert would be found in dun civilian's garb, shoulder to shoulder with the multitude on the sidewalk, studying the significance of the pageant. This strenuousness acted as a bar to popularity. Harry could count twenty friends to Robert's one. People called him by his given name at the second or third meeting. Women, in particular, circled about him like moths about a taper. But Floyd, who shunned no man's eye, sought no woman's. This may have been why the one girl to whom he had given his heart believed his nature to be of sterling gold.

There was much in the prison life to quicken the thoughts of so serious an observer, but all his attempts to record the impressions had ended in failure. He soon realized that no man can at once live and write. Our deeper experiences need to be mellowed by distance, just as we must back away to a certain focus before we can feel the sentiment of a painting. There was nothing left but to bide his time as patiently as possible, occasionally beguiling the long hours by conversation with Dobbs.

This scoundrel had an unctuous manner which was hard to resist. His quaint, infectious chuckle and pre-eminence in crime made him a favorite among the inmates of the ward—a popularity which he generously used to secure for Robert a certain immunity from insult. The young man could not help feeling grateful for this. Besides, the man's incurable asthma, which he attributed himself to "hexposure to cold night blarsts in the performance of perfessional duties," entitled him to sympathy. Indeed, he was often removed to the hospital for days at a time. During these intervals Robert remarked the cessation of a curious grating noise which seemed to come from his neighbor's cell.

"Blood's thicker than water, Bobbs. You and Hi are Henglish, you know. These 'ere bloomin' coves get red-'eaded over nothing. Don't catch me mutineerin' and violatin' the rules. Ho, no."

This was true. So far as outward behavior went, Dobbs was an exemplary prisoner.

"By the way, Dobbs, my name is Floyd," said Robert.

"Ho, you don't mind bein' called Bobbs, chummy. That's cute for Robert. Hi found out your name. We hall know wot you're jugged for. It's harson, eh?"

"Yes."

"'Ow did you set it?"

"I am as innocent of the charge as you are." Robert's tone was curt. He felt vexed to be the subject of discussion among this crew.

"That's just wot I told the judge, chummy, w'en ee politely hasked me if Hi 'ad anything to say. But it didn't work, chummy. Hi'm a-winkin' at you, Bobbs."

The invisible wink probably expressed incredulity, but Robert did not care to debate his own case with his neighbor.

"Hi knows it's a delicate matter, and some folks Hi wouldn't trust, neither. But Dobbs is your friend, Bobbs, and ready to prove ee's true blue. Do you know I like the sound o' them two names. Dobbs and Bobbs. Suppose we go into business together.

"DOBBS AND BOBBS
"ROBS FOBS.

"'Ow's that for a partnership sign?"

Dobbs exploded in a paroxysm of laughter and coughing over his own cleverness as a rhymester. The fit was continued so long that his neighbors began to protest in their ungentle fashion.

"Say, Dobbs, get into your coffin, quick," cried one. The same whose voice sounded familiar to Robert though he was unable to place it. It was a thick, uncouth utterance, as though the speaker's natural brogue were assisted by the presence of a ball of yarn.

"'Old your bloomin' breath for Longlegs," answered Dobbs.

The passage of the hated turnkey caused a diversion in

his favor. Longlegs was a tall man of remarkably bony strength. The convicts were only collectively brave against him. When not gathered in packs they avoided his stern visage as a lone wolf slinks away from the hunter. His right name was Hawkins, but almost nobody within these precincts escaped a sobriquet. Warden Tapp was "the Pelican," Turnkey Gradger was "Gimp" and a particularly vile denizen went under the name of "Parson." Dobbs explained his own escape quaintly.

"You see, chummy, Dobbs his a nickname halready. You can't forshorten it no more."

The visitor who accompanied Hawkins shared the unpopularity of his escort.

"Whoop, da, da, da!"

"He's a yellow aster."

"Lend me your monocle, Cholly, and don't be wude."

But the tall, blond-bearded man with the monocle sauntered leisurely along, looking into every cell until he reached the end of the corridor. Then he turned back and stopped before Dobbs, while Hawkins clanked his keys beside him.

"If God writes a legible hand, that man's a villain," he quoted from the old-time actor; "what name do you go by?"

"Bill Dobbs."

"Hand me out that pen and ink and I'll draw your picture."

"W'ere?"

"On your thumb nail. The right one. That's it."

It seemed scarcely half a minute before Hawkins was heard exclaiming:

"That's a stunning likeness."

"Take away this 'ere lookin'-glass o' mine, Longlegs, and bestow it on the poor. Wot use 'ave Hi for it w'en Hi carry my hown himage on the hend of my bloomin' thumb?"

"You've a face of great power and cunning," said the artist, "but there's one thing you lack."

"Wot's that?"

"Reverence. Some day I'll use you for a mask of Iago that I've had in mind."

"Thanks. Wot's your name, stranger?"

"Tristram March." It was our artist friend, rummaging for types in this out-of-the-way corner.

"You've a sort of a soft lip about you and a delicate horgan of hodor. But there's one thing you lack?"

"What?"

"Starch. Hi'm a-thinkin' Hi'll copy my make-up after you next time Hi play 'Amlet to the queen's Ophelia."

Tristram's good-natured laugh was the last thing Robert heard as he sauntered away.

A sculptor, friends called him if pressed for a definition. Yet in truth he had never yet executed a figure of life size, being a modern instance of talent without ambition, dispersing and dividing its strength. He modeled, painted, rhymed, composed—a many-faceted reflector of impressions; but everything he did was done by halvés and the most finished of his products were only brilliant sketches. His sister Rosalie's single gift, besides her beauty (which, to be sure, entered into it as a primary element), came to her less by nature than by ardent aspiration. But critics had compared her Rosalind to a perfect rose, blown into a bulb of glass; and she was still a patient learner, standing tiptoe on the vestibule of her art, with an untold future before her.

"'Ow did Hi begin?" said the cracksman, when the confusion had subsided.

Robert was again at the chink, like some penitent whispering through a grating to his father confessor. "Hi never began. Hi was born wicked. Wicked Willie they called me w'en Hi wasn't old enough to toddle halone. And 'ere's 'ow Hi earned it, Bobbs."

"How?"

"You see, my mother, who was a hinnocent woman and a Christian, took me out on 'er harms to see the lord mayor's procession, the lord mayor o' Lunnon wot 'as all the wittles to eat, you know. And w'ile they was all preoccupied admirin' 'is lordship's gold buttons, wot was Wicked Willie a-doin' of but leanin' forward in 'is mamma's harms and pluckin' a hear-ring w'ich ee liked, hout of a grand lady's hear. 'Ow!' says the lady, w'en it 'urt; and Wicked Willie 'ad 'is 'ands slapped, w'ich Hi say ee richly deserved, seein' as 'ow ee bungled the bloomin' job."

"From the cradle up you were a thief," said Robert, sadly.

"Ho, them bantam games don't count."

"When did you first begin professionally?"

"Do you count a gunniff a perfessional in this 'ere country?"

"A gunniff? What's that?"

"Don't you know wot a gunniff is, Bobbs? W'y. Hi'm amazed. Hi'll 'ave to present chummy with a Century dictionary in sixteen volumes w'ich we'll be hable to do w'en we get out of 'ere, w'ich won't be long. Hi'm a-winkin.'"

All the time that he spoke Robert heard a low scraping noise, softer than the rasping he had noticed in the evenings. Apparently it was close to his ear.

"A gunniff is a juvenile institution peculiar to our bloomin' hold Hengland."

"Leave out some of your bloomings, won't you, especially about England."

"W'y not, chummy? Ain't it in the dic? Is it a wulgar word?"

Robert did not reply, but he thought how many words as sacred and beautiful as this have been profaned to foul uses or cheapened to the vapidity of a Frenchman's "Mon Dieu."

"Hi beg your bloomin' pardon, Bobbs. If it's wulgar, Hi drop it, and with your leave Hi'll resume my hinterrupted hautobiography."

"You call yourself a gunniff?"

"Gunniff in general, but more particularly Hi was a snatcher, w'ich takes precedence of the mob by reason of the difficulty of 'is duties, of the taker as well as of the blokie and the moke."

"What's the English for blokie and moke?"

"The Henglish? W'y, Hi'm amazed. Don't tell me

you bilked 'em all so 'andily on settin' that 'ouse afire. Hi won't believe it of a chummy as hasks me wot a blokie and a moke is."

"I never heard the words before."

"W'y, the mokes do the scrappin' wen the gent 'as been relieved of 'is pocketbook, w'ich is too heavy for 'im to carry, by the willin' and accommodatin' little snatcher, w'ich was me."

"You began as a pickpocket?"

"Pickpocket? Wot does that mean? Hi never 'eard that word. We were hexpress boys. Is pickpocket the bloomin' Americanese for that? Hi'm a-winkin' at you, Bobbs."

This conclusion was invariably the prelude to a burst of laughter, which was so droll and self-satisfied that it put Robert in good humor in spite of everything.

"Four of us, Bobbs, and that makes a mob. First we picked out our gent, always a hold gent or a bloomin' swell, a-standin' in the crowd. Four of us playin', rompin', friskin', about 'im, as hinnocent little fellows will, bless 'em all, w'en, hall of a sudden, one bumps up against the bloomin' gent's pocket not with 'is 'ands, you know? The bloomin' gent might fancy ee was a hobject of hinterest to us if ee used 'is 'ands, w'ich ee hisn't, ho, no! That's the blokie wot does the bumpin'. Ee wears a thin shirt and a huncommonly hintelligent spine w'ich can feel a 'ard lump in a gent's pocket surprisin'."

"The blokie ascertains where his purse is located?"

"And the snatcher, w'ich was Wicked Willie, relieves 'im of it gently."

"How?"

"'Ow? By makin' a hopportunity. There's nothin' in this world like makin' a hopportunity for yourself, Bobbs. And if two little fellers get a-scrappin' and jostle a hold gent hover, and a crowd comes and the hold gent gets hinterested in separatin' the little fellers, and givin' them a moral lecture, 'ow's ee a-goin' to know w'ere 'is valuables went, unless ee reaches to present 'em with a 'alf-crown apiece, w'ich he don't."

"Is that common in London?"

"Run into the ground, Bobbs, completely wulgarized. No self-respectin' gent would bring up 'is bantams in that line nowadays. But hafterward, w'en Hi was a-lightin' my 'Avana cigars with the old lady's ten-pun notes, Hi always looked back on my rompin's with the mob as the beginnin's, 'umble but 'onorable, of a great and useful career."

During the talk it had seemed to Robert that the cracksman's voice was coming nearer.

"What's making that noise, Dobbs?"

"Wot noise, chummy?"

"That little scraping."

"You can 'ear it?"

"It's close to the chink."

"That's a rat's tooth gnawin'. Hi'm a-winkin' at you, Bobbs."

"Are you cutting into the wall?"

"Look 'ere, chummy. Dobbs 'as given hall the confidence so far, and Bobbs 'as given none. 'Ow is Dobbs to know Bobbs is true blue?"

This was a puzzler. Robert did not feel prepared to abet prison-breach yet, if that was the cracksman's aim, though his own feeling toward the authorities was anything but submissive.

"Hi'm 'urt, Bobbs. Hi've a sensitive nature and a large bump of curiosity, both of w'ich is offended by my chummy's lack of confidence in me. But Hi'll prove Hi'm true blue, wotever Bobbs says. Chummies is chummies and bobbies is bobbies, there's the distinction Hi draw. Do you 'ear the tooth?"

The gnawing sound became louder at Robert's ear.

"That's a hinstrument Hi hown w'ich Hi wouldn't show to the Pelican 'imself, but Bobbs shall see it and feel it if he likes."

"Is it a file?"

"A wery little file."

"How did you smuggle it in?"

"Just in a little plug o' smoke, Bobbs, w'ich a friend sent me for my 'ealth, w'ich is poor, as my bloomin' associates around me 'ere frequently observe. Nobody'd

look for a little rat's tooth laid crossways in a little plug
o' smoke, with the 'andle alongside of it, would they,
Bobbs?"

"Are you sawing the bars?"

"Ham I? It's all done."

"You've sawed them through?"

"And poor little hinnocent Bobbs never 'eard me."
Dobbs went off in a peal of laughter.

"But how do you hide the cuts in the bars when any
one comes?"

"Wot'll stop a leak in a gas-pipe? Soap. Wot'll 'ide
a slice in a sawed bar? Gum."

"Gum?"

"You see, chummy, the wentilation is poor in 'ere.
There's a green mildew on my floor and the bloomin'
spiders is too silent to be sociable company. But you
never 'eard me 'ollerin', Bobbs."

Indeed, he always lay low during the outbreaks. His
methods were more secretive. He was the villain by
trade.

"But my sympathy is with the bloomin' mutineers hall
the time. So I pick away with my rat's tooth,w'en the
others is 'ollerin' and even green little hinnocent Bobbs
cawn't 'ear me."

The rasping sound illustrated his meaning.

"Ee won't trust me, but Hi trust 'im. We'll see who
can keep a secret, and who leaks."

There was a sound as if something had been slid out
of the wall on the other side and of a sudden Dobbs'
whisper became startlingly distinct.

"Honly a few minutes, Bobbs. Hi 'old the plaster in
my pockets, and the rat's tooth in my fingers w'ile Hi
gnaw and gnaw." The tool began working rapidly and
dexterously. In a short time Dobbs spoke again:

"Tap 'em till you feel it 'ollow, and shove on the 'ollow
spot."

Robert tapped the wall.

"Shove 'arder."

Robert gave a stiff push with his elbow. The brick
was loosened and gave way.

"Now, catch it, chummy."

Slowly the Englishman shoved the brick toward Robert, till it protruded from his side of the cell. It would have fallen on the bed if Robert had not caught it. After the brick came a hand and the striped sleeve of a convict's arm. It was a characteristic hand, broad, with spatulate fingernails and a black star on the fleshy ball between forefinger and thumb. But the cracksman must have fallen out with his own likeness as Iago, for his thumb-nail was clean as a whistle. Between the fingers lay a tiny file of rarest workmanship. Its teeth were set almost as sharply as those of a saw, and the steel was tempered to the hardness of adamant.

" 'Ow's that for a tooth, Bobbs?"

Floyd took it for a moment, but a step was heard coming along the corridor. It was Longlegs.

"Quick, Bobbs, put back the brick."

Dobbs' voice grew hoarse with excitement. Robert replaced the block on his side, and heard the convict doing the same on the other. As Longlegs passed, Dobbs fell into a tremendous spasm of coughing. The turnkey hastened to the end of the corridor, jangling his keys as if deriding the derision with which he was greeted all the way. He had run his gantlet too often to heed the jeers and grimaces he met. There was a sound as if he were unlocking the farther door and then re-locking it from the outside.

"That's a very useful cough," whispered Dobbs to Floyd. It had ceased all of a sudden. "It drives undesirable acquaintances about their business and it procures me admission to the 'ospital, w'ich is a sociable and communicative quarter. Hi'm a-winkin'."

Robert was beginning to understand things. The cracksman was malingering. It was through the hospital that he communicated with his friends outside.

"And Hi 'ope that Dobbs 'as given ample proof to Bobbs that ee his deservin' of 'is confidence."

Robert looked down and started at the temptation before him. The file lay in his hand.

CHAPTER XV.

A TRIP TO HILLSBOROUGH.

The life of Emily Barlow during this balmy month of summer might be described as an oscillation in criss-cross between her home and the studio in one direction, and Shagarach's office and the state prison in the other. For in spite of Robert's protest she had returned several times to pour the sunlight of her sympathy into his cell, and the convicts, either because the latent manhood in them went out to a brave girl doing battle for her lover, or because Dobbs had exercised his influence in her behalf, offered no repetition of their first affront.

The point of intersection between these two much-traveled routes was a certain down-town corner, where Emily was already becoming a familiar figure to the policeman who escorted ladies over the crossing. A more disagreeable feature of her passage of this point was the frequent appearance there of Mr. Arthur Kennedy Foxhall. But Emily, like other golden-haired girls, was accustomed to rude glances from men, and had learned to tolerate them as we accept turbid weather, muddy streets and the other unavoidable miseries of life.

She had been riding in the steam car fully fifteen minutes before she could determine in what direction the hostile influence lay. It could not be the mere uncertainty of her journey. Even if Bertha were not with the Arnolds at Hillsborough, it did not follow that her sweetheart was lost. At first broadly pervasive, like an approaching fog, the malign presence had gradually begun to locate itself near her, and it was with a sudden shock, like the first splash of a long-delayed shower, that she realized she was under observation from the passenger in front.

He had never turned around since they had left the

station. To all appearances he was buried in a magazine.
There was not even a sidewise position to indicate that he
was keeping her within the field of his vision. Yet
Emily knew that every sense of the man was alert in her
direction, and that by a sort of diffused palpation, like
that of the blind, he was aware of her slightest gesture.
She thought of moving back to escape the oppression,
or forward into another car. But the station platforms
on either side lay in full view of the windows, and she
felt that the relief would be only temporary. He would
follow her out.

Who was the stranger? She was certain she had never
seen his round, shaven face before, yet she felt that it
was some one whose fortunes were bound in with hers,
some one whom she would recognize, when his name
was uttered, as a familiar. All efforts to dispel this dim
fear were fruitless. She tried to gaze out at the skim-
ming landscape, but some subtle force gripped her
muscles and turned her head to the front. She closed
her eyes, but the image still floated before her and she
knew it was there to thwart her purpose and work her
lover harm.

Fully fifty minutes of the ride had been rendered
wretched to Emily by these doubts and fears, when the
conductor entered to collect the tickets for Hillsborough.
The man in front seemed to jerk himself out of his fit
of absorption. He fumbled for his oblong blue card, on
which Emily espied the lettering "Hillsborough." But
the hand which delivered it struck a numbness in her
heart. It was broad and fleshy, with the fingernails which
are said to betray the professional criminal, and a star
worked in black ink on the protuberance between forefinger and thumb. Robert had described this peculiarity
in his cell-acqaintance, Bill Dobbs. If it were he, this
was a strange situation in which to find the solitary
cracksman. Perhaps it was one of his "hospital days."

"Hillsborough! Hillsborough!" came the announcement from both ends of the car, followed by the usual
banging of doors. Emily started for the rear exit, which
was the nearer. Once alighted, she walked leisurely

forward along the platform. A side glance upward revealed Bill Dobbs just leaving his seat and passing to the rear, exactly in her footsteps. When he caught her eye he smiled. It was true. He was pursuing her. Her spirits sank, and she did not quicken her pace. The engine stood champing like an impatient horse beside her, for she was almost abreast of the tender.

"All aboard!" the uniformed trainmen were crying. Emily glanced around. Bill Dobbs was just entering the station door, apparently taking no more notice of her than of the drivers soliciting his custom. But she knew that her least movement was under his cognizance. With a quick jump she placed her foot on the step, and, catching a conductor's hand, remounted the moving train. A backward glance, as she sunk into her seat, discovered Bill Dobbs sauntering up the road.

An interval of regret seized Emily when she reviewed her conduct calmly. Had she, indeed, escaped some unknown danger? Or was she the victim of a girl's foolish illusion? She was beginning to chide herself as a prey to superstition when the realities of her predicament suddenly forced themselves upon her by the reappearance of the conductor.

"What is the next station, please?"

"Elmwood."

"How far is that?"

"Two miles."

Two miles. To be carried two miles beyond Hillsborough into the neighboring township! Possibly the Arnold estate lay midway between, but it was more probable that she would be footsore and spent before she reached the house where Bertha was supposed to be living. There was an extra fare to pay, a brief whirling glimpse of woodland and meadow, and then the engine slacked up again before a cottage-like, rustic station.

A circle of 12-year-olds desisted from their romp to watch the sweet lady approaching them.

"Little boy, could you direct me to the **Arnold mansion?**" she said to the oldest.

"Arnold mansion? Don't know any Arnolds round here."

"They live in Hillsborough. How far is that?"

"Oh, I know," put in a tot in tires. "That's the lady that has the gardens way over on the Hillsborough line."

" 'Bout five miles from here, isn't it, Chester?" said another.

"Can't I get a carriage to drive me there?" Emily felt equal to five miles or twenty, now that she was once started, but if feasible she would have preferred to let some four-footed creature do the walking.

"Well," said Chester, "you see the coach is up at the academy and I guess it won't come down till the game is over. You might get a wagon."

"Oh, well, somebody may give me a ride. Which way does Hillsborough lie?"

"Follow this road straight along, till you come to the bridge. That's the Hillsborough line and I guess anybody over there will tell you."

Emily thanked her guides and sped off on her long trudge. Behind her she heard the boys' shrill chirps, mingled with the light soprano of girlhood, running up and down the bright gamut of pleasure. How melodious their joyous inflections were, compared with the harsh syllables she was accustomed to hear from the children of the pavements. How much richer and deeper this country stillness than the everlasting murmur of the city, which makes silence only a figure of speech to the dwellers within its walls.

But is not all silence figurative and relative, thought Emily, a mere hint at some magnificent placid experience, only possible in its purity to the inhabitants of outer space? Even the countryside was not still. Plump sparrows, dusting themselves in the road, never ceased their brawling. The shy brown thrush swerved across her path at intervals and bubbled his song from the thickets. The meadowlark left his tussock-hidden nest to greet the world proudly from the pasture rock, and far away the phoebe's plaintive utterance of his lost love's name pierced the sibilance of the trees.

"There's a loam for you," said an old gardener, spading an oval plot on a lawn. His bulbs and potted sproutings were arranged at one side. "Feel. 'Twouldn't soil a queen's hands. Dry as meal and brown as a berry. Same for two feet down."

Emily took up a handful to please the old man. It crumbled between her fingers like the soft brown sugar which grocers display in crocks, though not, as youthful customers sometimes think, to be scooped and paddled with by idle hands.

"I can see roses in that, miss," said the gardener, turning up a deep spadeful for her inspection. But time was precious and she shortened the commonplaces, breaking away toward Hillsborough.

All that was visible of Elmwood was a cluster of cottages about the station and a few outlying farms. A brick building crowning its highest hill was probably the academy to which her guides had referred. On both sides the country opened out in great reaches of level fertility, groves of dark trees rising at intervals where the pools lay that nourished their roots. Now they sprung up by the roadside and overarched her with drooping boughs.

Looking upward, as she walked, almost alone, Emily felt herself the center of a greater mystery, embracing, as it were, that in which her sweetheart was entangled. Nights of vigil had begun to overstring her nerves. That strange doubling of impressions which attacks us in such moods, making a kind of mirage of the mind, came over her. Everything about her seemed familiar, as old as her infancy, as the world itself. Elmwood! She had babbled the name in her cradle days, her earliest rambles had been through its grassy paths. Yonder silver-birch, whose delicately scalloped foliage rose and drooped in long strings, as if the foamy spurt of a fountain should be frozen in its fall, had it not printed itself on her memory somewhere a thousand times before? The three urchins passing her from behind, surely their faces were not strange.

It may be Emily was right about the urchins and that

there was no mirage in her recollection of them. She had been present on the morning when Ellen's body was found and they may have stood by her side in the crowd.

"I'm stiff, Whistler," said one of them in the broad drawl of the city gamin.

"Don't expect to be limber after ridin' twenty miles on a car truck, do yer, Turkey? What place is this, any-way?"

"I'll stump yez to come over in the swamp and get some little frogs," said urchin number three, who was no other than our crabbed young acquaintance, Toot Watts.

Emily wondered, as she saw them disappear down in the meadows, whether they had really been her fellow-passengers all the way from the city. How dingy they were! Not a point of color except the peachy cheeks of Whistler and the golden glow at the end of Turkey's cigarette.

When she reached the academy playground she thought she must have covered two miles. There was a game in progress between two baseball clubs of rival academies and the sight of sportive youths and cheering onlookers was welcome to her after so long a spell of solitude. She was unhappily ignorant of the rudiments of that most scientific of games. "Fly" and "grounder" to her were simply undistinguishable terms of a barbaric technical jargon. But the sparkle of eager eyes and the motion of active limbs, set off by graceful costumes, was, perhaps, more apparent to her than if appreciation of the spectacle had been overwhelmed by interest in the match. . What breeding in the salute, in the very tones, when one of the outfielders, chasing a hit out of bounds, begged pardon for jostling against her ever so little. For a mo-ment, admiring the liberal swing of his arm, as he made the long throw home, though the most womanly of wo-men, she envied men the bodily freedom which they deny to their sisters. Presumably the play was successful, for its result was greeted with plaudits, and the club afield closed in toward the plate.

Beyond the ball ground, under a clump of willows,

Emily was surprised to come upon her three fellow-passengers once more. They must have cut through the meadows on the other side of the academy. The grove made a screen completely hiding them from the playground, and there was no one else about. Against a rocky wall three bicycles were resting.

"Let's take a ride, fellers," said the one who had been addressed as "Turkey."

"Cheese it. There's somebody comin'," protested the Whistler.

"Come on. I'm sick of this. Them fellers can't play a little bit."

"On'y a little ride around. They'll never know," added Toot.

Turkey boldly led the way, mounting like a veteran. Toot followed quickly, and finally the Whistler, finding himself abandoned by his comrades, swallowed his scruples and joined them. His was a girl's wheel, but he overtook his companions easily.

"Boys! Stop!" Emily found herself calling out a remonstrance. All three turned their heads at this shrill command, but it only made them speed away more rapidly. The road was downhill here, and the pedals whirled around like the crank-shaft of a flying locomotive. Should she turn back and give the alarm? It was a good stretch for limbs already weary and with an unknown number of miles before them. Besides, this was probably nothing worse than a boyish prank. If only city-street boys were like country-academy boys, she sighed. Perhaps they would be if they all had natty uniforms to wear and a bicycle apiece. No doubt the gamins would soon turn about, although they acted as though her outcry had frightened them; and the last she saw of them they were pedaling for dear life toward the city, twenty miles away.

Circumstances were to be greatly altered when Emily met these young racers again.

CHAPTER XVI.

STAMPEDE AND AVALANCHE.

Is there in all the world a sight more wholesome and comforting to the tired wayfarer than a loaded hay-cart? When Emily spied one ahead of her she felt a little throb of pleasure in her bosom and at once hastened her step to overtake it. The farmer was asleep on the seat, with a sundown over his face.

"Perhaps I had better wake him," thought Emily. "Won't your horse run away?"

"Run away?" The peaked old face was wide open of a sudden. "Guess not, miss, not with that load on. Dobbin ain't no pony. Step aboard? How far are you baound?"

"I am looking for the Arnold mansion."

"Arnold mansion? This is just the kerridge you want to take. Mrs. Arnold's a putty close neighbor of aours."

Grateful for the offer, Emily climbed into the creaky seat under the fragrant, overhanging load.

"You b'long in Foxtaown, I s'pose?"

"No. I'm from the city."

"All the way from the city? Well, I declare. I thot I knew all the Elmwood leddies. I s'pose things are putty brisk in taown these days?"

"Oh, yes. We always have plenty of excitement. Too much, I fear. Some of us miss the quiet you enjoy out here among the meadows."

The rustic meditated upon this a moment, chewing a straw.

"Speakin' of medders, haow's hay sellin'?"

"I don't know, really," answered Emily. She was not informed on this utilitarian side of the subject.

"Just been shavin' my ten-acre lot daown the road. Did most o' the mowin' ourselves, me and Ike, that's my brother, with the Loomis boy. But he ain't good for much except forkin' it on. You wouldn't s'pose there was a clean ton o' hay on this wagon, would you?"

"No, indeed," answered Emily. This was true. She would not have ventured any supposition at all as to the weight of the hay.

"Good medder-grass, too."

"Do you live in Hillsborough?"

"Aour haouse jest abaout straddles the line, but wife goes to meetin' in Elmwood."

"I suppose she likes the services better?"

"Nao. You see the Elmwood parson takes all our eggs, and wife thinks 'twouldn't do to spile a payin' customer. Woa! Here comes wife's nephew, Silas Tompkins."

"Evenin', uncle," nodded the young man in the buggy.

"Evenin', Silas. Been down to the pasture?"

"Yaas."

"Well, haow are the oats lookin'?"

"Comin' putty green, Uncle Silas," drawled the other, speeding by.

Emily was wondering if a life of agricultural labor always gives such a vegetable cast to people's minds, when a clatter of hoofs behind caused her to turn her head. The cavalier was clothed in velvet of a soft, rich bulrush-brown. Just as he passed them his eye caught something afar and he shouted to the farmer:

"Here's a runaway! Hug the right of the road!"

They were turning a bend, but across the angle through the bushes a pair of coal-black horses could be seen heading toward them. The farmer's jerking at the reins was comical but effective. In a twinkling he had his nag squeezed against the wall which bounded the narrow road.

"Get up, Aladdin!" whispered the rider, and the horse, a powerful roadster or steeplechaser, yet with limbs like a stag's, cantered forward, as if to meet the wild blacks. But suddenly his master turned him about and began trotting gently back, keeping to the other side of the road and turning his head over his left shoulder toward the approaching runaways. As they slewed around the bend their coachman was flung from his seat into the grass border of the roadside.

"Rosalie!" exclaimed the waiting cavalier, cutting his horse over the flanks. It bounded away abreast of the team. Emily remembered a vague whirl of spangled reins and a frightened face of rare beauty blushing through its silver veil.

"He's killed!" she cried, dismounting and running toward the coachman. But the grass was like a cushion in its midsummer thickness, and he had already picked himself up uninjured, save for bruises and a tattered sleeve.

"It was the gobbler frightened 'em,' he said, starting off at a lame dog-trot after the retreating carriage. Emily turned just in time to witness a rare exhibition of coolness and skill. The chestnut had kept abreast of the blacks with ease. At the right moment his rider, clinging to the saddle and stirrup like a cossack, reached over with his left hand and caught the reins of the foaming pair. Then gradually he slowed up his steeplechaser, jerking powerfully at the bridles. The added weight was too much for the runaways to pull, and all three were ambling peacefully when they faded from sight in a cloud of dust.

"I guess we'll start for hum," said the farmer. Emily was standing with her finger on her lip, unconscious of his presence.

"Putty slick on a horse, ain't he?"

"Who?"

"Young Arnold. He kin stick on like a clothes-pin, I tell yew."

"Is that Harry Arnold?"

" 'Tain't no one else."

Emily remembered how his expression had changed when he recognized the lady in peril as "Rosalie," and felt like asking the farmer if he knew her. But Griggs (she now learned his name) was prosing on about his new barn, and she relapsed into silence. The rest of their road was an avenue of elms. Through their interstices

smiled the calm blue of the late afternoon sky, tempered
by contrast with the green of the foliage. It was the
first time she had ever observed this rare harmony of
colors.

"Woa! There!" said Griggs. "I'll set you daown
here. The Arnolds' house is up yonder over the hill.
They ain't p'ticler friends of aours, but the help come over
and buy wife's cream."

"Have they a girl in help named Bertha Lund?"

"I s'pose wife knows the women-folks. I don't," replied the old man, energetically reaching for his rake.

"A new servant, this is."

As if to answer her question, there came a loud bark
from the little woody knoll on the right of the road, and
a great St. Bernard came bounding down. It was Sire,
who had recognized Emily. She knew that he had been
left in Bertha's charge and probably the housemaid was
behind him.

"Sire! Sire!" her cheerful voice was heard calling
through the stillness. How fresh she looked with her
soft country bloom and a golden tan.

"Is it you, Miss Barlow?" cried Bertha, opening her
eyes in amazement. A cream pitcher in one hand revealed her errand, but Farmer Griggs was already half-
way to his new barn, which lay fifty yards off the left of
the road.

"Yes, Bertha," answered Emily, fondling Sire, who
seemed almost to know that she bore him a message from
his master. "I have come all the way out to meet you."

"How is poor Mr. Robert?"

"Not very well contented with his present quarters."

"He is still in jail? Ah, poor young man! What a
shame! And Ellen gone, too! It was the beginning of
trouble for all of us when the old professor died."

"It wasn't easy to find you, Bertha. You didn't leave
your address with Mrs. Christenson."

"Indeed I did not." Bertha gave an independent toss
of her head. "I had no wish to be chased by her and
coaxed to come back, and I'm very well satisfied where

I am, with my $5 and light duties and out of the city and as kind treatment as if I was a visitor."

Emily thought she might understand the reason of this bountiful hospitality.

"Mr. Shagarach, the lawyer, who is defending Robert, suggested that I come and see you. You were so near the fire when it broke out, he thought that you might know something that would help our side."

"That I'll tell heartily. They sha'n't tie my tongue."

"You don't believe Robert set the fire?"

"No more than I did or Sire."

Emily looked at the dog, who was crouched before them. He had lifted his head at the mention of his name.

"Ah, Sire, you know the solution of all this mystery, don't you? And you'd tell it if you could."

Sire barked an answer to this appeal and turned his head away, blinking, as old dogs do.

"But who could have done it, Bertha?"

"Nobody in all the world. It just happened, like the other fire before."

"Was there another fire before?" asked Emily, all eagerness.

"Two or three years ago we had a fire in the study."

"Tell me about it."

"Oh, the professor had just gone upstairs a minute and when I went in the big waste basket was blazing up."

"There wasn't much damage then?"

"If I hadn't opened the window and thrown it out on the sidewalk the whole house might have been burned. Why, the study was nothing but a tinder-box with the books on the shelves and magazines and papers always thrown about."

"After the fire had once started, I can see how it would spread. But the mystery is, how did it start? You never followed the first fire up?"

"Indeed we did. The professor was careful to follow it up, but they could find nobody then and they'll find nobody now. It was just the will of heaven."

"I wish you could have told about this other fire at the examination, Bertha."

"I had it in my mind to tell, but the little thread of a man made me so cross with his nagging, it all flew out of my head."

"Robert—was Robert in the house when the other fire happened?"

"Yes. I remember calling him, and he flew downstairs four at a time and stamped out the sparks on the carpet."

"What time of day was it?"

"I'm not good to remember time. It was daytime, I know."

"Forenoon or afternoon?"

Bertha's knitted forehead brought no clarity to her recollections.

"I've forgotten, Miss Barlow. I know it was the hot summer time, but forenoon or afternoon, that's all gone from me now."

"But you will try to bring it back, Bertha? It may be important. Mr. Shagarach is a wonderfully wise man who could build up a great explanation out of a little thing like that. You will tell him all you know if he comes to see you?"

"I'll be as free-spoken as I choose, and forty inspectors won't stop me."

"Could you describe the study again, Bertha, just as it looked when you were dusting it, with Robert standing over the hearth?"

"Why, you know the room, Miss Barlow—square, high-studded, with two windows, the professor's desk at one and the bird cage before the other. Shelves and books all round, hundreds of them, and magazines and papers scattered about. Chairs, pictures, the safe and the professor's things just as he left them—his slippers on the floor, his spectacles and bible on the desk, his dressing-gown over the back of the arm-chair——"

"And a waste-basket?"

"Oh, yes, the big waste-basket always beside his desk. The professor had so much writing to do."

"Was it full?"

"All full of black wrapping paper that came off of his books. The professor got so many books."

"And his safe with the papers in it?"

"Nobody ever touched it but the professor. At least, I never meddled with it."

Emily noticed the emphasis Bertha laid on the first person, but an unwelcome interruption prevented further disclosures.

"The knoll which Bertha and Sire had descended made a grade like the pitch of an old gable roof. Toward the top a tempting tussock of clover lay in sight, scenting the atmosphere and titillating the nostrils of the horse attached to Farmer Griggs' hay-cart. Dobbin was ordinarily a staid and trustworthy animal, who might be left alone for hours; but on this occasion his carnal appetite overmastered his sense of duty and led him gradually higher and higher up the grade toward the odorous herbage. The first hint the two girls had of the peril which was imminent was when they heard the voice of the farmer shouting from the barn.

Turning in that direction, they beheld him running toward them, hat in hand, as if racing for a guerdon, and brandishing a pitchfork. Whether they or some one else were the object of his outcries they could not in the confusion of the moment determine. But the doubt was speedily settled by the occurrence of the very catastrophe which Farmer Griggs was hastening to avert.

Dobbin had just climbed within reach and was relishing the first morsel of his stolen supper, when suddenly the top of the hay load, which was tipped up to an exceedingly steep angle by his ascent of the knoll, slid down like a glacier and deposited itself at the feet of the startled girls.

But this was not all. From the midst of it the figure of a man, badly shaken but unhurt, arose and straightened itself out.

Both girls gave a shriek in unison. Emily recognized, to her astonishment and dismay, the face of her train companion, the supposed Bill Dobbs. But Bertha's surprise was quickly converted into merriment.

"Why, Mr. McCausland, what a tumble!" she laughed, just as Farmer Griggs arrived.

CHAPTER XVII.

REPORTING TO HEADQUARTERS.

"McCausland!"

Emily bit off the exclamation just a moment too late. This, then, was the interesting convict who had tried to worm himself into Robert's confidence. This was Shagarach's vaunted opponent, the evil genius arrayed against the good, in mortal combat for her sweetheart's life. With Sire worrying his heels, Bertha holding her side in unchecked laughter, and Emily eying him with an expression of amazement gradually turning to scorn, the detective looked for a moment as if he would have resigned his whole reputation to be elsewhere. But suddenly he righted himself and led the horse around to the road, snatched Griggs' pitchfork and was tossing the spilled hay back into place before the fuming farmer realized what he was about.

"This is Miss Barlow," said Bertha. "But I suppose you don't need an introduction."

"We were fellow-passengers on the train coming down."

"Don't tell me, after that, we servants are the only keyhole listeners."

"Mr. McCausland makes eavesdropping a science," added Emily, who was not at all disposed to spare him.

"There!"

The inspector had finished his task. As the old farmer led his recovered property back to the barn he never relaxed his hold on the bridle and vented his wrath all the way on the offending beast. When he had disappeared inside his barn, they could still hear him scolding.

"Tarnal idiot! Yer fool, yer! I'll shorten yer fodder for yer! I'll teach yer to stand! Woa!"

"Eavesdropping! What nonsense!" said McCausland,

smiling. Shorn of its mustache his face looked more ferret-like than ever and one could excuse Tristram March's estimate of its owner's villainy. "I had to leave Hillsborough on the 6:21, and natural impatience led me to follow the lazy girl who went after the cream for my supper."

"It took you a long time to make up that fib," retorted Bertha, but she took the hint and went over to the farmhouse to fill her pitcher.

"Perhaps you will join me at lunch, Miss Barlow. You may be taking the same train and I shall have the pleasure of your company to the station in Mrs. Arnold's carriage."

"No, I thank you. I will not trouble Mrs. Arnold either for lunch or for the carriage."

"Or, Mr. McCausland?"

"Or Mr. McCausland."

Emily spoke in a tone which was meant to convey that there were too many unforgiven injuries between them to permit her to accept favors from either of them. She looked at her watch. It was 5:30.

"There is no other conveyance from here and the station is three miles," urged the inspector, with good humor.

"I can walk there in an hour."

"You must have walked a part of the way from Elmwood."

"Please do not press me, Mr. McCausland."

He muttered something about "spunk" as he looked after the girl's slight figure retreating. Then he gallantly relieved Bertha of her foaming pitcher and sauntered with her back to the Arnold mansion.

When Emily reached the Hillsborough station she was indeed a footsore girl, fully convinced that country miles are as indefinite as nautical knots, but in the few moments she had to spare before the train came by she purchased a lunch of fruit, which refreshed her a little. Before they were well out of the station Inspector McCausland came up and asked permission to occupy the seat at her side.

During her walk Emily had come around to a gentler

view of the detective's behavior. She could not look back on the afternoon's events without a certain complacency. For the true aspect of the case against Robert, as a grand chess duel between the criminal lawyer and the detective, was gradually dawning upon her, and surely in the discovery of Bertha's hiding-place and the unmasking of Bill Dobbs, white, her champion, had gained two positive advantages over black, the enemy's color. Besides, loyal as she was to her sweetheart, with that singleness of heart which we sometimes call womanly prejudice, there was a genial persistency in McCausland few could resist. So she forbore to fire upon his flag of truce and assented to the request.

They talked for the most part of irrelevant matters, and she herself did not like to broach the subject of all subjects. Only once did he appear to glance at his official relation to her.

"The fisherman, Miss Barlow, doesn't enjoy the death struggles of the mackerel in his nets," he said. "But he is obliged to see that they do not escape."

"Then you do disagreeable work from a sense of public duty?"

"And for the support of my family," he added. "But as we've arrived at the city perhaps I'd better return these now."

So saying, he laid Emily's watch, pocketbook and brooch in her lap. Dumfounded, she felt of her bodice, where these articles should be. The neck-clasp was missing, the watch-pocket empty. McCausland had picked her pockets while they were conversing.

"Set a thief to catch a thief," said the detective, still smiling, but raising his hat with respect. Emily smiled herself, less at the prank he had played than because she thought she had good reasons to be cheerful. But she did not communicate them to Richard McCausland, alias William Dobbs.

It happened that her course through town took her by Shagarach's office. It was nearly 7:30, but there was a light in his window still, and an impulse seized her to convey the glad tidings of her successful journey to the lawyer. So she picked her way across the street and tripped light-heartedly up the stairs.

"You bring good news, Miss Barlow," said Shagarach, a little heavily. He was standing at the window with his hands in his pockets and his back turned, but there was power in his very carelessness. If he could not pick pockets he could master men.

"How could you know?" she asked.

"I simply heard you coming. There is mood in a footstep," he answered, facing her and offering a chair, while he sat himself at the table with his arms folded expectantly. Through the open window where he had been standing Emily felt the cool evening air, dim with dew it held in suspension; and far away the hill-built capitol of the city, printed darkly against the blood-orange sunset, seemed lifted into the uppermost heavens, at an immeasurable height from earth. Had this been the object of Shagarach's contemplation?

"What is the result?"

"Bertha is found again."

"At Arnold's?"

"At Arnold's."

Knowing his taste for brevity, she condensed the story of her day's wanderings, not omitting, however, the incidents which seemed to connect McCausland with the pretended English cracksman.

Toward the end of the narrative she perceived an unwonted wandering of attention in her listener. A trio of street minstrels, with flute, violin and harp, had set up a passionate Spanish dance tune, just far enough away to afford that confused blending of harmonies which adds so much to the effect of carelessly rendered music. Shagarach's eyes had left Emily's face and strayed toward the window. Twice he had asked her to repeat, as though he were catching up a lost thread. At last he arose abruptly and shut down the sash, muffling the minstrelsy at the height of its wildest abandon.

"Our street troubadours distract you?" asked Emily.

"The violinist is a gypsy," said the lawyer, shutting his eyes. Emily remembered this saying afterward, and even now she began to understand why a certain compassion, mingled with the fear and admiration which this man so gifted, but so meanly surrounded, aroused.

"That is all?" he said. She thought it amounted to a good deal. "I fear Miss Barlow may not descend the stairs as gayly as she mounted them."

"What have I done? How have I blundered?" she asked herself.

"To have caught McCausland napping was a pleasant diversion, but of little practical value. He is merely playing the nest-egg game."

"The nest-egg game?"

"Dressing up as a convict, locating himself in the adjoining cell and confessing some enormity himself so as to induce his bird to lay. The trick has an excellent basis in psychology, since the second law of life is to imitate."

"And the first?"

"To devour. You think that crude?" he added, noting Emily's look. "Ah, fact is crude, and we must never shirk fact. But since Floyd is innocent it could have availed McCausland little to continue his harmless efforts to wheedle a confession out of him—which I presume you will now interrupt."

"Not necessarily," answered Emily, who would by no means be sorry to prolong the joke at the expense of the subtle inspector.

"But that our discovery of Bertha's hiding-place should be known to McCausland is a little unfortunate. She may be removed at once, this time beyond our reach."

"Is he so suspicious a man?"

"When fighting wealth."

"But we are not rich."

"You forget the $5,000,000 and McCausland's point of view."

Emily colored slightly. This was the bitter fruit of her wasted afternoon, her six miles' walk, her long fast. But she kept these things to herself. And Shagarach did not look at all perturbed. John Davidson had told her that he was accounted by some a trifle slack in the preparation of his matter, trusting overmuch to his power in the cross-examination to bring out the truth. His record, however, showed that he did not overrate his own skill. As certain clever exhibitors, blindfolded, will take the arm of a reluctant guide, and, by noting his resistances, compel him to lead them to some article in hiding, so Shagarach followed the windings and subterfuges of unwilling testimony, bringing witnesses at last face to face with the truth they had striven to conceal.

"Our cause has assumed a novel aspect," said the lawyer, opening a drawer and producing three or four letters. "I am the victim of an anonymous correspondent."

Emily glanced at the envelopes. Their penmanship appeared to be that of an illiterate person, the "Shagarach" in particular bearing a strong resemblance to the four priceless if illegible autographs which are the only relics left us bearing the immediate personal impress of the man of Stratford.

"The earlier epistles merely threaten me with death in its least desirable forms if I do not surrender my brief for Robert Floyd. The writer appears to cherish a grievance against your friend. Had he any enemies?"

"Not that I know of."

"Very well. It appears I was to suffer martyrdom for his sake. Today's mail, however, discloses a change of policy. The handwriting is the same, but sloped backward to disguise it."

He passed a letter over so that Emily might read the wretched scrawl.

"Dear Mr. Shagarack: I mean to let you know that I have discovered a important klew which will save your cliant. Pleeze be at the bridge, the Pere leading over to the island Fort, at 8 o'clock (8 P. M.) sharp To-morrow, and I mean to let you know my klew for nothing. If you do not cum, yore life is not worth living. You will be torn into on site."

A rude skull and crossbones was figured in place of a signature.

"Don't you think the writer's brain has a flaw in it?" asked Emily.

"Possibly. There is something not entirely consistent

in the promise to rend me in two if I do not accept his assistance."

"Or hers?"

"You do not recognize the handwriting?"

"It might be that of any very ignorant person. There is almost no style or character."

"Rather masculine. It may be some irresponsible being, as you say. But there is a singular accent of sincerity in the earlier letters; a genuine hatred of Floyd."

"You will not venture to the meeting-place at that hour?"

"I hardly fear Mr. Skull-and-Crossbones."

Shagarach drew a delicate revolver from his lowest drawer. It lay like a toy in his small white palm, but Emily could not repress a shudder.

"You do not value my advice. You ask it, but you will not follow it?"

"The chance of seeing and studying my correspondent is too good to be lost."

"Do you really read minds, Mr. Shagarach?" asked Emily.

"Not in the charlatan's sense, certainly not. But the dominant thought in every man's soul—self, money, pleasure, fame—is written plainly on his face. The trained psychologist can predict much from a photograph."

Eight! The ringing bells recalled Emily to thoughts of home. Almost simultaneously a knock on the door ushered in a visitor, who proved to be Mr. Arthur Kennedy Foxhall. The opium-eater was feathered in peacock fashion this evening, but no brilliancy of plumage could offset the undervitalized appearance of his tenuous form and sallow cheeks. He started on recognizing Emily and appeared confused, but lifted his hat with a sweep meant to be grandly courteous.

"I beg pardon. Shall I be so fortunate as to have the privilege of an introduction?"

"I was just about to leave," said Emily, passing him without a glance. "Good-evening, Mr. Shagarach."

"Good-evening."

Shagarach attended her to the door with the deference he habitually showed, and she felt his strong presence like a zone of protection thrown around her.

"You are punctual, Kennedy," said Shagarach, returning to the newcomer. He had clicked his desk to and donned a hat and coat while the other was drawling out an answer.

"The Dove-Cote is just about on."

Meanwhile Emily, as Shagarach predicted, had descended the stairs much more doubtfully than she had mounted them. But she clung to her woman's faith that even the interrupted conversation with Bertha might yield items which would germinate at a later stage; and, empty though it were, her victory over the great McCausland was one of those successes which give cheer to a young campaigner.

Sustained by these hopes, she rode home at last and related the whole story of her day's adventures and misadventures to her wondering mother over the supper that had been cold for two hours.

CHAPTER XVIII.

INSIDE THE DOVE-COTE.

"Here we are!" cried Kennedy.

The sudden flood of light dazzled Shagarach's eyes. Glittering chandeliers threw prismatic reflections upon the twenty or thirty occupants of the room, many of them in full evening dress, like his escort, and several adding the sparkle of diamonds to the iridescence of mirrors and cut glass around them. Across one corner stretched an arc-shaped bar, from which two colored waiters served liquors to the patrons, while others at intervals disappeared behind curtains and reappeared balancing platters of light delicious viands for the men who chatted at the tables. These were octagon-topped and covered with plush. The carpeted floor yielded like turf to the feet. The conversation ran low. The servants whispered their requests and answers. It was an atmosphere of stealth and suppression.

The getting there had been a story in two brief chapters. This palace of fortune owed its name to its location on the uppermost floor of one of those tall, slender structures, like dominoes set on end, which illustrate the reaching upward for space in our cities when horizontal expansion becomes no longer possible. It fronted on a blind passageway in the heart of the hotel district. Its proprietor was a jovial man-about-town, rather prone than averse to the society of police captains. On the ground floor a commercial agency conducted its business quietly. Tailors rented the second and third flights, but the fourth story was always unoccupied and never advertised for hire. Applicants covetous of its advantages were frightened away by the rental asked. It was at the head of the stairs leading from this landing up that Kennedy had pressed the three white bell buttons in the massive door.

The door immediately swung open, and the pair found themselves in front of a second door, similar to the first except that the opaque panels were replaced by glass. Through these the stairs could be seen beyond. Kennedy repeated his signal, this time, however, reversing the order and beginning with the lowest knob. A slide opened at the head of the stairs, and the two men were the object of scrutiny for awhile. Shagarach's sponsor was evidently persona grata to the sentinel, for the second door now swung in and they were free to mount the stairs.

"Sure it's true-blue, Kennedy?" said the sentinel, when they passed him.

"Sure," answered the manikin, but his smirk was forced. "Wine, Sambo."

Kennedy began breaking the ice in this manner for his companion.

"Not a life-long votary of the fickle goddess, I should judge," remarked a man introduced as Mr. Faught.

"This is my initiation into her mysterious rites," answered Shagarach, sweeping the room for Harry Arnold.

"Ah, then, it is not too late for you to withdraw. The ceremonies are trying. I myself am only a neophyte of low degree. Perhaps, being a student of character, you have observed as much from my appearance?"

"I should have known that you had not lost a fortune this evening, at least."

"There is one simple rule to escape that."

"Not to bring one here?"

"Precisely."

Shagarach had indeed been contrasting Faught with the other habitues, most of them men of fashion, still young in years, but middle-aged in the lines of their faces. Several beardless youths appeared to be college students. Two or three wore the style of confidential bookkeepers or bank cashiers. As many more were flush-faced veterans, with wrinkled pouches under their worldly eyes and gray mustaches of knowing twist. Against such a gathering, smiling, but irritable withal underneath from the nervous tension, the large man of bland visage and ironical phrase certainly struck a discordant note.

"Come to the altar and I will explain our ritual."

They moved toward the table in the middle of the room, which was the center of all interest. If men appeared to be chatting absently in a corner, their heads were constantly swiveled this way, their ears caught the announcement of every result.

"None of that, Perley. It was on Stuart's spot," cried a harsh voice from behind the table.

"The needle was on the line," protested Perley, reckless-looking and sadly young. "I say, the needle was on the line, Reddy."

He had missed the prize by a hair. Perhaps the bill he had laid down for this turn was his last. But a friend led him away, still muttering, by the arm, and the gap in the circle which his removal made was quickly closed. The man called Reddy gathered the pile of bills together, separated a small portion, which he swept into the till, and passed the remainder to Stuart.

"Reddy runs things," whispered Faught, not so low but that the bank-tender heard and looked the newcomer over suspiciously. "Comes from the west, a desperado. Just the man to keep them down."

"The bad blood breaks out sometimes?"

"Would if there wasn't a strong hand at the needle."

There was certainly nothing weak about Reddy. He sprawled sidewise in his chair, with his left elbow on the table and his right arm free for a variety of uses—a big-boned ruffian with a sandy face and an eye apparently riveted on the disk before him, but really sweeping in the whole compass of the room. Overhanging eyebrows veiled these furtive glances. As a rule he spoke quietly, in a sepulchral bass, warning the players to adjust their stakes more evenly on the spots, or announcing the winners of the prizes. The recent jar with Perley was something uncommon in the mute and decorous chamber over which Reddy presided.

"It's a new game—roletto; simple as odd or even," explained Faught. "The circle is segmented off into black and white rays, or spots, as we call them——"

"And red?"

"Those are used, too. You see, they are numbered like the others. But they are specially colored for the game with the bank. In the ordinary game some one proposes a stake and puts it down on its lucky number. Then the rest follow suit. Would you like to try this round? It's only a $10 trick."

"Very well."

Shagarach laid his stake down on one of the spaces.

"That starts it. See them join in. Twenty-four spaces, black and white, and twenty-three filled. My ten spot quits it out. Now thank your stars if you see that bill again."

The gamblers stood near while Reddy reached toward the needle. A squad of grenadiers at attention would not be more rigid. They were frozen with suspense. But something paralyzed Reddy's wrist. He had caught the full glance of Shagarach. It was several seconds before he twisted the pointer. For several more it spun around,

gradually slowing up and coming to a rest over Shagarach's number.

"Twenty!" called Reddy.

"Mine!"

Shagarach coolly smoothed out the bills and folded
them in his pocket, while the unsuccessful players eyed
him greedily. Eleven-twelfths of the stakes went to the
winner, and 2,000 per cent would be considered a fair
profit in any speculation. But the return to the bank
was still more liberal, being the steady harvest of two-
spots. It was easy to see how the luxuries and free
accessories of the Dove-Cote could be provided.

"Try again," said Faught, shaking Shagarach's hand.

"Perhaps that is enough for an experiment," answered
the lawyer, a little undecided still whether Faught were
a decoy of the establishment.

"A hundred dollars even I come out whole to-night!"
cried a voice at the door. It was Harry Arnold.

"A little quieter, gentlemen," said Reddy, tapping on
his desk. "This isn't the stock exchange."

"It's a more respectable place," answered Harry, sur-
rendering his wraps to a servant.

"I take you," said several, picking up the gantlet he
had thrown down. Faught had spoken first and Kennedy was chosen stake-holder. Shagarach, meanwhile,
had retired to a table in the corner and ordered some
wine.

"One thousand to ten I break the bank," called Harry
as loudly as before.

"I will debar any man who uses that tone again," said
Reddy, never moving a muscle. His eyes were as cold
and steady as the barrels of two Derringers in the hands
of a Texan train robber, and the young bravo, though
his lip curled, did not reply. His second bet was taken
and the game resumed amid its former silence.

The losers repaired to the sideboard now and then
and renewed their courage with stimulants, but one or
two who called for brandy were told that no strong
liquors were allowed. The little outbreak over Perley's
protest showed the wisdom of this rule. Harry Arnold's

purse seemed to be well lined to-night, for he led the play higher and higher.

Shagarach held his wineglass toward the chandelier, so as to shield a searching glance at the young man's face. Under the artificial light it was brilliantly beautiful, the face of a man who could say to almost any woman "Come" and she would follow him to the ends of the earth.

"Do you know young Arnold?" asked Faught of Shagarach, who had just lowered his wineglass. He began to take some notice of this large, quiet man, who, all unobserved, was making the rounds of the room.

"By sight," he answered, suppressing a yawn. "You took his bet, I noticed?"

"Only a hundred, and as good as mine already. He's bucking the reds."

"Gad, Harry, you have nerve," Kennedy's pipe was heard exclaiming.

"I see you don't understand," continued Faught. "There are four red spots, you remember. Ordinarily these are not used. In the common game it is impossible for the bank to lose, though one of the players may win."

He smiled in allusion to Shagarach's maiden try.

"But sometimes the bank condescends to take a risk. Then the stakes are high. Each player lays a thousand opposite one of the four reds. If the needle stops over white or black, Reddy scoops the pot. But if it favors a red the man on the spot opposite gets $5,000 from the bank and the others quit whole. You see it's perfectly fair. Twenty blacks and whites and four reds, that makes the odds five to one against the players. So the bank, if red wins, quintuples the stakes all round."

"But the bank twists the needle," said Shagarach.

"Oh, that's all open and above board."

"Do you see Reddy looking down?"

"He is watching the checker board."

"Why not a mirror under the table?"

"What would it show?"

"Two slender bar magnets crossed under the disk. His foot can rotate them so as to underlie any four of the

spots; and the needle is of steel." Faught opened his
eyes.

"Bravo!" an exclamation burst from the crowd.

"That's number one," Harry Arnold was heard exult-
ing. Followed by Kennedy and the taker of his second
bet, he crossed over to the bar.

"Has Arnold set the place on fire?" asked Shagarach.
It was said during a pause of the hum and he raised his
voice. In one of the facets of his wineglass he saw Harry,
who had just passed him, start and turn, but it was impossible to tell whether the expression of his face had
altered. Certainly it was no more than a glance and he
took no notice of Shagarach. The lawyer's low stature
diminished at a distance the effect of his splendid head
and eyes, which were so powerful at short range. On
the present occasion, if disguise were at all his purpose,
this insignificance was useful.

"He has beaten the bank," said Faught.

"A Pyrrhic victory," answered Shagarach, "and a Par-
thian flight." His companion rose and sauntered behind
Reddy, but either the mirror was hidden or the bank-
tender was too wary to be caught. Suddenly his harsh
voice was heard again.

"Put that down, Perley."

Every one looked in the direction of the youthful gambler, who had been the center of the dispute when Shagarach and Kennedy entered. He had brooded moodily
since his loss, sitting alone at a corner table, and was
just raising a revolver to his temple when Reddy's command checked and bewildered him. Instantly Harry
Arnold, who was nearest, wrenched his wrist and some
one else secured the weapon. Perley writhed like a madman, so that it took several minutes to quiet him. When
at last his contortions were helpless his spirit seemed to
give suddenly and he burst into tears.

Shagarach felt a deep pity in his breast. The youth
looked weak rather than wicked. Possibly others, whom
he loved, would suffer by his recklessness this night. An
aversion to the whole tinseled exterior, gilding over soul-
destroying corruption, came upon him and he longed for

the sight of something wholesome and pure—if only a basketful of speckled eggs or a clothes-press hung with newly lavendered linen. But his purpose in coming was still unfulfilled, so he merely stopped the youth as he was passing out in dejection, accompanied by a friend.

"I was luckier than you," he said, taking out the roll of bills he had won. "Will you accept my first winnings as a loan?"

Perley halted irresolutely.

"They amount to $200 or so. You may have them on one condition."

"What is it?"

"That you go immediately home."

"I will," said Perley.

From now on the play became more and more exciting, as the champagne began to work in the veins of the gamblers. Once again Harry Arnold won, then lost and lost again. Still he laid down bill after bill from a bulky roll, sometimes leading at the simple game, oftener challenging the bank. As luck turned against him (if luck it were) his temper changed. He grew hilarious, but at the same time savage. Once or twice his differences with Reddy promised to culminate in a serious quarrel, but each time the coolness of the experienced bank-tender prevailed. Shagarach paid no attention to Kennedy, little to Faught. He was studying the soul of Prince Charming.

When Harry came over and demanded brandy and struck the bar with his clenched fist because he could not have it, every one knew that his wad of crisp bills had shrunken to almost nothing. But still he would not surrender.

"The whole pile," he cried, laying the roll down opposite a red spot. It was the same one he had played all the evening. Reddy counted the money coolly.

"A thousand is all we go," he said, returning one bill to Arnold—the last poor remnant of Rabofsky's loan.

"I challenge you to play higher. I dare you to give me my revenge."

"There's only a hundred over and you'll need more

than that to settle your outside bets with," answered
Reddy, as if victory for the bank were a foregone conclusion. Three others, carried away by the force of play,
put down stakes of $1,000 each and all of the reds were
covered. Reddy snapped the needle with his forefinger
as carelessly as a schoolboy twirling a card on a pin.
Four necks craned over, four lungs ceased to draw
breath, while it slowly, slowly paused.

"Mine!" exulted Harry, stretching forth his hand; but
Reddy intercepted it.

"The bank!" he growled.

"It's on the line," said Harry, flushing.

"By the rules I am judge, and I say the bank!" Reddy
lowered his voice to its most sepulchral register, while
Harry raised his to a shriek.

"Between man and man, but not between a player
and the bank. I leave it to these gentlemen if it wasn't
on the line."

"Always," answered Reddy. He snapped the needle
again. Whether the bar-magnets below had been carelessly adjusted, whether the pointer had really rested
over the line, that was a matter upon which arbitration
was now rendered forever impossible. Then he reached
for the money.

"You swindler!" shrieked Harry, striking at his face
across the table. Instantly Reddy's right hand, the free
hand, opened a drawer and presented a cocked revolver.
His finger was on the trigger to pull, when Shagarach
gave the shout of warning.

"Spies!" he cried. It was a word to strike terror. Perhaps it saved Harry's life.

During the confusion, observed of none but Shagarach, a whistle had been heard from the outside, and the
quiet man, Faught, had passed over to one of the windows. There were only two, and these were protected
by iron shutters, which closed with a latch. The first
sound heard was Faught lifting the latch and throwing
the shutters apart. A uniformed man dropped into the
room, followed by another and another. Faught rushed

behind Reddy and the second window was soon opened. All the officers carried lanterns and clubs.

"The first man who moves his little finger dies," said the foremost of the invaders, advancing. `His tone was easy and his pistol covered Reddy. The whole room looked toward the desperado as if expecting him to do something. He turned his revolver's muzzle quickly as if from Arnold to the officer, but instantly his right hand was knocked up by Faught. With his left he pressed an electric button for some daring purpose. Then the pistol shot rang out, a moment too late, and the room was in total darkness.

The slides of the officer's lanterns, however, were opened at once, and in a jiffy the door was guarded. Through the yellowish light Shagarach could see tussling groups and hear cries of anger and pain. He himself was seized and handcuffed. Presently the uproar quieted down and the voice of the spokesman was heard ordering one of the negroes to light up.

But it was a different sight that met Shagarach's eye when the chandeliers blazed again. The roletto table had disappeared, probably carried downstairs by a trap-door at Reddy's touch of the button. This was the use for which the vacant fourth story was reserved. All around among the smaller tables the gamblers stood like lambs, trembling and pale in the grip of the law. In the middle of the floor lay Reddy, the blood bubbling from a pea-sized hole that divided his left eyebrow and gathering in a thick pool on the carpet. McCausland's bullet had flown true to its target.

Only one of the gamblers was missing.

"He must have climbed out of the window," said Shagarach, sotto voce.

CHAPTER XIX.

LEX REX.

Stupefaction is a weak word to express the feelings of Saul Aronson when a messenger awakened him at 1 o'clock Thursday morning with a request from Shagarach that he would come to police station No. 5 at once. The attorney's assistant was never a sluggard, but the celerity with which on this occasion he scrambled into his street clothes would have done credit to a lightning-change artist.

The police captain received him courteously, explaining, as he conducted him to Shagarach's cell, his hesitancy about discharging the lawyer without permission from McCausland, who had maliciously disappeared. Both he and Shagarach were agreed that the most judicious course was to accept a temporary release on bail, and later to secure a quashing of the charge by an explanation to the district attorney. So Aronson set out again to secure bail, and at 4 o'clock had the joy of seeing his master pass down the station steps with his bondsman.

It was fortunate that the affair turned out so well, for the very next day had been set down for the hearing in the Probate court on the settlement of Benjamin Arnold's estate.

Hodgkins Hodgkins, Esq., flanked by the other two members of the firm of Hodgkins, Hodgkins & Hodgkins—namely, his brother and his nephew—was already on his feet to address the court when Shagarach, as representative of Robert Floyd's interest, arrived and pushed to the front. Except for the fact that he was Prof. Arnold's oldest acquaintance in the city, it was hard to understand the selection of Hodgkins for the responsible position of executor over a property of $10,-000,000.

A tall, withered specimen of nearly 70, thin-whiskered and jejune of speech, you would have looked instinctively for the green bag at his side if you had met him on the street. "Whereas" and "aforesaid" and a dozen other legal barbarisms disfigured his rhetoric and the trick of buttoning his coat with an important air over documents mysteriously shuffled into his breast pocket was as natural to him as crossed legs to a tailor.

But all this pomp, ridiculous as it was, gave no promise of the disloyalty that was to follow. From the first words of his address it became evident that Hodgkins Hodgkins, Esq., was there not to execute the will of his friend but to oppose its execution. Like many another intrusted with the same office, he had transferred his allegiance from the forgotten dead to the living who had bounty to bestow. Mrs. Arnold, sitting among the spectators, alone, might well congratulate herself upon a clever stroke in engaging the services of the quondam executor for her son.

"As counsel for the petitioner, Mr. Harry Arnold," said Hodgkins, ahemming huskily, "I desire to explain to the court briefly my relation to the case. As your honor has been informed, I enjoyed the privilege of the testator's—or, more properly, the intestate's—acquaintance during a period of nearly fifty years. During that period nothing, I believe, ever occurred to mar our mutual trust and confidence. Up to six weeks ago the deceased had never expressed any desire to alter the natural distribution of his property after his death. Up to that time, although approaching his seventy-ninth birthday, my honored friend had been entirely satisfied, entirely satisfied, I repeat, with the prospects of a division of his estate according to the laws of descent in this commonwealth."

"A statement which we deny," broke in Shagarach, sotto voce. Hodgkins was a little nonplussed.

"Am I to understand that Brother Shagarach, representing, I presume, the interests of the other nephew, refers to some previously existing testament?"

"Not at all. I refer, your honor, to oral expressions of an intention to will his entire property to the nephew who lived with him, Mr. Robert Floyd."

"There was a will drawn, which is not extant, I believe?" inquired the judge.

"There was a will drawn," answered Shagarach, "but since unfortunately destroyed, by which Floyd was disinherited."

"I opine, then"—Mr. Hodgkins frequently opined—"that Brother Shagarach concedes the destruction of the document and is here——"

"To argue for its upholding."

The whole firm of Hodgkins, Hodgkins & Hodgkins looked as if a thunderbolt had struck them at this announcement. Shagarach was throwing away Robert's share, amounting to $5,000,000.

"We were not aware of this intention," said the senior member, after a consultation, "and as to the alleged oral expressions of a purpose to leave the—the accused nephew sole legatee—er—er in any case we should have contested such a will on the ground of undue influence. Six weeks ago," Hodgkins was now frowning as formidably as possible, "I received a letter from my honored friend, informing me that he had made a will and requesting me to assume the function of sole executor—a request which I felt it a duty, as well as an honor, to accept."

"May I see the testator's letter?" said Shagarach, breaking in.

"I trust the court will accept my assurance——"

"It is no question of your word. I desire to see the terms of your appointment as executor, and request that the letter be read."

"As the first step toward establishing the existence of a will," said the judge, "upon which, I believe, both parties,.all parties"—there were several other lawyers present—"are agreed——"

Hodgkins and Shagarach bowed.

"The letter had best be read in evidence."

There was a great diving into green bags for awhile among the Hodgkins firm, at the end of which the senior member read the following letter:

"Friend Hodgkins: You are the only one of your cursed tribe to whom I ever got nearer than swearing distance, and our intimacy began before you were admitted to the vulpine crew. Here I am, a youngster of 78, anticipating death by thirty years at least and indulging in the folly of will-making. Can you conceive anything more absurd? I might as well think of getting insured so early in life. But I was always excessively cautious, you know—hence my odium advocatorum, I suppose. Can you superintend the job? Most of my hoard goes elsewhere, but there will be some for the executor to distribute, and you will find legal pickings in it that will pay you. Write at once.   "BENJAMIN ARNOLD."

This eccentric epistle raised a smile among the lawyers, but Shagarach was busily occupied drafting a verbatim copy while Hodgkins continued his plea.

"I was remarking," he repeated, one of his favorite introductory formulae, "that upon receiving this request I made haste to indite a favorable response, as I felt bound in duty and honor——"

"And the prospect of pickings," added Shagarach, sotto voce, still copying the letter. The senior member glared.

"It is needless to relate the unfortunate circumstance, in which Brother Shagarach's client is so deeply implicated, which has relieved me of this welcome if laborious trust. The will under which I was to serve in the capacity of executor has been destroyed—destroyed, presumably, by the party whose hopes of a fortune is cut off, and we stand here to-day facing the same status which existed up to six weeks ago. I say the same—I am in error. There is an important, a melancholy difference. Six weeks ago my friend's nephew was not an accused and all but a convicted murderer."

Hodgkins paused, as if expecting a rejoinder from Shagarach, but the latter appeared profoundly absorbed in a telegram which Jacob had just brought him.

"The property now stands in no man's name. There

is no person to whom its dividends, its rents, its interest, constantly becoming due, can safely be paid. Under the laws of descent its title vests equally in the heirs-at-law, the nephews of the deceased. But there is need of an administration, in order that the two shares may be apportioned in a satisfactory manner. I need not again allude to the circumstance which renders a joint administration improper and impossible, the circumstance which explains the absence of Brother Shagarach's client——"

"I do not see Brother Hodgkins' client in the court-room," Shagarach retorted to this sarcasm. As he spoke his eye fell on Mrs. Arnold's haughty face.

"It is certain, however, that he is not occupying a felon's cell," answered Hodgkins. "Briefly, your honor, there is only one course open. An administrator is urgently needed for this immense estate. In the absence of a will, the heirs-at-law, being of age, would naturally be selected, but under the circumstances I respectfully suggest that the younger of the two nephews is debarred and that your honor's choice should fall upon the elder, a college graduate, a young man who moves in the highest social circles, and who has not, I believe, the honor of an acquaintance with the inmates and turnkeys of the state prison."

Hodgkins had hardly sat down after this acrid peroration when Shagarach was on his feet.

"I have only a few words to say at present. The case is by no means so simple as my learned brother imagines. My learned brother assumes that the physical destruction of the will has involved the extinction of its contents. So mature an advocate does not need to be reminded that parol proof of the contents of a will, of its accuracy in technical form, and of its existence unrevoked at the time of the testator's death, are equivalent in law to the presentation of the document itself.

"We have in the court-room today a number of witnesses who will testify to the contents of the will. We have the witnesses who signed it to prove its compliance with statutory requirements as to form; and I do not understand that Brother Hodgkins denies that the paper was in existence until destroyed at the Arnold fire."

"You object, then, to the issuance of administration papers to Mr. Harry Arnold?" asked the judge.

"Emphatically. We desire to uphold the will. Brother Hodgkins has introduced evidence as to the making of a will in the letter which he read. I should like to put in evidence now the testimony of the three witnesses to the signature."

When the three witnesses had sworn to Prof. Arnold's acknowledgment in their presence of the will, to their own attestation of his signature, and to the date, June 7, of these occurrences, another lawyer, who appeared to act in concert with Shagarach, briefly announced his guardianship of the interests of the heirs of Ellen Greeley, a legatee in the sum of $1,000. After recounting the long and meritorious services of the dead domestic, he called upon her sister to testify to several conversations in which she had referred to the professor's generous remembrance of her in his will.

"It is proper to state at this point," said Shagarach, "that the other servant, Bertha Lund, is not represented here by counsel, but there is evidence to show that she was remembered in the same manner as her colleague."

Mrs. Christenson was thereupon called and deposed, exactly as Ellen Greeley's sister had done, to the several conversations in which Bertha had referred to her employer's liberality.

"Until yesterday evening," said Shagarach, "Bertha Lund was employed in the country house of Mrs. Arnold at Hillsborough. A telegram, however, sent to the station-master at that place, brings the answer that Miss Lund took the outward-bound train at 5:21 this morning, being alone and accoutred with a large baggage trunk. I doubt, therefore, if this important witness as to the contents of the will can readily be found."

While he made this statement Shagarach searched Mrs. Arnold's face. Her gaze shifted and she perceptibly whitened. Then the rise of still another lawyer, also seeming to act in concert with Shagarach, drew attention to the court. The new attorney represented, as he immediately informed the judge, certain charitable institutions which had been remembered under the clauses of the will —namely, the Duxborough institution for the blind, of which the professor, who had himself been operated on for cataract, had been throughout his life a conspicuous supporter; the Woodlawn home for consumptives, the dipsomaniac hospital, the Magdalen reformatory, the asylum for idiots and the Christian orphanage. Letters were read from Prof. Arnold to the superintendents of each of these institutions, requesting them to accept legacies of $20,000 each under the will which he had just drawn. The letters were couched in a stereotyped form and all dated alike.

But the most significant testimony of the day was contained in the last document which this attorney presented —a letter.

"Dr. Silsby himself," he explained, "is detained from attendance at this hearing by important scientific labors in the west."

The mention of Dr. Jonas Silsby's name caused the eyebrows of the Hodgkins firm to elevate themselves unanimously in a manner which amusingly accented the facial resemblance of the members. Jonas Silsby had been a pupil of Prof. Arnold and was at present the most distinguished arboreal botanist in the country. Along with some of his master's eccentricities, such as vegetarianism, he had imbibed much of his independence and noble honor. He was, moreover, Robert Floyd's most intimate friend, bridging, as it were, by the full vigor of his fifty-odd years, the great gap of half a century which separated the boyish nephew from his octogenarian uncle.

Mrs. Arnold's quick smoothing with her finger of an imaginary loose lock—the characteristic feminine gesture of embarrassment—did not escape Shagarach's lustrous glance. The letter was worded as quaintly as the other:

"My Dear Jonas: Rob has gone back on me, God bless him, the rogue, and you've got to take my dollars. I know you don't want them, but I'm going to commit inverse larceny just the same. I'll grab you by the throat and stuff your pockets with gold, though you bellow like an ox. You know what it's all about. We've talked it over often enough. And I want it called the 'Arnold academia,' too. If agriculture stops going to the dogs in this country through the preaching of the dons my hoard keeps in shoe leather, then I want the credit of it for my ghost downstairs. It'll need some comfort, Jonas. But don't suppose I dream of quitting you yet, my boy, and don't expect all of the pudding I've baked. There will be some plums for the asylums, and some for the servants, and Rob, the young rogue, has got to be provided for, willy-nilly. This is only a hint, but verbum sap. We'll talk it over when you come east again, with your pouches full of seeds. Here's good luck to you, Jonas. It is God's world, anyway, and not the devil's. Your old friend,   "BENJAMIN ARNOLD."

"Dr. Silsby explains," added the lawyer, "that the allusion in the text to an academia refers to a cherished project for elevating the position of the American farmer. The idea was to establish a great agricultural university. It had been a frequent subject of discussion between them, and nothing could be more natural than that Dr. Silsby should be selected as president of the institution."

"And trustee of its funds," added Shagarach, looking at the senior member of the bewildered firm of Hodgkins, Hodgkins & Hodgkins. Then the court adjourned for lunch.

CHAPTER XX.

TWO STEPS FORWARD AND ONE TO THE REAR.

At the afternoon session Mrs. Arnold was found at her place, still unaccompanied by her son. Five lawyers had already outlined their standpoints to the judge, but still there were new complications in store. Lawyer Howell was Shagarach's earliest opponent, the Goliath of his first great duel. He contented himself with stating his intention to attach Floyd's share of the property in behalf of the insurance companies and proprietors who had suffered loss through the crime with which he was charged. He was of opinion that the evidence offered

to uphold the will lacked particularity and was insuffi-
cient——

"Brother Howell is not here as associate justice." Shagarach was on his feet in a flash. "His opinions are impertinences, too manifestly dictated by his interests. Naturally the insurance companies and burned-out proprietors desire to break this will, in order that Robert Floyd
may take the $5,000,000 which he does not want and they
may join the hue and cry of the other conspirators
against an innocent man."

Howell was protesting against such a suggestion, when
he was interrupted by a roar from one of the learned
brethren who had been impatiently waiting his turn.

"I speak for the murdered girls," he cried, "whose
pure young blood stains the hands of that guilty monster, and in the name of their bleeding corpses and young
lives, ruthlessly done to death, I utter my protest against
the imputation of innocence to their slayer."

The auditors, who had begun to drowse over the technical details of the case, were stirred to attention at once
by this declamatory opening. Even Saul Aronson,
sleepy from his restless night, checked a yawn midway
with his fingers and turned around. The new speaker
was a middle-sized, burly man, whose most conspicuous
feature was a projection of the flesh beneath the outer
corners of his eyebrows, so as to bury the eyes and give
his whole face an expression almost Mongolian in its
cunning. His clothes were seedy, and his remarks punc-
tuated by amber-colored shots at the cuspidor. Altogether it was a decidedly rakish craft and the look on
Judge Dunder's face was by no means propitious.

"It is an axiom of law," said the orator, waving his
hand and executing a demi-volt toward the spectators,
"that no man can take advantage of his own tort. I
hereby accuse Robert Floyd of the murder of my
clients——"

"Who are your clients?" interrupted the judge.

"Mary and Florence Lacy, two virtuous maidens, the
sunshine of a happy home, the pride of a loving and
admiring circle of friends"—just here came one of the

orator's punctuation points, which produced a sadly anti-
thetical effect—"the comforts of a bereaved mother's
heart——"

An old lady in the audience burst into tears. Presumably it was Mrs. Lacy. This tribute to his eloquence
warmed the orator to a mighty outburst.

"Woe, I say, to that ruthless hand! Perdition gripe
that marble heart——"

"Will you kindly make your statements relevant?" The
judge's manner was arctic. "We are considering the
disposition of Benjamin Arnold's estate."

"I beg to interpose." Hodgkins had seen a ray of hope
in the utterances of the last two speakers. Slack, the
grandiloquent, was a bibulous shyster, who made a
precarious livelihood by imposing on just such victims
as Mrs. Lacy, but at this juncture he might prove a useful ally. "Brother Slack is not unnaturally, I may say
most creditably, carried away by his feelings on behalf
of his clients; and I, for one, heartily join him in oppos-
ing the efforts which have been made here today to put
the means of redress for those—er—unhappy victims
beyond their reach—or, rather, to reduce them to a
paltry $20,000."

"Twenty thousand dollars!" shrieked Slack. "Who
dares insult the sanctity of human life by estimating its
value at such a bagatelle. I say not $20,000,000 would
recompense that weeping mother for the loss of the children of her bosom."

With pointed finger he held up the grief of the now
blushing and embarrassed woman to the curious gaze of
the crowd. Then, wearied of his vulgarity, and confident
of a case already complete, Shagarach rose and immediately drew all eyes and ears.

"Brother Slack has unwittingly uttered the strongest
argument of the day in favor of the request which I
make—a request, be it understood, for postponement
only, until sufficient time elapses to permit the contents
of this will to be demonstrated. Brother Slack assumes
the guilt of my client in a criminal cause now pending.
Brother Howell assumes it; Brother Hodgkins, in ask-

ing you to exclude him from the administratorship, also
assumes it. This is a new doctrine of law, to adjudge a
man guilty without according him an opportunity for defense. I ask your honor to consider the stigma which
the choice of Harry Arnold as sole administrator would
cast upon Robert Floyd, and the prejudice it would work
him in the cause I have mentioned.

"But, aside from this, I ask you to consider the chain
of evidence presented as to the will itself. Let us keep
in mind that will is only legalized wish. I am aware
that great particularity is required in such cases as ours.
But when your honor reviews the statements of Martha
Greeley, of Mrs. Christenson, of the six superintendents
of institutions of charity, and of Dr. Silsby—yes, and I
will add the letter to Brother Hodgkins, who, it now
appears, was to stand as executor only of that small resi-
due of the estate which did not go to the founding of
the Arnold academia—when your honor reviews these
I am convinced that you will agree that the disposition of
this vast property is not a matter to be hastily determined.

"My brother has referred to the supposed advantage
reaped by Floyd from the destruction of the will. Floyd
is not here to speak for himself, but he has contended
consistently that the reduction of his legacy to $20,000
was made at his own request, and that even that small
sum was in excess of his wishes. Read as I read them,
the expressions of endearment in the letter to Dr. Silsby
support this statement. They are not the language of an
irate testator, used in reference to a disinherited heir.
Allow me, moreover," Shagarach was now looking
straight at Mrs. Arnold, "to point out that Robert Floyd
was not the only gainer by the destruction of Prof.
Arnold's will. What atom of evidence has been adduced
to show that the testator remembered Harry Arnold?"

Mrs. Arnold started and reddened at the mention of
her son's name. Then she put her handkerchief to her
lips and coughed nervously. Shagarach's glance was just
long enough to avoid attracting general attention toward
her.

"For these reasons I ask that your honor schedule a second hearing of this important cause, to take place after a complete survey of the evidence shall have demonstrated that not Robert Floyd but another is responsible for the death of Mary and Florence Lacy."

Mrs. Arnold's trembling was painfully apparent, and there was nothing in Hodgkins' feeble and desultory reply to give her hope.

"I will take the matter under consideration," said Judge Dunder, when he had closed, and Shagarach knew that a severe blow at Robert's reputation, as well as a timely relief to the Arnold purse, had been prevented by that morning's work.

There were fewer clients than usual in the office when he returned. One of them, a large man, immediately arose.

"I am Patrolman Chandler," said he.

"What can we do for each other?"

"Not much, perhaps." The policeman drew an envelope from his pocket and showed a lemon-colored glove inside. "Will that help you any?"

"Perhaps. It has a story?"

"A short one. That glove's been in my pocket ever since I was taken to the hospital when the girl fell on me. Never thought of it; hardly knew it was there. Had broken bones to think of, you know."

"I read of your bravery at the fire."

"Pshaw! Well, here's the history of that article. I know Floyd; have known him ever since I took that route. Things look blue for the boy, but I never heard harm of him before, and says I to myself, yesterday when I found the glove, perhaps Mr. Shagarach can turn this to good account, and perhaps he can't. It's worth trying, and if it saves Floyd's neck, why, it's no more'n I'd like to have him do for me if our positions were just right about."

"That's the golden rule, stated in the vernacular. Where did you find this?"

"On the stairs in the Arnold house."

"After the fire?"

"When I went into the house at the beginning."

"How was it lying?"

"About the middle of the staircase, I believe."

"A little to the left, with the fingers pointing to the door?"

"Exactly—close to the wall."

"It is a right-hand glove. He was carrying it in his left hand and dropped it when running downstairs." Shagarach said this sotto voce, as if to himself.

"Who? Floyd?"

"The incendiary."

"I don't know that I ever saw young Floyd with gloves on except in winter. Seems too loud for him anyway— more like some swell's."

"You will leave this with me?"

"Glad to, glad if it helps you," said the officer, rising to go. Shagarach took his hand and thanked him, then tried on the glove and studied it for fully five minutes before admitting his regular clients. If it were Floyd's the case had neither gained nor lost. But he felt that the kid was too fine, the make too fashionable, for the eccentric young radical, who, as Chandler had noticed, never wore gloves except for protection against the cold. There was no hint of identity about it. Had it belonged to Harry Arnold? If so, how did it happen to lie on the stairs of his uncle's house immediately after the fire?

*　　*　　*　　*　　*　　*　　*

The island fort was a many-angled specimen of ancient masonry, following the shore line of an islet in the harbor. It was useless now. No flag streamed from its pole. Passing vessels no longer saluted it, only a lame old sergeant being about to protect the property. By an arrangement with the local authorities it had been converted into a pleasure-ground and connected with an adjacent peninsular of the city by a pier or bridge of half a mile's length. This was the rendezvous mentioned by the anonymous correspondent.

When Shagarach stepped from the car on his way to meet Mr. Skull-and-Crossbones he found that he was early. It still wanted twenty minutes to the appointed hour. The humanity of the district was just rising from its supper tables in teeming tenements to enjoy the cool liberty of the twilight air, and Shagarach listened to the sayings of the multitude whose current he found himself stemming. They were flowing to an open-air concert at some point behind him. The correspondent had timed his evening well for a lonely conference.

As he approached the pier the crowd thinned and at last he found himself walking near the water alone. Ships were putting into port, with red and green caution lights hung aloft. The sea, now violet, melted into the sky and a gathering dimness subdued everything to one tone. Only the black tree-masses and the outlines of the houses stood out somberly distinct.

"We violate nature," said Shagarach to himself, "with our angular, unsightly houses, but she puts her own fairer version on all at last—mosses the manse, curves the beach, litters the ruin, bathes the hard carpentry and mason work of the city with soft twilight balm." He looked back upon the sad accumulation of misery, amid whose foulest reek he was doomed to live. A greenish tint hung over it where the sunset had sunk. It was a rare hue for the heavens to wear—something bizarre yet beautiful, like yellow roses.

Thus far Shagarach had walked alone. Leaning over the railing on the right, he saw three boys fishing in a dory below. One of them was just lighting a lantern, for the thick dusk had begun to gather. The penetrating silence favored their occupation and he paused a moment to watch the silver-bellied mackerel slapping their bodies in the basket. A little farther on an oafish monster stood against the railing on the left. Shagarach thought he leered mirthlessly when their eyes met.

Then at the middle of the pier he came to a closed gate, shutting off access to the island.

"No admission to the fort after 7 p. m.——" He had started to read the placard, when suddenly he felt himself seized from behind. A hand over his mouth throttled the outcry he launched. It was too late to reach for the revolver. A brief, fierce trial of strength and he found himself forced over the railing into the water. The shock, to one who had never entered the ocean before, was icy as death.

His senses did not depart from him. He made an effort to lie still on the surface and to hold his breath. A hideous face projected over the railing, printed itself on his memory, and then disappeared. He knew that he clutched his assailant's cap in his right hand, and that the lights of the city were dancing before him as he rose and sunk. Then the only thing he felt was the gurgling of the deep, dark water nearer, nearer, nearer. How to fight it off? His hands wildly strove to push it away. All the sweetness of the world he was leaving flashed through him in one pregnant second, whereupon his resolution yielded. He opened his lips to utter the fatal "Help!" of the drowning man, and the element rushed in and made him its own.

CHAPTER XXI.

THE BREWING STORM.

Friday was to be the last day of Warden Tapp's tenure, and Robert was aware that the convicts had determined to celebrate his removal by some demonstration of their joy. Everybody was dissatisfied with his government— the public, his deputies, his charges, alike. Stalking about with that inveterate preference for his own company which had won him the nickname of "The Pelican," he gnawed his huge mustache in a manner that seemed to betray that he was not oversatisfied with the results himself.

The prison which he had taken from his predecessor, as orderly as any barracks the world over, he left to his successor (a military man) slovenly, rebellious and tunneled with secret avenues of communication to the outside world. He had begun with leniency and a smiling face. Vice, indolence and a thousand weedy growths flourished up under his elevated chin. When he awoke at last his rigor in uprooting them was intemperate and ineffectual. Several felons escaped. A riot broke out and the warden had been helplessly holding the reins behind a runaway horse ever since.

He had flogged men for not saluting when he passed, yet he was hooted at every time he showed his head to the crowd. He had strung three brushmakers up by the thumbs for idling, yet every shop except the harness-makers, in spite of free labor, showed a deficit for the last half-year. The cells were so littered with storage that it was almost impossible to enter them. Contraband tobacco, gift books, tools, bird cages, shirts and shoes smuggled from the workshops, even knives and revolvers, were found in them.

The "block," or dark dungeon, was always full. If some dozen of the conniving deputies had been sent there, Warden Tapp might have had less to extenuate.

"It's quiet this evening," said Robert to Dobbs on Thursday.

"That's the lull before the storm, my boy," said the cracksman.

"You think we'll have trouble, then?"

"Keep your 'ead in, my boy, when it rains. These 'ere coves 'll get a wetting that'll spoil their Sunday duds. They 'aven't no hart."

"No what?"

"No hart, no hingenuity. They hask first and then try to take it. We'll take what we want first—honly a little fresh air, Bobbs—and then we'll hask for it, as a matter of form. Hi'm horfully punctilious on forms, Bobbs."

Dobbs chuckled at the prospect of writing a letter to the warden, requesting his release from the safe distance of 3,000 miles.

"Hi ain't the fool of the family, ham Hi, Bobbs?"

"Who's that talking now, Dobbs?"

"The thick-mouthed cove wot gets choked with 'is hown Adam's happle? That's Quirk."

"Quirk?" It was the familiar voice he had often tried to place, but Floyd knew nobody named Quirk.

"What is he grumbling for? Is he a ring-leader among the men?"

"Ring-leader, ho, no. Ee lost 'is temper the first time ee saw 'is mug in the quicksilver and ee's never found it since."

This conversation had been conducted face to face in the dark through the aperture formed by the removal of four bricks on each side of the partition. Dobbs had already outlined a general plan to Robert by which they were to escape. He was only waiting, he said, for his "chummy" to "drop the sweet hinnocence game and hown up ee wasn't a lamb."

"So you expect me to climb through that hole, Dobbs?"

"If you won't gnaw your hown bars, you must."

"It's too small."

"Then we'll stretch her till she fits, as the 'aberdasher said when 'is royal 'ighness' trousers didn't meet round 'is royal 'ighness' waistband."

"I doubt if even six will be wide enough. The bricks are only eight by four apiece, and I think I'm more than sixteen by twelve."

"Can a cat jump through a keyhole? No-sirree. But a corpuscle can wiggle through a capillary."

About 11 o'clock the next morning the entire prison force was summoned to the rotunda to hear the farewell address of the warden. The rotunda was a great round hall at one end of the bastile, or prison proper, communicating through two double doors with the warden's office, from which it was only a step to the street. Looking around at the desperate gallery of 600 faces, all shaven, but ill-shaven, and most of them brutal from the indulgence of hateful passions, Robert thought how small a chance the forty keepers stood if that sullen herd should ever stampede.

But the walls of the rotunda were undressed bowlders of granite and the windows all around were double-barred with iron rods that looked strong enough to hold

up a mountain. Only the rear doors were vulnerable
at all, and these simply led through the kitchen to the
cells, or right and left into the yard, at the end of which,
and all along one side, abutting the rotunda, were the
workshops, while the other side was impregnable with
its twenty-foot wall.

Flanked by Gradger and Longlegs, the Pelican rose
to address his mutineers. At his approach there was
such a tremendous joggling in the crowd, that for a
time it looked as if the volcano would burst then and
there. But three spokesmen who had wriggled their
way to the front stepped forward with their hands clasped
over their heads as a token of peaceful intentions and
requested the privilege of a word to the warden. They
were all marked men, undergoing long sentences and
recognized as dangerous criminals. The difference of
type between them was conspicuous as they stood in
front of the surging crowd—Dickon Harvey, the Right
Spur and Minister Slick.

Dickon Harvey was a diamond thief, polished in
person and of fluent address. Like those madmen in
asylums whom the casual visitor finds perfectly rational
and indeed delightful companions, Dickon Harvey
never failed to convince callers at the prison of his moral
sanity. He admitted past misuse of undeniable talents,
though stoutly denying the particular crime upon which
he was sentenced. His legends of early temptation and
ambition to reform had softened the heart of many a
philanthropist to pity. But his cold eye glittered with
a point of light sharp enough to cut the Koh-i-noor, and
a turnkey of exceptional ability was assigned to the ward
which contained Dickon Harvey.

The Right Spur derived his sobriquet from his position
as head of the rooster gang. There was little of what
Dobbs called "hart" in his line of work, which consisted
simply in sandbagging and garroting picked-up
acquaintances or passers-by. But in the crude occupation of the footpad he had displayed a brute daring that
had surrounded his name with associations of terror, and
this diabolical halo had been brightened and enlarged

by his turbulence in jail.　He was middle-sized and bar-
rel-built, with the complexion of a teamster, a wicked
smile and a scar.

Minister Slick's career would be pictured by a line
more excursive than the diagram with which Sterne represents the history of Tristram Shandy.　His criminal
twist had begun just where most men's end.　Up to the
age of forty he had been able to delude several con-
gregations into a belief in his fitness for the sacred min-
istry.　His sermons had been noted no less for unction
than for orthodoxy, their only heresies being grammat-
ical ones.　Then came a fall, sudden and irretrievable.
In a few months he had developed unusual skill as a
confidence man, in which he was aided by a certain
oiliness of manner and insinuating ease of speech.　He
was tall and dignified, with a long gray beard, which
Tapp permitted him to wear on account of a chronic
quinsy, though his kennel-mates whispered this was all
in your eye—a strange location to be sure, for a clergyman's sore throat—but minute veracity was never expected of Minister Slick.

"Mr. Warden," said Dickon Harvey, "I am desired,
with my fellow-spokesmen, by the entire community,
to tender you our deepest respect upon your retirement
from the office whose duties you have so conscientiously
fulfilled."

Tapp's lips quivered.　Was this irony or praise?

"If you have not always met with success, if our
interests and yours have seemed to clash at times, believe me there are few among us who do not appreciate that the fault is in the system and not the man."

"The system, the system," there rose a murmur among
the men, which died away like a stifled cry when Longlegs raised his gun.

"We have read with interest the article on 'Prison
Discipline,' contributed by you to the last number of
the Penological Quarterly, and the petition we present
is, we believe, in line with most of the reforms you
suggest."

"You desire to present me a petition.　Of what value

is that?   Col. Mainwaring enters to-morrow.   It belongs
to him."

"A recommendation from yourself, Mr. Warden," answered Minister Slick, "would surely have great weight."

"What is the burden of your document?"

Dickon Harvey removed a paper from his "budge."

"A seriatim schedule of the reforms which we respectfully ask to be enacted."

"Take the paper to your office," whispered Longlegs
to the warden, but the obstinate official only flushed
angrily at his presumption.

"I will hear what you have to say," he said, weakly
clutching at this last hope of favor among the convicts.
Dickon Harvey proceeded to read his production.

"To the Warden of Georgetown State Prison: We, the un-
dersigned, being inmates of your institution and the chief suf-
ferers by its irregularities of government, hereby offer and
present the following schedule of reforms which we regard as
necessary——"

"Necessary," emphasized the Right Spur, and nearly
500 heads wagged approval.

"Necessary to the quiet and welfare of the community.

"1.   That the grotesque, degrading, uncomfortable and un-
healthful striped garb which we are at present condemned to
wear be exchanged for a uniform of gray woolen goods.

"2.   That the practice of shaving, designed to destroy our
self-respect and efface all evidences of our former and better
identity, be abolished, and each man allowed free choice in the
matter of his personal appearance, which concerns himself so .
deeply and nobody else at all.

"3.   That intervals of conversation be allowed among the
whist parties. (This was the local name of the shop-gang, who,
under the existing system, were compelled to work amid a
silence as absolute as that of a Trappist monastery.)

"4.   That the dunce-cap rule be suspended and workers who
happen to be unemployed for a few moments be allowed to sit
at their benches instead of standing face to the wall.

"5.   That the cat-o'-nine-tails and thumb-screw be abolished
and punishment limited to the block or extension of sentence,
and that the rules for shortening of sentence on account of
good behavior be made more liberal.

"6.   That the tobacco rations and weekly prune stew be restored.

"7. That the cells be lighted until 9 o'clock with a gas-jet in each, and reading or writing allowed.

"8. That Ezra C. Hawkins, Kenneth Douglas, Murtagh Mc-Morrow and Johann Koerber be discharged for inordinate and unnecessary severity and cruelty."

This article was greeted with a swell of cheers and taunts which Tapp seemed impotent to quell.

"9. That favoritism and privilege shall be a thing unknown."

Another bellow greeted this, and Floyd knew from the glance that the clause was a blow at himself. The cell he occupied was known as "the parlor" from its greater width, its ventilation and its possession of a reading-table and cupboard. There was jealousy, moreover, because he had been allowed to do light work about the greenhouse (which he was entirely competent to supervise, from his botanical knowledge) instead of being put at a bench. They forgot that his status was different from theirs. The labor was quite voluntary.

"10. That the indeterminate sentence be put into effect, so that through the specious pretext of punishing crime, the abominable crime of depriving peaceable and perfectly harmless citizens, who have bitterly atoned for some past peccadillo and earnestly desire to demonstrate their change of spirit to the world, be not committed under the sanction of law."

Harvey handed the petition to Tapp. It was, on the whole, an enlightened document. Two of the men who prepared it were probably as able as any of the officials of the prison. Robert could see the different hands at work in its composition. The "past peccadilloes" were Dickon Harvey's "flim-flam" adventures, while the demands for more tobacco, for Hawkins' removal and the reduction of his own "privileges" were a concession to the ruffian element, represented by the Right Spur of the Rooster gang. Yet several of the recommendations were as wise and sound as though all the prison associations in the country had indorsed them.

"Prisoners——" Tapp started to reply.

"No gammon," interrupted the Right Spur, scowling, while a hundred other scowls immediately gathered on the foreheads of his particular followers.

Tapp colored again. His obstinacy was aroused. He was not a timid man. "It would be a breach of courtesy toward my successor to offer him such suggestions. I do not propose to recommend the discharge of employes whose only offense is their fidelity to duty; neither do I propose to constitute myself the spokesman of a mob of law-breakers."

A hiss—the most hateful sound that issues from the human throat, with its serpentine suggestions and its vagueness of origin—greeted this challenge. The keepers gripped their guns, awaiting an order, but the Pelican stood helpless, furious, perplexed.

"To the shops!" he cried at last, and the triumphant convicts were driven like a herd of cattle to their tables and tools. There were muffled yells from the offenders buried in the block when they passed it; and at dinner, when the men filed up to the kitchen slide and carried off their platters of bread and pork, a dozen unruly boarders were only subdued to moderate quiet at the rifle's point.

CHAPTER XXII.

A BATTLE IN THE ROTUNDA.

At 2 o'clock the alarm bell rang out thirteen ominous notes. This was the fire-box of the prison. The flames had broken out in the wicker-workers' shop, where the younger and lighter convicts plaited summer chairs, flower-stands and all kinds of basket articles. On a high throne set against the middle of one wall sat Johann Koerber, the deputy in charge, overseeing everything, pistol in hand. He was a Titan of 300 pounds, who might have proved admirable in his proper work of putting maniacs in strait-jackets. But his selection as overseer of the work-rooms was another instance of Tapp's want of judgment. For all his formidable strength, Koerber lacked the power to govern. The slenderest boy did not fear him, while even "papa," the giant negro who loaded the teams, stood in awe of "Slim" Butler, the lightweight deputy who had charge of the harness-makers. Right under Koerber's eye, the match was applied in several places, and almost before he smelled smoke the canes and osiers were on fire.

Then came the wild riot. In every shop but "Slim" Butler's the officer in charge was overpowered before the alarm bell had ceased ringing. Butler held his men down by sheer strength of will, until the sight of others rushing about in the yard below drove the men at the windows to frenzy, and with the loss of one of their number the brave deputy was disarmed, mangled, crushed. Brushmakers, tailors, shoemakers, saddlers, teamsters and handy men, all streamed from the work-shop doors, making by concert toward the wire pole in the middle of the yard. Here the Right Spur was executing a dangerous but ingenious maneuver.

Astride of the cross-bars of the pole, which he had climbed in full view of a dozen deputies, he was cutting the thick telephone wire with a huge pair of shears. The thing could be done in twenty seconds if his confederates mobbed the keepers below, and it might mean a delay of twenty minutes in the arrival of re-enforcements from the nearest station. Stupefied and absorbed, the convict crew were gazing upward at their chief on his perilous perch, when the tall form of Hawkins was seen striding down from the bath-room entrance. The other deputies had contented themselves with fronting the crowd, shoulder to shoulder, rifles leveled, like a herd of musk-bulls with lowered horns defending their females against wolves or men. Hawkins raised his rifle and fired.

The bullet missed its mark and the crack of the powder roused the convicts from their stupor. With a bestial cry and faces on fire, the forward rank, pushed on by those behind, swept down on the group of deputies. Chisels, mallets, hammers, tools and weapons of all kinds from a wheel-spoke to a blunderbuss were brandished in their hands. One volley and the deputies fled—all but Hawkins. Almost simultaneously, it seemed, the second barrel of his rifle hurled its missile, the Right Spur was seen to drop from his post, dragging the severed wire with him to the ground, and "Long-legs" himself was felled, bleeding and senseless, with a heavy bottle.

The mob would have been glad to outrage his body, but time was precious and Dickon Harvey had already sped to the north corner of the "bastile" and was beckoning and summoning his men to follow. They rushed in his wake, turned one corner of the bastile and then another, gave a great shout of joy as they saw the wide outlet of freedom before them.

The bastile was the great granite castle which contained the cells, a continuation of the rotunda. It projected into the yard, leaving a wide space at one end and at both sides. On the opposite side from that in which the shops were located stood the greenhouses, where Robert Floyd was accustomed to work whenever he wearied of writing. He had been crouching under the slant glass roof of the conservatory, snipping off the dead leaves, when the alarm bell sounded. The cries on the other side of the bastile brought him out on the open grass plot, and he was standing there, scissors in hand, when the convict pack swept toward him around the angle 100 yards away. At the same time he heard the impatient bells of the fire-engines jingling up the street.

The riot had been ably planned. Over on this side of the yard stood the entrance for teams. It was this point that the fire engines from without and the convicts from within were making for together. The alternative offered was that of letting the workshops burn or of emptying the jail of its inmates. Outside there was a ponderous iron gate, guarded by a deputy. Within this a stout one of oak wood, which a convict was detailed to open and shut. This convict was no other than Minister Slick, who had persuaded the warden to assign him to this light duty on the score of advancing age and feebleness.

Minister Slick's door was only open a crack. He was too cunning to give the deputy outside a view of the convicts racing down the yard. Not until the outer iron gate was swung back and the fire horses came galloping along did he throw his own gate in, without any marked evidence of "feebleness." The fire engine burst through; the convicts were at hand. Before the heavy iron gate outside could be shut they would be down upon its guardian and he would be swept aside like a sapling before the moose.

Floyd was quick to take in the situation and quick to choose his course of action. The deputies were flying in every direction before the victorious mob. A hundred yards can be covered in a very few seconds, even by men who are not professional sprinters. The wooden gate must not remain open.

The fire engine shielded him from the gaze of Minister Slick, who had drawn a revolver, but, not daring to attack the outside deputy alone, stood awaiting the onset of his fellow-prisoners. Robert was upon him in an instant and drove the greenhouse scissors into his neck, then thrust him aside, swung the door to with a mighty shove and turned just in time to dodge the rush of the maddened convicts.

Fifty of them flung themselves against the gate. It groaned but held firm. The original oak had buffeted winter gales fiercer than this, when the sap was in its veins and its green leaves rustled about the spreading branches. Like a wave of ocean breaking into foam against a cliff the oncoming mob scattered and reeled back in indecision. Several of them made at Robert, hurling their weapons at his flying form. Others ran along the great wall, like tigers along their cage bars, as if feeling for an opening. Only Dickon Harvey, from the moment that the inner gate clanged, had stood still in the middle of the clashing throng, turning his head to and fro and studying the situation. He was not slow to make up his mind.

"Out by the rotunda!" he shouted, waving his hand, and the whole rabble was making for the rotunda before

the fire-horses had rounded the angle of the bastile at
the other end of the yard.

Now Robert, hemmed in by a broad line of 400 armed
opponents, had already chosen this outlet of escape for
himself. He had foiled their plan and it would go hard
with him if he and they should remain within these
prison walls alone. There was a possibility that the flying deputies had left the rotunda doors ajar, since they
were so heavy as to require several seconds to open and
shut. So through the kitchen, up the iron stairs and
across the tiled floor of the rotunda he sped, with the
foremost of the pursuers almost at his heels. Only one
deputy, Gradger, opposed himself to his progress, gun
in hand, and Robert eluded him with the ease of a foot-
ball dodger.

Both doors were ajar, the outer one, however, only a
dozen inches or less. Perhaps twenty feet lay between
him and safety. He had almost flung himself upon the
knob, when a man coming toward him from the outside
forestalled his purpose and drew the door to with a
clang. It was Tapp, who from his office, unable to rally
his routed deputies, was rushing to the scene of the riot,
determined to retrieve by a last act of courage the num-
berless shortcomings of his administration.

Robert's predicament was fearful. The door barred
egress, the dogs were at his heels. Something of the
cowering awe that benumbs the stag when his legs at
last tremble under him and he turns to face the baying
pack swept through his breast for an instant. But it was
no more than an instant, for the young man's blood was
roused and it was not unmixed with iron. With a leap
at the knob and a mighty tug he drew the inner door
between himself and the criminals.

A snarl, hardly human, burst from hundreds of throats
when they saw this last avenue closed. The thick glass
of the door was splintered in a jiffy and vicious hands,
armed with bludgeons and cutting tools, stretched
through the bars at the traitor who had twice cheated
them. As green displaces yellow in the chameleon's
coat, so a wave of revenge suddenly swept aside the hope

of escape in the temper of the crowd. Fortunately the space between the two doors was so wide that Robert could back away and avoid the blows intended for his vitals.

But he had not reckoned on Dickon Harvey. Harvey had been the first to hurl himself on the door that Robert drew between the convicts and himself. Without a word, without a moment of hesitation, he had turned back diagonally, the others making a lane for him, and thrown himself on the turnkey Gradger. The struggle was fierce. Had Harvey been alone, he would have gone down underneath in the bout. But he was not alone. Twenty hands reached at the keeper and presently Harvey came pushing through the others, waving a huge bunch of keys over his head with a shout that the whole hall echoed.

Robert looked behind him through the outer door. Tapp had disappeared into his office. There was only the clerk and some idlers about and none of these, if they could have opened the door, dared to exercise the power. It was only a question of time when Dickon Harvey would find the right key. He could see the weapons waving in bared right arms and the shouts of the rabble once more had a hopeful ring. He said nothing, did nothing. There was nothing to do. But a rippling in his cheek showed that his teeth were clenching and unclenching. Instinctively he spread his arms out, backing against the outer door, clutching the bars and facing his hunters. It was the attitude of crucifixion.

"Ha!" Dickon Harvey was silent as death, but the shriek of exultation told that his wrist had turned on the handle of the key. It fitted the wards. Slowly, all too slowly for the convicts, all too quickly for Floyd, the inner door was drawn ajar and the foremost men crouched to spring. Then came a crash in the glass behind Floyd at his very ear. A long tube of steel passed by his cheek, and, turning, he looked into the eye of Warden Tapp sighting along the barrel of a rifle. The report rang out and Dickon Harvey fell forward, the keys jangling at his feet. Robert wrenched them from his unclasping hand. They were his only weapon. He had lost the scissors.

At the fall of Harvey the men recoiled for an instant. Quickly another rifle, and another, and another were thrust through the bars behind Robert, and he was cautioned to stand motionless. Like a mountebank's daughter, whose body outlined against a board the father fringes with skillfully cast knives, each missing her by only a hair, the prisoner stood with his arms outspread, protected by the chevaux de frise of protruding guns. Several of the defenders were kneeling and one thrust his muzzle between the young man's legs.

"Retire!" said Tapp. "Clear the rotunda!" The men sullenly stood.

"One! Two——"

Before the fatal "Three" was added they broke and turned. Then the muzzles were drawn in, the door behind Robert opened and the warden, at the head of half a dozen deputies and a dozen policemen who had just arrived, charged in upon them. The odds were twenty to one, but with the Right Spur lying senseless under the telephone pole, Minister Slick wounded at the gate where Robert had stabbed him and Dickon Harvey dead on the threshold to freedom, the rabble was merely a torso of Hercules, formidable in physique but powerless without head or limbs. The clubs of the officers made heavy thuds and the red blood starting here and there splashed curious spots of color in the dingy crowd. At one stairway Robert saw the tall form of Hawkins, bleeding but revived, thrashing around with an empty gun barrel. Then the mob was driven down the stairs, dividing itself into two portions in the right and left yards.

"Open the team gate," cried Hawkins, leading the deputies and officers to the left, through the kitchen, instead of to the right through the bath-rooms, whither Tapp had started. This time the warden was content to follow and the reason became at once apparent. The solitary fire engine stood over against the burning shops, helpless without its hose. From the outside several streams were playing on the buildings and the firemen, mounting by ladders, were climbing along the roof. But access from within was necessary if any headway were to be made. The engines stood outside the gate, occupying the interval of delay by getting up their fires.

Hawkins stationed his men in a cordon across the gate and admitted the engines and hose carriages and ladder trucks. One by one they dashed by till as many as could be supplied with water from the hydrants in the yard had entered. Then the tall deputy locked the others out, detailed one squad to guard the rotunda and another to close all doors of the bastile. With the remainder of the company, re-enforced by more policemen and keepers, he began to corral his steers.

In order to do this it was necessary that his own men should maintain the solidarity of a phalanx, while deploying out like a line of skirmishers from wall to wall. Spread over the width of the yard at one side, they began their march with rifles and revolvers ready. The stragglers fled before them. Their gait was slow. Turning the upper angle, an ambush was to be feared, but the spirit of the convicts was broken and they only hurled their weapons and fled. Hawkins wheeled his line to the right, making the pivot-mark time, and passed along the end of the yard, which was deserted. Turning the second angle, a more desperate resistance was shown. Here all was confusion, the engines and burning shops offering places of refuge, while the presence of the firemen made it impossible to shoot. Hawkins halted his command.

"All firemen in the yard fall behind this line!" he shouted. The firemen left their engines, several of them only tearing themselves away by force. Three were captured and held in front by the convicts. The others, seeing this murderous purpose, could hardly be restrained from rushing to their rescue.

"Club guns!" cried Hawkins, and the breeches instead of the muzzles were presented to the mob. But they seemed to dread this end of the weapon as much as the other, for they released the firemen and slowly withdrew,

Hawkins' line continuing its Macedonian march. Suddenly from a thick nucleus among the rebels, a spokesman started forward with a white handkerchief tied to a pole. Hawkins motioned him back and the march was continued. The men were penned up against the bath-room entrance, leading into the rotunda and the bastile, where four deputies with leveled rifles prevented escape. Hawkins had cleared the hydrants and the firemen resumed their work.

"Deputies at the bath-room door fall back and guard the stairs leading up to the rotunda! The prisoners will file into their cells in the bastile!"

This was the last straw. A yell of rage burst from the mob. To be flung back into their kennels with the bitter crust of disappointment to gnaw, and the prospect of punishment for the day's misdoings, this was too much to endure without a last resistance. They turned upon their keepers with the courage of the beast at bay.

"Now!" cried Hawkins, and his line rushed forward. The hand-to-hand struggle of the rotunda was renewed more equally, for there were resolute men in the mob, men reckless of life and maddened by the goading around the yard. Nor was their accoutrement of iron tools despicable. Dozens slipped through the line, and policemen as well as convicts were seen staggering under blows. But the timid ones speedily fled into the bastile, and, thinning the multitude, robbed it of that consciousness of numerical superiority which had given it confidence. At last not more than twenty desperadoes remained, backs to the wall, in front of the line.

"Club them down!" cried Hawkins.

There was no choice but to obey. The men were of that mettle which breaks but does not bend. One by one they were beaten to the ground.

The whole of the afternoon was required to lock the mutineers up properly. With the aid of those prisoners who had not joined the riot the fire in the shops was finally put out and a good deal of the property was saved. Only one life had been lost, that of Dickon Harvey, but the hospital beds were full that night.

When Warden Tapp called Robert to the office and thanked him in person for his behavior at the team gate and in the rotunda there were tears in the proud man's eyes. This was a shameful legacy of ruin and rebellion which he was leaving to his successor.

Passing out of the warden's room, through the rotunda, Robert heard the familiar voice which had puzzled him so often.

"Aisy, Misther Butler, aisy, for the love o' heaven," the uncouth fellow groaned.

Floyd turned and looked. "Slim" Butler, the overseer of the harness-shop, was superintending the transfer to the hospital on an improvised stretcher of the prisoner whom he had shot when his section rose against him. His own head was bandaged and his clothes were burned. The firemen had rescued them both with difficulty. But the face of the prisoner caused Robert to start, for he recognized in the convict whom Dobbs called Quirk his uncle's coachman, Dennis Mungovan.

CHAPTER XXIII.

THREE OF A KIND.

"I've got him! I've got him! Take his other arm, Toot!"

"Let go; she's tipping!"

"Will I let go and see the bloke drownded? You're a spunky feller, Toot Watts. Anybody'd think you never rocked a dory before yourself. Get up in the stern, Turkey. Now pull her in to the bridge and hold on to the logs. That'll balance her."

With one hand the Whistler held the drowning man's arm, while with the other he lifted his chin out of the water. It was a dangerous position, leaning over the bow in this manner, but the man in tow was unconscious and could not struggle. In a half-dozen strokes Turkey had brought the dory's stern up against one of the piles of the pier. This support he clasped with might and main, while Toot and the Whistler drew the body over the bow. Both were breathing hard when it was finally boarded.

"Turn him over," cried the Whistler. "You take the oars, Turkey, and row like fury for the beach. Get the bloke's head around, Toot, up against the bow. That's it. Now work his left arm up and down; I'll take the right—not so fast—about like this. That'll make him breathe."

"Do you think he's dead?" asked Toot in an awestruck whisper.

"He ain't dead. I felt of his heart."

"I seen a bloke at the bath-house that was in the water half an hour and they brought him round," said Turkey, panting at the oars.

"Keep the arm going, Toot. Never mind if you're tired."

"Are we near the beach?" asked Toot. He was the youngest of the trio, not much more than a child, in fact, and even the slum child, precocious in many kinds of knowledge, does not peep without tremors behind the veil of the mystery of mysteries. No one answered his query. An answer was not necessary, for over his shoulder the white line of the surf could be seen. When they got near the Whistler jumped to Turkey's side, seized the right oar and gave the added impetus of his lithe young arms to the headway of the boat. The water hardly rippled the glorious ribbon of moonlight behind them and wind and tide were set toward shore. Under these favoring circumstances the dory was carried high and dry upon the sands.

"Lift him out," cried the Whistler. Shagarach's body was laid upon the beach, dripping and disheveled. "You run up to the refectory, Toot, and tell the cop there to bring some whisky. Turn him over, Turkey, and let the water run out. Now slap his cheeks. Slap them hard."

"He's breathing."

"How did he tumble in, I wonder? Gee, didn't he come down flopping?"

"P'raps he was loaded."

"Lucky he didn't hit on them rocks there."

"He would if the tide was dead low."

Neither the Whistler nor Turkey had checked their vigorous efforts to resuscitate the limp body. Even the catching of their boat on a high-crested wave did not seduce them from their work.

"I'll swim after her," said the Whistler, watching the dory drift slowly off the sands.

Soon Shagarach's eyes opened and his lips muttered indistinctly. Presently he moved his arms. How cool the air was! He had often longed to lie like this on a soft, white sand, and let the·shallow water play over him, while he pierced with his gaze the deep blue sky. But the stars were above him now—not pendulous tongues of flame such as throbbed in the oriental heavens of his childhood, but the smoldering embers of the northern night, paling in the moonlight. And whose were those two strange faces thrust darkly over the golden disk?

"Are you better, mister?" It was unmistakably an earthly tone, the voice and accent of the city gamin, but warm with that humaneness of heart which a ragged jacket shelters as often as a velvet one.

"Take my coat, mister. You're shivering," said the Whistler, suiting action to word, so that Shagarach found himself embraced by a garment, not dry by any means, but more grateful than the soaked apparel which was chilling his skin.

"If you can get up, mister, and run around, it'll warm you. Toot'll be here soon with some whisky."

Shagarach gathered his strength to rise, but the effort was fruitless.

"How did I come here?" he gasped.

"You fell over the bridge, right near us. We were fishing for smelts and rowed over and saved you."

"That was fortunate. I thank you," murmured Shagarach.

"Can't yer swim?" asked Turkey in a pitying tone, but Shagarach was preoccupied with his recollections. He had made a mistake of judgment. He should have declined the rendezvous. But who and what was the assailant, the leering oaf he had passed on the pier? Was it some agent of the Arnolds? The anonymous letters pointed to that source. They were all seamed with allusions to the trial of Robert Floyd. And they formed his only clew. Stay, the hat he still clutched in his hand. He raised it feebly—for the mental energies of the lawyer were more elastic than the physical—and his teeth were still chattering though his brain was clear. It was a round, rimless cap of a common pattern.

"Here comes Toot." The Whistler, who was all eyes, had been the first to espy him, running at the top of his speed. Out of the darkness behind him loomed the powerful form of a policeman.

"The cop's comin', fellers. Here he is," cried Toot.

"Gimme the whisky," said the Whistler. "Take a swig, mister. It'll warm you up."

Shagarach applied his lips to the bottle and took a sparing draught.

"Well, how is the gentleman?" sang out the policeman, cheerily.

"He's all right now," answered the Whistler, a strange uneasiness coming over him.

The officer stooped down to the man's face.

"Why, Mr. Shagarach——" Surprise prevented him from saying more and Shagarach looked up at hearing his name.

"You're not on the old beat now?" he said.

"No, I'm on the park force till I get strong again. This is a bad accident. Coming round all right, though, by the look o' things."

"Yes, give me a hand and I'll try to rise."

Officer Chandler's great hand swung Shagarach on his feet. For a moment his knees sunk. Then he shook himself like a draggled dog. The liquor was working its way to his marrow and banishing the deep-seated chill.

"I owe my life to these boys," he said.

"Hello, what are you stripping for?" asked the officer, turning around.

"My dory," answered the Whistler. He had already reduced himself to the minimum of wearing apparel and stood ankle-deep in the surf.

The dory was twenty yards out, showing a dark broadside against the moonlit waves.

"Oh, all right," laughed Chandler. "Give me your arm, Mr. Shagarach. We'll furnish you a new outfit at the refectory. How did it all happen?"

"One moment, till the boy comes back." Shagarach knew that his assailant had had time to escape and that search for the present would be useless, but he saw no advantage in keeping the incident to himself. So he sketched the story of the letters, the rendezvous and the struggle, in his curt, forcible style.

"Find the head that cap fits and you'll do me a service," he concluded, showing Chandler the headgear.

"There was nobody on the bridge?"

"Nobody but the oaf I described."

"Wade out, Turkey," the Whistler was calling to his barefoot companions. He seemed shy of putting his boat ashore. Since the arrival of the officer all three urchins had become singularly distant and distressed. Was this only the natural awe which slum children feel in the presence of the police? Or was it conscience that made cowards of them all?

"Come ashore, young feller. The gentleman wants to thank you," said Chandler.

"We must look for the fishing-pole under the pier," answered the Whistler. It was true that he had thrown his rod away when they heard the loud splash of Shagarach's body in the water. But his manner indicated that while what he said might be true, it was not the fact. Turkey and Toot also had shown unseemly haste in wading out to the dory with the Whistler's outer raiment. The Whistler was digging the blade in for his first stroke when Shagarach addressed him in a tone that made him pause.

"My young friends, I am too weak to thank you to-night. To-morrow is Saturday. Could you call at

my office in the morning, 31 Putnam street? Mr. Shagarach. Can you come?"

"Yes, sir," answered the boys, with more submis-
sion than gladness in their voices. All the gamin's impu-
dence melts at a touch of true kindness. The boys
waited a moment, then disappeared into the night, while
Shagarach, with the policeman's assistance, made his way
through the gathering crowd to the refectory.

It was the misfortune of Jacob, Shagarach's office boy,
to be the owner of a most preposterous nose, the consciousness of which led him to fear society and shun
the mannerless multitude. Boys of his own age in
particular he dreaded, as a tame crow is said to fear
nothing so much as a wild one. So when our three mis-
chiefmakers entered the office the next morning and
seated themselves till Mr. Shagarach should return, the
poor lad began squirming by anticipation in his chair as
if its seat were a pin cushion with the points of the pins
protruding. As a matter of defensive tactics, this was
the worst possible attitude to take, as it courted assault.
But Jacob was not a strategist.

Before long his torture began, first by side comments
and giggles, suppressed in deference to the decorum of
the surroundings. Then he was subjected to a running
fire of personal questions, the tone of which speedily
began to mimic the muffled nasals of his own richly
accented responses. This would have been acute torment to a sensitive lad and a spirited one would have
ended the comedy by an appeal to arms. But poor
Jacob was stolid and peaceable. So his tormenters
had things their own way. The Whistler especially
seemed to have neither conscience nor reason in his
make-up, but an enormous funny-bone which usurped
the functions of both. It was not until Aronson came
in that Jacob was able to make his escape.

Saul Aronson was not a musical young man. If he
yawned down the major chord twice or thrice at bedtime
this was the nearest he ever got to singing. But when
the Whistler raised his flexible pipe, at first softly, then
loudly, with wonderful trills, breaking into still more

wonderful tremolos, with staccato volleys, and ascending arpeggios that would have put a mocking-bird to shame, it is no wonder that he gave up the attempt to insert the metes and bounds correctly in a quit-claim deed and contented himself with furtively watching the o-shaped orifice from which this flood of melody issued. This was his occupation when Shagarach's form, crossing the threshold, sent him back to his copying and checked the Whistler in the full ecstasy of an improvised cadenza.

"You have saved my life," said Shagarach to the boys when they had followed him into the inner room. He used the plural number, but his gaze seemed to be attracted to the Whistler, whose neatly brushed hair told of a mother's hand, and whose restless blue eyes, fringed with heavy dark lashes, centered a face oval, high-born and sweet, which gave out in every contour the glad emanation of a youth which was natural and pure. There was less in the others to make them distinctive. Turkey seemed to be a hulking clod and Toot was wizened and shrill-voiced and sharp.

"You have saved my life. How can I repay you?"

"I don't want any pay," spoke up Whistler. "I on'y came here to tell you about the fire."

"What fire?"

"Turkey said you was defending the bloke that set fire to the house on Cazenove street."

"Do you know something about that?"

"We seen a blo—a man coming out of the house," answered the Whistler.

"Then you come to make me still more obliged to you. But you must let me discharge a part of my other debt first. I have just come from the bank. Here are fifteen double eagles. You will each give me your mother's name and address and I will send her five."

Turkey and Toot showed no reluctance in doing this, but the Whistler still held back.

"My mother doesn't want any reward," he said. All three of the boys had just graduated from the Phillips grammar school, and could place their negatives correctly when they chose.

"This is not a reward. I only ask you to allow me to be your friend. At your age I had never seen this amount of money."

But still the Whistler blushed and shook his head till Shagarach perceived the boy's principle could not be shaken.

"You will give me your mother's address? Perhaps I may be able to get you work. Wouldn't you like to go to work?"

"Oh, yes, sir." The Whistler's face, which obstinate refusal, even for so honorable a scruple, had clouded with a trace of sullenness, brightened at once and his blue eyes smiled. Shagarach copied the address carefully and determined not to lose sight of the boy who knew how to say no so decidedly.

"And now——" he pushed the memorandum book aside. "I am defending Floyd. What did you wish to tell me?"

"We was the first at the fire," said Toot, eagerly.

"And we found the body of the servant," added Turkey.

But Shagarach's eyes never left the Whistler.

"Just when the fire broke out," said the Whistler, "we were coming through the alleyway side of the house."

"Yes."

"A big bloke—I mean a tall man—was running down the alleyway into Broad street. I noticed him, because the alley was narrow and he knocked me down."

"Where?"

"In the alleyway."

"Near Broad street?"

"Yes, sir."

"Ran against you and knocked you down?"

"Yes, sir, and said: 'Darn it, get out of the way.'"

"Was he running?"

"Well, half-running."

"We was running," added Toot; "'cause we heard them yelling 'Fire!'"

"What kind of a looking man was it?"

"A big, brown man, with a black mustache."

"He looked like a dood," added Toot.

"You didn't know him?"

"No, sir."

"Would you know him again?"

"Oh, yes," answered the Whistler. "I seen—I saw him last week pulling a single scull up the river."

Shagarach remembered having seen a portrait of Harry Arnold displayed in a fashionable photographer's showcase—shaggy cape-coat and fur cap setting off his splendid beauty. Immediately he wrote the address on a card, and, summoning Aronson, bade him obtain a half-dozen copies of the photograph.

"He was a handsome young man, then? About how old?"

The three guesses varied from 21 to 27. Either of these ages seems fabulously advanced from the standpoint of 14.

"Did you notice anything about his hands? Were they bare or did he wear gloves?"

"His right hand was bare," answered the Whistler, "'cause his fingernail scratched me when he thrun me—when he threw me down."

Shagarach drew forth the glove which Chandler had brought him and was studying it profoundly. Apparently he forgot the presence of the boys, so deep was his meditation. Then at last he started out of the reverie, thanked them again and with kind assurances of friendship shook their hands in parting at the door.

"Ain't he a dandy bloke?" whispered Turkey on the stairs.

"Why didn't yer take it, Whistler?" said Toot.

But the Whistler held his peace.

CHAPTER XXIV.

DEATHBED REVELATIONS.

When Emily Barlow ran down to Shagarach's office at noon this Saturday she was accompanied by her friend, Beulah Ware. Beulah Ware was as dark as Emily was fair. In temperament, as in complexion, the two girls offered a contrast, Beulah's carriage having the recollected dignity of a nun's, while Emily's sensibilities were all as fine as those Japanese swords which are whetted so keenly they divide the light leaves that fall across their edges.

"We should like to leave a note with the flowers, Mr. Aronson. Could you furnish us paper?"

Aronson was only too eager to furnish not only paper, but envelope, ink-well and a ready-filled pen. When the young ladies went out he thought a cloud passed over the arid chapters of his Pickering XII. This was the note, pinned to a graceful bouquet, that Shagarach read on his return:

"My Dear Mr. Shagarach: You must have read of the riot yesterday in which Robert behaved so nobly. But he is even more pleased with a discovery which he made during the affair. It seems that one of the wounded convicts, who has been passing under the name of Quirk, is no other than the coachman, Mungovan, whom none of us could find. Could you manage to call at the prison to-day? The poor fellow is seriously injured and may have important evidence in his possession. Yours truly, "EMILY BARLOW."

The violets seemed to move Shagarach far more than the note, momentous as its revelation might be. His hand trembled when he reached to clasp the stems. Then he withdrew it and stood irresolute. A procession was passing through the street below. From the window he could see the tilted necks of a line of fifers. Was it a horror of music that made him shut out these sounds so often? A dread of perfume and loveliness that made him leave the room at once with brief directions to Aronson? The casual observer would have said that he merely hurried to obey the suggestion of Emily's note, for he took his way at once to the state prison across the river.

When Col. Mainwaring took hold of the prison that morning it was expected that two out of every five of the convicts would have to be bastinadoed before peace could be restored. Against the advice of all the deputies, including Hawkins, he had summoned his wards to the rotunda and outlined his course of action in a cool speech. The burden of it was that he intended to begin with a clean sheet and to look out for their interests rather than their sensibilities, or, as he expressed it, "to give them hard words but soft mattresses."

The matter and manner of the address had a tranquillizing effect and some of the shops that day wore as quiet and decent an aspect as any factory-room in the state. Moreover, as soon as it became known that the colonel had resolved to adopt several of the reforms demanded in Dickon Harvey's petition, even the moodiest of the ring-leaders felt that they could submit without any hurt to pride.

Stretched on a hospital cot, whispering with contrite eyes to a black-robed clergyman, lay Dennis Mungovan. The look on his face was peaceful and exalted. His hands were clasped. The groans of patients and the odor of drugs which filled the chamber did not reach his senses. He had just finished his deathbed confession and stood upon a secure footing on the terra firma of faith, awaiting the summons from above.

"A lawyer to speak with Quirk," announced the attendant.

"Not Quirk, but Mungovan," said the clergyman, making way.

"And must you lave me, father dear?" besought the

patient, stretching out his hands as a cold man in winter reaches toward the fire.

"I have a wedding to perform, my son. Remember, your hours in this valley of tears are few, and you have left everything worldly behind you. Thank God, who in His infinite mercy has given you the grace of a happy death."

"I do, father, I do," cried the pallid sufferer.

"And an opportunity to repent of your sins. God bless you. Good-by."

The clergyman bowed to Shagarach and departed—from the deathbed to the wedding service, from the grave to the cradle of life, so wide was the compass of his ministrations.

"You are dying, then?" asked Shagarach.

"Wid a bullet in me breast, misthur, that the doctors can't rache. Och, they murdhered me wid their probin'. And all for what? All for nawthin'. What was I to be mixin' in their riots for? Wirrasthrue! Wirrasthrue!"

"You know Robert Floyd is in the prison here?"

"Robert Floyd! For the love o' heaven, misthur, don't tell him it's me. Tell him I'm Quirk. Och, that lie is a sin on me sowl."

"The truth will be best when you are so near death," said Shagarach, quietly. "Perhaps it would be better at all times. Besides, Mr. Floyd knows you are here."

"Misther," the dying man drew Shagarach toward him. "Misther! Do me a favor for the love o' doin' good."

"What is it?"

"Will you do it—an' I'll pray for your sowl before the throne, so help me——"

"I will if I can. What is it?"

"Keep it from Ellen."

"Keep what?"

"My name, my disgrace. Never let the poor girl know. She was my wife."

"Your wife?" Shagarach was puzzled a moment. "You mean Ellen Greeley?"

"Ellen Mungovan, before God."

"Ellen Greeley is dead. She perished in the fire."

The man started up in his bed so violently as to burst the bandage of his wound. His blood began to stain the linen and Shagarach was obliged to call an attendant, who adjusted it and tucked the patient snugly in. Still his glassy eyes were fixed on Shagarach and his muttering lips seemed to say over the word: "Dead! Dead! Dead!"

"She was burned to death in the Arnold fire. Robert Floyd is accused of setting it and causing her death."

"Burned to death!" The man's brain seemed bewildered.

"Didn't you know these things?"

"Shure, how would I know them, misther, all cooped in here like a bat in a cave?"

"How did you come here?"

"Och, the foolishness came over me, wid my head tangled in dhrink. What does a man know in dhrink? He can't tell his friend from his inimy. And me that had a dacent mother in the ould counthry and a dacent wife in the new, look at this, where it druv me."

"What crime are you charged with?"

"Wid breakin' and enterin', misther; and, sure, it was the stableman put me up to it that night I was full, and they got away and I was caught wid the watches on me and I was so shamed of Ellen and me mother at home, says I, I'll niver disgrace them, says, I, and so I gev in me name Quirk, and none of them could tell the differ."

"When was it you were arrested?" asked Shagarach.

"It's three weeks and three days yesterday, misther; that I know by the scratches I made in me cell."

"Can't you read?"

"Only the big, black letthers, misther."

This explained Mungovan's ignorance of Floyd's arrest. It seemed to be an accident that the two had never met in prison. Though they occupied cells in the same ward, their daily work carried them to opposite parts of the yard, Mungovan's to the harness-shop under "Slim" Butler; Robert's to the greenhouses near the team gate.

"Misther!" The poor wretch clasped Shagarach's wrist and drew the lawyer's ear to his lips again.

"Misther, will you bury me where Ellen is buried?"

"I'll see if that can be done."

"Misther!" The man's eyes were glazing. "Look!" He fumbled with aspen fingers in his breast, finally drawing forth an envelope. From this he removed a ringlet of black hair, probably a love-lock of Ellen's. Then he showed the inclosed writing to Shagarach. It was not addressed.

"Read it," he whispered. "Ellen gev it me to carry."

Shagarach opened the envelope and read in a servant-girl's painstaking hand the following words:

"The peddler has not come for two days, so I send you this by a trustworthy messanger. As I rote you in my last, the professor said in the study, 'Harry gets his deserts.' That was all I could hear only he and Mr. Robert talked for a long time afterwards. The will is in the safe in the study. If I hear ennything more I will let you know, and please send me the money you promised me soon."

There was neither address nor signature to this document.

"To carry where?" asked Shagarach, but the man's brain was all clotted with a single idea.

"Will you bury me by Ellen's side, misther, in the green churchyard under the soft turf that the wind combs smooth like in my own dear counthry? Will you bury me beside Ellen I disgraced so, misther? She'll know I'm wid her there. Will you bury me, misther?"

"I will. I will. Where did Ellen bid you carry the letter?"

"The letther? Och, I carried the letther in me mouth. Sure, I wouldn't be afther givin' up Ellen's letther to the warden."

"I mean——" But the man was passing through the delirium that precedes the last fainting calm. Several times his lips moved, murmuring "Ellen." His fingers clutched the love-lock to his breast. Once he turned his head and asked for "Father Flynn." But Father

Flynn was ministering now at another ceremony as opposite to this as laughter is to tears.

Toward the end a smile of singular sweetness irradiated his rough face, made delicate by the waxy color of death. Were his thoughts playing back again among the memories of childhood, in the beloved island, perhaps at the knee of that honest mother whom he feared to disgrace? Or were they leaping forward to the joy of the cool bed under the churchyard daisies at Ellen's side? Shagarach, holding the shred of paper in his hand, brooding over the answer to his unanswered question, could only watch the flickering spark in reverential awe.

But he did not default his side of the pact they had made, he and Dennis Mungovan, with clasped hands in the hospital alcove. At a great sacrifice of time he sought out Ellen Greeley's sister, explained the secret of Ellen's marriage and Mungovan's repentance for his follies, and, with the help of Father Flynn, persuaded her to consent to an interment of the couple together. He even went to the pains of communicating the death to Mungovan's worthy mother, having obtained her address from Ellen Greeley's sister and heir. But the circumstances and place of the "accident" which killed him were humanely concealed.

In return for all this solicitude the lawyer had an unaddressed and ambiguous scrawl in his possession. Three facts were established in relation to the person for whom it was intended. In the first place whoever it was he knew that Harry Arnold had "got his deserts" under his uncle's will. Secondly, he had employed Ellen Greeley as a spy upon the doings in the professor's household. Thirdly, he was in league with the missing peddler, who seemed to act as a go-between for Ellen and her correspondent.

CHAPTER XXV.

THE NEST-EGG HATCHES OUT.

"St! Bobbs!"

The sound was at Robert's left ear. He had been dreaming of Emily arrayed in bridal white and kneeling at his side before the altar of joy. Uncle Benjamin in a clergyman's surplice was pronouncing a benediction upon them. The good old custom of a nuptial kiss was about to be observed, when the warning whisper and his prison nickname rudely awakened him to his surroundings. The sweet vision melted into a black reality, the wide arches of the cathedral contracting to narrow cell walls and the loved faces of Emily and his uncle cruelly vanishing.

"Bobbs! Do you 'ear?"

"Yes!" Robert rubbed his eyes as if to restore the illusion and his answer was slumbrously indistinct.

"Count that bell."

A distant clock was giving out two strokes faintly but with vibrations prolonged in the silence.

"'Ear the hother coves snoozing."

The deep breathing of the convicts grew more and more audible as Robert's senses became sharper and he sat up on his couch.

"Hi 'ear you, Bobbs. Hare you making your toilet?" inquired the facetious cracksman.

"Yes."

"Leave your bloomin' boots be'ind as a keepsake. We haren't pussy-footed, me hangel."

"All right, I'm ready."

"Now, take out the blocks, me boy, and 'andle with care. If they falls on your toes they might 'urt, besides disturbin' the bloomin' deputy, which we must be werry

careful to havoid, Bobbs, out of consideration for 'is
feelings. Sh!"

A footstep was heard coming along the corridor, and
the re-enforcement of light told the prisoners that the
turnkey had a lantern in his hand, the dim gas jet at
one end only sufficing to deepen the shadows in the
cells. Robert lay back on his ·pallet and closed his
eyes till the steps retreated. In a half-minute the turnkey would be back. He was a new man, both Gradger
and Hawkins being still on the sick list from the blows
they had received in the riot of the day before.

"St, Bobbs, hare you ready?"

"All ready."

Robert had removed six bricks and carefully muffled
them in his bedquilt, leaving an aperture not much larger
than the door of a kennel. The light came nearer and
nearer and suddenly he heard the cracksman groaning
piteously. The turnkey raised his lantern, approached
the cell from which these sounds issued and peered in.

"Somebody bludgeoned yesterday," thought he. But
"somebody" was standing at the front of his cell, with
his hands firmly grasping two bars. As the turnkey
stooped and brought his eyes nearer, the two bars were
wrenched out and clasped around his neck. Being a
sturdy fellow, his instinct was to struggle rather than
to cry. But his struggle availed him nothing in the surprise of the moment, with the odds of position against
him. His head was drawn down through the bars and
he nuzzled a soft substance on the cracksman's breast.
Then a strange odor got possession of his senses. He
gasped, fought, gasped again, and finally fainted away.
When his writhings had ceased the cracksman removed
his lantern and laid it lightly on the floor outside.

"Climb through, Bobbs—not that way."

Robert had stood on the bed and thrust one leg
through the aperture.

"Head foremost, as the little feller dives."

Robert reversed his position, and with a terrible
wrenching of his shoulders worked the upper part of his
body through the opening, Dobbs giving him loyal as-

sistance and encouragement meanwhile. The turnkey hanging helpless into the cracksman's cell, his body outlined against the lantern, caused him to start back.

"Ee's hall right. Hi nursed 'im asleep on my breast-pin. Hain't it daintily perfumed?"

Attached to the cracksman's breast was a large sponge saturated with chloroform. The turnkey had inhaled this and was soundly asleep.

"Now for running the gantlet, Bobbs."

Dobbs' motions were lightning-like. First he laid the turnkey softly outside, then climbed through the cell-bars, this time feet foremost, for the cuts had been made nearly two feet apart vertically and the bars were not set close together. Once outside, he motioned to Robert to follow him, while he detached the prostrate man's keys from his girdle, dabbing his nose now and then with the sponge. Squeezing them tightly so as to avoid clanking, he coolly selected one of the largest.

"That comes of watching Longlegs w'en the others were 'ollering," he whispered to Robert, holding up his prize. It was the key to the door at the blind end of the corridor, which a turnkey passing through with the intention of going out into the yard would naturally select from his bunch and carry separate. Hawkins' habit of swinging his keys nonchalantly had not escaped Dobbs' observant eyes.

"Now," whispered Dobbs, making for the blind end of the corridor. There was no time to remove the lantern and the chloroformed turnkey from sight. Most of the convicts were still asleep, but two or three, awakened by the noises, started up in their night clothes and stood behind the bars, making gestures but uttering no sound.

Thus far Dobbs' plan had proved successful. There was no other outlet than the one he had chosen, since the cells were backed against the middle of the bastile and were impregnable at the rear. There remained two strong doors in the opposite wall to force. One turn of the key in its wards slipped the lock of the first. Before the second Dobbs waited and listened. A rhythm of receding footsteps was heard outside. Suddenly they seemed to cease.

"He's turned the corner," whispered the cracksman, immediately opening the outer door.

"Pull the inside one to, me boy."

Robert did as he commanded.

"Out with you now."

Robert preceded his confederate into the deserted yard, while Dobbs closed the great outer gate softly and sprung its iron bolt. Pursuit from within was thus cut off.

"Now run, me boy."

Robert followed, easily keeping up with his leader. As they approached the end of the bastile, Dobbs slowed his pace.

"Tiptoes, now," he cried stealthily working his way up to the corner of the building, where he stood crouching as if in ambush. Their shadows were thrown forward beyond the corner, so that the cracksman could not get within a yard of the edge.

"The hother cove Hi greased, but this one we'll 'ave to sponge, Bobbs," he said, taking the sponge from his breast and sprinkling it anew from a tiny vial.

"'Ere ee comes a-waggin' of 'is 'ead, but this at 'is beak will set 'im snoozin', Hi fawncy."

The footsteps came nearer and nearer, as monotonously regular as the ticking of a clock, but slow and heavy, as if the sentinel were a man of size. Dobbs stood ready to spring, the sponge in his right hand, his left free to disarm the deputy if he should present his gun. The form of a man turned the angle. It was Koerber, the giant, whom Col. Mainwaring had transferred from the caneshop to this less responsible duty.

Luckily Dobbs caught him in the midst of a capacious gape, and the great sponge stuffed into his open mouth served at once as gag and smothering instrument.

"'Old 'is harm," cried Dobbs to Robert, who leaped to his side and held down the powerful right arm of the German Titan. Koerber kicked and fought with desperation, bruising each of his assailants, but the sponge muffled his outcries and gradually he sunk in a stupor, Dobbs, with a strength no one would have suspected, breaking the fall of his body and laying him gently on the ground.

Another long application of the sponge and again he sped away. Koerber's beat stopped at the middle of the end-section of the yard, where he and the other sentinel must have met and saluted. But no one had come to his aid, and when the two fugitives crossed the "left yard," as it was called, making directly for the wall, no one impeded their progress. Eighty yards away, near the greenhouses, the back of a deputy could be seen marching in the opposite direction. Was this the man whom Dobbs had "greased?"

The cracksman had made a bee-line for the twenty-foot wall. How did he hope to surmount such a barrier? It was as smooth as a planed board, with hardly crevice enough at the cemented seams to give a cat's claw footing.

"'Ere's a hinstrument of my hown inventin', which I call the 'andy 'inge," said Dobbs, removing from his bosom an iron thing coiled around with rope. Unreeling the rope with lightning twists, he displayed for a second a plain, strong hinge, very broadplated and sharp at the inner angle. With a cast that no professional angler could excel, he flung this far over the top of the wall, and drew it taut, by means of the rope. The edges of the wall being drilled off perfectly square, the hinge must have caught on the other side, and the security of the apparatus as a means of ascent was only limited by the strength of the rope. The device was as simple, yet as ingenious, as the clock-face.

"Climb, me boy," said Dobbs.

Robert was up in a few seconds, the rope being thick enough to give his hands good purchase, and the cool night air and exhilaration buoying his strength. Dobbs climbed with more difficulty and was puffing heavily when, with Robert's help, he reached the broad top of the wall.

"Hi'll 'ave you gazetted hensign in the royal navy, Bobbs, next time Hi confab with 'er royal 'ighness," he smiled, his humor never appearing to desert him. "Such climbing would do credit to a powder monkey."

Just then, with the two figures standing on the top of the wall, a loud clang smote the silent air. It was followed by another and another till the world seemed awake once more.

"The alarm bell!" cried Dobbs. "They're after us! Drop!"

Both men were on the ground in a second, Dobbs coiling his "handy hinge" as he led the way running. Fear lent him wings and though he panted and his voice grew husky, he managed to keep abreast of his fleeter companion. The prison wall skirted a long, ill-lighted alley, which debouched in an unfrequented street. Here the houses were scattered, barren lots intervening, and a glimpse of the river breaking into the background now and then. It was broad moonlight, and the trees and fences afforded little shelter to the runaways.

Any policeman who met them would have been justified in shooting down two men, one in convict garb, fleeing from the direction of the prison. Doubtless Dobbs had prepared himself for this emergency, but luck favored him here and his reserve resources were not called into play. To left and right and left again he turned, finally climbing a low fence and crossing a stableyard that bordered on the river. A second fence to climb and Robert found himself on the rocky embankment of the stream.

How dark and beautiful it was in the moonlight! "Free, and I know not another as infinite word"—the line of the poet came back to him, and for an instant he felt in his veins all the glory of that treasure for which nations have thought rivers of their purest blood no extravagant price. But there was little leisure now for meditation. The alarm bell could still be heard sounding distinctly at the distance of a quarter of a mile and Dobbs was peering down the embankment, which cast an inky pall over the water in its shadow.

Presently he whistled. An answer came, some fifty yards to the right. Clutching his comrade's arm, the Englishman ran along the bank to the spot from which the response proceeded. A light keel-boat with a single occupant was moored in the gloom below, but so far below that to jump would surely capsize her, for the tide was at its ebb and the stream had sunk like an emptying canal lock.

"Shall we plunge in?" asked Robert, not averse to the bracing midnight bath.

"'Ardly, with a four-mile row in wet clothes before us, me hangel," answered the cracksman, "and the 'andy 'inge still lovingly clasped to my bosom."

Scooping out some earth at the rim of the flags which crowned the embankment wall, he made a hollow for the hinge and threw the rope down into the boat. The corner to which it clung had not been chiseled off clean like the edge of the prison wall and there was some chance of its slipping, but the risk had to be run.

This time Dobbs descended first. Robert followed him nimbly. All through the adventure he had reflected and even echoed the cracksman's humorous mood, and had displayed as little nervousness as if it were a student's lark upon which he was engaged instead of the grave crime of prison breach. So when the hinge slipped, just as he was dangling midway, and he fell plump into Dobbs' arm, with a coil of rope and an iron implement behind him, he only laughed as delightedly as a high-perched tomboy after climbing a forbidden fence.

"Well, that gives us back the hinge," he said. "We might have had to leave it."

Evidently the serious-talking young radical had a vein of drollery under his thoughtful exterior.

"You didn't 'urt yourself?" asked Dobbs, gathering his own dispersed members together.

"Not a bit. You're as good as a feather bed. I'd just enjoy tumbling on you four or five times a day."

But Dobbs, ruefully rubbing his barked shins, only ordered the boatman to "give way," which is nautical for "pull straight ahead," and in three or four strokes they were clear of the embankment and out in the full current of the flowing tide.

CHAPTER XXVI.

ITS CHICK PROVES PECULIAR.

Have you never lain back at midnight in the bow of a Whitehall, with your hands clasped behind your head and your legs lazily outstretched—no comrades but the oarsman amidships, and the fellow-passenger facing you from the stern, no sound but the gurgle of your own gliding, no sensation but the onward impulse of the boat, as gentle as the swaying of a garden swing, and the scarcely perceptible breeze aerating the surface of the river? Then the moon has never tinted the atmosphere for you with such voluptuous purity as it did for Robert Floyd that night, and the sparse, dim stars have never announced themselves so articulately as the lights of a grander city than that whose gloomy masses and scattered lamps they overhung. Even Dobbs' lighting of a cigar—no cosmic event, surely—did not jar upon the grand totality. The tiny flame, drawn in and then flaring up, gave flash-light glimpses of a face unmatched in the shrewdness and humor of its lines.

For fully ten minutes not a word was spoken. Suddenly Dobbs' voice snapped out:

"The hother duds, quick, chummy. There's a bobby on the draw."

A pair of black trousers was thrown toward him by the oarsman and Dobbs drew them on over his prison garb.

"Now the coat."

He was turning his striped blouse inside out.

"Now, let's 'ear you in the chorus," said Dobbs, who immediately set up a sailor's song about Nancy Lee. Robert and the boatman swelled the chorus as desired, with rollicking "Heave ho's."

"Quit your caterwauling there!" cried the policeman above. The pseudo-sailors at once hushed as if much frightened and rowed swiftly under the bridge, while the policeman, satisfied with this display of obedience, stalked along on his lonely beat. Above the bridge the river narrowed and the banks were no longer of granite, but of arable loam scalloped into a thousand little inlets. An hour must have elapsed and three more bridges had been passed, when the boatman turned into one of these coves and drove his keel against a grating sand bank. The passengers jumped out and shook the cramp from their limbs.

"Is that all, Mr. M——"

A finger on Dobbs' lips checked the boatman's sentence half-way and a nod gave the answer to his uncompleted question. Robert was not paying attention, but when Dobbs touched his arm and led the way up to the road, he promptly followed. By this time the milkmen and marketmen were about. A rattle of distant wheels broke the silence now and then. The dawn-birds trebled their matin greeting and a pearly flush located the eastern quarter of the sky. After a few turns, Dobbs approached the side entrance of a large house, not unlike an inn. The waiter who answered his tap appeared to have been expecting him.

" 'Ere we are, Bobbs, me boy. 'Ere we'll shift our duds and 'ave a talk over the breakfast victuals. Whew! Hi'm tired! Fetch a lamp, Johnnie, into the guest chamber. We haren't clemmin' on you, we've got rocks. Hey, Johnnie?"

The white-aproned waiter grinned and led them into a private room with a table in the middle.

"The porker, Johnnie, and plenty of good hold hale with the fixin's."

Dobbs had drawn his chair up to the table, set Floyd

opposite him, and made one hand wash the other with the true gourmand's expectancy while he gave this savory order.

"Well, you bloomin' old milksop! Hi suppose you'll put me in your prayers now, hey? Hey? Hey?"

Dobbs poked Robert under the ribs in a fashion which the young man might have resented in any but a familiar and a benefactor. Apparently his acknowledgment of his obligation was not warm enough for the cracksman, who began grumbling in an injured tone.

"Thankful? Wot's thankful? A word. Hi don't want words. Words is for magistrates and ministers and such like 'ipocrites. Hi want a mark of confidence. 'Asn't Dobbs trusted Bobbs?"

"Yes, he has."

"Well, w'y won't Bobbs trust Dobbs? Are we mismated? Do we work at cross-purposes? Hi need a pal, Bobbs—upon which you may remark w'ere is the shillin' comin' from wot's payin' this piper? But there's pals and pals! And if Hi offer my friendship to a honorable associate Hi made the acquaintance of while we was both serving in Col. Mainwaring's regiment, wot's Jim Budge got to say? Cut and run, Jim, says I, and much obliged for your 'elp. 'Ave a glass, Bobbs?"

The waiter had brought in several bottles of ale. Robert filled out a glass of the brown, foaming liquor and poured it down with a gusto that seemed to cheer Dobbs immensely.

"The uniform, Johnnie, and, don't overtoast the porker."

Johnnie seemed afflicted once more with his grinning fit, for he stuffed his apron in his mouth when he got to the door.

"What are your plans ahead, Dobbs?" asked Floyd, nibbling a pretzel, while the cracksman helped himself liberally to the ale.

"My plans is Chicago. Hi'm going into business as a reformer."

"Ha, ha; what will you reform—yourself first, I suppose?"

"Hi'll begin on the police force. You haren't a-drink-in', Bobbs. Your 'ealth, me boy, a-standin' toast to the 'ealth of Dobbs' pal. Hip, hip, hip-oh, 'ere's Johnnie, with the porker."

Johnnie seemed to have caught a sharp glance from Dobbs on the threshold, for his grin subsided and he was obsequious in his attentions to the breakfasting pair. Dobbs accepted them as a lord would the bows of a lackey, but Robert felt constrained to brush off the importunate caresses which he had no means of repaying in coin.

"If there's one meat in creation wot's sweet and savory," said Dobbs ecstatically, digging a fork in the dish just brought, "it's a juicy little 3-months-old baby porker, swimmin' in greens and gravy."

Robert could hardly help smiling while Dobbs carved the young pig, smacking his lips prodigiously mean-while.

"A hearty breakfast, me boy; we've a long ride be-fore us."

"Where to?"

"Pitch in and don't spare the gravy—w'ere to? W'ot say to the Hargentine Republic, w'ere you can sue for your uncle's money by proxy, hey?"

"My uncle's money?"

"It's your'n, now the will's busted."

"I don't want the money and never wanted it."

"Then wot are you 'ere for?"

"Only the fresh air and the trip. I thought they might do me good."

"See 'ere, Bobbs, if you think Hi'm a-fishin' for a slice o' your bloomin' pile, Hi'll show you Hi'm straight as a flag-pole. Them's not the harticles of partnership Hi propose."

"I never said they were, Dobbs."

"But your heye says you suspect me, and it don't pay to be too suspicious, me boy. Hi'm opposed to suspicion, bein' of a hinnocent nature myself. 'Aven't you learned that, Bobbs, halready? 'Aven't Hi trusted

a hutter stranger with my rat's tooth and gone 'alvesies
with 'im, doublin' the risk and not doublin' the enjoyment?"

"You've placed me under a great obligation, certainly.
I wouldn't have missed this night for the world."

"'Ere's a 'ealth to it, Bobbs—a standin' toast—and may
we never bunk in the bastile again. Hip, hip, hip—"

"Here are the clothes, Mr. Mc—"

The crashing of a beer bottle on the floor cut the name
off at the initial letter, and for some reason Johnnie did
not finish it after he had picked up the fragments.

"Lay the duds on the chair, Johnnie; we haren't done
discussin' the porker." A black business outfit, including
headgear and footgear, bore witness to the cracksman's
foresight. "Bring us some more hale. 'Ave a pretzel,
Bobbs (hic)."

Bobbs was undeniably succumbing to the influence of
his potations, but Robert knew the thirst-creating prop-
erties of salted cracker, so he declined the proffered morsel.

"Won't break bread with me! Hi say, Bobbs, this is
a houtrage—a houtrage. W'ere'd you be this minute if
it wasn't for me? Afore a tender little juicy porker, a-
sprawlin' of your legs under the table and a-facin' a hail
jolly Johnnie, w'ich is me? Or snoozin' in a ten-foot
kennel, with sweet dreams o' the swingin' gallows?"

"I wouldn't be here, certainly, Dobbs."

"You wouldn't be 'ere! That's so. A glass on the 'ead
of it. Your 'and, Bobbs, and your 'ealth. Bobbs says
(hic), and Bobbs is a gemman (hic), Bobbs says he
wouldn't be 'ere. But afore we part," here the cracksman sat down again, "Hi 'ope ee'll show ee's a gemman
and not mistrust 'is pal. Hi ain't no psalm-singer, Bobbs,
me boy. Wot's more natural, with a blank check before 'im, than for the confidential clark to facsimilate 'is
marster's hautograph? Wot's the hodds? Hi'll drink
with 'im hall the same—and a glass on the 'ead of it,
Bobbs."

Dobbs was rapidly becoming incoherent and his incoherence took a boastful turn.

"Ho, Hi cawn't 'elp a-grinnin, w'en Hi think of old Koerber a-wakin' up and a-roarin' for 'elp. Didn't Hi do 'im brown, Bobbs (hic)?"

"He was no match for you, certainly."

"Ee? Koerber? Lemme tell you there's few in the fawncy stand as 'igh as Bill Dobbs. Wot's Jim Budge? A hordinary bloomin' safe-cracker as must 'ave a pal. Ee cawn't stand alone, no more'n one leg of a scissors, which is the Hirish for bachelor. Barney Pease (hic) is truly great, Hi own. For sleight-of-'and work ee 'as no superior in the three kingdoms."

"Not even the solitary cracksman?"

"Not even the solitary cracksman, w'ich is me. But sleight-of-'and hisn't hall, Bobbs. It's sleight-of-'ead! Do you fawncy Barney Pease could 'ave got you over that sky-scrapin' wall? It was Bill Dobbs' 'andy 'inge done that. Lor' bless us! We'll be famous for this 'ere night's outin'."

"I've a notion you'd be a bad man to cross, Dobbs, eh?"

"Do you fawncy Hi'd 'urt you, Bobbs, me hangel? Hi wouldn't 'arm you no more'n a wadge-dog would bark at a baby. Hi'll (hic) Hi'll protect you, Bobbs."

Floyd smiled at the cracksman's offer of patronage. But this time he thought it better not to seal the compact with a bumper.

"Not drink?" Dobbs' temper had changed again. "Won't drink and won't give me no mark of 'is confidence—"

"What is it you want, Dobbs? A confession?"

"Confession? Hi? Ho!" the cracksman laughed as if the joke were a rich one. He was far gone, as indeed any man might be after taking so many quarts of ale.

"Confession, ho, ho—wot do Hi want of a confession? Hi 'ad a natural curiosity to know 'ow you set it, and"— his voice assumed reproachful quavers—"a natural mortification to find that my pal (hic) wouldn't trust me."

"Well, the truth is, Dobbs—"

"Wot is the truth?"

"Is this house safe? Walls have ears, they say."

"Safeazherown (hic)."

"I'm afraid—couldn't I write it down—that waiter, you know—" Robert walked uneasily to the door, but the waiter was not eavesdropping.

"Waiter," Dobbs rung the bell and Johnnie appeared.

"Bring me pen and paper." They were brought with expedition.

"Zhall I 'old the lamp, Bobbs?"

"It's almost lightsome enough to see, if you draw up the curtains."

"Hi'll 'old the light, Bobbs."

"Steady, now, you'll drop it."

Dobbs staggered over behind Robert, with the lamp in his trembling hand and stood over the young man's shoulder while he wrote the following confession:

"When you pick a lady's pocket on a railway train next time, do it with your left hand, Mr. McCausl—"

Before he realized what was happening the lamp had been shattered against the opposite wall and he found himself forced to the floor, with a cold circle of steel at his temple.

CHAPTER XXVII.

BEHIND THE VEIL.

"My mother has your flowers," said Shagarach. "She would be delighted if you would come to see her."

It was in response to this invitation that Emily had selected an appropriate dress from her modest wardrobe and kissed her mother good-by for the evening. She was at first not a little alarmed when a young man sidled up to her from behind and began uttering incoherent avowals of devotion, which not even her chilling glance and hastened step could check. Kennedy had disappeared for some time,—probably busy extricating himself from his

Dove-Cote scrape,—and she had congratulated herself on good riddance of the lovesick manikin. But here he was, bolder and more nauseously enamored than before.

She felt like summoning a bystander to her aid, but as she was walking close to the edge of the sidewalk, with Kennedy on the very curbstone, this appeal for help was rendered unnecessary. A quick, firm shove with her brave little hands sent the shadow of a man topsy-turvy into the gutter, while Emily, with burning cheeks and quickened pulse, made on to the car corner.

An old Hebrew housemaid answered her ring and ushered her into the tiny parlor of the tiny house, none too large for even the three persons who occupied it—and three is the smallest number that can be called a family. It need not be said that Emily was all a-flutter with the privilege of admission to the great lawyer's private acquaintance and that she cast a curious glance upon the surroundings. There was something oriental about them, even to the barely perceptible odor of musk in the air.

The carpet was clocked in a Turkish pattern, though the bough birds woven in the corners suggested that it came from one of the countries further east, where the shah, not the sultan, rules under Allah, and the admonitions of the prophet are less literally observed. The lamp was a silver fantasy, brazed with arabesques in gold, and the furniture in its scroll-work and the embroideries, like gossamer, all whispered of a taste exotic and luxurious.

Yet the articles were few and severely disposed in their places. A bust of Swedenborg over a massively carved bookcase, filled with volumes of royal exterior, attracted Emily's eye. On the opposite wall were several shelves, crowded with plainer books, as tattered and dingy as a schoolboy's algebra. A portrait of Spinoza reclined on an easel, and a well-thumbed Marcus Aurelius, of pocket size, with flexible covers, lay face down and open on the table. It was a far cry from the Swedish mystic to the imperial stoic of Rome.

"You are welcome, Miss Barlow, to my home," exclaimed Shagarach, extending his hand and sunning her with his great warm eyes.

"Pardon my curiosity. I am a woman and a book-lover," said Emily, who had been standing before Shagarach's gorgeous volumes when he crossed the threshold.

"They are not secreted from those who can handle them without danger," answered the lawyer, opening the bookcase..

"I call them my meeting of the masters."

Emily marveled at the range and judgment of the selection. Here were Homer, Dante, Shakespeare and Goethe in the original tongues, which her own studies just enabled her to distinguish one from the other; the Koran, the Talmud, the Zend-Avesta; Camoens, Luis de Leon and a dozen others from the hidalgo land; Maimonides and all the great mediaeval Hebrews; Keats, Wordsworth and Coleridge—whatever richest remnants remain from the cultured nations of Europe and western Asia. What rare powers of acquisition, what hermit-like seclusion from the busy world, were implied in the ability to read and enjoy these treasures!

"And which are your especial favorites?" asked Emily.

"The Persian poets," answered Shagarach, pointing to the uppermost shelf, where the titles were in characters she could not read, resembling odd curves of beauty and flourishes of a draughtsman's pen. "Firdusi, the weaver of the magic carpet, who spurned back the treasure-laden caravan of the shah; Sadi, the nightingale of a thousand songs, planter of the rose garden and the garden of trees; Hafiz, the sugar-lipped dervish of Shiraz, whose couplets are appealed to as oracles by the simple, and whose legion of commentators surround him like the stars clustering around the orb of the moon."

Was this the criminal lawyer, the granite-lipped reasoner of the immobile forehead, forever pacing to and fro, folding his arms in solution of problems?

The memory of the barren law office was vivid upon her, and of the austere occupant, the last being in the world from whom dithyrambics would be expected. She found it hard to reconcile the task-ridden Shagarach with this praiser of Firdusi, the half-fabulous minstrel who had loved to recline on silken divans, smothered with roses and waited upon by his hundred slaves.

"Inspect them," said Shagarach. Emily reached for the Persian shelf. The books stuck a little, and when they came away she was surprised to find that they were attached together in sets of five; still more surprised when she turned them over and saw a fine chain of steel running from edge to edge through the covers, just where the clasp of an album fits, and meeting again in an exquisite padlock at the middle volume. All this splendor of beauty and thought was sealed as effectively as if the pages had been bathed in glue.

"The keys to the padlock?" she looked interrogatively.

"There is only one," said Shagarach, a divine smile for the first time breaking the set curve of his lips. "It fits them all, but the dragon is jealous of its possession. My mother, Miss Barlow."

The lady who had entered approached Emily and greeted her warmly.

"My son said you were beautiful," she said.

Emily blushed. She was usually disconcerted by praise, but somehow the entrance of the mother put her more at her ease. Standing beside her son, the lady appeared to be taller than he, though this may have been more in looks than in inches, since the standard of stature for women is lower. The resemblance between them was marked. It was from her that the son inherited his beauty, for she must have been queenly in her maidenhood. Even now her coloring was autumnally perfect, the rich dark skin, oxidizing like an old painting, having gained in mellowness a part of what it had lost in brilliancy.

"We live plainly, you see," she said, speaking with a strong accent, as if she had learned our stubborn language too late in life ever to master it.

"I admire your furnishings," answered Emily, "but your library amazes me most of all."

The son and mother exchanged a sparkling glance, while Shagarach replaced the Persian set on its shelf. But he did not explain the mystery of his padlocked treasures.

"Miss Barlow has been wondering at my taste in the poets," he said, diverting the conversation a little. "She forgets, perhaps, that we are orientals, a long way back. And still in my dreams at times I feel the rocking rhythm of the camel ride and the winged bulls of the Assyrians seem to haunt me like familiar sights."

All at once Emily remembered that she had often divined a more emotional and mystical side to the criminal lawyer.

And then in a flash many things became clear to her—Shagarach's constant repression of emotion, his frugality and tireless toil, his shutting out of the gypsy violinist's strain that day when she brought him the news of Bertha—all these told of some great resignation, the ruthless division of a dual nature and the discarding of one part, perhaps the better beloved, and the abandonment with that resignation of almost all that was personal to him in life—leaving only the restlessly energizing intellect, the ethical strenuousness as of a modern Isaiah, the filial love and these sealed mementos of a more congenial but probably less successful past.

"And this is Spinoza—the greatest of our race," added Shagarach. "Not the least refined of human faces."

"My ancestors were his kinsmen," added the mother, not without pride. "We were Spanish once and my son can claim the title of count in Spain if he chose—"

"And many a castle in that country besides," added the son, smiling the rare, sweet smile which he reserved for this privacy of his home.

"But my mother speaks the truth, Miss Barlow. She is an accurate historian, as you see. An ancestor of mine rose to power in the court of Ferdinand and left his wealth to two sons. The elder, bearer of the title, chose exile when our people were harried from Spain. The younger, by apostatizing, succeeded to his name and property, and the heirs of that brother still survive in Valencia. That makes us feel for Spinoza, who was also an exile—and a heretic," he concluded, in a lower tone.

"This way, Miss Barlow," the mother led Emily through portieres into a rear room, not unlike the parlor in its furnishings. "Here are the flowers which you were so good, so thoughtful, to send. I have changed the water twice every day, and last night put them out to drink in the rain, for they love the rain from heaven, it is manna to them." The mother fondled them as if they were living things, and gave them to Emily to smell. They were indeed wonderfully fresh, considering the number of days they had been kept.

Shagarach stepped to the cleft in the portieres and excused himself to answer a ring at the doorbell. Emily was left chatting alone in the dim light with his mother. From flowers to other subjects of feminine interest the transition was easy, and the old lady's vivacity, strong sense and above all her warmth of heart made the minutes pass delightfully for the sensitive young girl. She had not been conscious of any unusual merit in offering Shagarach a simple bouquet, yet it had deeply touched the lonely son and his devoted mother, both of whom seemed to regard her now with that intensity of friendship which the Arab lavishes upon the stranger whom he admits to his hospitality.

It was while they were alone in the rear chamber, and Shagarach was conversing in low tones with the visitor behind the drawn portieres—probably a client calling in the evening—that Emily's attention was called to a tapping noise which seemed to come from the window. She thought it best not to speak of it, though it continued for almost a minute. Besides, she remembered having often arisen in the night to investigate the origin of just such a tapping, and lifted the sash to find nothing and hear nothing, not even a departing sparrow, who, perched on the sill, might have been feeling his way along the transparent glass. Shagarach's mother was talking herself at the time and probably the sound of her voice obscured the interruption.

"Is it not pleasanter in here, mother?" Shagarach had

thrown the portieres aside and stood again in the cleft, widening it for the ladies to pass. His visitor had been dismissed, but it was a few moments before he recovered his earlier manner. By a graduated ascent, however, his conversation rose to its former glow of enthusiasm, and Emily could not help contrasting its richness and elasticity with the sententiousness, the compressed statement, bare of all accessories, which characterized him when at his desk in the office. Probably this was the style he had used in addressing his caller, and the transition to and fro was not easy.

" 'Try how the life of a good man suits thee,' " Shagarach began reading from his Marcus Aurelius; " 'the life of him who is satisfied with his portion out of the whole and satisfied with his own just acts and benevolent disposition.' That is the advice I gave to my visitor and charged him nothing for it."

"It was Simon Rabofsky's voice?" asked the mother keenly.

"Yes," answered Shagarach.

"Then you did wrong. You should have charged him double. He is a rogue."

"For the emperor's wisdom?" smiled Shagarach.

"What mischief is he about?"

"He wishes to sell Mrs. Arnold's jewels. It is his legal right, since she has defaulted in the payment, but I have counseled a postponement of its exercise."

"And will he postpone it?" asked Emily, sympathetically.

"He? My dear, you do not know him," said the mother. "He is of the tribe of Aaron, who worshiped the golden calf."

Emily wondered if some of the proud Spanish blood had not become mingled with the Hebrew in her veins. Scorn of petty avarice was betrayed in every line of her noble face. Yet Emily felt sure that it was she who had called Shagarach away from the companionship of the Persian poets and impelled him to write his signet on the living world in letters of self-assertion and honorable achievement.

CHAPTER XXVIII.

AN UNBIDDEN GUEST.

"What tainted people you have to deal with!" she exclaimed, unconsciously continuing her vein of silent thought. "I should crave another environment, I think." "Your Christ lived with sinners and publicans. And they are not all tainted, my dear," added the mother, smiling so that Emily might know whom she meant to except. "There is so much in common between my son and Mr. Floyd. Both proud, serious, too serious, I tell him, and both true Castilians in honor. But the one looked about wisely and found him a—lady; and the other—"

"The other will grow gray by his good mother's side, I fear," said Shagarach, gently kissing the laughing and delighted old lady. Emily smiled herself to see John Davidson's sphinx, whose reticence outside was indeed a mask of stone, unbending thus to the frankness and simplicity of a child. The mother's ways were more demonstrative, but with deep reserves of dignity.

"But you are right, Miss Barlow. The lawyer's profession is one shade more distasteful than the surgeon's, for he handles the moral sores of humanity."

"Handles them to cure them," cried Emily, shifting about, like a true woman.

"Possibly. Though for my own part I agree with those who hold that the law perpetrates no less wickedness than it punishes—were it not that it prevents more than it perpetrates," he added, smiling, "we should live in a very troublesome world. It is a profession which uses the conscience as a whetstone upon which to sharpen the intellect. I attribute the venality of our congress and legislatures partly to the disproportion among them of lawyers."

"But surely there are exceptions?"

"In the criminal courts," answered Shagarach. Emily asked herself if this was Shagarach's destiny, to continue as a criminal lawyer. As if in answer to her question, he added:

"There alone one can feel at all times that he is either protecting the innocent or punishing the guilty. This is my working library," he pointed to the thumbed volumes on the shelves. Emily noticed that most of them were treatises on psychology, the old and the new.

"I do not carry the keys for those," said his mother, gayly.

"Light to illuminate our case," Shagarach took down one of the books. "By the way, my correspondent, Mr. Skull-and-Crossbones, has honored me again."

The two ladies started and the mother seized her son by the arm.

"A black-edged letter, apprising me that I am marked and doomed." Just then Emily heard the strange tapping that had startled her before. It came from the window of the front parlor this time. She shuddered in a sudden terror and drew closer to Mrs. Shagarach. The old lady had heard the sound and blanched a little, but her voice was firm when she spoke:

"Is that a mouse in the wainscoting, my son?"

"I thought it was a tapping at the window, mother."

"Go and look. There may be a stranger in the yard."

Shagarach raised the curtain and looked out, then opened the window. The cool night air flowed in and heightened Emily's tremors so that the elder lady took pity on her.

"There is no one in sight, mother, but I will put on my hat and go out the back door."

In a few minutes Shagarach returned by the street entrance.

"I thought I heard footsteps in the passageway and followed them around, but there is no one. The yard is empty."

"I will inform the policeman to-morrow," said his

mother. "There are many loiterers about in these bad times. And you should acquaint them with the letter you received."

"I have done so, mother. I have considered it strange," he added, turning toward Emily, "that the parties opposed to us in the Floyd case should resort to murder. It is a confession of guilt."

"If they are caught."

"Murder will out. Moreover, I do not work alone. I have engaged the assistance of—whom do you think?"

"Of Mr. McCausland," said the mother, breaking in. "It was my suggestion."

"McCausland investigating Harry Arnold!" exclaimed Emily.

"Is it not amusing? But he will not allow that Arnold is at all open to suspicion, and of course I have not laid all my evidence before him."

"But surely the letters are connected with our case, and who else could it be?"

Since the finding of the glove and the testimony of the three gamins Emily was coming around to Shagarach's view of Harry Arnold's possible guilt and the attack on Robert's lawyer had aroused her sympathies so as almost if not quite to convince her.

"Mr. McCausland is very keen—a wonderful man—of deceptive exterior, but like the rest of us, he sometimes makes mistakes," said Shagarach. "His defect is that he uses the logical method only and ignores the psychological. It is necessary first to find out if the accused is capable of the crime. I first became sure of Robert Floyd's innocence when I saw him through the cell-bars of the jail. He is incapable of the crime."

"My son so admires your lover," added Mrs. Shagarach.

"These other friends of mine," continued her son, taking down the thumbed volume which he had put back when the tapping startled them, "commit the opposite error. They are strictly physiological. They predict too much from a man's physical peculiarities."

The book he opened for Emily was a treatment on criminology, illustrated with villainous heads in profile and full face. It was in Italian, so Shagarach exchanged it for another.

"Behold the brands of the true criminal—'enormous zygomae,' 'ear lobes attached to the cheek,' 'spatulate fingernails——' "

"That takes in Mr. McCausland," said Emily, roguishly. She had got over her fright by this time and the allusion to spatulate fingernails recalled the whole train of events which had ended in the inspector's discomfiture.

"The refutation of such theorists," said Shagarach, "is simple. We need only point to the fact that the greatest crimes are committed by men who are not professional criminals at all and who do not belong to the criminal type."

"Like this man," said the mother, going to a closet at one side and drawing forth a bundle of photographs. One of them she showed to Emily. It was Harry Arnold, bold and handsome, with the shaggy cape coat thrown carelessly over his shoulders.

"Has he enormous zygomae, ear-lobes attached to his cheek?" she asked.

"I wish I could see his fingernails," laughed Emily.

"Arnold's face in repose does not show much capacity for evil. But it lights up badly. I have seen him crossed and in passion."

"I think he looks as if he were veined of evil and good," said Emily frankly, studying the portrait long, as she loved to do. She had seen Harry once when he was at his best. Besides, her service in the photograph studio had made her something of a physiognomist, too, though not, of course, such a soul-reader as Shagarach.

"His crimes are of the preventable order and therefore the more culpable. There are men born to crime, as the theorists argue; others driven to crime. For both of these classes it is hardly more than a misplaced emphasis, a wrong direction of energies."

"Here is another volume—I am showing you all my workshop. Does it fatigue you?"

"Nothing which helps to clear up the mystery is dull to me," answered Emily.

"This treatise deals with 'Incidental Homicide.' Rather legal than clinical. The cases are all parallel to ours. The indictment, by the way, has just been given out. The weakest count charges Robert Floyd with arson and murder in the second degree. The punishment for that is only imprisonment for life."

"Only! Robert says he would rather be hanged."

"Let him have no fear of either," said Mrs. Shagarach, cheerily.

"The newspapers tell us that the government offered much new evidence," said Shagarach.

"I should like to know what it was," cried Emily, eagerly.

"So should I. Ordinarily, the grand-jury room is leaky enough, but Mr. McCausland, who is the government in this case, appears to have found a way to seal it hermetically."

"Perhaps he padlocked the jurors' lips," suggested Emily, whereat all three were merry.

From time to time during the conversation relapses of the old shudder had come back to Emily, though the tapping had utterly ceased since Shagarach investigated the yard. He had left the curtain half-raised, so that any one approaching the window would be visible from within. It was just at this moment that she happened to change her seat, bringing her face around to the darkened window. Before the others could catch her, she had risen, pointed to the window and fallen to the floor with a terrified shriek.

Shagarach started to raise her, but the terrible detonation of a pistol rung out, sacrilegiously invading their quietude. Then all was darkness, a noise of crashing glass telling that the lamp had been shattered and extinguished. Another report followed and another. Mrs. Shagarach, trembling, heard her son quickly crossing to the window. The panes seemed to be broken, and there were sounds of a scuffle, mingled with a gnashing of teeth and growls more animal than human. Suddenly, with a ripping sound, the scuffle ceased, and rapid footsteps were heard pattering away. Then her son spoke to her in the loud, firm voice which he used in all practical affairs.

"Light the little lamp, mother. It is safe now. There are matches on the mantel."

"Are you hurt, Meyer?" she asked, anxiously, while lighting the lamp.

"A little," he answered.

"You were shot, my son?" she cried, embracing him.

"No. Let us revive Miss Barlow. Some water, Rachel," he said to the old servant who had come to the door.

When Emily came to she found Mrs. Shagarach sponging her forehead, while her son was washing his hands in a basin of bloody water.

"Wrap the cotton around them quickly, Rachel," he was saying. "I must notify the police."

"Meyer, it is not safe."

Emily heard the mother protesting, then swooned again. When full consciousness returned the lawyer was gone and the three women were alone in the room. Rachel began picking up the fragments of the lamp. Only its chimney and globe had been broken, the metal being still intact. The windowpanes showed great ragged holes, which explained the laceration of Shagarach's hands.

"Poor lady," cried the mother. "This is ill treatment we give you. But we are not to blame. It is the wicked enemies who are pursuing us all—your lover and my son." With terms of endearment she petted the weak girl back into a coherent understanding of her position. But every now and then the remembrance of something would cause her to shudder again visibly; whereat the elder lady would renew her caresses.

"I have notified the policeman. That was the best I could do," said Shagarach, re-entering. He looked extremely grave. It was a narrow escape for one or more of the three. "This is all I have to identify him by. It was detached in the struggle."

He laid a common coat button down on the table, with a piece of cloth adhering.

"That face! Who could ever forget it?" cried Emily.

"You saw him, then?" asked son and the mother in one breath.

"Shall I call it 'him'? Was it a man?" answered Emily. "Rather a monster, no more than half-human."

"It had the form of a man," said Shagarach, "as I felt it through the glass."

Rachel was busy bandaging his cuts with plaster during this conversation, but they bled through, calling for the surgeon's thread.

"But it snarled like a tiger," said the mother.

"Oh the wild, blue eyes! They were staring at me through the cleft of the draperies. And the demon leer, and the forehead, retreating like a frog's——"

"It is the oaf I passed on the pier," cried Shagarach, interrupting Emily. "We have found Mr. Skull-and-Cross-bones."

"Oaf? What is oaf?" asked the mother.

"An idiot, a monster."

She shuddered.

"A man of that description cannot long elude search," said the son in a more hopeful tone.

"They are often very cunning," replied the mother.

"Can it be Harry Arnold would employ such an agent?" asked Emily, still trembling.

"Twice," said Shagarach, as if speaking to himself. "A cap and a button. Men have been captured on slighter clews."

"You will give the button to Mr. McCausland," said the mother.

"Yes; since it fits with the cap."

"Maybe he will help you to bring Harry Arnold to justice."

"And so to acquit Robert Floyd," said Shagarach, smiling to cheer his guest.

The mention of her lover restored the wilted girl, who was brave enough when there was anything definite to be done. Shagarach showed her the book on "Arson" which he had been holding when the first shot was fired. The bullet had pierced it on its career toward the lamp.

"The bullets will be evidence also," he said, "and I will measure the footprints before the rain comes down and washes them away."

"You will wish to go home, poor child," said Mrs. Shagarach to Emily. "Not yet, but soon, when you are stronger. Rachel!"

The soothing words of the mother warmed Emily quite as much as the wine which Rachel brought. Meanwhile two policemen entered and began to examine the premises. Shagarach visited the yard in their company and soon returned with a tape measure and a paper block, on which he had recorded the lengths of the footprints.

He was assiduous in his regrets and inquiries toward Emily and insisted on accompanying her home in a carriage, which the mother, however, would not allow them to enter until she had exacted from her visitor a promise that she would come again on an appointed evening, and pressed upon her in true oriental fashion a certain rose-embroidered gossamer scarf for which Emily had expressed admiration.

At her own door the sweet girl heard Shagarach order the hackman to drive to Dr. Lund's, and she guessed that his cuts would be somewhat worse for the delay in stitching them. That night she saw gorgon faces leering in at her window, and her dreams were of new-moon scimiters and the rocking of the camel ride.

CHAPTER XXIX.

JACOB AND DELILAH.

"Put your wrists together!"

The voice was totally different from Dobbs' whine; a strong, deep register, like a ledge of the basal rock peeping out from a smiling meadow. For the first time Robert felt the veiled strength which resided in the detective's character. There was no option but to obey.

"Pull up the curtains, Johnnie."

The servant had been attracted by the crash of the lamp. A faint stream of daylight entered the chamber, and the noises of the city could be heard in the distance. McCausland's face seemed to have altered in every line.

"Get a hack! Jump into those shoes!" He tossed a curt order right and left, one for Johnnie, the other for Robert.

"To the county jail," was his direction to the hack driver. Robert wondered at this, but he sat back smiling and said nothing during all the ride.

"Here's your prisoner," said McCausland when they arrived. It was not yet 6 o'clock, but the sheriff was up and showed no great surprise. Robert wondered at this again and his amazement was not abated when they assigned him to his original cell in murderers' row. However, the change was to his liking, for the surroundings were less presageful of permanency.

"You missed your vocation as a character actor," was his parting shot at McCausland.

It is easy to imagine the dismay in the prison that morning when the escape was discovered. Col. Mainwaring was a very different man from Warden Tapp, and for a time it looked as though McCausland might lose his badge. But when he showed an order from the sheriff empowering him to bring the body of Robert Floyd from the state prison back to the county jail, which had now been put in repair, Col. Mainwaring saw a light; and when McCausland pointed out that he had laid his finger precisely on certain weaknesses of the bastile, frequently suggested without avail to Tapp, the new warden thanked him pleasantly.

The story at first was given to the public that Inspector McCausland had captured the fugitive, Robert Floyd, and for a time not only did the detective's cap wear a bright new feather but all the credit of Robert's conduct during the riot was canceled by this outbreak, which was construed as a confession of guilt. But of course the truth leaked out, and the failure of his "nest-egg game," with its brilliant but desperate climax, was made the occasion of much chaffing to the contriver.

"Has Bill Dobbs been taken yet?" a brother-in-buttons would ask him; and the two lovers had many a good laugh over the game which they had played and won. For the first time since the great shadow fell across them they were as happy and hopeful as lovers should be, and for several days little smiles of reminiscence would creep into the corners of Emily's lips while she was touching out the blemishes in some negative destined to pass from young Amaryllis to her Strephon or old Darby to his Joan.

Meanwhile Shagarach, too, was interesting himself in the study of photographs.

"Have they all been returned?" he asked Aronson one morning.

"All but Meester Davidson's."

"And none of the neighbors saw Arnold coming out?"

"They all shake their heads and say no, they don'd know that face."

"Very well. Jacob may put them in his desk. We shall hardly need them again. Go over to the second session and answer for me in the Morrow case. I am expecting Mr. McCausland."

"Speak of angels," said the inspector, entering cordially. "You know the rest of the saying."

"Good-morning. Be seated."

It did not escape even modest Saul Aronson what a contrast the antagonists made, sitting with the table between them. McCausland had, apparently, not glanced around with more than casual interest, yet, if blind-folded then and there and put to the test, he could have surprised those who did not know him with the minute and copious inventory of the office, not excluding its occupants, which this glance had furnished him. It was this, with his almost infallible memory, which made him so formidable an opponent at whist. Shagarach was hardly his equal in mere perception, perhaps not his superior in analysis, when the subject was within McCausland's range. His advantage lay, if anywhere, as he had said himself, in his deeper insight into the human soul, in his psychological reach.

"Sorry I was out when you called the other day," said McCausland. "I've been looking up your matter."

"With what result?"

"These clippings may interest you."

Shagarach glanced rapidly over the newspaper scraps.

"The Broadbane murder—I remember that well."

"It occurred about a week before your first attack. You remember Broadbane lured the young woman to a lonely bridge in his carriage and threw her into the river."

"The circumstances were similar to my adventure. The second item is strange to me."

"It's from a New York paper, dated July 28—the very day before your second attack. The circumstances are closely similar this time again. A jealous husband shot his wife through the window of her room."

"Our monster reads, then."

"He is a lunatic (puff)," said McCausland, who had lighted his invariable cigar.

"You believe so?"

"The evidence convinces me. They have an itch to imitate, as you are aware. This man is a victim of homicidal mania, of which you have unfortunately become the object (puff)."

"Why Shagarach and not another?"

"Newspaper notoriety. You should see my crop of cranks. This particular crack-brain has aimed his illusion at you. We must strait-jacket him before it goes further."

"You expect, then, to have him soon?"

"Sooner or later (puff). Let us know if you hear anything. I see you were hurrying off as I came in. Goodday."

McCausland had been deputed to investigate the attacks on Shagarach, because they connected themselves so manifestly, through the threatening letters, with the Floyd case, which he was handling. Neither he nor Shagarach had objected to this opportunity to meet and possibly force each other's hands a little.

"I shall be in the Criminal Court, second session, Jacob. Remain here till Mr. Aronson comes." Shagarach was gone and Jacob left alone to his meditations.

To judge from his expression, they were never very pleasant. Perhaps, like Job of old, he daringly questioned the power behind human destiny, why he showers cleverness and attraction on one boy of 14, while another is afflicted with a manner of nose preposterous, conspicuous and undisguisable, to carry which is a burden. That godlike young man in the photograph, how he would like to be as handsome as he! Was there no way to attain it? He took the bundle of photographs out of his drawer and laid them on his desk to study and admire.

While thus engaged the jingle of harness outside attracted him. He knew by the sound that the carriage had stopped before his door. It wasn't often that equipages, sprinkling sleigh-bell music in their course, paused at the door of the dingy old business building. So Jacob became interested enough to approach the window of the inner office languidly and peep down into the street.

There stood a covered black carriage, as polished as a mirror, with a buff-liveried coachman holding the reins. His seat was perched so high that his legs made one straight, unbending line to the footrest, and his back was as vertical as a carpenter's plummet. Mrs. Arnold was not careless of these niceties. It would have shocked her sense of the fitness of things almost as much to publish the fact that her coachman had knees, as if her own lorgnette should stray from the proscenium box higher than the first balcony—an impropriety which had happened only once to her knowledge, and that by inadvertence, on an opera night.

"This is Mr. Shagarach's office, I believe," said the grand lady to Jacob.

"Yes'm," he mumbled, abashed.

"He is out, I perceive. Does he return soon?"

"No'm."

"About when could I see him if I should wait?"

"He is trying a case'm, over in the second court'm, criminal session," answered Jacob, mixing things badly in his confusion.

"Couldn't you send for him?"

"Mr. Aronson will be here soon. Perhaps he would know."

"I will wait a few minutes," said the lady, sitting down with hauteur in the cushioned chair which Jacob pushed toward her. After a spell of silence she addressed him again in a gentler tone:

"What is your name, little boy?" she asked.

"Jacob," he answered. Servants and office boys grow to think of themselves as having only one name.

"Jacob. That is a very old and dignified name. Are you Mr. Shagarach's clerk?"

"No'm."

"His errand boy, then?"

"Yes'm."

"It's too bad you had to leave school so young. I suppose you give all you earn to your mother?"

"Yes'm."

"Haven't you any father?"

"No'm."

Jacob thought he had never met such a kind lady. How sympathetic she seemed and was it not gracious of her to inquire about his father and mother? How much more agreeable it was to deal with real ladies and real gentlemen who never, never would call vulgar names. He would have given almost half his week's spending money to oblige this sweet-tongued lady then, and his only regret was that he could think of no better answer to her questions than "Yes'm" and "No'm."

"If you are an errand boy perhaps you could do a little errand for me," said the lady sweetly after a pause.

"Yes'm," answered Jacob, putting a world of eagerness into the word.

"You are sure you can do errands and not make a mistake?"

"No'm—yes'm," he replied, a little puzzled as to which of the two words which seemed to constitute his whole vocabulary fitted into his meaning here.

"Then, perhaps, I will let you take this for me."

She drew out the tiniest, daintiest purse Jacob's eyes had ever beheld, and, opening its clasp, gingerly fingered forth a bill.

"I want very much to have this changed. Mr. Shagarach will not be back immediately, you say?"

"No'm."

"Then perhaps you can spare a moment to run down to the corner and get some silver for this."

"They'll change it upstairs," said Jacob, at last finding his voice.

"Upstairs? Very well, you make take it upstairs and bring me back small silver, Jacob."

With a skip of elation Jacob mounted the stairs. There was a little delay in the mission, to which he had repaired. When he came downstairs, the silver clutched in his hand, his heart rose to his mouth at discovering that the office was empty. To think that he had kept the kind lady waiting so long! Probably she had become disgusted with him. He stood a moment in perplexity. Then glancing at his own desk, he opened his mouth in horror.

"My pictures!" cried Jacob. The photographs were gone.

If there was one being that Jacob reverenced and feared

it was his master. To feel now that he had betrayed him at the prompting of a grand lady, who deceived him with honeyed words and was undoubtedly one of his master's enemies—how could he ever face Shagarach again?

"My pictures!" he cried a second time, running into the entry. But here at the head of the stairs a dubitation seized him. Shrill and re-echoing through the narrow passage came the flute-like warble which Jacob knew only too well. It was the precursor of torment for him. True, the Whistler himself had almost ceased to pick on the office boy and even taken him under his wing of late, but Turkey Fenton and Toot Watts were as implacable as inquisitors turning a heretic on a lukewarm gridiron.

Turkey's tyranny was of the grosser order, as became an urchin who in Jacob's presence had swallowed a whole banana, skin and all. Toot's nature was subtle and spiderlike. He possessed the enviable distinction of being able to wag his ears, and his devices of torture were correspondingly refined and ingenious. During the last visit of the boys he had played a small mirror into Jacob's eyes all the while behind Shagarach's back, and it wasn't until they were going out that Jacob discovered why he had been dazzled almost to blindness.

If he took the stair route down he would be stopped and teased and the wicked lady would get away. Perhaps she was already gone—gone with the photographs which should have been securely locked in his drawer. Why had he ever taken them out?

The emergency was desperate and Jacob met it heroically. Rushing to Shagarach's window, he saw the grand lady just crossing the sidewalk and waving her parasol to the coachman. In a moment she would be ensconced on the cushions within and the disaster would be beyond remedy. The window was open, and there was a little piazza outside. Jacob stepped out and shouted. The lady looked up and hastened her pace. Leading down to the first story from the piazza was a flight of steps, and from the first story down to within twelve feet of the ground, another—an old-fashioned fire-escape.

Down these steps Jacob scrambled, scratching his
hands and nearly losing his balance, to the first piazza
and thence to the lowermost round, where the awful fall
of twelve feet checked him. But the sight of the coachman mounting his box nerved his courage and he released his hands. For a moment he felt dizzy. But the
horses were already started. With a flying leap he caught
the tailboard in his hand, and after being dragged along
with great giraffe-like bounds for nearly a block managed to draw himself up to something like a sitting position.

There, through an eye-shaped dead-light in the back
of the carriage he obtained a dim view of its occupant.
His master's stolen pictures were in her hand. What was
she kissing them for—and crying? But Jacob was determined to have no pity upon her. He had just resolved to
call out and demand her attention, when the crack of a
lash made him turn and his lip began to tingle. The
coachman had discovered his unlawful presence on the
tailboard and had reached him with just the tip end of
his whip.

Probably he had meant only to frighten the lad. If
so, he had thoroughly succeeded. Again the whip curled
backward over the coachman's shoulder and snapped like
a pistol shot close to Jacob's ear. To add to his dis-
comfort a great St. Bernard, which had been running
under the carriage, had become aware of his intrusion,
and began rearing at him in a manner more alarming
than dangerous, to be sure, but sufficient to make a peaceable lad tremble. Between the whip and the dog's teeth
his ride had begun to be worse torture than the gantlet
of the stairway, flanked by the three gamins, would have
been, when the ordeal was brought to a sudden end by the
stopping of the carriage at a great brick railroad station.

Jacob's time had come. Disregarding the St. Bernard,
he jumped down and stood on the sidewalk. The dog
growled and the coachman spoke to him roughly as he
opened the door with practiced alacrity for his mistress.
But Jacob was now within his legal rights.

"I want my pictures," he said, catching the grand lady by the arm. Mrs. Arnold looked down at him with amazement not unmingled with fear. It was the same stupid little boy she had bribed to go upstairs in the office where Harry's photographs had been lying—for no good purpose, her instincts told her.

"What does this little ragamuffin say?" she asked.

"I want my photographs," said Jacob, doggedly, as the coachman shoved him aside. He ran after Mrs. Arnold, the tears in his eyes, and clung to her dress. A scene was imminent. The policeman approached, doubtless to render assistance to the lady in distress. But Mrs. Arnold did not desire his assistance just then. With a quick motion she removed a parcel from her pocket and placed it in Jacob's hands.

"Take back your things, then, and don't bother me," she said, with a flushed face.

Jacob gloated on his recovered treasures. Then his hands likewise sought his trousers pocket, and he jingled a handful of silver into Mrs. Arnold's hand.

"Take the money, Joseph," she said to the coachman. "These small storekeepers are so ill-mannered."

The policeman gave Jacob a hard look as he passed him, but the office boy was obliviously counting his pictures.

When he returned to the office the gamins were gone and Aronson was there alone. To Aronson's question where he had been, Jacob, not being an imaginative boy, gave an answer which was strictly truthful, whereupon Aronson, not being a humorous young man (for such are always grave), laughed immoderately, and proposed that the fire escape henceforth be known as Jacob's ladder.

CHAPTER XXX.

CUPID TAKES AIM.

"Mother, my friend, Miss March."

Mrs. Arnold came forward on the rose-embroidered veranda. An old look crept into her face. Her brow darkened. Her heart froze. But love conquered jealousy, and for Harry's sake she took both hands of the young woman whom she knew he loved, and smiled.

"And Mr. Tristram March."

"Welcome to Hillsborough. Will you not come inside?"

"Let's sit on the veranda," said Harry, throwing himself on a seat. "It's cooler here."

The others became seated and submitted their foreheads to the cool caresses of the breeze.

"I enjoy your road from the station so much, Mrs. Arnold. It winds like a river all the way," said Tristram March.

"A narrow river, I fear, and rough in parts," answered the lady.

"Do you know I like a soft country road. It seems padded for the horse's hoofs," said Miss March.

"Rosalie is a philanthropist, you know. She is vice-president—one of the vice-presidents—I believe there are nineteen—of the ladies' league for the abolition of race dissension in the south by the universal whitewashing of negroes."

"Mrs. Arnold knows better than to believe that."

"A chimerical plan, I should call it," said Mrs. Arnold.

"Not at all," added Tristram. "Most scientific. The whitewash is indelible. All charity fads must be scientific nowadays."

"Brother Tristram plays the cynic, Mrs. Arnold," said Rosalie. "But he has an excellent heart of his own."

"It is a burned-out crater," said Tristram, solemnly, at which Harry burst into a laugh and the sister smiled.

Watching her furtively, Mrs. Arnold saw that she was as exquisite a masterpiece as nature had ever put forth. Her figure was virginal and full; her manner, auroral; her age, Hebe's, the imperceptible poise of the ascending ball before it begins to descend, which in woman is earlier by a decade than in man; her coloring, a mixture of the wild rose and gold. Art seconded nature; she was faultlessly dressed. In that instant of inspection the mother knew that her son's heart had been weaned from her forever. She had always felt that it would be a blonde woman. Are they charged with opposite magnetisms from northern and southern poles, that they attract each other so, the dark type and the fair?

"Will you never be serious, Tristram?" cried Rosalie.

"Well, dear, the crater has humming-birds' nests built along its inner sides, like the old volcano of Chocorua, and the little winged jewels flash out sometimes and land in Sister Rosalie's lap."

"What is this?"

"You prefer rubies. I picked those up at a sale in the city. Did you ever meet such stones—perfect bulbs?"

"How can I ever rebuke you again?"

"Then I needn't try to be serious?"

"Oh, if it's a bribe——"

"Look at the name on the plate behind—'Alice.'"

"That will have to be changed," said Harry, coming nearer to glance at the brooch. "Why!" he snatched at the jewels, but caught himself in time. His mother looked at him in an eloquent appeal for silence.

"Where did you get them?" he asked.

"Rabofsky. An old bric-a-brac man. Why, do you fancy they're stolen?"

"Oh, no. I congratulate your sister. The name made me start. It is my mother's, you know."

"I was Alice Brewster," said Mrs. Arnold.

"Speaking of philanthropists, Rosalie," said Tristram, to change the subject, "how did you like the noble Earl of Marmouth?"

"The most overbearing person."

"With the courtesy of a snapping-turtle," said Tristram.

"And the humor of a comic valentine," added Harry.

"Still there is something grand about the title of earl," said Mrs. Arnold, who chose to forget that the original Brewster of Lynn was a yeoman.

"Mme. Violet interested me more," said Rosalie. "Rumor is linking their names, you know. I feel that she and I might become friends."

"She has just the saving spark of deviltry that you lack, Rosalie."

"It isn't every brother who can call his sister an angel so happily," said Mrs. Arnold.

"Nothing was farther from his thoughts than to compliment me, Mrs. Arnold. You should hear him abuse me in private. I am a philistine, a prude. But I grow accustomed to his taunts."

"Dear Rosalie, you are only not esthetic because you are so divinely moral. Just think, she objects to my marble cupids, that they are not ashamed of their innocence."

"Surely that is going far," interposed Harry, who had long been silent. "The modeling was capital. Most little cupids are just doughy duplicates of each other. But yours have character—baby-face wisdom—Puck and Ariel linking arms."

"Say two Pucks, Harry, or Rosalie will moralize. Ariel was a wicked little sprite. He used to go on bats."

Rosalie lifted a finger of reproof.

"But from my standpoint a dash of wickedness is just the sine qua non in art. How fascinating the Inferno is! And how tame the Paradiso! In art, do I say? In religion itself? What the horizon line is to the landscape— a rare pageant you have before you, Mrs. Arnold—such is the fall in the garden to the faith of our fathers."

"Do you mean that it separates earth from heaven?" laughed Harry.

"You would think, to hear this grumbler, it was his strait-laced sister and not his own laziness that prevented him from—" Rosalie hesitated.

"From amounting to something. Say it out. Ah, Rosalie, you have indeed achieved. Your Rosalind is divine, Carp says—and surely Carp knows."

"And Portia," added Harry.

"While my medallions——"

"Would be glorious if they were ever finished. But come," continued Harry, "I must dress for my wager. Where's Indigo?"

"He is about the house, Harry."

"What a name! Your valet, I suppose?" asked Tristram.

"And secretary. That is, he answers my duns."

"And so spares you the blues?"

"Punning again, Tristram," said Rosalie. "And you profess not to consider word-plays respectable."

"Right, always right, Rosalie."

The party passed inside, and the Marches were escorted to their rooms, while Harry went in quest of Indigo. When he returned he found his mother alone in the front room. She seemed to be awaiting him.

"The rubies, mother?"

"They were mine. Sit down, Harry. I must speak with you."

Her manner was sad, and Harry thought in the strong light her face looked careworn.

"We are very much pressed for money—temporarily, of course. As soon as your uncle's estate is settled our income will be larger than ever; and even without that, Mr. Hodgkins has hopes——"

"But mother, you did not sell the rubies?"

"I have sold all my jewels, Harry."

Harry stood up. His mother gave him a long look. She had made this sacrifice for him. He understood and colored when he remembered the fate of the money his mother's rubies had brought. It was luck alone which had saved their name from a blot on the evening when McCausland raided the Dove-Cote.

"I must curtail my expenses," he said, rising to go.

"There is another matter, Harry," said his mother, still sadly but gently. "I saw Mr. McCausland in town to-day. He desires you to testify at your cousin's trial."

"Testify against Bob!"

"It is in relation to the will—the disinheriting of your cousin."

"Why, he admits that himself."

"He may deny it if his conviction hangs upon that point. Mr. McCausland wishes to leave no weak link in the chain."

"Hang it, mother, I don't want to be mixed up in it. Think of the looks."

"All he wants is a word. You heard your cousin say he was disinherited under the will."

"Yes, that is—why, of course, I knew it. He told me at the jail that day."

"Then I will write to Mr. McCausland that your testimony covers that point——"

"No, but mother——"

Rosalie March re-entered at this moment. Her first glance was toward Harry and his toward her. Their thoughts had been traveling the same route and meeting half-way all during the talk on the veranda, when Harry was so unwontedly silent. Alas, he knew well that he was unfit even to look at her.

In their outward demeanor to each other he was embarrassed and she reserved. The religious difference seemed likely to be permanent. For Rosalie was a Catholic, the daughter of an eminent Maryland family, as historic and proud as the Brewsters and more wealthy than even the Arnolds. But this barrier between them only acted with the charm of a material fence over which or through which a rustic couple are plighting forbidden troth.

"All ready to win my wager," cried Tristram, following

his sister in. He, also, had changed his attire, and looked very handsome in his curling Vandyke beard of the cut which artists affect.

"What wager is that?" asked Mrs. Arnold.

"We passed the river coming down, and I offered to canoe the rapids."

"And the river so low, Harry. It is rash."

"Would you have them set me down a boaster?" Harry was eager now. His mother knew "them" meant "her," and her heart yearned more and more to the son who was drifting away.

"Indigo!" he cried out the window to his valet.

"But the danger—was it not there the canoeist was drowned last year?" said his mother, anxiously.

"Hang the danger! It's the prospect of scraping the bottom off my new canoe that troubles me."

"Old age is privileged to prate, I suppose," said Mrs. Arnold, feebly attempting to smile.

"Cut the fingers off that lemon-colored mitten, Indigo, and get me some salve double quick. My oar blister's worse than ever."

Indigo sped up stairs for the scissors, and the party was soon on its way.

At the bridge Harry left them, proceeding alone to the boat-house, up-stream, while Indigo led the others to a rock below the rapids, where they were to witness the feat. To look at the long slope, nowhere steep, but white from end to end with foam, it did seem incredible that any craft could live through such a surge. The murmur was audible far away in the still countryside, and the air, even where the three onlookers stood, was moist with impalpable spray.

"Looks as though that wager was mine," said Tristram. "He might as well try to swim Niagara."

"Ought we not to have a rope in case of accident?" said Mrs. Arnold.

"By all means," cried Rosalie, and for an instant the two women were one in sympathy.

"Indigo," said Mrs. Arnold, "go over to Farmer

Hedge's and procure a stout rope. If anything should happen——"

"Nothing will happen," said Indigo. But he obeyed her command, and departed in the direction of the nearest farmhouse. The moments were long drawn out with anxiety before he returned, until at last even Tristram's sallies could not draw a smile from the two ladies. So he coolly took out a pad of white paper, sharpened his pencil and sketched off the rapids.

"There he comes," cried Rosalie, peering up-stream.

"Harry!" murmured Mrs. Arnold, as her son rounded a bend of the river into view. Already he was coasting down without using his paddle. His brown arms rested on the handle before him and his muscles, seemingly relaxed, were tense for exertion.

A great log which had preceded him down had been whirled around like a chip and finally submerged, reappearing only in the clear water forty yards beyond. A similar fate surely awaited the light cockleshell which bore the beloved life.

As his canoe half-turned, Harry pushed his paddle into the water. Evidently it met a rock, for the prow righted at once and swept down a narrow channel where the rush was swiftest, but the foam seemed parted in two. Here again it caught, poised and spun around. It was fast on a ledge, and the young athlete was straining every sinew to push it off. While he was struggling in this peril, Indigo came down, staggering under a coil of thick rope.

"Indigo," said Mrs. Arnold, excitedly, "throw him the rope."

Indigo stood on the bank, but instead of obeying, ran farther down to a rock that jutted over the clear water where the rapids ended. On his way he heard the ladies shrieking.

"His oar is broken."

"But he has worked himself free," said Tristram, nonchalantly sketching. "He will win, confound it! Yet it's worth losing once to see that play of his right deltoid."

Harry's paddle had indeed broken in the last successful shove, but it was a double blade, and the half in his hand was used to good advantage. As he came sweeping down, his eyes intent on the prow before him, Tristram raised his hat and the ladies leaned forward, waving their kerchiefs. Harry answered their salute by standing up in the boat. It was a superb piece of bravado.

* * * * * * * * * * * *

"He doesn't always wear a glove canoeing?" asked Mrs. Arnold of Indigo. Harry had just put ashore an eighth of a mile down stream.

"No, the mate to that one's lost," replied the valet, "and Mr. Harry told me to cut it up for his hand."

"When lost and where?" said Rosalie.

"I don't know that."

"Let me tell you."

"What a sibyl!" exclaimed brother Tristram.

"It was on Broad street, the afternoon of the fire. Don't you remember, when we saw him crossing the street so hurriedly and I remarked he had only one glove on."

"You must be mistaken," said Mrs. Arnold. "Harry was ill at home all that day."

CHAPTER XXXI.

MATER DOLOROSA.

Honora Riley, who washed for Mrs. Barlow, lived in a ramshackle, desolate district of the city which was appropriately known as "the Barrens." Colliers, sooty to the eyerims, trudging home; ashy dump-pickers; women cowled in drab shawls from beneath whose folds peeped pitchers brimmed with foam like the whipped surface of the milk pail, but the liquor was not milk; such were the sights Emily noticed when she called at Mrs. Riley's

to inquire whether it was a spell of illness that had prevented her from coming to wash that Monday.

"Come in," a feeble voice answered her knock. "Oh,
is it you, Miss Barlow?"

Emily saw that the supper on the table, laid for two,
was untasted, and that the eyes of the woman who sat
on the chair clasping her knees before her, were red.

"We thought you might be ill, Mrs. Riley," she said.

"It is heartsick I am, and too broken-hearted to work,
dear. Land knows I have good reason or I wouldn't
fail your mother."

"It isn't the pneumonia again, I hope."

"Shame and loneliness have come upon me in my old
age," said Mrs. Riley, wiping her tears with the corner
of her tidy apron. "They've taken Walter away."

"Who took him away?"

"The officer came with a warrant this morning—and
he my only child, and the kindest boy to his mother, with
no harm or wickedness in him at all, at all."

Walter was Mrs. Riley's only child, the last of seven.
All the others had preceded their father to the grave,
narrowing the resources of the little family with contin-
ual illnesses and funerals. Finally her husband himself,
an honest roofer, had been fatally injured in a fall and
had passed away, kissing the six-months' infant who
would never know a father. This was long ago. For
this child the good mother had provided by her willing
labor, and he had grown to be her pride and hope, a
promising boy of 14.

" 'It was a bicycle he stole,' said the officer, 'away out
in the country.' 'But I never meant to steal it, mother,'
says Walter, and the boy was that truthful he never lied
to a soul that breathes. 'I never meant to steal it, mother,' he says," repeated Mrs. Riley softly, her grief over-
mastering her.

"Did you say Walter stole a bicycle?" asked Emily, a
vague reminiscence coming back to her.

"It was the bad company I warned him against, especially that Fenton boy and Mrs. Watts' little imp that

has more tricks in him than a monkey. 'Keep away from them, Walter,' says I, but no, he would choose them for companions. And 'tis old Bagley, the junkman, I blame most of all. Upon my word, I believe he put them up to the trick. What would three little boys travel out to the country like that for, and ride away on three bicycles and then sell them to Bagley?"

"Walter sold it, then?" said Emily, thoughtfully.

"Indeed, Walter did not. 'Mine is safe and sound in the club-room,' says he; that's Lanty Lonergan's back kitchen he lets them use for a meeting place. 'It's in the club-room,' says Walter, 'and I wouldn't sell it, mother, but I was afraid to give it back; only I never meant to steal it.' "

"That I believe, Mrs. Riley, for I saw him take that bicycle."

Mrs. Riley's tears stopped flowing for a moment in her surprise. Then Emily related the story of her trip to Hillsboro and the conversation of the boys which she had overheard, not forgetting to explain her own share in frightening them away.

"So perhaps by my officiousness I converted an innocent prank into something more serious," she concluded.

"If it was the price of it only, I'd give double that, and land knows I've no stockingful, like some that go to the city for help, for I'd rather rub my knuckles off than beg," said the good woman.

There was a piece of old carpet stuffed in one window-pane, adequate in summer, no doubt, but hardly impregnable to the winter winds—and Emily judged from the table before her that more than once the mother and son had sat down to a Barmecide feast, in which the imagination had to be called on to help appease the palate. So it was by inheritance that the Whistler came by his aversion to Shagarach's charity.

"I think it strange Walter and I have never become acquainted."

"Indeed he knows all your goodness to me."

"Is he still at school?"

"Graduated this year, and his masters recommend him for the best-tempered boy and as innocent—but full of the old Harry, like his father, that would always be dancing, even with seven children between him and his youth."

"What a pity if he should turn out bad now after you've made so many sacrifices for him."

"Oh, for the sacrifices, Walter's willing to take his share. With his paper route he would bring me in sometimes $2 a week, and there was nothing he wouldn't do, distribute handbills, deliver baskets in the meat-market on Saturday nights. Look, here's the shoeblack's kit he just bought. Come in, Miss Barlow."

Emily entered the small side room which completed Mrs. Riley's suite.

"There's the blacking-box. Bought it himself with his own savings."

"But he was too changeable. I should think he would have done better to stick to one thing."

"That's what I told him. But you know how a boy is fickle-minded. 'Get me something good, mother,' says he. There's the little cradle I rocked him in that I kept all these years—" Emily herself could hardly check her tears at thought of the mother rocking this empty memento.

"His Aunt Mary gave it to me—not that we couldn't afford it—plenty and to spare I had when my husband was alive, but it wasn't lucky to buy a cradle for your first baby, she said, and so I rocked them all in hers, and now six of them are in heaven with their father, God ha' mercy, and Walter, all that was left me, is in the lockup this night with the bad people."

Walter's little room was bare but not squalid. A knockabout suit hung on pegs at one side, and a washbowl stood on a cheap commode, like a prophecy of cleanliness in the occupant.

"Don't worry, Mrs. Riley. Since I helped Walter into this scrape, I am bound to help him out of it."

"Heaven bless you, if you can save my Walter—and

I know you would try if you knew him. The lovingest boy, full of mischief like his father, but he'd give the blood out of his heart to a soul in trouble. Oh, well I knew he had something on his mind all these weeks. For he wouldn't run up stairs two steps at a time, as he used to, and whistle so that it was sweeter and louder than a cage full of canaries. When I heard him whistle low I knew it was something troubling his mind. 'Yes, mother, it is,' says he, but that was all I could get out of him."

"Suppose I bring a very great lawyer to be his counsel," said Emily, deeply moved by the lonely mother's sorrow, and haunted, too, by a dim remembrance of the central face among the three gamins—a frank boy-face, with red lips and cheeks. "Wouldn't he stand a better chance of getting off?"

"Just as you say, Miss Barlow," answered the sad woman, brightening a little.

"He is very busy, but I feel sure that he will attend to this if I ask him. I'll see him to-night. Don't brood over it too much and never mind about the washing. I will have Mr. Shagarach call at the station and talk with Walter, and then let you know. Good-night."

"Good-night and bless you," said Mrs. Riley, holding the little candlestick high at the landing. Emily picked her way down two crazy flights of stairs and a doorway barred with sprawling children on to the sidewalk. "While we wink, the lightning may have flashed," was a motto she had copied out of an old book of maxims and embroidered into her life; so, without taking time even for a wink, she hailed a passing car that would carry her near Shagarach's house.

Not all that Mrs. Riley had said of her boy, the Whistler, should be set down to a mother's partiality. Mischievous Walter was, if the unquenchable avidity for excitement which reigns at fourteen entitles a boy to such an aspersion. The five hours' rigid confinement at a school desk especially provoked him to perpetual fidget, and no teacher had yet been found who could make him buckle to his books so long. Yet he was a favorite with one and all, less because of his deft hand at the drawing lesson than because of the real salubrity of his nature, which made him exceptional among the slum children who were his fellow-pupils.

To these very schoolmates Walter figured as a hero, an Admirable Crichton, invincible at all games and master of most things worth knowing for boys. There was no swimmer of his age could equal him in grace or speed, and his dive from the top of the railroad dock was famous in local annals. So was his successful set-to in the brewery yard with Lefty Dinan, the Tenth street cock-of-the walk.

Yet for all his proficiency in the art of give, take and avoid, Walter was the least combative of boys, being, as his mother said, "loving" in disposition. The great gray Percherons with shaggy fetlocks, that drew the fire-engines, knew this, and admitted him to a brotherly comradeship, bowing with delight when he patted and stroked them. Mechanics found him handy beyond his years, and often employed him at odd jobs. For he had a carpenter's eye for short distances and a surveyor's for long, and there was no tool that did not fit his fingers. If he had run away to join the circus last summer, that was not the unpardonable sin.

Shagarach heard Emily gravely.

"An important witness for our cause," he answered, when she had finished. "We surely cannot suffer him to be thrust into prison." Emily knew that it was unnecessary for her to press the matter further, so she spent a brief evening in conversation with the quaint, affectionate mother, rarely alluding to the Floyd case or the mysterious oaf who had so alarmed her in that oriental room.

The following noon she ran down to the jail to see Robert, half-expecting to hear him playing the violin which she had sent him the day before. Robert's own Stradivarius, with all his other personal effects, had been destroyed at the fire, so Emily, having begged the sheriff's permission, had pinched herself to buy him a new one as richly toned as her slender means could purchase. Her own instrument was the piano, whose keys turned to silver beneath her touch, and it had been in the ensemble classes of the conservatory that she and Robert (through Beulah Ware) first met. When Dr. Silsby, the botanist, who had just come home from the west, called yesterday, she had insisted on his taking the violin to Robert, without betraying the giver's name. However, Robert's corridor (murderers' row, the name made her indignant) was silent when she approached it, and she searched his cell vainly for a violin box.

"Dr. Silsby has been to see you, Robert?" she asked, after the greetings due from sweetheart to sweetheart.

"He came in yesterday to cheer me."

"His usual method of cheering, I suppose."

"Oh, yes, said he had never expected me to outlive uncle; I always acted so much older than he did," laughed Robert.

"He is such a droll tease," said Emily, who never could be brought to admit that Robert was overserious for his years.

"But I made myself even with him before he went. He promised to read an article I had written while in prison, and took the manuscript under his arm, little suspecting what was in store for him. You know how he abhors my social heresies."

"And the article was——"

"My 'Modest Proposal for a Consumers' Trust,' socialistic from kappa to kappa. How Jonas will writhe! The last words he spoke were a thrust at my 'fad.' Yet every letter-carrier and uniformed employe I meet," added Robert, returning to his natural gravity, "contented and useful, convinces me more and more that the world is moving toward co-operation."

"But the reading will be torture to Dr. Silsby."

"It ought to do him good. How hard that lumper works!" Several negroes were staggering down the corridor, shouldering huge sides of beef for the jail cuisine.

"And in fifty offices within a radius of a mile men are receiving large salaries for dawdling at elegant desks two or three hours a day."

"There are no sinecures at $10 a week," sighed Emily, drawing upon experience for this generalization. "But did Dr. Silsby have nothing with him when he called?"

"I believe he had—a violin box."

"Just so," said a cheerful voice behind them; "a violin-box, and forgot to leave it. You see I had the jacketing of that birch tree so much on my mind," it was Dr. Silsby himself, "everything else slipped out. You remember my speaking of the birch tree, Rob?"

"At least seven times," answered Robert.

"Cruelty, Miss Barlow, positive cruelty. That fine silver-birch in the jailyard—you saw it, I suppose, coming in—all peeled and naked from the ground as high as my reach. Wanton cruelty. Think of the winter nights. It will die. It will die."

One of Jonas Silsby's eccentricities was his keen sympathy for arboreal life, to which his rugged nature yearned even more than to the delicate products of the flower garden.

"I complained to the sheriff. There ought to be an ordinance severely punishing the barking of trees."

"Don't they fine the boys who mutilate foliage in the parks?" asked Emily.

"Fine! Horsewhip them! Rattan their knuckles! I'd teach them a lesson or two! The young barbarians! Well, cut it short, thinking of the trees, I forgot your violin. So last night I ordered a jacket made, good canvas cloth, that'll interest you, Rob, if you haven't forgotten all your botany in your wild——"

"How did you like my essay, Jonas?" asked Robert, mischievously.

"Quackery! A poultice to cure incurable diseases. Bah!"

"But you brought the violin to-day?" asked Emily, smiling.

"Yes, with the canvas jacket. You see it's Miss Barlow's present——"

"What!" cried Robert.

"There! Thunder! I've let it out. She was going to blindfold you and let you guess the giver."

"And the violin is in your vest pocket, I suppose?" asked Emily, innocently, on the brink of a peal of laughter.

"The violin! Jupiter!" exclaimed Dr. Silsby, thunderstruck. "It's a box of bulbs. I thought they were rather heavy."

Emily and Robert had a merry time over the botanist's absentmindedness, but he insisted that the original fault lay with the young barbarians who had upset him by unbarking the birch tree.

There was little news to exchange except the arrest of their "important witness," and the lunch hour at best was only sixty minutes long, so Emily was soon forced to make her adieus and leave Robert with his second best friend.

CHAPTER XXXII.

EMILY STRIKES A MATCH.

Beulah Ware called that evening to talk over their plans for a trip to the provinces, which Dr. Eustis, the Barlows' family physician, had imperatively ordered for the wasting girl. Could he have looked into her brain while she was preparing to retire in her chamber, and seen the velocity of the thoughts which were coursing through it then, he would surely have lengthened the weeks to months.

"Would the will be upheld?" she asked herself. Dr. Silsby's oral evidence was strong in its favor and Shagarach had spoken hopefully of late. The least that he could expect was a postponement until the trial was concluded. Since the evening she spent at his house, the

lawyer had applied himself, if possible, more sternly than
ever to the case, and his manner was more than ever that
of a man repressing all lightness of spirit to make room
for weighty thoughts.

What a mesh they were all entangled in. Shagarach
as well as Robert, with the monster reaching again and
again at his life! And McCausland—she hated his eter-
nal smile. As if this business of life or death were a
comedy for his amusement or the display of his superfine
powers. She had begun to doubt whether their triumph
over the false Bill Dobbs had been as genuine as they
first supposed.

"A lie will travel a league while truth is putting on his
boots," old John Davidson had said, shaking his head,
when she described the adventure to him. And the result had proved him right. Although the truth leaked
out, the original impression that Robert had really
broken out of prison was never quite corrected, and of
course it did him no good with the public.

In spite of herself, Emily could not help feeling that
both these powerful minds were overreaching themselves
by their very fertility and keenness, like the colossus of
old, which tumbled by its own huge height. For the
hundredth time she set their theories before her, trying
to imagine how a jury would look at them.

Her rambling drowse naturally brought back the whole
trip to Hillsborough and her conversation with Bertha.
She tried to recall every word that the housemaid had
uttered, rendered doubly precious, as it seemed to Emily,
by the impossibility of consulting her again until the
trial. What she had said of the previous fire especially
struck Emily now. She tried to form a vivid picture on
the curtain of darkness which surrounded her of that
fatal study. The books all upright on their shelves, the
canary bird singing, the waste-basket, the slippers under
the arm-chair, and the dressing-gown thrown over it,
the dog—suddenly Emily's heart stood still. She started
up in bed and sat on its edge.

A minute later she was feeling for the match-box. As

she stood before the mirror, her image came out slowly, slowly, emerging by the sulphurous blue flame. Lighting the gas, she drew the curtains. The bark of a watchdog broke the silence, or the footsteps of tardy homecomers, and now and then the shrill, faint whistle of a distant steamer, ocean-bound. But her ears were closed to outer impressions. She snatched at a volume of the great encyclopedia which she kept in her room, and, sitting on the bed, laid one knee across its fellow for a bookrest. In this posture she read eagerly, then exchanged the volume for another, and that for another, until she had ranged through the entire set and peeped at every letter from Archimedes to Zero, with long and very attentive stops at many curious headings. It was after 1 o'clock when she turned out the light and nearly 3 when her brain stopped buzzing. Next morning she limped in her left knee where the heavy encyclopedia had rested and her eyes were dull at their work.

The idea was so bold, so novel, that she waited a day before submitting it to Shagarach. Beulah Ware was her first confidant. Beulah took it up enthusiastically, and was for developing it farther before giving it out at all. But Emily judged this secrecy unjust to her lawyer, and, besides, was eager to know his opinion. He listened with interest to her "maybes" and "might bes" and commented in his usual tone of conviction.

"There are a great many 'ifs.' You depend entirely upon Bertha, and she is not at hand. When she does appear it will be so late that you will have little time to work up your idea. This is not said to discourage you; only to point out the obstacles you must surmount. By all means follow out the thought."

This was not the worst that Emily had feared, although she understood that it meant "There are at present only two theories, McCausland's and mine. Those are the horns of the dilemma between which the jury must choose." Seeing that she did not reply, Shagarach turned the subject toward Walter Riley's case, which was more serious than his mother knew.

The robbery of the bicycles was only one of a series of thefts which had been traced to this youthful "gang." In the club-room at Lonergan's, not only the Whistler's bicycle, which he had refused to sell, but a store of cigars, whisky, cheap jewelry and ladies' pocketbooks had been found, and the junkman, Bagley, was under arrest for acting as a "fence" to the thieves.

Walter asserted his innocence of other thefts, and also his ignorance of all the articles excepting the bicycle, which they had urged him to sell. His refusal to do so was corroborated by Turkey and Toot. On this very head he had had a falling out with the crowd and had ceased to visit the club-room, but, although it was frequented by as many as twenty youngsters, some of them half-grown men, no one had dared to heed Bagley's suggestion and dispose of Walter's abandoned property.

"Riley's act at its worst was no more serious than breaking a window or plucking pears from the tree. With your help he may get clear and be put on probation."

"Oh, must I testify?" asked Emily.

"Next Monday the case will be heard. You can be of service to the boy. I shall recommend short terms for Fenton and Watts."

Emily promised to be present. While she was returning to her studio old John Davidson overtook her in his carriage. She was glad to meet his kindly glance again and accept his proffered seat, especially as she espied the manikin, Kennedy, crossing the street in her direction. It was only a few blocks to her destination, but before they arrived she had poured out her new theory to the marshal, as if he were her father.

"Don't you think it's possible, Mr. Davidson?" she appealed to him, craving a morsel of sympathy.

"Possible? Of course it's possible," he answered cheerily; "I've met things a hundred times stranger myself."

But Emily's heart sunk a little, for she saw that he only spoke so out of kindness and that he did not really believe in her idea. And from that day she followed Beulah Ware's advice and hardly mentioned it, except to Beulah.

CHAPTER XXXIII.

M'CAUSLAND'S AMMUNITION.

It is no wonder at all that Emily Barlow should have come to regard Inspector McCausland as the villain of the drama in which she was taking a part. Although whenever she tried to formulate his theory of the case it seemed to her too frail to hang a kitten by, yet she had moments of doubt in which his great reputation and clean record of victories oppressed and appalled her. And these moments were rendered frequent by a quality which McCausland seemed to possess in common with other satanic characters, his ubiquity, in which he was only surpassed by Mr. Arthur Kennedy Foxhall. In justice to McCausland, however, it should be stated that he did not make a practice, as the manikin did, of writing bi-weekly billet-doux.

The first time the detective's shadow fell across Emily's path—after her discovery of his identity—was on one of her visits to Senda Wesner. Who should be coming out of the bakeshop but chubby Richard in person? His bow was gallant and his smile serene.

"My weekly call," he said, stopping to chat for a moment. "A sociable little magpie, that one," jerking his thumb toward the bakeshop girl. Emily thought this uncomplimentary. From Miss Wesner she gathered enough to lead her to suspect that he was trying to connect the peddler in the green cart, who was certainly no peddler and who had eluded all pursuit thus far, with the slamming of the rear door, which must have been done by some one else than Floyd.

A few days later she had called at the office of the Beacon, the newspaper for which Robert wrote special articles, to obtain some papers from his desk. The desk was indeed there, but all its drawers had been removed and the managing editor explained that they might be found at the office of Inspector McCausland.

Twice she had met the inspector climbing Shagarach's stairs, but passing by the lawyer's door and mounting to the top story. The second time she had heard his voice in conference with a throaty falsetto she thought she knew, and the black mask of Pineapple Jupiter, appearing at the head of the stairs, confirmed her suspicions. Without scruple she entered the mission herself one day and expended all her arts to pump the old negro. The moment McCausland's name was introduced, however, his loquacity was checked of a sudden, then took dizzy flights of irrelevance.

"Oh, dese chillun, chillun," cried Jupiter, puttering away at a broken pane, "dey done gone break my winders."

"The stout, ruddy gentleman, I mean," persisted Emily, but Jupiter was so absorbed in his hymn tune that he did not hear her.

Sharper heads than Emily's had failed to force McCausland's hand when he chose to shut it tight. The newspaper reporters, whom no ordinary walls can bar, had bestirred themselves to secure for an inquisitive public the "new evidence" that the government had presented before the grand jury in the Floyd case, but absolutely without avail. Where such experienced allies owned themselves beaten, the gentle maiden might surely do so without dishonor.

As Shagarach foretold, Bertha had been spirited away. Mrs. Christenson, the intelligence offices, the Swedish consul, the Lutheran pastor, were all visited and revisited by Emily, especially since the new inspiration seized her, but none of them knew the address of the housemaid since she left Hillsborough that morning on an outward-bound train. The only rumor of her whereabouts was that vague report, coming from the bakeshop girl, which Dr. Silsby had set out to investigate.

With regard to the Arnolds' coachman, who had driven their carriage on the day of the fire, Emily considered

Shagarach to be curiously indifferent. He had promised to subpoena the man for the trial, but that was all. Yet his testimony was crucial, since he must know whether Harry was with his mother in the vehicle.

This was a peculiarity of Shagarach's, in which he differed again from McCausland. Though he prepared his defense with consummate painstaking, when it came his turn to prosecute an unwilling witness, he seemed satisfied to know the truth in his own mind, relying upon his genius to extort a confession during the cross-examination. With a perjurer before him he wielded the lash like a slave-driver, and perhaps he was justified in this case in omitting a rehearsal which would only put the Arnolds on their guard.

But Emily's greatest disappointment came in what seemed to her the one weak point of Robert's defense, the axis around which the entire prosecution revolved. Time and again she had conferred with Shagarach on the subject of her lover's reverie after the deed. To think that he could not remember a face he had seen, an incident, a word spoken, during those four hours—nothing but a vague itinerary of the afternoon, which came out with difficulty each time, and the course of his own meditations, which, to tell the truth, was clear and copious enough, but worthless for the purpose.

At her last visit to the lawyer's home he had entered into this more deeply. Apparently the method of attacking the enigma, which he had hinted at possessing from the very first, was now ripened. For he loaned Emily a ponderous volume on "Diseases of the Memory," and asked her to bring in all the evidence possible showing the mutual affection of nephew and uncle, not failing to wear the water lily from time to time, as he had suggested before. But she was not satisfied with this, and, knowing Robert had visited the park, spent one whole Sunday making a tour of that district, questioning each of the gray-coated policemen.

At last she had found an officer who recollected "something of such a young man as she described." He

"couldn't swear to it," but "had an idea he noticed him."
In fact, his recollection grew vaguer and vaguer the more
they tried to make it specific, and to Emily's chagrin,
when they brought him to the jail, he asserted positively
that Robert was not the man. This disappointment was
sharpened tenfold by her meeting Inspector McCausland,
passing out of the corridor, arm in arm with a car conductor.

"I am certain that was my passenger," the conductor
was saying. To have her own failure and McCausland's
success thus brought into contact accentuated both and
gave Emily a miserable day.

The case of the old chemist was not so bad, and besides, was none of Emily's doing. John Davidson, the
marshal, had taken up Shagarach's theory of Harry Arnold's guilt with remarkable zeal and had borrowed one
of the photographs, so as to see if he could be of use.
One day he came in, greatly excited, and asked for the
lawyer.

"Got some evidence that'll surprise you, brother," said
the marshal.

"Then it must be extraordinary," answered Shagarach.

"What do you think that young rascal did?"

"Who?"

"Arnold. Went to a chemist, a friend of mine, fellow-
townsman, too, Phineas Fowler, and bought a big heap of
combustible powder, a day or two before the fire.
Sprinkled it over the whole room, probably."

"He wasn't so foolish as to leave his name, however?"

"Oh, Phineas knew the photograph. Spotted him right
away when I fetched her out. Lucky I took it now, wan't
it? 'That's the man,' says Phineas."

"I believe I have your friend's address already," said
Shagarach, and in two or three days he was paying a
long-delayed visit to Phineas Fowler.

Amid the compound odor of chemicals sat a shriveled
pantaloon, with a long, thin beard whose two forks he
kept pulling and stroking. Shagarach was about to state

his business, when a stranger at the window came forward and interrupted him.

"The young man who bought the combustion powder was identified in jail yesterday," said Inspector McCausland, smiling. "It was only Floyd, on that matter of the bomb."

That matter of the bomb! Perhaps it would be harder to explain than Emily thought.

But McCausland was not always out beating the bush for evidence. Occasionally the mountain went to Mahomet. The reward of $5,000, which Harry Arnold had advertised, drew a dribbling stream of callers to the inspector's office. There was the veiled lady, who had seen the crime with the eyes of her soul, and would accept a small fee for a clairvoyant seance, and the lady with green glasses, whose card announced her as "Phoebe Isinglass, metaphysician." The moderation of her terms could only be accounted for by her scientific interest in the matter. She asked only $1,000 if she proved Floyd insane, $500 if she proved him sane, and $100 (merely as a compensation for her time) if the case baffled her skill.

Prof. I. Noah Little, the conchologist, paid McCausland the honor of a call and even brought his whelk-shell with him. With this occult instrument at his ear he had been known to make the most remarkable prophecies, declaring to gullible girls the names of their future spouses, and even portending the great snowfall of May 21 in the year 1880.

As for suggestions by mail, the office porter's spine grew bent with emptying the waste-basket which received them. Hypnotism was the favorite explanation with a large majority of the correspondents, followed by a somnambulism and various ingenious theories of accident. The pope and the czar were named as authors, and the freemasons were accused in one epistle of a plot to burn up the ocean with some diabolical explosive, to procure which they had all sold their souls to the devil, though what this had to do with the Floyd case was a greater mystery than the fire itself.

Out of all this chaff the inspector sifted a solitary grain. One morning he was joking in the office with Hardy, Johnson and Smith, three of his brothers-in-buttons. Hardy handled sneak-thieves and shoplifters, Johnson swindlers of a higher order, such as confidence men, and Smith the gangs of forgers and counterfeiters. They were all, like McCausland, common-looking men. This enabled them to slouch through life quietly, taking observations by the way.

"Well, Dick," said Johnson, "I hear you've been appointed confessor-general to Col. Mainwaring's sinners."

This was received with a hearty laugh, for they were a jolly four, these men of iron.

"That arson case is a puzzler," put in Smith. "Why didn't you send a bottle of the smoke to Sherlock Holmes?"

"With a blank label," added Johnson, "for the incendiary's name."

"Would he notice such an A B C riddle?" laughed Hardy.

"A lady for Mr. McCausland," announced the mulatto policeman, and the brothers-in-buttons quickly found other business.

CHAPTER XXXIV.

HONEY, NOT WITHOUT STING.

She looked so timid and demure, with the blue straw bonnet which framed her sweet face, the red band lettered in gold, "Salvation Army."

Eyes, lifted slowly, of deep, dark blue, and the level brows laid over them for a foil. Beautiful eyes, we male observers say in our rough, generic fashion, but the finer perception of our sisters discriminates more closely. Not the iris alone makes the beauty of eyes. Lashes long and thick, lids of bewitching droop, brows penciled in the bow curve, any of these may be the true feature that starts our exclamation of delight. But in Miss Serena Lamb (as the girl gave her name) nearly all these marks were blended, and they overhung a feature which used to be fashionable and is still, when perfect, divine—the rosebud mouth.

She might well be timid in those surroundings—revolvers and handcuffs to right of her, medals and canes to left; shutter-cutters, winches, chisels, diamond drills, skeleton keys, wax molds, jimmies, screws, in the glass case in front—an elaborate outfit of burglar's tools, the trophies of McCausland's hunting expeditions, for the inspector's specialty was burglary. On one side the portrait of the true Bill Dobbs looked out from the center of a congenial group, and a tiny plush case kept the file made from a watch-spring with which the famous Barney Pease had cut his way to liberty. All this was formidable enough in itself, to say nothing of the huge bloodhound that lay half-asleep, with his jowl on the hearthstone.

"I thought I ought to tell you," said Miss Lamb, modestly, "although it may not be of importance."

"And yet it may," said the inspector, politely. "We often work from the merest trifles."

"It concerns the fire in Prof. Arnold's house."

"Ah!"

"You know our labors often bring sinners back to the fold and many of them insist on unburdening their past misdeeds to us. It is very distressing to hear, but it seems to ease their consciences."

McCausland mentally registered a great broad mark in her favor. She had not begun by asking for the reward.

"One day a young convert of ours came to my house and spent an hour with me. We sung hymns and conversed, and I truly believe he has heard the word. Hosanna! Alleluia!"

McCausland fidgeted a little at these transports, but the sweet face in the blue bonnet kept him respectful.

"I am young," she hardly looked 18, "but I strove earnestly with him that night. Moved by the spirit, he

told me a guilty story, which I put aside until reading
about your case stirred my memory, and I felt in duty
bound to relate it. Alleluia!"

"Proceed, Miss Lamb."

"The young convert had been in his early days a locksmith and a great sinner before the world. One day a
stranger proposed to him a reward if he should enter a
certain room and open a safe which it contained. The
temptation was great and he yielded, for he was poor in
the riches of earth, and knew not then of the treasures
of heaven. Alleluia! Praise!

"Weakly he consented to accompany the stranger, and
on a certain Sunday, during the early hours of evening,
suffered himself to be led into the room, where he found
himself alone with the stranger. It was the name of this
man and the description he gave me of the room which
led me afterward to think that his action might have a
connection with your case."

"What name?"

"Robert Floyd."

McCausland took a cigar from his pocket and bit off
the end.

"And how did he describe the room?"

"A library, he said, with a bird cage before one window
and a desk in the corner."

"And the safe?"

"He could not open it at first, but tried again and
again. Something alarmed them, however, or so I gathered. For you must know his accent was very hard to
follow and—and"—(Serena blushed)—"he was very much
agitated while he told me. But I gathered that they were
interrupted and put off their wicked work."

"I must see this young convert. He may have sinned
to good purpose that time."

"There comes the strange part of it. Since he made
the confession I have not seen him again. He has not
come to our meetings, as he used. Perhaps he has fallen
back into the evil ways of the worldly minded. Perhaps
the wicked ones have punished him."

"The description is certainly similar," said McCausland, shutting his right eye, so as to fix more keenly on his visitor's face the other, which was the one reputed microscopic in its powers.

"So it seemed to me, reading the papers, which are full of profane sayings, alas! But where sin is there must be the workers in the vineyard."

"I am glad you read them and you did well to come. But—do you know the convert's name? Without some clew, I fear——"

The young girl hesitated awhile, then answered:

"Aronson!"

McCausland started. It was not a common name.

"A young man, you say? And spoke with an accent?"

"Yes, slightly."

"Can it be Shagarach's man?" said McCausland to himself, reaching for the city directory. "There was something shady about his record." Then he rung a bell.

"Have the criminal docket looked up about four years ago for a case against one Aronson—larceny of an overcoat, I believe," he said to the mulatto officer.

"That was all," said Miss Lamb, arising to go.

"One moment," said McCausland, running his forefinger up the directory page. "Was his first name Saul?"

"I don't remember. I remember very little about him."

" 'Saul Aronson, law student.' Let's look farther back," said McCausland, restoring the 1895 volume to the shelf; " '94, '93, '92, '91," he drew out the last. "It would be queer," he said to himself, "if Floyd's junior counsel should turn out to be an accomplice."

"Aronson," he read aloud. "Isaac, Jacob, Marks—Saul! 'Saul Aronson, locksmith'!"

CHAPTER XXXV.

A BACK-STITCH.

This was how Aronson made the acquaintance of Serena Lamb. One day there resounded through the Ghetto (where Aronson lived) the pounding of a violent drum. Tum, tum, tum! Tum, tum, tum! Tumtyty, Tumtyty! Tum, tum, tum! And every now and then its bass companion marked the ictuses with a cavernous "Boom!" Then Moses and Samuel ceased their buying and selling for a few moments and the coats, vests and trousers which draped their window-fronts swung idly in the wind. And the little Samuels swarmed from their hiding-places till both curbstones were fringed two deep with humanity, eying the musical invaders. For the notes of the bugle burst out after this percussion prelude and a mixed choir of voices lifted a strange refrain.

Motley singers they were! Shabbily dressed men, with exaltation in their faces, and women of all ages and types, uniform only in their costumes. Raising the song, they clapped their hands together, like bacchants or chory-bantes dashing cymbal on cymbal in the ecstasy of the dance. But such bacchants! Bacchants in blue bonnets, like grandmother's sundown! Bacchants with pure faces of undefiled girlhood! Bacchants with crone-faces all wrinkled and yellow! And away at the rear, chanting with might and main, though bent nearly double under the bass-drum which rested on his back, proudly marched Pineapple Jupiter.

Frowns gathered on the foreheads of Moses and Samuel when the import of this procession became clear, and many a portly Rachel clucked warningly to her brood. But youth is frivolous and inquisitive even in Israel; so the square was jammed with onlookers when the army set up its standard in the very heart of the

Ghetto. True, not all these were children of the tribe. The slurred consonants of the Italian, vainly trying to smooth and liquefy our rugged tongue, were heard; the muffled nasals of the Portuguese; the virile drawl of the Celt; and a youthful accent which seemed to be a resultant of all this polyglot mixture. And to these others also the army was an abomination even as to Samuel and Moses.

Therefore, when the music ceased and the army formed in a wide ring with hands joined sisterly and brotherly, a great pandemonium took up and prolonged the last note of the dying bugle. The cock crew, the cat called and the bulldog barked at these devoted soldiers. But they only blessed their enemies and danced round and round as if rejoicing at persecution. Whereat the multitude fringing their circle danced with them, too, and staid Saul Aronson, who was passing, found himself whirled perforce in a maelstrom of larking boys, full-grown hoodlums and petticoated hobbledehoys.

When the first sister stepped forth to give her "testimony" the face beneath her bonnet compelled silence. Her voice was gentle, her figure petite. Her eyebrows lay across her forehead straight and dark, and she spoke from a rosebud mouth. No wonder the nearest onlookers leaned forward and the idlers on the outskirts inclined their heads to one side and hollowed their hands at their ears so as to catch the utterance which promised so fairly to their eyes.

To Saul Aronson it was a vision of paradise. The lashes of her modestly drooped eyes lay in dark half-moons on her cheek, but once when she lifted them a blue light seemed to flash down into his very heart; and that organ, amorphous before, grew suddenly crystal—a great blood-red ruby which he longed to lay at her feet. This was what she said, this lily of the morass:

"I give thanks to the Lord,"—her utterance was slow, her shrill voice pierced the stillness, "that He has led me away from my sins."

"Alleluia!" murmured the chorus.

"That He has poured into my heart the grace of His love and made manifest the wonder of His works. Are ye weary, sinners, weary of the way ye tread? Oh, come to the true way, where ye shall find life and light and joy and peace, as I have found it."

"Bress de name ob de Lord!" said Pineapple Jupiter, loudly. Whereat several tittered and a discreet sister whispered "Hush!"

"It is not to-day for which we live or the things of to-day—not for bread, or for gold, or for fame, which are perishable things. Not for to-day nor for to-morrow should we strive, but for eternity! Not for the approval of men, but of Him who is the just Judge everlasting. Holy! Holy! Holy!"

"Alleluia!" murmured the chorus.

"It is written in the word, which cannot lie, that the keys of the kingdom are given to Peter. Therefore, when ye go forth to the labor of your days, ask yourselves not what will men say, but what will Peter say when I knock at the golden door for admittance. Will he welcome me as a true child or will he spurn me to the outer darkness? Ask yourselves this, oh, sinners, each and all. What will Peter say, Joseph? What will Peter say, John? What will Peter say, Christian soul?"

This conclusion seemed to be the refrain of a hymn which the circle took up:

> "What will Peter say, Christian soul,
> When the last great trumpet sounds?"

The trombone here drew forth a sepulchral note, representing, no doubt, the trump of doom, and Saul Aronson could almost feel its vibrations in the earth beneath him. He could have pummeled the irreverent knot of gamins who mimicked it grotesquely. Such courage, such loveliness, such sincerity, imposed reverence even for opposite opinions. Never before had he seen their performance in such a light as now. For performance it was. One after another of the brethren stepped into the circle and recited "testimony" to the jeering crowd

around. Each testimony was followed by a hymn, in
regular alternation. Not even the curiosity about the
different sisters and brothers could prevent this evangel
from becoming monotonous. So the captain varied it
with more and more ecstatic exhibitions.

"Volunteers to clap hands!" he would call and four or
five brothers jumped into the middle, clapping hands to
the verses of a simple hymn, repeated ten or fifteen times.
Brisker and brisker the tempo became, till the captain
and his volunteers found themselves galloping around
the ring, with sweet bonneted faces eagerly chanting their
accompaniment. Aronson marveled but he did not
sneer. For his gaze was on the rosebud mouth, whose
"Alleluias" (adapted from his own liturgy, he knew)
seemed to him the sweetest music mortal throat ever gave
forth, the distilled honey of sound.

After more than an hour of such missionary effort, the
captain called for a show of converts. "Hands up, all
that have the love of the Lord in their hearts!"

Two seafaring men and a darky had the courage to
show their palms, and they were standing very near the
circle.

"How many souls love Jesus who died on the cross?"

Aronson, still at his post, felt a traitorous gladness
when a dozen more of the crowd gave the signal of as-
sent. This meager harvest of souls was the result of their
labors. Then Pineapple Jupiter again bent his back under the heavy bass-drum, and the army reformed. Tumtyty, tum! Tumtyty, tum! Tumtyty, tumtyty, boom! The
ringing bugle revived the languishing interest of the mob.
One Jew of the Jews followed the music for nearly a
mile. When he finally fell to the rear the rosebud mouth
was still singing:

"What will Peter say, Christian soul?"

and he felt as if a great light had come to him and then
vanished again, leaving a deeper darkness than ever.

Next morning he awoke with a rapid pulse. "What
will Peter say, Aronson?" he asked as he drew on his

garments, and when he sat down to copy a brief for Shagarach, "What will Peter say, Aronson?" the question again recurred. Strangely enough, it always took the clear, shrill accent of the girl. "What will Peter say, Aronson?" was the prayer for success he offered, when a week later, he mustered up courage to cross the mission threshold and ask Jupiter her name.

From that day Saul Aronson was an altered youth. The least beat of a drum in the Ghetto found him ready to quit dinner or company or work and fly out of the house with a hasty snatch at his hat in the entry.

Sometimes he returned with a rueful look and then his mother knew it was only the Garibaldi guard parading. But at other times it was a subject of remark how long he stayed and how moody he returned.

There was a family living in the rear of the Aronsons, with a divine little 8-year-old girl. Saul knew she was divine, although he had never seen anything but the back of her head. For at noontime when he came to dinner, or in the evening when he returned from work, she would be sitting in the swing her father had built for her, with her back toward him—swinging, singing, in blissful ignorance of the eyes that doted on her through the slats of Saul Aronson's blinds. She had one song of "the Savior" which she delighted to croon. Her voice was like that of a fledgling lark and her carols were made sweet with little improvised turns which often threatened to fail but always came out true—so sure was the child-singer's instinct, feeling the way before her. Nothing reminded him of Serena so much as this earthly angel, and he loved her for the image she called up.

Serena always looked at him. That is to say, her blue eyes pierced him through, accused him, reproved him, every time they were lifted toward the onlookers. But it was not until the day he raised his hand among the converts that she noted down his face for remembrance. He knew its features were not fascinating, especially the red mustache that bristled out horizontally from his lips, with the ends trimmed off as clean as a scrubbing-brush.

But no one else, he felt sure, could worship her with such reverent adoration; and now she had deigned to notice him. What if Simon Rabofsky scowled at his raising his hand? Not "What will Simon Rabofsky say?" but "What will Peter say, Aronson?" was the question of questions. But I fear Peter was confused somewhat oddly in Saul's mind with the possessor of a certain rosebud mouth.

One night Aronson dreamed of Serena Lamb as his bride and the next morning announced his conversion to Pineapple Jupiter, at the same time asking for an introduction to blue eyes.

CHAPTER XXXVI.

A RECANTATION.

Saul Aronson was not the only person who found pleasure in the company of Miss Lamb. There were others, with eyes not glamoured by any golden mist of love, who would have found it hard to select an adjective strong enough to express their approbation of the petite devotee. About a year before she had come down from the country to be a companion to her aunt, Mrs. Wolfe, who had just lost her husband.

Mrs. Wolfe (according to neighbors' gossip) had been no more than a moderately loving wife, but she made a devoted widow. She had the waist of a wasp and a temper to match it. Her frame was angular, and her disposition, too, revealed shoulder blades and elbows. If she loved anything in this world it was her marbled cat, which was hated by every boarder in the house, and a pariah among its tribe. From constant visiting of her husband's grave her manners had assumed a cast which would have been appropriate to a cemetery, but was most depressing in everyday converse. Even her smile had something acrid about it, like a shopworn lemon, and the acidity of her scowl would have reddened blue litmus paper.

People wondered why her niece, such a tender little body, should be doomed to the martyrdom of waiting upon "Old Tabby Wolfe and her boarders." Mrs. Gubbins, who was the landlady's most intimate crony—probably because among her other virtues she had a keen sense of the doleful—spread the report that Serena would inherit her aunt's property, and that her own mother, Mrs. Wolfe's sister, had had an eye to this when she parted with the eldest of her household. However that might be, the girl put up patiently with all the widow's quirks and oddities; entered into religious work enthusiastically, and in six months had rubbed off the slight rusticity with which eighteen years of choring on a farm, before she came down to the city, had touched her accent and manner.

There were hardly any traces of kinship between aunt and niece. To be sure, Serena had the slenderest slip of a waist that nature ever fashioned, and just the least suggestion of cheek bones, too, which were not at all disagreeable, however. When occasion demanded, she could give a sharp order, much as she may have rebuked Spot and Bossy for switching when she milked them in the cowshed at home. But to the boarders these bursts of impatience only gave their sweet waitress a piquancy · like the tartness of the full-ripe strawberry.

With them she was a general favorite. They used to declare that she put yeast in their beds, for they were like pans of dough, feathery and white, when she made them of a morning; and Serena, spinning the pie-plates round, scalloping the edges of the crust with a four-tined fork, or knitting in the sitting-room from a ball of pink yarn that danced on the carpet as she unraveled it, was a spectacle of domesticity at which they never tired of gazing. Yet her dignity, which was far beyond her years, prevented their making her a plaything. Though cordial, she was very reserved. Young ladies called her set; young men, seraphic but cold.

You may imagine how Aronson's heart hopped in his bosom when Jupiter presented him to this goddess.

"I have seen you at our meetings, Mr. Aronson," she graciously observed. She had noticed him, then. He knew it before, but the assurance from her lips gave him measureless joy. But this joy swelled to rapture inexpressible, such as only the saints in the ninth heaven and happy lovers on earth are privileged to know, when she invited him to call upon her and pressed his hand a second time on bidding him adieu. The thrill of her fingertips did not die out all that day; but it was a week again (for Aronson was a bashful youth) before he presumed to accept her invitation.

His mother marveled why Saul furbished himself up so carefully that evening. He had risen from the supper table prematurely and spent exactly fifty-five minutes smoothing his hair, tidying his cravat and drawing on his new pair of gloves. When he went out, instead of soliciting admiration for this array, he seemed to avoid it.

As he drew toward the mansion whose door-plate still bore the name of the departed Ephraim Wolfe, an unwelcome surprise met Aronson. There in the doorway, silhouetted against the hall lamp, was the form which he knew to be Serena's. She was admitting a visitor—a youth. The door quickly closed and a rosy light came through the tinted curtains behind. But Aronson's spirits had sunk, his resolution departed. Instead of crossing the street, as he had planned to, and ringing the bell, with a little speech of greeting all prepared, he walked on to the next corner and irresolutely turned back.

This time a shadow fell on the white curtain of the front room. It was Serena rocking herself placidly in the rocking-chair. Every forward inclination brought her sweet profile into view, every backward one removed it. Her lips moved. She was conversing, doubtless, with the youth whose stolid shadow occupied the center of the opposite curtain. Eight times Saul Aronson passed and repassed that house-front before he could tear himself away and return home to divest himself downheartedly of all his finery.

Two days later, however, he saw Serena again; and she renewed the invitation. This time, when he approached, there was no hostile youth at the door. Serena herself admitted him to the portals of the paradise which she inhabited in common with Mrs. Wolfe and the seven boarders, and 10 o'clock had long ceased striking when, incoherent with ecstasy, Saul Aronson uttered his last lingering doorstep adieu and promised to return.

He never returned. As she informed Inspector McCausland, Serena had never looked on that lovelorn visage again.

This was how he came to break his promise: One Sunday afternoon a messenger came to the Aronson door with a request from Simon Rabofsky that Saul should favor him with a visit. The young man had misgivings, but he dared not disobey.

Up a squalid flight, into a dingy back room, Aronson took his way reluctantly. The clamor of voices died when he crossed the threshold and six pairs of inimical eyes, he thought, were lifted to his face. At a table in the midst sat Rabofsky, his yellowish earlocks dangling beneath his skull-cap and a great book spread open before him.

"Peace be with you, Saul Aronson," he said in the jargon.

"The angel Dumah spare you, Simon Rabofsky," answered Aronson.

"I rejoice to see that you have not forgotten the holy salutations."

The twelve eyes sharpened their glances at Aronson and he knew the ordeal was come. They were six of the strictest in the congregation, from old Silberstein, who sat on the left of the ark and led the recitation of the eighteen psalms of a morning, to young Cohen, the Jewish butcher, a zealot of zealots, than whom none more devoutly beat his bosom in prayer or observed the allotted holy days.

"Brother Silberstein was just proposing that your place

in the synagogue be disposed of. It is a pity to see a seat vacant, when so many must stand. But I bade him not be hasty, for perhaps you had been ill of late."

"Why play the innocent, Simon Rabofsky," broke in Cohen, "when you know as well as we that he has been consorting with the gentiles?"

"It is because I am loath to believe it," answered Rabofsky, in a sorrowful tone, as if rebuking Cohen. "I am loath to believe one of Isaac Aronson's household would turn away to bow before the idols of Babylon."

"Is it forbidden to search for wisdom?" said Aronson.

"You do not search for it in the book where it is found," said Rabofsky, laying his finger on the book before him. It was printed in Semitic characters, but the language was the jargon, for Rabofsky was no master of Hebrew and Aramaic, "the divine talmud, which our fathers have preserved through their hundred persecutions."

"But its wisdom is obscure," answered Aronson.

"Are there not doctors to explain those parts which are dark?" rejoined Rabofsky. "And behold, in this edition, which a Hebrew so enlightened as Saul Aronson should possess, are not all the lengthy passages shortened and the unnecessary omitted by the labors of that light of Israel, born at Cordova, Moses ben Maimon, whom the gentiles miscall Maimonides?"

"Why plead with the apostate?" cried Silberstein, angrily. "He is no longer a Jew. He toileth on the Sabbath. He goeth not down to the waterside to lament."

"It is false," said Aronson, hotly.

"I said so," nodded Rabofsky.

"Who are you to reprove me, Simon Rabofsky," continued Aronson, "because I cannot lie idle two days in the week? Do you rest from your money-getting on the Sabbath? I think your wife, Rebecca, could answer me that. Did I not see her selling jewels to a Christian on the seventh day of this very week?"

"It is written," answered Rabofsky, his steel-blue eyes contracting, "that the high priests in the hour of necessity made food of the bread of the tabernacle. So saith the holy book," he laid his finger again on the page, "which Jehovah hath covered with the wings of His protection so that torches could not destroy it. Behold it has arisen from a thousand burnings uncharred!"

All the Hebrews plucked their garments and with bowed heads muttered a prayer, in which Aronson found himself joining.

"Too many of our youth are beguiled by the flatteries of the gentiles," continued Rabofsky, not unwilling to divert the conversation.

"But such are only the lax ones, who worship no God," said Cohen. "Few grovel before idols, like this one."

"And hath Saul Aronson done this?" asked Rabofsky, as if in surprise.

"Did you not see him yourself at the gentile ceremony raising his hands?"

"You wrong the Christians," protested Aronson. "They are not all cruel and there is much sweetness of love in their doctrine."

"Not cruel!" rejoined Cohen. "How have they not poured out our blood in the ages!"

"Jehovah hath stored it up," added a gentler voice, piteously. It was Abraham Barentzen, the patriarch of the colony, who had not spoken before, but kept looking at the backslider kindly, as if more in sorrow than bitterness.

"Sweetness of love!" cried Silberstein. "Love indeed and enough. How they love each other! Sect embracing sect! Pah!"

"They hate us; they mock us, and our children court them," droned another in a minor key.

"They call us cheats and usurers," cried Cohen, "because we make wealth out of the waste they cast away."

"Psh!" said old Barentzen, raising his hands. "Be just. Those are only the few."

"Perhaps it is some gentle girl that is tempting Saul Aronson, even as the Philistine women of old weakened the faith of Samson," said Rabofsky, keenly.

"Are there not black-eyed daughters of Israel," cried old Barentzen, mild-voiced and reproving, "who will make him a home? If he wants a wife comely, buxom, well-dowered, modest, a good housekeeper and free from tittle-tattle, are there not such by scores in the neighborhood?"

"I fear it is Meyer Shagarach's doing," murmured Silberstein.

"Not so," spoke Cohen, sharply. Though young, he seemed a leader. "Shagarach is lost to the fold of Israel, but does he chant with cracked voice out of a tattered hymn-book? Pretty soon we shall see Saul Aronson shivering in the waters of baptism, and then he will change his name to Paul, like that other traitor, the firebrand of Tarsus?"

"Traitor yourself!" cried Aronson, stung by Cohen's irony.

The word has terrible force in Israel. The whole past of the race is vivid in the minds of the wanderers, and recollection of its sorrows makes a bond so strong that no temptation can break it. Aronson paused to think. The dim traditions, all tears and fire and blood—the exodus from Egypt, the Babylonian captivity, the burning of Jerusalem, the dispersion, the persecutions without number—could he forget all those, snapping ties so sacred?

"After all, I think Saul Aronson's heart is not with the gentiles," said old Barentzen, in a soothing voice. "Would he rather be buried when he dies under some idolatrous mound stuck with the symbol of him whom Judas righteously delivered——"

"There never was such a Nazarene," broke in Cohen impetuously. "It is all a fable and the text in Josephus was written in by the gentiles."

"I say the Christ was real and rightly condemned as a creator of sedition," said Rabofsky, with authoritative pomp. Like the misers of every race, he was both devotee and formalist.

"He is not mentioned in the talmud," argued Cohen.

"Nor elsewhere, until the history of our race crosses the
history of the pagans. It is all an invention."

Thereupon the two zealots wrangled and jangled till
Aronson's ears ached. But his mind was dwelling upon
old Barentzen's saying and sadly acknowledging its
truth. His heart was not really with the Christians.
What did he know of their teachings? He had been given
a bible, but it was locked in his office drawer, unread.
Besides, these were deep questions. Who was he to
dispute the great doctors, like Moses ben Maimon?

"So be it, obstinate youth," said Rabofsky at last, waving his hands to end the discussion.

"I had begun to ask Saul Aronson a question," resumed Barentzen, in a tone of rebuke. "Would you not
rather lie like your fathers with the shards on your eye-
lids and a handful of earth from the land of Israel thrown
over your resting-place?"

Aronson hung his head.

"Enough of this pleading and coaxing," snarled Cohen.
"He is stiff-necked, I see. I will put his name with the
other traitors. There are twenty in all. They shall be
published in the next issue."

"Stay," said Aronson.

"On the first page," said Silberstein. "And the first
page shall be hung outward in my store window."

"That the very children may know them for apostates
and greedy hypocrites," added Rabofsky, to clinch the
threat.

"Hold," cried Aronson. He foresaw the fatal result
of his misstep. He could hear the storm rising around
him; the clamor of children on the streets, the pointed
fingers of men and women, the ironical comments from
the doorstep groups when he passed, the sly digs at the
supper table, the estranged glances of his mother. "It
is all wrong," he cried.

"Then, why do you haunt the gentile mountebanks?"
asked Cohen, seizing his sleeve.

"Fangled like a fop!" said Silberstein, catching his
lapel.

"And shun the blessed synagogue?" added another, fumbling at his vest buttons.

"Are you a gentile of a Jew?" questioned Rabofsky, as chief inquisitor.

"I am a Jew!" cried Aronson, in honest wrath, tousled and clapperclawed until his patience had given away. Then he rushed from the room.

The list of "traitors" appeared in the Jewish Messenger without Saul Aronson's name. The old, old conflict between love and honor had ended with another defeat for the imperious boy-god. But it is no discredit to Serena Lamb that her influence yielded to a passion which is hardly second to any in the world for intensity—the Israelite's devotion to his race. All that she retained of the young convert from whom so much had been expected was a confused memory of the conversation in her sitting-room. What had Aronson told her in his agitation during that confidential interview? It would seem that he had been too frank. At least, for several weeks after Serena's visit to McCausland, he was strangely conscious that some one was dogging his footsteps, both at home and about the office. Naturally, he ascribed this espionage to the sacred brotherhood, whose power is great in Israel, and, fearing their vigilance, redoubled his evening invocations and waxed regular in his attendance at the synagogue.

CHAPTER XXXVII.

THE WRATH OF SHAGARACH.

Walter Riley, Thomas J. Fenton and Arthur Watts had a separate trial from the other members of the "club," which resorted to Lanty Lonergan's back kitchen. There was only one charge against them—to wit, the larceny of three bicycles and their sale to one Timothy Bagley, aforesaid, dealer in junk.

The government had little difficulty in proving its case. First, one of the owners of the bicycles testified to having recognized his wheel, cunningly repainted, in a stranger's possession, to following up its rider and tracing it finally to an auction sale at which he had purchased it cheap. From the auctioneer to Bagley, from Bagley to the "club," was easy work for the officer detailed to investigate the theft. Walter's unsold wheel was confiscated, together with all the other stolen property on the premises, and no fewer than seven of the boys placed under arrest. But the only charge against Riley, Fenton and Watts was the theft of the bicycles.

Bagley, the junkman, who was involved in the affair, had made a singular confession, candid enough in most particulars but with great hiatuses here and there concerning the disposal of certain articles, principally articles of value—a watch, a meerschaum pipe and the third of the bicycles. No threats or promises in private had been able to wring from him a confession concerning these points. But at the mention of a pipe Shagarach had raised his head and, crossing over to the prosecuting attorney, secured a description of the missing object.

"You admit, then, that you offered Riley $10 for the bicycle which he had ridden?" asked Shagarach of Bagley on cross-examination.

"Yes, sir."

"How often did you repeat this offer?"

"Several times—about four or five times."

"And the boy each time refused?"

"Yes, sir."

"What language did he use?"

"He said the wheel wasn't his."

"Which you knew very well, didn't you, without being told?"

"Yes, sir."

"And when you proposed that Fenton should ride the bicycle over to your shop, what was Riley's conduct then?"

"I don't know of my own knowledge. But they told me that he wouldn't have it."

"He threatened them, then?"

"Yes, sir, you might call it threatening."

"Then Riley would appear to have put forward some claim upon the bicycle, although he denied that it was his. Would you not say that he seemed to regard himself as its custodian rather than its proprietor? That he was storing it in Lonergan's kitchen until the occasion should arise when it might be returned to its owner?"

"Well, the boys said he was sorry for taking the wheel and that he never meant to steal it."

"That is all—all on that point, I mean." Bagley had started to leave the stand. "There is another matter, however, with regard to the third bicycle—the one which has not been recovered"—Bagley shifted uneasily to the opposite foot. "How does it happen that you, the sole repository of the secrets of these young law-breakers, can tell us nothing of that?"

"I know nothing about it."

"And about the gold watch stolen from Mr. Merchant's window?"

"I don't know, sir."

"And the meerschaum pipe—of rare coloring, according to the connoisseur who testified in the previous trial?"

"I know nothing about the watch and the pipe, sir. They are not in my line. I couldn't dispose of such articles."

"Ah! But you might be acquainted with somebody who could, might you not?"

"I suppose I might——"

"Some second-hand dealer, let us say?"

Bagley's eye dropped and he looked pale.

"Have you been visited, Bagley, by any one, since you were let out on bail?"

"Only by my bondsman."

"What is your bondsman's name?"

Bagley hesitated so long that the judge finally had to order him to answer.

"Mr. Rabofsky," he stammered.

"Kindly subpoena Mr. Simon Rabofsky," said Shagarach to Aronson. "It is that gentleman just starting to leave the room. He will remain for a few moments."

The writ was made out and handed by the awe-stricken Aronson to the money-lender, who glared at him furiously. But he could not escape.

"Mr. Rabofsky is a second-hand dealer, I believe?" continued Shagarach.

"I think so."

"Of a higher class than yourself?"

"Oh, yes sir. Mr. Rabofsky's reputation is first class."

"How much money did Simon Rabofsky offer you to keep him out of this scrape?" was the next question. The witness looked over at the money-lender in terror; then back at Shagarach, and his terror was intensified.

"No money," he finally gasped.

"Would you be willing to swear that if Mr. Henderson, the owner of that pipe, should call to-day at 84 Salem street and request Mrs. Rebecca Rabofsky to sell him the colored meerschaum which her husband was showing to a customer yesterday, when Mr. Shagarach called, he would be told that no such article was in the store?"

Either the length of the question or its import confused the witness.

"No, sir," he answered.

"You would not be willing——"

"Yes, sir, I mean—that is—how do I know?"

"Mr. Henderson," said Shagarach, turning to a gentleman present, "will doubtless be interested enough to try. He could be back in half an hour. That will do, Bagley."

During the half-hour Shagarach put on, as witnesses for the defense, Walter's schoolmaster, who told an anecdote of his truthfulness and another of his generosity, which were better than the warmest words of general commendation; and Emily Barlow, whose story of the theft accorded exactly with Walter's own, which was honestly told, with a correctness of language that his former master did not fail to notice.

"Only I never meant to steal it," he said finally. "We all clung together and I was sorry before I got home. I read the papers to see if the owners' names were given, but they lived too far out of town. If I knew whose it was I would have ridden it out to him again."

To all this the judge listened coldly. He was a new appointee, fearful lest the balance of Libra on his unpracticed fingertip should incline too much one way or the other. Just as Walter concluded, Mr. Henderson returned and Simon Rabofsky was summoned to the stand. He muttered in his beard and flashed a glance of hatred at Shagarach.

"What do you know of this case?" asked the lawyer.

"Nothing."

He looked furtively at Mr. Henderson.

"That will do for the present. Mr. Henderson, will you kindly testify as to the result of your search?"

Mr. Henderson's testimony was brief and pointed. He had visited 84 Salem street, stating that he came from Mr. Rabofsky and desired to see a colored meerschaum pipe. The lady had shown him his own pipe. He had priced it. Twenty-five dollars. She had procured it, she said——

"One moment," interrupted Shagarach. "Will you kindly remain awhile, Mr. Henderson? Mr. Rabofsky again."

Rabofsky returned.

"You have heard Mr. Henderson's testimony?"

"I have heard it. If you had sense enough to ask me, I could have told you that without sending him off on a wild-goose chase."

Shagarach knew that Rabofsky was excited, because his accent came out so strongly.

"Go on," he said, giving him the rope to hang himself by.

"I know nothing about this case. That pipe I took from a woman who wanted money. I lent her $25 and she never came back. All I ask is what I paid for it, no more, no less, and so I wash my hands of all of you."

"Not yet," said Shagarach. "You are required by law to record the names of persons who pawn articles. If we should send an officer down to your shop would he find the woman's name in your book?"

"She would not give me her name."

"But you loaned her the money?"

"She cried and was so poor I took pity——"

"Enough," said Shagarach in temper. "Mr. Henderson!"

Mr. Henderson replaced Rabofsky a second time.

"You were about to say that you inquired of Mrs. Rabofsky where her husband obtained the pipe, were you not?"

"Yes, sir, I asked her that."

"What was her answer?"

"That it was his own pipe he had smoked for eleven years."

This statement produced a visible effect on the spectators. It concluded the defense for Walter Riley. After the prosecuting attorneys had pleaded for sentence, Shagarach briefly addressed the judge.

"The real criminals in this case, your honor, are the last two witnesses—adults of responsible years, and one of them, at least, enjoying a reputable position. They were the receivers of the stolen goods and the encouragers of the crimes. Were I prosecuting attorney, I should suspend the cases against the young defendants until justice had been done to both of these maturer thieves.

"I cannot look upon the deed committed on the lonely roadside at Hillsborough as a serious offense, for which our code provides a penalty. It was a prank, played in the ebullient spirit of mischief, but given an ambiguous color by Miss Barlow's well-meant outcry of warning. Evil resides in the intentions of the mind. Not until Fenton and Watts disposed of the property which was not theirs was their misdemeanor consummated and an unhappy practical jest warped into a legal theft.

"Even then, I might recommend clemency to all three

offenders, on account of their youth and the restitution of the property. For I have no doubt that the missing bicycle will be found installed beside the meerschaum pipe in Simon Rabofsky's back room. But, considering the evil associations which these boys have formed, and their unfortunate homes, Fenton having no mother and Watts an intemperate one, I believe that a short period of retirement, under the regular discipline of the reformatory, would be of advantage to them.

"But the case of Riley is different. His character is better than that of the others. He is fortunate in possessing an excellent mother, who depends upon him in part for support. Moreover, the refusal on his part to dispose of the bicycle, against a pressure few boys of his age could resist, shows a moral courage which is exceedingly rare in my experience, and which only needs fostering to develop its possessor into an admirable man. I, therefore, respectfully suggest that Riley be placed on probation."

If the judge were not so new to the bench he would have known that Shagarach's addresses were always brief. But, knowing the great lawyer only by reputation, he judged that the brevity of his plea denoted a perfunctory interest in the case. The sentencing was deferred until 4 o'clock, when a whole batch of prisoners filed into the "cage," one after another, to receive their punishments.

"Ochone!" cried a maundering old woman after every sentence, and even the court officers whispered to each other:

"Perkins is having a picnic to-day."

But there was little severity in the sentence accorded to the white-faced youth who came just before the three gamins. Emily recognized in amazement Mr. Arthur Kennedy Foxhall.

"In consideration of your social standing," said the judge, "of your promise to reform and of the fact that your weakness is one which injures only yourself, I will mitigate the penalty."

Then the clerk read out a fine of $20 and costs. The opium parlors of Hi Wong King had recently been

raided. That is to say, four tall, youngish men had entered one evening and called for dinner. For Hi Wong
King's restaurant was open to all. Chicken wings had
been served them and an aromatic salad. Jelly pats had
been dropped over their heads into dainty plates, on
which droll baboons scratched their heads and tigers
grimaced fiercely. Such is the art of the orient. Tea
leaves newly steeped in a bowl had taught them their first
lesson in the needlessness of sugar and milk; and they
had practiced with the merry chopsticks, a pair in each
hand. Then, by way of diversion, they broke through
the painted screens into Hi Wong King's rear parlors
and arrested eight opium smokers, Mongol and Cau-
casian, of both sexes; among these one who was dreaming
over a peculiarly elegant pipe proved to be Emily's ad-
mirer.

"Riley, Fenton and Watts, stand up," said the clerk.
Walter's cheeks were burning red, as he stood between
his companions. They seemed to feel the disgrace less
keenly and looked at the clerk with sheepish and cunning
glances.

"Fenton and Watts, you are sentenced to the reform
school during your minority, and Riley for the space of
one year!"

"Ochone!" broke out the maundering old woman and
a chill fell on Emily's heart. Then the voice of Shagarach
was heard in wrath. The building seemed to quake with
its power. It was such a voice as that Roman tribune
may have owned who could make himself heard from
end to end of the forum.

"Sir, you have just imposed a nominal fine on a mature
man, who has not only, as you speciously alleged, ruined
himself by a degrading vice, but done what example
could to spread its contagion. Immediately after you
sentence three poor children to long terms of imprisonment. Are you ignorant that four in seven of all who
enter those institutions return to them sooner or later?
Do you see no possible spark of reform in the natures of
these boys, no means of tiding over the danger period of

youth, the formative years, the sowing season? Or do you think to scatter seeds inside a jail and reap some other crop than crime? Sir, it is not my sense of justice that social standing should condone offenses and social obscurity magnify them."

The ticking of the clock could be heard when Shagarach paused. Officer looked at officer, as if they expected immediately to be called upon to execute a sentence of contempt on the audacious lawyer. But Shagarach's reputation was great, and Judge Perkins could not afford to inaugurate his session in the Criminal Court by a conflict with such a man. He only stroked his chin nervously and pulled at his severe legal whiskers.

"I do not know which is the more deserving of censure," continued Shagarach, "the dangerous laxity of the one judgment, which virtually acquits a convicted lawbreaker, or the atrocious severity of the other, which condemns to a year's whole punishment the innocent act, already more than atoned for, of a boy for whose uprightness I would pledge my personal word."

"Oh, if you are willing to vouch for the boy's good behavior," said the judge, "I will put him on probation and reconsider the other sentences."

"I will accept the charge," said Shagarach.

Emily's heart leaped for joy, and Mrs. Riley could not be restrained from rushing forward and embracing Walter in rapture. But the most touching moment came when Walter walked over to Shagarach and, with tears in his eyes, but a stanch voice, said: "I want to show you I am grateful."

CHAPTER XXXVIII.

COUNT L'ALIENADO.

"Here is the substitute I promised you, Rosalie. Miss March—Count L'Alienado."

There was a vacant seat in the barouche that stood before the Marches' villa. It had been destined for Tristram, but even behind the black glasses he wore the August sunshine dazzled his eyes, so he was compelled at the last moment to excuse himself.

"Mme. Violet—his lordship, the Earl of Marmouth."

Count L'Alienado was thus informally presented to his other two riding companions. There was just a suggestion of Spanish reserve in his obeisance, and he bowed a graceful adieu to Tristram before mounting to his seat.

It was curious that Tristram should have been the first to break the count's incognito. He had arrived at Lenox a few days before, attended by a single valet, and registered at the hotel as M. L. L'Alienado, Valencia. Though not imposing in stature, he exhibited a head of rare distinction—the black beard trimmed to an exquisite point at the chin and the curled mustaches setting off a pair of glowing eyes which riveted the beholder from the moment he met their gaze.

As the artist spoke Spanish, they had become friends in an afternoon.

"We have flattered ourselves that the coaching party is something purely American," said Rosalie, who sat beside him, to the stranger.

"I am glad of it for the color. That is an element I have observed to be generally a little lacking in your life."

"Color and lordliness," sighed Mme. Violet. "Ah, there are no troubadours, no spurred cavaliers, no mailed knights in this busy America—not even scarlet soldiers parading. You men are so dingy, dingy in your black propriety. Why be so funereal? My heart goes out sometimes to a very mountebank, all spangled and jingling like a tambourine when he moves. Color! Give me color. Ah, it is not we who have taste, it is the canaille! It is Victorine, my lady's maid, with her bonnet-ribbons flaunting all the colors of the rainbow."

A silk banner lay outspread in Rosalie's lap, throwing warm blushes against her throat. It was the prize for the gentlemen's steeplechase, which was to close the programme of the afternoon.

"Scarlet, sea-blue and gold," she cried, stroking the tasseled fringe which justified the last addition. "Are not these the primary hues, the major chord of color, and the white their perfect blending?"

The Violet laughed. When addressing her directly or referring to her in her own presence, people carefully called her Mme. Violet. But to the world, out of earshot, she was simply the Violet, just as Cleopatra is Cleopatra. It was taken for granted that her blood was French, but Count L'Alienado, noting her fawn-brown eyes and the strong black hair, which made Rosalie's fluff appear like carded golden silk—thought he detected the marks of the Romany. Yet the full mouth hinted at a Spanish cross. She was not very young, or, at first sight, very beautiful, but she possessed a diablerie stronger than girlhood or beauty, and gossip said the Earl of Marmouth was succumbing to its spell.

"The signal!" cried Rosalie, as the notes of a hunting-horn pealed, faint and mellow, from a distant quarter. "It is time to start."

For several minutes the occupants of the barouche lay back, reveling in the luxury of the cushions and in the changing view which the drive afforded. Other equipages swept into the main road here and there, from cottage and mansion and by-path, each freighted with its cargo of flower-raimented beauty. Marshals in velvet hunting garb galloped up and down, with low salutes to the passengers and brusque orders to the coachmen. On the top of a little hill there came a pause while the procession was arranging itself, and the conversation rippled out again.

"The color is overdone," said the Earl of Marmouth. "It smacks of Latin degeneracy."

"Such as appears in the canvases of Titian?" asked Count L'Alienado quietly.

The Violet, sitting opposite him, caressed her bronze-eyed spaniel to her cheek, so that she might survey the newcomer more closely. His lordship, at her side, alone of the party had sat upright during the ride.

"You are Spanish, not Italian, I am told," he said, much in the tone of a hotel clerk demanding the settlement of an overdue bill. The Violet's eyes met the count's interrogatively.

"Question me in Castilian," he smiled.

"Where are your estates?"

"In Valencia."

"I was there last autumn. I seem to have overlooked the L'Alienados."

"Our estates are in dispute with another branch of the family."

Marmouth grunted.

"The title is very old?" asked Rosalie, to blunt the edge of his impertinence.

"Not very old," answered Count L'Alienado, gently, but looking full at Marmouth. "Before Columbus set out from Palos my ancestor was knighted by Ferdinand the Great—for honorable services."

"We are moving at last," growled the earl, as if personally grieved at the delay. His own title was less than 200 years old and the services for which it was granted, by the second Charles, though historic, could not possibly be called honorable.

"Ah, this is joyous!" cried the Violet, as the sensuous pleasure of the ride stole over her. A quick-step, taken from the start, gave the party a gentle jolting, just sufficiently softened by the padded carriage upholstery. Up hill and down dale, through the riches of midsummer, the route chosen wound. Forest and meadow sailed leisurely by them. Handkerchiefs waved from piazza and window wherever they passed a dwelling house, and at every cross-road stood a group of the fresh-faced country-folk to give them greeting. At the end of an hour the road recurved on itself along a hillside overlooking the valley of the racing park and the pageant bent its length into the form of a letter S, so that without the delay of a formal review each carriage was permitted to inspect the others.

Count L'Alienado saw barges filled with maidens, like living flowers, four-in-hand tally-hos, crowded with sportive collegians, odd jaunting-cars and donkey-carts got up by the wags, staid family coaches with footmen faced rearward to enjoy the retrospect, and open drags like his own without number, all brilliant with lovely womanhood.

The Violet stood apart from the others, sensuous and exotic—like an orange lily in a garden of snowdrops. But, supreme over all, like a bright light, enhanced by re-flectors, shone the loveliness of Rosalie March—pure, placid and faultlessly costumed as ever. The jockeys whispered to one another when her vehicle entered the racing park. An eager look at that moment chased away the slight hauteur of her expression—not unbecoming in one so clearly removed from the common order, and far from approaching disdain. She turned her head toward the stables expectantly.

"Paradise," said the Violet, when they had entered and the carriages circled around the great oval.

"This is something like England," said the earl.

"None the worse for that," smiled Rosalie.

"No. Most of the good things I have seen here are derived from the mother country."

"Do you agree, Count L'Alienado?" asked Rosalie, appealing to the stranger.

"Candor is too sharp a sword to carry about unsheathed," answered Count L'Alienado.

Mme. Violet smiled archly, bringing her Gainsborough brim close to the earl's great face and caressing her spaniel with provoking abandon.

Rosalie's little abstraction since they passed through the gate might easily be understood, for Harry Arnold was entered in the steeplechase for gentlemen riders.

"There they come!" she cried, but it was only a group of motley jockeys for the ring race. This passed off quietly enough.

"Now for the steeplechase," cried Rosalie. "There's Harry!" She instinctively plucked the Violet's hand. Then, remembering they were not alone, she colored. Harry led the group of riders who came from the stables, mounted on strong-limbed steeplechasers.

His uniform was of the bulrush brown velvet he
liked, and his horse a bright chestnut, which pranced as if
proud to carry such a master. Even at a distance his
splendid seat gave presage of victory.

"Mr. Arnold is the favorite," said Count L'Alienado.

"Although he gives away forty pounds to Leroy,"
added Rosalie, the technical terms of the track coming
strangely from her lips. It was fortunate for her peace
of mind Tristram was not there to hear them.

"Now they start!" she cried, alive with interest; but
it was only Harry Arnold who spurted his curvetting
chestnut across the turf, then reined him up on his
haunches with a sudden jerk, as you may have seen an old
cavalry sergeant perform the trick. But Leroy, who, as
Rosalie said, weighed nearly half a hundred less, wisely
reserved his white horse's strength.

"Now!" repeated Rosalie, unconsciously clasping the
flag, as if eager to bestow it. The horses, six in number, .
had started in a bunch and kept together easily till the
pistol flash. Then each bounded as if cut with a whip,
and rider and horse bent forward.

"Hurrah!" shouted the ring of onlookers about the in-
closure, as all six took the first low wall together. The
course led straightway across the oval, up a hill at one
end, then out of sight for a circuit of a mile, and back
by another route, over ditch and mound. Harry Arnold's
chestnut and Leroy's white could be seen a length in the
lead of the others and neck and neck, as they struggled up
the hill and sunk to view on the other side.

"How glorious! How delightful!" cried the Violet, in
the interim of suspense. "It is better than the wild Indians that rode in the coliseum last year. Your full-
blooded racers, they are too lean, like grasshoppers. Oh,
the steeplechase is better. I believe, after all, you owe
something to old England, which bequeathed you this
legacy."

"You remember the horse-race in 'Anna Karenina?'"
asked his lordship, much mollified. "One of the most
ethical of books, in the broader sense of the word."

His question seemed addressed to Count L'Alienado.
"I have not read the Russians," he answered.

"You are behind the world, senor. And where may your diversions lie?"

"My favorites," he answered, "are the Persian poets."

Rosalie desisted for a moment from scanning the black crest of the distant hill with her great eyes full of eagerness. Then she recovered herself suddenly, and cried out, in a piercing voice:

"They are coming!"

"Who is ahead?"

"The chestnut and the white are even," said the count.

"Oh, I hope he will win!" prayed Rosalie, clutching the prizes she was to award. Down the slope they strained, heading toward the goal. Only a close side view could have disclosed the advantage in favor of either.

"Harry Arnold will win," said Count L'Alienado. "Leroy is whipping his horse."

The count's judgment proved correct. Almost immediately the chestnut began drawing away from the white. A nose, a neck, half a length, and the clear ground intervened. Harry did not touch whip or spur to the sides of his mount, until the last leap, when a high wall and a long ditch had to be taken together. On the very rise of the jump he switched his chestnut's flanks, and just as the conductor's baton seems a wand visibly producing the swell of the orchestra, so this light motion seemed to give the impulse to the horse's spring. The clatter of his feet on the hard turf beyond announced him the winner amid cheers. Leroy's white took the ditch gallantly, too, but the blood showed red in its nostrils.

Instead of reining up at the goal, Harry executed a characteristic caprice. The fence surrounding the race-track was nearly five feet high. Careering on at full gallop, the victor urged his animal toward this obstacle. A great shout greeted him as he cleared it, the chestnut's hind hoofs grazing the boards. Then, swiftly turning to the right, he cantered up to Rosalie's carriage, gracefully backed his horse and saluted. Leroy joined him through the gate, and stood at his side, while the losers straggled in, haphazard and blown.

"That was for you, Rosalie," said Harry in her ear as she laid the flagstaff in his hand. It was meant for a whisper, but others heard it, and on the morrow the news had spread all over Lenox that Harry Arnold and the beautiful Rosalie March were definitely betrothed. When it reached Mrs. Arnold in Hillsborough, as though by special messenger, she retired at once to her room.

The coaching party paraded out and dispersed amid merrymakings freer than before. Mme. Violet was bewitching during the journey home, making up by a double stream of effortless prattle for Rosalie's unwonted silence.

"But Poe," protested the girl, as if waking suddenly, when the earl, who had got back to book talk again, inveighed against the poverty of our literature.

"Ting-a-ling," said his noble lordship. The carriage had just stopped to leave Count L'Alienado at his hotel.

CHAPTER XXXIX.

THE PURPLE TEA.

"The Earl of Marmouth sends his regards. He will be unable to join us." Tristram March held a coroneted note in his hands while he made this announcement to the company. There was a faint salvo of regrets, meant for the Violet's ears. Only Miss Milly Mills was heard remarking, sotto voce:

"I'm glad the old bear is chained for once."

"But the grizzly is grand in its den, dear," chided Dorothea Goodbody, a little louder.

"True. We do not fit everywhere," said the Violet, who had overheard them. "Imagine Thoreau in a salon."

"Or Talleyrand in the Walden woods," added Count L'Alienado.

More than one of the company had noted this as the third occasion on which his noble lordship avoided a meeting with the count. Was it that in the reserved Spaniard he had encountered a force which he could not overbear? Or was he jealous of the count's attention to the Violet? Twice at the Ryecroft's hop she had inadvertently answered the slender foreigner and turned her smooth, brown shoulder to the Englishman.

"Well," said Tristram, "the menagerie must perform without its lion."

"How flattering, brother!" cried Rosalie. Harry Arnold was leaning over her chair. "You compare us to wolves and panthers."

"Not unhappily," said the Violet. "Mine host is clever. He will put us all in an apologue like Aesop's. I am curious to see how I shall be transformed."

"The mood is wanting," cried Tristram, while the young ladies seconded the suggestion. "I am savage. I should affront you all with some furious satire."

"Imagine Tristram furious," said Harry.

"A smothered volcano. I have committed to-day the sin against the Holy Ghost. Guess what that is?"

"Success," said the Violet.

"Candor," the count.

"Bachelorhood," Miss Milly Mills.

"Punning," his sister Rosalie.

But Tristram shook his head drearily at each response.

"Well, then, tell us," cried a chorus of impatient voices.

"I have prostituted art to lucre—having disposed of my great design of Ajax's shield—for what purpose, do you think?"

All the guesses were wild again.

"For a bed-spread," said Tristram, and there was a chorus of laughter, amid which the circle broke up into little moving knots, all electrically united, however, so that the talk flew from one part of the room to another.

It was one of Tristram's soirees, which were the events of the season in Lenox. The flavor of art was substituted for that of artificiality, and usually some souvenir, bearing the touch of the host's own fanciful hand, was carried away by each of the guests. The coveted invitation for this night's affair announced "a purple tea," and the furnishings verified the description. Rich muslin shades over the chandeliers (Rosalie's work) purpled all the atmosphere of the parlors. Purple hangings here and there carried out the suggestion, but not too obtrusively, and each of the guests appeared with some purple garment.

Among the ladies these generally verged toward the wine-colored shades, for they were all too young to carry well the full warmth of the Tyrian. Thus the Violet's mantilla, Rosalie's cloud, Harry Arnold's sash, were all steeped to the same dye, now the crimson, now the blue element prevailing in the mixture. Count L'Alienado alone appeared to have evaded the rule until, raising his right hand to smell a rose, he scattered a pencil of purple light from an opalescent stone which none present were learned enough in lapidary science to name.

"Let's have tableau charades!" cried Miss Milly Mills, who flitted from person to person, from subject to subject, like a butterfly, and was accused of a partiality for spruce gum. The suggestion was taken up with approval, and nearly every one present acted out the first word that came to him on the spur of the moment.

Tristram gave what he called a definition of himself in lengthy pantomime which no one could fathom. So he was obliged to explain that meed—eye—ochre—tea, summed up "mediocrity," at which one and all protested. Most of the other attempts were quite as laborious. But when the Violet stepped forward and trilled an upper C, then buzzed like an insect and put her right foot forward, there was a unanimous cry of "Trilby!" and the flatness began to be taken out of the game.

Then the pleasures grew more miscellaneous and Count L'Alienado found himself for a time alone on the outer balcony with Mme. Violet. The sky was starlit above, the shadows lay deep in the garden bushes below, and the diamonds burned amid her braids. They talked of the Persian poets till the light voice of Tristram within interrupted them and a ripple of laughter from the purple interior reached their ears.

"Ah, this is not fair; that our wisest and wittiest should impoverish the company by their absence. Your places are waiting and the bell is tired of tinkling to you."

"We were lost among the stars," replied Count L'Alienado.

Opposite the count sat Harry Arnold; opposite the Violet, Rosalie. Waiters were serving refreshments, and a purple tea was poured into the wine-colored cups. On each table lay a souvenir containing verse or prose by Tristram March, with fantastic decorations in the border. Harry Arnold was just passing the souvenir of their table to Rosalie. It contained a caricature in profile of Tristram himself, and a brief "Autobiography," which Harry read aloud:

> "I went to school
> To Ridicule.
> He taught me civility,
> The peacock humility,
> Depth and subtility
> Feste, the fool.
>
> Meeker and meeker becomes my mood
> From studying Conscious Rectitude;
> And if my speech be firm and pat,
> Madam Garrulity taught me that."

"Oh, I hate sarcasm," burst out Rosalie. "Why won't you be literal, commonplace, something positive, if it's only a woman-hater?"

"An abominable fault, brother Tristram," said Harry, sternly.

"Hideous!" cried the others, drowning poor Rosalie's homily in a flood of irony more heartless than Tristram's own.

Then Rosalie gave him up as incorrigible.

"I wonder if Count L'Alienado's jewel has not a legend attached to it?" said some one.

"It is an alamandine ruby from Siam," began the count.

"Oh, do go on," cried Miss Milly Mills from the rear, who had been listening over her shoulder. "Tell us the story. I'm sure it will be better than Cleverly's last book."

"Oh, if it isn't better than that——"

"But the setting was fresh," said Tristram, who was Cleverly's friend. "He rehangs his gallery well, even if the portraits are familiar."

"This talisman of mine has indeed a story attached to it," said Count L'Alienado at last, "but you may read hundreds better in any book of oriental tales. Its quality, however, is curious. You know that mesmerism has long been known in the east, and that many of the occult feats of the Hindoo magicians are ascribed to that power. It was an Arab caliph who first attributed to this stone the quality of securing immunity to its possessor from the magic trance. As a matter of fact, I have never been hypnotized while I wore it."

"A challenge, Harry," said Tristram.

"You possess the power?" asked the count.

"So I am told," laughed Harry.

"People go to sleep at his bidding," said Tristram. "He is the surest recipe I have seen for insomnia."

"Except the Rev. Dr. Fourthly," whispered Miss Milly Mills, but at this Dorothea Goodbody looked shocked.

"Shall I hypnotize you, Rosalie?" smiled Harry to his sweetheart.

But Rosalie shook her head with a little shudder.

"The count," said the Violet.

"The count! Hypnotize the count!" a chorus echoed.

"Very well," said the Spaniard; "a moment till I invoke the genii of the carbuncle. Now."

"Are you ready?" said Harry, laughing a little awkwardly. He made one or two cabalistic passes with his hands, looking straight into the eyes of the count. They were large burning eyes, the like of which Harry had never met before. Gazing into their depths, he seemed to feel a new spell. They were drawing him, drawing his soul away. Other objects disappeared. Rosalie, Tristram, the Violet—he clutched at them, but they were gone. The count himself grew shadowy. Only his eyes —fixed, haunting, luminous—remained, centering a vast drab vault, which was all that was left of the populous world and its occupants. What could Harry do but surrender his faculties and be absorbed like the rest?

"It is Harry who is hypnotized," cried Tristram. Rosalie fixed her gaze on her lover's face.

"Raise your right hand," said the count. Harry obeyed. His stare was glassy, his lower lip stupidly dropped.

"Do you know this glove?" asked the count, raising a lemon-colored kid.

"I do," came the answer, mechanical, monotonous.

"Try it on."

Harry drew the glove on his right hand, his eyes never leaving those of the count.

"Button it tightly," said the Spaniard. Do you remember where you wore this glove last?"

"I do."

"Can you see the side door opening from the passageway?"

"I can."

"Do you recognize the youth who is entering?"

"I do."

"Is it Harry Arnold?"

"It is Harry Arnold."

"Does he listen cautiously?"

"He listens cautiously."

"Does he climb the stairs softly?"

"He climbs the stairs softly."

"Does he enter the study?"

The young man's face twitched and convulsed. His eyes started from their sockets. The foam rose to his lips as they worked.

"Harry!"

It was the agonized cry of Rosalie March, throwing herself upon her lover and turning defiantly at Count L'Alienado, whose fierce insistence had amazed the onlookers. The spell seemed to be broken, for Harry sunk from his chair, supported by Rosalie's arms.

"Some wine," cried Tristram, chafing Harry's forehead and gently striving to unclasp his sister's arms. But she clung to her sweetheart with love in her eyes.

Count L'Alienado approached the unconscious man, the crowd parting before him.

"Wake!" he said, "and forget!" Harry's eyes shut naturally and then opened. He drank the wine which Rosalie pressed to his lips. In a few minutes he was erect, eagerly questioning the company.

"Call it a faint," said Count L'Alienado, quietly. "It is better that he should not know."

"But what was it all about?" asked Miss Milly Mills, on tiptoe with curiosity.

"Only an experiment in clairvoyance," answered Count L'Alienado.

CHAPTER XL.

THREE TIMES RUNNING.

Shagarach's office was a hive of industry the next time Emily Barlow called. Walter Riley, installed in Jacob's place, looked smartly clerical, with a pen over one ear, docketing some papers, and Aronson was knitting his brows over a decision in the digest. But the lawyer himself, she thought, did not appear to have profited greatly by his fortnight's vacation. His cheek was worn and his manner betrayed an unusual aberration at times.

He had returned only the evening before. When she entered the parlor to greet him his mother found the padlock chain of the Persian poets torn through their edges, and her son face down on the carpet buried in a volume of Hafiz, with Sadi and Firdusi scattered near. She trembled, but she did not disturb him.

"Our cause progresses," he said, in answer to Emily's query. "Important links have been discovered since we last conferred."

The sweet girl lifted her eyebrows and waited.

"In the first place we shall put Harry Arnold on the stand. I have traced him to the door of the study a moment before the fire was set."

Emily bit her lip just a trifle in disappointment, for her own cherished theory would only be embarrassed by the presence of Harry Arnold there.

"The other points?" she asked.

"You remember the peddler in the green cart, alluded to in Ellen Greeley's letter, who carried messages to some person unknown?"

"Perfectly."

"Three witnesses stand ready to swear that a peddler in a green cart cried his wares through the roads of Woodlawn about the time of the fire and frequently stopped at the house of the Arnolds."

"That connects them legally," said Emily, still more discontented. "How soon do you expect a trial?"

"In less than two weeks. I am sorry you will have to shorten your vacation."

"Oh, it is better over; the suspense is agony."

"The door, Walter," said Shagarach, as she passed out. Pretty soon he went home to his own midday meal. Aronson was called away to look up a title and left the Whistler in charge.

Walter had already caught just a little of his employer's decision of manner, which sat oddly on his rosy face, but was no more, after all, than a laudable aspiration toward manfulness. The lawyer had discovered his skill with the pencil and his mechanical interests, and had set him to work evenings copying the designs in a drawing manual. Meanwhile, his gamesome impulses had quieted a good deal, and it was only when the office was empty, as now, that the old rich whistle was heard. Shagarach and Shagarach's suggestions seemed to consume that whole fund of adolescent energy which formerly had overleaped all bounds in its search for an outlet.

He was just in the middle of a skylark solo, interrupted by bites at the contents of his lunch-box, when a white-bearded old man entered. At first Walter, hearing the limp on the stairs, took it for old Diebold, the pensioner, one of Shagarach's clients. The lunch-box vanished like magic and there was a hasty brushing of crumbs and swallowing of a half-masticated mouthful before he turned the knob.

"Is Mr. Shagarach in?" asked the stranger, glancing around with a senile leer.

"Not now, sir, but I expect him soon," answered Walter. "He's gone to dinner. Won't you be seated while you wait for him?"

"How long?" said the old man, mumbling his words, as if he were toothless, and nodding at the boy over and over again.

"How long before he comes back? Oh, he never stays away long. He'll be here in five minutes, I guess."

The old man sat down feebly in the chair. Such a strange old man, thought Walter. His white beard almost covering his face and reaching down on his bosom, and long white curls coming out from under his hat. He must be almost a hundred, said the boy to himself. Yet his eyes rolled around quickly and his skin wasn't wrinkled at the corners of the eyes, nor did he have those time-scored furrows in the neck that soldiers call saber cuts.

"Buy a pencil," he said to Walter, taking out a bunch from his pocket.

Walter shook his head in some disappointment. It was only a peddler, after all.

"Two for five," persisted the visitor.

Should he show him the door? Mr. Shagarach did not like to be troubled with peddlers, but this one was so very old. Walter hesitated about dismissing him. Besides he had asked for the lawyer. Perhaps he had some business, too.

Just then Shagarach's brisk step was heard in the entry, and the little man came flying across the room to his desk in the inner office.

"That is Mr. Shagarach?" asked the gray-beard, jerking his thumb and leering again.

"Walter," said Shagarach. Walter jumped and was preceding the visitor in when a terrible snarl of rage caused him to turn. The white-bearded old man seemed to have been transformed into a beast, glaring with his wild blue eyes and gritting his great teeth at Shagarach. He raised a bottle in his hand and hurled its contents at the lawyer. But Walter had caught his arm and pulled it down with all the might in his bourgeoning muscles. The liquor hissed where it fell, and several drops spattered on his neck and bosom, causing him to shrink as if touched with a caustic. Still he tore at the old man's face, and covered the mouth of the bottle with his palm so as to intercept the hot shower.

Shagarach had been looking down at some papers when he first heard the sound of the old man's breath forced between his teeth. As quick as thought he reached for the paper-weight and hurled it with all his force. It struck the stranger full in the forehead, cutting a ragged gash with its edge. Then the lawyer sprung from his chair, following up his missile with the quickness of a cat. But just as he reached across Walter's body the boy fell back in his arms with a shriek of pain, the stranger's white beard coming away in his fingers.

"The oaf!" cried Shagarach, but the assailant was gone in a flash.

"Water! Water!" shrieked the office boy, writhing in his arms.

The lawyer glanced around. The wainscoting was charred where the liquor had fallen. The boy's jacket was eaten away in holes. It was vitriol that had been thrown.

"A quart of lime-water at the nearest apothecary's," he shouted to Aronson, who had just come back. "And the first physician you can fetch. Don't lose a second."

Aronson was off like the wind, while Shagarach unbuttoned the boy's vest and tore away the saturated portions of his undergarments that were clinging to his shriveled skin. Already great blisters rose under the action of the acid.

"Will you telephone central 431, Inspector McCaus-land," he said to the tenant opposite who had been at-tracted in by the noise. "Ask him to call at once, and state that I have been attacked again."

It was the physician who arrived first, then Aronson. Walter's burns were bathed profusely with the lime-water, and the blisters pricked open by the doctor's needle. After the first agony he bore the pain without a groan. His breast and palm would be scarred for life, but the only wound on the visible parts was a long, pear-shaped cor-rosion extending along the side of his neck. You may imagine how tenderly Shagarach nursed him and how ex-citedly Aronson ran to and fro fetching whatever was asked for.

"It is time this should be stopped," said McCausland, entering. But he was not alone. He held a great blood-hound in leash. "It was the same customer, I suppose? Can you give me any article belonging to the man? I picked up this in the doorway."

He held up a white wig.

"The false beard," cried Walter, holding it out from the stretcher on which they were bundling him.

"Better the blood drops," said Shagarach. "Search the stairs. He was wounded."

McCausland rushed out, his hound tugging strongly at the leash.

"Smell, Wolf, smell," they could hear him saying, and then a half-trip and a clatter down the stairs told that the dog had caught the scent and nearly pulled the inspector off his feet.

"I am glad it is no worse, Walter. The doctor will do all that skill can to soothe your pain. You have saved my life twice," said Shagarach, pressing the boy's hands, which were clasped over his bosom, where the lint lay on his burns. Gently the ambulance men carried him down the stairs, with never a cry from his brave lips tightened over the sound.

"I will call to-night, Walter. May you be better then," said the lawyer, giving the driver Mrs. Riley's address.

The physician climbed into the spare seat and the wagon drove off with its suffering passenger.

"A cap, a coat button and a false beard," said Shagarach. "And still we grope in the dark. Yet an anatomist will reconstruct a mastodon from a fragment of his tooth!"

"Lost again," said McCausland, re-entering with his bloodhound, which nosed about in corners of the room. The inspector sat down, puffing and looked thoroughly disgusted.

"You lost the trail?"

"Never fear Wolf for that. Lie down, Wolf! No; the hound kept his track through all the cross-scents of the city—something to boast of, that—there was blood dripping here and there, that I knew by his yelping. By the way, you must have struck him hard."

"The paper-weight is heavy," said Shagarach, picking it up from under the desk where it had rolled. As he did so the hound gave a roar and a bound, and stood up to reach it with his forepaws.

"Down, Wolf! Lie down!" cried McCausland, sternly. "There is blood on the edge. That may help us another time."

"Take it," said Shagarach. "But you lost the trail, you said."

"It vanished into the air. Wolf took us to the northern station, running me off my feet all the way—through the waiting-room, up and down the platform twice, inside track gate No. 5, and then—flatted fair and square. You know the random way he runs about when he's lost the scent? Our man had taken a train."

"The western express, 12:59," said Shagarach.

"How did you know?"

"I have had occasion to take the same train at track No. 5 on a visit to Woodlawn. Had he purchased a ticket?"

"No man with a cut on his face, or of our description."

"Then he has a trip ticket and lives there."

"Where?"

"At Woodlawn," said the lawyer. "Near Harry Arnold."

McCausland smiled incredulously.

"Is Woodlawn the only station between here and Albany?" he asked. "However, I telegraphed along the route to have the runaway stopped."

"What time did you send the telegram?" asked Shagarach.

"At 1:19 by the station clock."

"Just a minute too late. The express reaches Woodlawn at 1:18. It is the first station."

"Heigho! Here's a to-do. What about Woodlawn?" asked a cheerful voice. It was Dr. Jonas Silsby, brown as a berry, with a broad-brimmed straw hat and a basketful of botanical specimens under one arm. The casual observer would have taken him for an uncommonly good-looking farmer, bringing some choice greens to market.

CHAPTER XLI.

A HUT IN THE FOREST.

"Who's talking of Woodlawn? Just where I came from, and if the fronds of those ferns aren't as fine-cut as petals, then I don't know an oak from a gooseberry bush."

"Dr. Silsby—Inspector McCausland."

The men clasped hands

"Didn't meet a maniac with a gash in his forehead on the way back, did you?" laughed McCausland.

"Maniac—well, no; but I've rooted out a peeping Tom there, that's been frightening the women."

"How was that?" asked Shagarach.

"It was those ferns did it. Aren't they beauties, though? Feel! Silky! Maidenhair! Rare variety."

"They helped you find the peeping Tom?" said Shagarach, who knew the botanist's tendency to forget.

"Oh, yes," said Dr. Silsby. "I was just about to tell

that story. You know the hemlock forest back of the blue hills in Woodlawn—marshy place thereabouts, lots of clay in the soil—some of it on those boots, eh? Well, those ferns came from there. Didn't walk in of themselves, I guess. No, I had to wade for them. Pretty boggy, but not quite up to the Dismal swamp. Well, I was feeling about, pulling up things, when I came on the hut."

"A hut?"

"I call it a hut by courtesy. Begging your pardon, said I, and tumbled in the sides of it. Hadn't any door that I could see—only two loose boards—and was mighty poor carpenter work all over. Just a roof and three sides, the whole thing backed against a pudding-stone ledge that juts out into Hemlock lake."

"Had it an occupant?" asked Shagarach.

"Three squirrels," answered Dr. Silsby, "investigating a can of corn."

"Nothing else?"

"Some old newspapers, a blanket, a stool and a mighty ugly collection of instruments, I tell you, including this article, which I confiscated."

He removed a pistol which lay at the bottom of his basket, handling the specimens as carefully as if they had been wounded kittens.

"Is it loaded?" asked McCausland, taking it in his hand and unhinging the butt. The backs of three cartridges stared out from the cylinder.

"You kept the second bullet, Shagarach, I believe," said McCausland, removing a cartridge. Shagarach rolled out a flattened bullet from a pen box in his drawer.

"Same caliber," said McCausland. "This looks like the pistol that was aimed at you that evening."

"So you know peeping Tom, then?" asked Dr. Silsby.

"Mr. McCausland and I have two of the three bullets that round out his pistol's complement," answered Shagarach, "and the third is lodged in my ceiling at home too deep for the probe to reach."

"I thought the hut had a human atmosphere. There

were fresh tracks around, and the station-master spoke to
me about a scoundrel that's been frightening the country-
folks—frightening them by running away from them, as
far as I could see. But you don't suppose he was fern-
gathering down in that swamp, do you?"

"Hardly," said McCausland. "Could you take us there
now?"

"Now? I've my lecture at Hilo hall—A Study in In-
gratitude; or, the Threatened Extinction of the Great
Horned Owl."

"It is an important piece of evidence in the Floyd case,"
said Shagarach, though McCausland still smiled incredulously. "We want the occupant of that hut."

"Robert's case. Command me," said Dr. Silsby. "Sorry
Mr. Hutman wasn't at home when I called. I'd have had
him here dead or alive."

"Wolf!" said McCausland. The great dog started up,
wagging his tail. "Smell." He offered him the revolver.
butt. The hound barked and smelled his way to the door
again, but McCausland pulled him back.

"It is our man," he said, thrusting the paper-weight in
his pocket.

"My pathfinder, Aronson," said Shagarach, who sprung
to his desk.

"The next train for Woodlawn doesn't leave till 4:03."

"We can go more quickly by team," said McCausland.
"I will have one here in ten minutes."

Then he departed with his hound, and Shagarach sent
Aronson to announce at Hilo hall that an imperative
summons compelled the defender of the great horned owl
to neglect for once the cause of that calumniated biped.

"This is where I left the road," cried Dr. Silsby, an hour
later. "A good, smart journey lies before us."

It's uncertain when we'll return," said McCausland to
the driver. "Probably not before 6 at the earliest. You'd
better drive home. We'll take the train into town."

The driver wheeled his team and drove away, while the
party of three—Shagarach, McCausland and Silsby—
crossed a bush-skirted meadow with the bloodhound still

in leash. But they were not destined to remain long unattended. The curious folk had got wind of their intention to unearth the peeping Tom, and the sight of an officer in buttons emboldened many to follow in their wake. Several men offered to help in the search, and McCausland did not refuse their assistance.

"The more the merrier," he said, whereupon not only men but women trailed behind them.

Among these followers was one young woman, familiar to two of the three leaders of the party.

"Good evening, Miss Wesner," said Shagarach and McCausland almost together, and the great inspector was not above entertaining that somewhat vulgar curiosity many of us feel as to the relationship of any chance couple we meet. For Miss Wesner was attended by an exceedingly attentive young man. Courting? Engaged? Married? The question rises as naturally as a bubble in water. In this case the truth lay midway. What more natural than that she should spend her afternoon off with Hans Heidermann at the picnic park in Woodlawn?

"Now you've left the cheap bombast of the town behind you," said Dr. Silsby, looking at the great trees as if he would embrace them one and all. "Isn't this grand? Isn't this Gothic? Pillars, gloom, fretted roof—don't tell me art's cathedrals are any improvement on nature's."

The bloodhound interrupted his rhapsody.

"We may leave Dr. Silsby behind, if he chooses, as well as the town bombast," said McCausland. "We shall not need his guidance any farther. Wolf has caught the trail again."

Two or three times on the march the inspector had held the glass paper-weight out so that the dog might smell the blood-clot on its edge. His joyful bark and eager straining at the leash announced that he had scented the fugitive.

"Not I," said Dr. Silsby.

Pulled on by the hound, McCausland and his two companions were soon trotting far ahead of the plodding laggards behind them. Their talk had died away. The heart of each was tense. Not a sound broke the mid-forest silence save the harsh screams of purple jays resenting their intrusion, and the snapping of twigs and branches.

"There are the ferns," said Dr. Silsby.

"Are we near?" asked McCausland.

"Within a hundred yards, I should say. This is the hemlock grove."

"Step on the moss. It will deaden our footfalls," said the detective. "Slow, Wolf, slow!"

He reined in the impetuous animal as best he could and his companions crept behind him softly.

"I see it," whispered Shagarach, pointing through the trees. It was nearly 5 o'clock and the light was beginning to slant more dimly through the aisles of the forest. But following his finger, the eye of the detective made out a rude shelter, sharply distinct by the smoothness of its boarded walls from the rough bark surfaces around. It seemed to lean against the steep ledge which Dr. Silsby had described and the roof derived most of its support from the projecting arms of two great trees whose roots spread up into the crevices of the rock. Osiers and strong withes took the place of nails, and the chinks were stopped with moss. No log cabin or camper's shed was ever more roughly joined. It had every appearance of being recent and temporary.

"We must surround it," said McCausland. The loud barking of the hound, re-echoing in the stillness, had betrayed their presence to the occupant. Shagarach and Dr. Silsby stationed themselves each at one side, the former empty-handed, the latter clubbing his stout cane. McCausland waited for the followers to arrive through the woods, but most of them hung back at a safe distance, only three or four of the men coming close to the besiegers.

"Who is inside there?" asked the detective loudly.

The silence succeeding his question was intense and prolonged.

"We have come to take you in the name of the law, and we will take you, living or dead," said the detective. There was no response but the rustling of the leaves. Song-birds were few in the deep recesses, and these few had been frightened from their nests. A creeping fear entered the hearts of the ring in the background and they edged farther away. For the gloom was gathering swiftly. Only one patch of sky was visible, above the steep ledge, and that lay toward the darkening east.

"I prefer that he should be taken alive, if possible," said Shagarach in a low voice to the detective. The latter gave three strong raps with a bough on the trunk of a mighty tree, then cried again to the secreted fugitive:

"Once more, I will state our errand. We are officers of the law. You are wanted for the murderous attacks you have made on Meyer Shagarach——"

A hoarse snarl of rage burst from within the hut, causing some of the distant spectators to turn in alarm. But it angered the bloodhound, as the spur a proud horse, and with an answering roar he burst loose from his leash and sprung at the hut, forcing a loose plank in with his impetus. Then a sharp tool was seen to descend in the opening—apparently an adze—and the hound's head sunk under the blow. He leaped from side to side in agony, and as he ran back whining to his master the blood dripped into his eyes from a hideous wound that had bared the bone of the skull. McCausland swore furiously and the lingering shadow of a smile vanished from his face. He unwound the rope which he had brought along and secured one circle of a double handcuff to his left wrist.

"We'll march home Siamese fashion or my name is Muggins," said the inspector, between his teeth. Then he began gathering brushwood in a heap before the hut.

"What are you at, man?" cried Dr. Silsby.

"Smoke him out," said McCausland.

"And fire these woods? Are you crazy?" The botanist was greatly excited.

"Confound your woods! Good Wolf! Poor Wolf!" said the inspector, alternately petting the hound, who, amid all his pain, licked his master's hand, and throwing fagots on his pyre.

"But—but—name o' conscience, man," stammered Dr. Silsby. "This is the finest hemlock grove this side of the White mountains."

"We could demolish the walls, I think," said Shagarach, "and capture him with a rush."

"Where are the axes?" asked McCausland.

"Poles will do." There were heavy boughs and light saplings lying about, which would make excellent impromptu crowbars. Without a word Shagarach seized one of these and wedged it into the crack between two of the boards. The roar of rage within told them the occupant was watching.

"Fall to!" said McCausland, scattering his brush-heap with an angry kick. The three men began prying the boards apart. Several of them creaked and gave way, and soon nearly the whole front lay in ruins.

"Surrender!" cried the inspector, pointing his revolver into the cave-like gloom. There was no reply. The three men peered in, then entered. The hut was empty!

CHAPTER XLII.

THE SECRET OF THE POOL.

Suddenly a shout from the onlookers behind called them back to the breach.

"The roof!" they cried. "He is climbing out by the roof!"

McCausland and Silsby stepped back to see the top of the hut, while Shagarach rushed in once more and reached at the ceiling with his bough.

There on the top of the hut, his body half emerging where the planks had been shoved aside, McCausland for the first time saw the long-missing oaf, and Dr. Silsby his peeping Tom. But Shagarach was groping within, vainly smashing upward in the darkness.

With wonderful strength the fugitive raised himself erect, sprung from the insecure footing of the slippery boards, and began clambering up the ledge.

"After him, Wolf!" cried McCausland, and the bloodhound, nerved by his tones, tore up the ledge in the monster's wake. McCausland and Silsby clambered as best they could on all fours, and presently Shagarach, hearing the outcry, followed them. The crack of the inspector's revolver was heard once, but the fugitive had turned like lightning and hurled his adze. McCausland uttered a sharp cry as the pistol was struck from his hand. The fugitive then stood for a moment on the crest, twenty feet above them, outlined in hideous distinctness against the pale patch of sky. But, espying the hound at his heels, he had given a mad plunge, and the onlookers, who had drawn nearer, heard a heavy splash behind the ledge. The bloodhound paused at the summit.

"After him, Wolf!" urged McCausland, and the dog's plunge was heard, as heavy as the man's.

"It is a pool," said Shagarach, gazing into the black water below him.

"Hemlock lake," answered Dr. Silsby. "The land beyond it is marshy for miles."

"And no boat?" asked McCausland.

"One at the upper end, a mile or so, kept by a farmer."

"Then it all depends upon Wolf," muttered the detective. The water side of the precipice afforded no stair for descent, and the party slowly picked its way down the ledge which it had climbed, and made a circuit, so as to stand on the grassy edge of the pool.

"Wolf!" cried McCausland. The dark heads of man and dog had long vanished from sight. No answer came but the night sighing of the trees that fringed the dark lake. A pale quarter-moon arose in the open sky and lent a translucent gloss to its opaque surface. The swallows twittered high in air, reduced to the size of a bee-swarm. But the lake gave back no tale of the two that had entered it.

"Wolf!" cried McCausland, again and again. He whistled till the woods echoed. He clapped his hands with a hollow reverberation. A plash close by startled the listeners. But it was only a pickerel rising to his food or a bullfrog plunging in. Again the mysterious terror invaded the hearts of the pursuers, and the women clung nearer to the men, clutching their bosoms.

Had man and dog reached the other side in safety, there to continue their terrible race? Had they fought their death struggle in the water, and one or both of them sunk to his doom? Who could tell? The lake guarded its secret.

"It is dark," said Shagarach, but McCausland lingered on the bank, shading his eyes with his right hand. In his left the empty handcuff clanked.

"We have failed," said Dr. Silsby. Then McCausland started with a jerk.

"To-morrow," he said. "To-morrow may tell."

"The way back will be hard to find," said Shagarach.

"Light these," said Dr. Silsby, cutting a pitch-pine bough. It blazed up almost at the touch of a match, and as the others followed his example the forest was strangely illuminated, weird shadows playing about the party. One coming upon them might have taken them for some brigand band en route to their mountains with plunder.

"We'll miss the guidance of the hound going home," said Shagarach, and the women shuddered at the prospect of being lost in the forest at nightfall. It was an unfrequented place. But there were boys present whose holiday ramblings might now be turned to good account.

"Yes, we shall miss Wolf," said McCausland, looking behind him, as if still hoping for a signal from his faithful hound.

"Let us explore the hut," proposed Shagarach, entering.

"And tear it to pieces," cried Dr. Silsby.

Instantly the roof was torn from the rude pile, and its

remaining timbers, hardly more than rested on end, almost fell asunder of themselves. A strange heap was revealed by the flickering torches. A stool, a sheet of tin laid over a clam-bake oven, some cans of prepared food, half-empty, an old coat, a blanket and a collection of knives, spikes and other weapons, picked up or stolen, that would have made a formidable array in the belt of a pirate. One of the lads, who had lighted a dry rush for a torch, was about to touch off the newspapers that lay about in great profusion, when McCausland sharply checked him.

"Bundle those up," he said, and the boys obeyed, while the inspector curiously scanned one of them by Dr. Silsby's torch.

"I thought so," he cried in triumph, motioning to Shagarach. "This is dated, like the others, only two days back—a New York paper again. The ——" he pointed to the name. "He knew where to look for sensations, you see."

"A vitriol-throwing case?" asked Shagarach.

"Read it for yourself," said the detective.

"At my leisure. We may as well start."

"Has any one a compass?" asked McCausland.

"Nonsense," replied Dr. Silsby. "Do I need a compass with the flora to guide me? There is the fern bed ahead of us, and, by the way, I think I'll gather a few more specimens."

"Not now, doctor," remonstrated Shagarach, and the frightened women echoed him.

"Tut, tut," said the botanist. "Have I slept out o' night in the woods since I was so high to be frightened by a little miscalculation of time? Who asked you to come?" he said to the followers, and the coolness with which he rooted up several ferns actually reassured his timid companions. "I'll take your newspapers to wrap them in," said he to one of the boys, but McCausland interposed.

"Something else, doctor."

"My hands, then," said the botanist, cheerfully. And

in fact he guided them out by his trained remembrance of the vegetation he had passed almost as quickly and surely as the hound had led them in by his scent.

It was then Miss Senda Wesner proved to Shagarach that for all her reputation as a chatterbox she could be prudent on occasion. For she selected a moment when Shagarach was bringing up the rear, to slip off the arms of her escort and pluck the lawyer's sleeve.

"Do you know who he was, Mr. Shagarach?" she asked.

"Who?"

"The crazy man, I saw him plainly on the top of the rock. It was the peddler in the green cart that used to come to Prof. Arnold's."

* * *

CHAPTER XLIII.

AN OLD SINGING SOLDIER.

"What will remind me of the summer while you are away, dear?" Robert had said to Emily one morning, little thinking that the sweet girl would treasure the saying for a whole day and end with a pitiful accusation to herself of "selfishness" for leaving him. Could she have consulted her own wish she would have put off the excursion then and there, but a stateroom had already been booked in the Yarmouth, Beulah Ware was looking forward joyfully to the trip and Dr. Eustis' orders had been imperative. So good Mrs. Barlow sensibly stamped her foot at the notion of her daughter's withdrawal and the maternal fiat went forth finally and irrevocably that Emily must go.

But Emily determined that while she was away the bare cell in murderers' row should not wholly lack touches of the midsummer of whose passing glories Robert, their loyal votary, was cruelly denied a glimpse.

And so one day the carpenter came and plotted off a

space over a foot wide at the side of the cell, and the florist followed with a load of beautiful long sods rolled up like jelly cake, and little potted plants all in bloom. And the sods were laid down in the trough the carpenter had made, and places scooped out with a trowel for the roots of the plants, and presto, there was a flower bed all along the side that got the sunshine, for Robert's window faced toward the south.

There were twiggy verbenas and fuchsias of tropic coloring, the nappy-leaved rose geranium, less highly rouged than its scarlet-flowered sisters, and blue oxalis along the border, plaintively appealing for notice with its spray of tiny stars. And lest these should not insinuate the odor of the country sufficiently into Robert's senses a pot of sweet basil was suspended from the ceiling to give out fragrance like the live coal in an acolyte's censer. Robert had complained of sleeplessness. What was better for this than a pillow stuffed with prunings of a fir-balsam at night and a sweet-clover cushion by day, when he sat at his table and wrote down his thoughts on "The Parisian Police Theory of Concentration of Crime," or some other such momentous topic.

But the last day, when the finishing touch had been placed on this narrow bower, over which the shadow of the scaffold so imminently hung, while Emily was sprinkling the beds with her watering-jar, Robert had laid aside his pen and was drawing forth sweet music from the violin.

"How divine it will be, Emily," he said. "The ocean sail and the week at beautiful Digby!"

"I wish you were coming, Robert," she answered, sadly.

"We may arrange a voyage in September. That is the month of glory in the provinces."

Robert had never admitted entertaining a doubt as to his acquittal. It must have been the confinement and the ignominy that had worn him down and converted his nights into carnivals of restless thought.

"But I will be with you in imagination," he added,

while Emily silently poured the fine spouting streams over thirsty leaf and flower. Poor little green prisoners! They, too, would miss the air and the sunshine and, perhaps, would reproach her, when she returned, with wilted stalks and withering petals.

While she hung her head a far-away voice stole over the high jailyard wall, through the narrow cell window, into the lover's ears. It was a tenor voice, not without reminiscences of bygone sweetness, though worn, and still powerful as if from incessant use. Something in its tones told the listeners that it was no common youth of the city trolling a snatch. For when do such sing, except in derision of song, with grating irony that is ashamed of the feelings to which true song gives expression? We are ashamed of our best impulses and proud of our worst, we cynical city folk! But this was a street singer, a minstrel, musical and sincere. Straining their attention, the lovers caught here and there the import of this ballad. Or was it a ballad repeated by rote? Was it not rather a recitative improvised as the impulse came, both words and music?

He sang of the southward march of armed battalions. Their ranks were full, their banners untattered, and the men shouted watchwords of joy when they beheld the battle-ground before them. A great chieftain stood mounted and motioned them into place with his brandished sword. Grant! Grim Grant! They echoed his name. Then came the thunder of artillery from distant hills, and the lines of the enemy's rifles were seen glistening as they advanced. The defenders did not linger, but rushed forward to meet them and their embrace was the deathlock of Titans. Hurrah, the chivalry of the south give way! It is cavalry Sheridan who routs them! Then the sun stood at its meridian. It was the noon of all glory, for the northern crusaders, doing battle in the just cause. Oh, the chase, the rallies, the heroic stands, and the joyful return, with plunder! But the corpse-strewn field checked their paean. Sire and son lay clasped in death, facing each other. The garb of one was gray, of the other blue. Ambulances issued empty from the hospital tents, and rode back groaning with the wounded. Nurses knelt with water cups at the dying hero's side. And until night closed over, sorrow mingled with joy in that bivouac by the fresh-fought field.

A loud salvo of applause told that the singer was done. Emily could see in her mind's eye the ring at the sidewalk edge, arrested in the course of meaner thoughts or idle vacuity by his heart-moving story. The gift of Homer, in a humble degree, was his; and men to-day are not unlike what they were 3,000 years ago. Robert had long since hushed his violin and stood with bow suspended in air.

"Emily!" he said in a strange tone.

She looked at him and started. He was eying her so eagerly.

"Emily!" he repeated.

The bow dropped from his hand. He reached forward as if he would touch her.

"What is it, Robert?" she asked.

"The water-lily. You are still wearing it?"

"Still wearing it, Robert. I put it on this morning."

Robert uttered a cry.

"It comes back! It comes back!" he said. "The old singing soldier that I met at the park gate. He is blind and wears a brown shade over one eye. His hair is white when he takes off his cap and passes among the crowd. I see him again! I see it all!"

Robert's gaze was far away. He was not looking at Emily, yet he heard her voice.

"When was this all, Robert?"

"That day, the day of the fire. I could not remember before."

She repressed a throb of joy. Was it indeed returning? God was good. He had at last answered her prayers.

"And the water-lily, Robert?"

"Do you not remember, Emily, that I brought you one that evening? It was the first of the season, I told you."

"I do—I do!"

"Search out the old gardener, who lives in the lodge at the west angle of the park. He will remember. 'This is the first of the season,' he said. He will remember the date. He will have kept some memorandum."

"And you talked with him, Robert?"

"We are friends of old. He will remember the incident—our stroll into the glen where the little pond glistens, my noting the one white flower floating among the pads, our poling the flat-bottomed boat from the bank and the courteous speech of presentation he made. 'For your sweetheart,' he said. Oh, it is as plain to me now as the sound of my own voice, Emily. How could I ever have forgotten?"

"It is Providence who sent us the old singing soldier," said Emily. "Let us thank Him for His mercy."

Then Robert ran over detail after detail of that afternoon, when he rambled from the house, burdened with the fresh grief of his uncle's death—seeing little, hearing little, mechanically following a familiar route, all his outer senses muffled, as it were. The great shock of the calamity when he came home late at night had canceled even the feeble impressions that lingered, and not till the voice of the old singing soldier came to his ears once more was the impediment removed.

Now the events rushed upon him, few in number, but clearly, microscopically outlined. The sight of the lily brought up the image of the gardener. He could no longer be suspected of hiding himself after the fire or of secret escape with confederates, or of other conduct that might require concealment and a mask of affected forgetfulness.

"The last link of his chain is broken," said Emily, joyfully, meaning, no doubt, the great inspector's. This happy turn of affairs reconciled her more than anything else to her vacation trip, and it was a gladsome farewell the sweethearts took that day.

On her way through the city she heard again the chant of the old singing soldier and a gush of gratitude impelled her to follow him. He was indeed blind and wore the brown shade as Robert had described. A little girl clung to his coat and guided him when he walked, and the cap he held out bore the initials of the Grand Army and was ribboned with silver cord. The bystanders stared at the sweet-faced lady who laid a bill in the maiden's hand and hurried off without waiting for her "Thank you," hurried off to acquaint Shagarach of the glad, good news.

It was not until she reached the upper flight of the office stairs that she remembered that it was Shagarach's suggestion that she wear a pond-lily now and then so as to start if possible the clogged wheels of her lover's recollection, as we shake a stopped watch to make it go.

There was a similar case, too, in "The Diseases of Memory."

"But it was heaven," she said, "that brought us the old singing soldier."

CHAPTER XLIV.

THE OCEAN NIGHT.

"Tristram!"

The artist started at his sister's voice. He had been lounging over the steamer's side watching a full-rigged ship in the offing. Its majestic sails glistened as white as snow, but the heaving motion from bow to stern was apparent even at that distance. For the sea was all hills and hollows, and the Yarmouth herself lay darkened under the shadow of a cloud.

"Let me break in on your reverie. This is my brother —Miss Barlow—Miss Ware."

"We shall have a storm," said Tristram, after the formalities.

"Oh, I hope not," cried all three ladies. They had become acquainted while watching the patent log on the saloon-deck stern, which Beulah Ware, who knew almost everything, had explained for Rosalie's information.

"It was due when we started," said Tristram.

"And you never told me," cried Rosalie.

"You would have postponed the trip, my dear."

"Make everything tight," came the cheery voice of the captain. "Get your wraps on, ladies. It's going to pour in a hurry."

"Do let us remain outside," cried Beulah. "I've nothing on that will spoil, under a waterproof."

The others assented, and Tristram and Beulah disappeared for a few moments, returning with mackintoshes and rubber cloaks.

"There, you look like fisher folk," said Tristram, when the ladies had pulled the cowls of their glazed garments over their heads.

"And romantic for the first time, I suppose," said Rosalie. "Tristram is a great stickler for barbarism, you know."

"Esthetically," said Tristram.

"He has positive ideas."

"Of negative value."

The rain had begun to spatter the deck beneath them and the cool wind was working its own will with their garments. They were almost alone on the quarter-deck. An officer eyed them loftily.

"That is the first mate," said Tristram.

"How can you tell?" asked Rosalie.

"Because he is so far off. The captain is always approachable. The first mate is rather distant, the second mate more so. The third mate is rarely visible to the naked eye."

"Hear that bell," cried Emily.

A ding-dong clangor resounded through the ship.

"Supper! All hands to supper!" piped the steward. "Early supper! Captain's orders! Early supper!"

"Hang the captain's orders!" said Tristram. "This is better than supper."

But the foamy crest of a great wave that was level with

the bow was caught just then by the wind and hurled up in their faces. The ladies sputtered, drenched with the spray, and the water seethed at their feet. Of course they shrieked and there was nothing for it but to descend and repair to their staterooms to prepare for the supper.

The dishes were clattering and dancing like marionettes. Capt. Keen had acted wisely in ordering an early supper. If the sea increased it would soon be impossible to eat at all.

"Isn't this superb?" cried the enthusiast again, as the vessel perceptibly rose under them, but she fell so suddenly that he probably bit his tongue. At least for a moment his eloquence abated.

"Now to go above again," he said when at last the tipping of the dishes made satisfactory eating no longer possible. "What a rare quality portability is! The portable arts—music and poetry; the portable instruments—fiddles, flutes, etc.; the portable eatables (excuse the unhappy jingle)—oranges, bananas, biscuits."

Suiting the word to the action, he laid in a liberal supply himself and pressed as much more on each of the ladies. He was not so unpractical as he seemed, our friend Tristram, with all his badinage and transparent sophistries.

"But you are not seriously going out on deck?" cried his sister in some alarm, when he made for the stairs.

"And surely you are not going to remain in?" answered Tristram in feigned astonishment. "Lose this glorious sea picture? Atmosphere, nature's own murk; canvas, infinity; music furnished by old Boreas himself, master of Beethoven and Rubinstein; accompaniments, night, sleet, danger and the lightning."

"I fear we are philistines," said Beulah Ware; "we prefer painted storms and the mimic thunders of the symphony."

"Accompaniment, dry dresses," added Rosalie. Whereupon Tristram gallantly saw the ladies housed in his sister's cabin and left them, lunching on his portable eatables, but not a little anxious while he himself climbed up to his perch on the quarter-deck. The sea tumbled over the steamer when she cut her way into a billow, but Tristram had drawn on thick boots and felt prepared to rough it.

"Better lash yourself down," cried the captain warningly. The artist's answer was lost in the tempest.

There was little sleep for the passengers on the Yarmouth that night. Stewards and matrons passed about reassuring them. The boat was seaworthy; everything was locked in; they could lie on their pillows with an absolute certainty of rising on the morrow with the Nova Scotia shore in view. Only they wouldn't. They dared not. And as Rosalie looked as timid as any one, her new acquaintances conspired to remain with her in her stateroom, all three sharing the two cots and getting what naps they could.

They had run out of talk and were almost drowsing when the great crash came. Have you felt your heart jump when a pistol-shot smites the silence? No crack of land ordnance could inspire the fear that resounding bump did in the breasts of the apprehensive girls.

"A rock!" was the thought of each, but they only expressed their terror in an inarticulate shriek. Then the whimpering of women and the cries of men were heard in the saloon.

"We are sinking!" cried some one, and the girls rushed out. A hundred white-clad forms darted to and fro like gnats in a swarm, or clung together, wringing their hands in misery. Some of the men fought to unbar the doors. But they were bolted from the outside. The whole cabin was penned in there to drown. Then each one felt for his dearest.

"Tristram!" moaned Rosalie, knocking at his stateroom door. "Tristram!" But there came no answer. "He is out on the deck! He is swept away and drowned!" she cried, with truer tears than the imagined sorrows of Desdemona had ever drawn from her eyes. But Tristram was safe in the pilot's box, where Capt. Keen was signaling the engineer to reverse his engines; and the engineer, shut in amid the deafening clangor of his machinery, ignorant of what had happened but trained to his duty, obeyed promptly his bell and forced the great vessel back.

The headlights of the Yarmouth had been doused out long before, and there was no lantern that could live in that surge, even if it were possible to hang a second one aloft. From time to time the captain had ordered a rocket sent up, to warn approaching vessels, for the air was densely opaque. Only out of the gloom before them, just before the shock came, Tristram could see a long row of lights, feeble and flickering. His imagination constructed the broadside of a steamship about them and once it seemed that he really did catch a vague, shadowy outline. But the reality became certain to another sense. Before the Yarmouth's engines were reversed and her bow disengaged itself, a wail of terror reached him out of the night, and a tearing as of parted timbers. Then hoarse shouts were heard from the emptiness soaring high above the wind.

"We stove in her side," said the captain. Then a signal rocket, hissing into the quenching rain, told him of his fellow's distress. The Yarmouth still receded. The double row of lights was withdrawn into the gloom. But the wailing increased and from the covered cabin below rose the responsive clamor of the passengers.

"Say that we have struck a vessel," telephoned the captain to the steward. After several repetitions the message was understood and it quieted the half-clad throng a little. But anxiety was legible on every face.

Twice more the signal of distress went up and the captain answered it, though helpless to assist. Then the air was blank.

"Head her east," said the captain to the pilot. He knew by the lights that the other vessel was pointed to the larboard when she crossed his bow. He could not back forever or heave to in that sea. He must circumnavigate the vessel or the vortex if she were sunk. So he nosed his prow oceanward into the teeth of the wind. Under these circumstances the headway of his boat was slow.

"Ahoy!"

Was it a voice from the darkness? A huge wave rose over them like a cliff and hurled itself against the strong glass of the pilot's window. In a moment they were soused and the wind blowing in upon them told them that their brittle sheath was shattered. But the electric globes still cast their white gleams over the foredeck and revealed a dark object that was not there before.

"A boat!" cried Tristram.

"Save them!" shouted Capt. Keen, rushing down the steps, with the artist at his heels. It was indeed a lifeboat, which had been carried on the crest of a billow clear over the Yarmouth's gunwale and left high, if not dry. Only five forms could be seen—three of them stirring, the other two motionless. All were men.

"Climb!" shouted Keen, seizing one of the limp bodies in his arms. Tristram caught up the other and staggered back in the direction of the light, the three wrecked men following and grappling at them in their bewilderment. Another wave like the last and they were lost, all seven. But these great surges come in rhythmic intervals. Rescuers and rescued reached the pilot house in safety.

"Who are you, shipmates?" asked the captain, pouring brandy down the mouths of the unconscious men. The others answered in German.

"The Hamburg liner, Osric," translated Tristram. "She broke her rudder and was driven off her course by the gale."

"Heaven save us from meeting any more such driftwood," said the pilot unsteadily with a hiccough.

"Were any other boats out?" asked Capt. Keen. Tristram interpreted question and answer.

"Two others, but they were swamped. All on board are lost."

A thrill went through the strong men. Usage does not render sailors callous to the perils of the sea. Death under the ocean is still the most awe-inspiring of fates—

the doom of the irrecoverable body, of the skeleton lying on the bottom, like a coral freak.

"Mostly immigrants from Germany and Sweden," answered the spokesman to the next question. All five were common sailors. They had waited their turn and the captain had ordered them into the lifeboat when it came. He himself had stood by his sinking ship to the end.

In a lull of the breaking seas, Tristram and Capt. Keen picked their way down into the cabin. The captain's appearance was a signal for a cheer. He addressed the passengers briefly, outlined the terrible event and assured them that, as lightning never strikes twice in the same spot, they might turn in and count on a clear voyage oceanward for the rest of the night. He could not control the weather or promise them sleep. But he felt so safe himself that he had just come down to retire for his own spell of slumber.

This little lie was one of those which the recording angel will blot away with tears. The old salt would no more have slept that night than he would have taken a dose of poison. Even for the few minutes he was below he had been as uneasy within as a young mother when she sees her baby in the arms of some one whose carelessness she has good reason to dread. The pilot was in liquor, and Capt. Keen, making a quick tour aft so that every one might get a view of him and a cheery word, together with a brazen repetition of his salutary invention, simply turned into the cook's room forward and swung himself out by its skylight-hatch. Meanwhile Tristram elbowed his way through the crowd to Rosalie. His reappearance soothed her, but she was still hysterical, and the good offices of the other two ladies were found seasonable during the night.

CHAPTER XLV.

ON DIGBY SHORE.

Daylight rose, gray and hollow-eyed, on the Atlantic. The sun was merely a moving brightness in the sky. Ocean, the blind Titan, still heaved and roared, playing his part in some grander drama than ours of flesh and blood—ingulfing sailor or bark as we crush the poor gnat toward whom neither pagan sage nor Christian doctor enjoins mercy—cruel without enmity, indifferent without contempt, divider or uniter of continents according to his chance-born mood.

The storm had scarcely begun to die. But with a clear outlook forward it was possible once more for the sturdy Yarmouth to resume her course. With Capt. Keen himself at the wheel, she steamed into the narrow harbor of the little city whose name she bore, situated on the nearest eastward tip of the Nova Scotia peninsula, half a day late, but with her 300 passengers safe and sound.

Several days later, our party of four were peacefully rowing across the calm waters of Digby bay—that isleless harbor of purest ultramarine, where the Bay of Fundy has cloven its way through peaks still wooded to the water's edge and lifts and lowers its huge tides as far north as Annapolis, at the head of the valley of Evangeline. Chance would have it that this resort was the destination of the Marches as well as Emily and Beulah; and the acquaintance made on shipboard under such unusual circumstances was already ripening into something like friendship—perhaps more than friendship—between Tristram and Beulah Ware.

She was his opposite, his complementary color, as he said to Rosalie, and so she harmonized with him and perhaps comprehended him, as Rosalie at times did not. In only one thing did she agree with Tristram's sister. She misunderstood his irony; for her own speech was yea, yea.

"Let us cross over to the camp of the Micmacs," proposed the artist, resting on his oars.

"Are they real Indians?" asked Emily.

"Full-blooded. See their tepees." A cluster of conical tents could be seen rising from the dark foliage on the hillside. For Digby rises from the water with a slope like a toboggan slide all the way up to the white cottages on its crest.

"There is a specimen," said Tristram, as a canoe skimmed by them. "Isn't he noble? The great face, the grim mouth, the high cheek-bones, the straight hair—it is a bronze mask of Saturn. I may utilize him."

"When?"

"When I carve my life group for the Academy's grand prize."

"Have you chosen your subject?"

"Driftwood Pickers at the Sea Level."

Beulah Ware looked up. She had suggested it the day before, while strolling alone with the man of hazy purposes.

The boat was beached without difficulty and the ladies stepped ashore—Beulah Ware collectedly, as usual, but Emily and Rosalie as warily as you may have seen a lame pigeon alighting.

"Let us follow my leader," said Tristram, meaning the brown canoeist, who had shouldered his craft and was climbing the beach.

"What is that?" cried Emily, pointing to an object that was tossing on the sands.

"A body," said the others, recoiling, but Tristram walked in the direction indicated. It proved on closer inspection to be the body of a woman, stout and tall. Her long yellow hair floated in the surf, but the features were swollen beyond recognition. It was impossible to tell whether she was old or young. Only her clothing, which was thick and of foreign style, denoted a woman of the poorer class.

"Is it a body?" asked Rosalie, apparently doubting the evidence of her eyes. The quick assemblage of a crowd rendered an answer unnecessary. There were men and women watching all along the Nova Scotia coast in those weary days. Schooners and smacks had put out before the storm, perhaps to be blown far out of their course and suffer the hardships of hunger and shipwreck, perhaps to founder in midocean and never to return. So the body rolling in the surf at the water's edge had been espied by others before the party of four landed, and there was a converging stream of searchers from bush and cottage, and even from the lonely tepees.

"Search her pockets," said one, and the woman's dress was torn open. A packet of papers came out, but the ink had run and the paper was as soft as jelly.

"She has been in the water a week," cried another.

"Perhaps it is a body from the Osric," suggested a boy.

The party of four shrunk in greater horror. There were rumors of lifeboats that had been launched and swamped from the sunken steamer. Could one of the bodies have been carried up the Bay of Fundy on its swift-running tide, forced by a current through Digby Gut, and cast ashore on this unfrequented beach?

"See if her linen is marked?" asked a woman who held a baby. But the search proved fruitless. No stenciled initials, not even a brand on the shoes, to identify the unfortunate. A truck was suggested to carry her up to the town.

"One moment," said Tristram, "her ring may be engraved."

The slender gold circlet was deeply imbedded in the flesh, but a fisherman ruthlessly cut it loose with his knife. Tristram held it up to the light and read a name from the inside.

"Bertha Lund," he read.

Emily Barlow turned pale and glanced at Beulah Ware. If she could have looked across the ocean to the city just then and seen Inspector McCausland closeted

with the district attorney, she would have been confirmed in her fears. The detective was scanning a list of
the passengers on the Osric.

"Bertha Lund, Upsala, Sweden. That is her birthplace.
She was to return on the Osric," he said, uneasily.

"Then it must be she," answered the district attorney.
"It is most unfortunate. However, we have her testimony at the hearing. We do not rely solely upon her."

But Emily did rely solely upon Bertha's knowledge,
and her heart sunk within her. Without Bertha, there
was only Robert to describe the room as she wished it
described. And would people believe Robert in so novel,
so miraculous, a junction of circumstances as her theory
demanded?

"Read that again, please," she cried to Tristram.

"Bertha Lund," Tristram seemed puzzled a moment by
the third word, "Bertha Lund, Upsala."

CHAPTER XLVI.

TURNPIKE TOLL.

"So to-morrow is the day of the trial, Miss Barlow?"

Mrs. Riley was pinning the bandage on Walter's neck,
while Emily buttoned his jacket. She and the quondam
Whistler had become fast friends, especially since the day
of the struggle in Shagarach's office, and now that his
burns were healing and he was able to get out they had
arranged a Sunday afternoon excursion to Hemlock
grove, with some vague hope of visiting the site of the
demolished hut, if Walter's strength could carry him so
far. There would be no lack of guides, for the spot had
already become locally famous.

"Yes," answered Emily, "the talesmen have been sifted
down to twelve at last."

"May the good Lord put mercy in their hearts," prayed
Mrs. Riley.

"I wish it was a jury of ladies," said Walter.

"Why, ladies are never selected for the jury," cried his mother.

"Jurywomen is a word not yet included in the dictionaries," smiled Emily.

"But they are all so kind," said Walter simply, but in such a way that his mother and Emily might each take half of the compliment. The bright slum boy was already losing all trace of his plebeian associations, as the innate aristocracy of his nature asserted itself. How luckily he was placed, if he could have foreseen. To begin at the lower-most round of the ladder, but with the unconquerable instinct in him to climb; and so at last, on the topmost round, to have the whole of life for a retrospect.

Mrs. Riley bade them a proud good-by and watched them from her window boarding the car. The downtown ride on a Sunday is always curious, for the desertion of the usually crowded streets gives them a foreign appearance. Emily was commenting on this when Walter called her attention to something in the sky.

"Look, it's a man," he said, pointing almost vertically upward.

"Where?" she asked, leaning forward.

"On the top of the Amory building. He is calling for help."

The Amory building was the tallest structure in the city, the tenants in the sixteenth story enjoying a view that swept in the entire harbor and flattened the men walking in the avenues below to the dimensions of crawling flies.

"We can change cars here, Walter. Let us get off and see."

From the sidewalk Emily could distinguish the minute figure of a man leaning over the parapet around the roof, and shouting through his hands to attract attention.

"Perhaps it is on fire," she said in alarm, framing the thought that lay uppermost in her mind.

"I think he wants to get down," suggested Walter, although not a word of the man's vociferations could be heard.

"Let us speak to the policeman," said Emily, just as a large hat came sailing down on Walter's head. It crossed her mind that the broad brim had a familiar look. The patrolman followed her index finger with his glance and presently there was a knot of passers-by doing likewise. Then the knot grew to a crowd, and the crowd to a multitude. Meanwhile the officer had hunted up the janitor of the building and both entered through the great carved doors. About five minutes later they came down, with a heavily laden, portly gentleman, who seemed taken aback when the crowd hurrahed him.

"Dr. Silsby!" cried Emily. He looked about in surprise.

"Miss Barlow," he said, shaking his head, "here's a to-do. I suppose you'll go right over and tell that Rob."

"Tell him what?"

"Tell him I got lost in the heart of the city I was born in," grumbled the botanist so that she could hardly help laughing. "Well, what are you sniggling at?" he shouted at the crowd, who fell back a little at this.

"And were you lost up there?"

"Haven't had a bite to eat since yesterday noon. Made a call on that ninny, Hodgkins, about his confounded will. Judge is going to decide against him and we'll have our academia after all."

"Good! Good!" cried Emily, clapping her hands.

"Office on the sixteenth floor. Ninny was out. Took my specimens up to the roof. Got worked up. Scribbled notes for my new lecture on——"

"I know. Rob told me. On the beneficent activity of the great horned owl. How interesting!"

Dr. Silsby glared.

"Janitor missed me. Didn't notice the time. Locked out. Slept four hours all night, and now I'm hoarse from bawling ten. What's the matter with Sleepy Hollow? Are they all in bed?"

"Why, this is Sunday morning," explained Emily, repressing her merriment.

"They ought to have ladders up there, so a man could climb down," grumbled Dr. Silsby.

Walter thought this a somewhat unreasonable demand.

"You might have descended by the mail chute," said Emily, laughing outright, "and then the postman would have collected you just before breakfast."

The learned doctor made no reply, so they left him shuffling away in search of a restaurant.

"I do hope Judge Dunder will allow the will," she said; and it took the whole ride to explain the why of this hope to her eager auditor.

At Woodlawn they were directed to Hemlock grove and wandered among its dark trees, peace-breathing in themselves, but haunted for them by the vague pervasive shadow of a tragedy. The hut was too far for Walter's strength, so they turned off at an angle, following a foot-path which they knew would lead to some road. Once or twice they heard a murmur of voices, seeming to come from the left. It was very deep and indistinct and not unlike the mooing of a cow. But her bell would have tinkled if it had really been a stray tenant of the milk-shed.

"What is it, Walter?" asked Emily. It had sounded again, this time more humanly and close to their ears. They had been moving toward it unawares.

Walter only clutched her arm in answer.

"Look!" he said, and she saw his eyes white with distension of the lids. "It is the oaf."

Through a parting in the boughs Emily saw the sight. There was a little cemetery near by, unpretending but neat with scattered headstones. In the midst of it, kneeling with his forehead bared and his eyes up-lifted, was the human monster who had woven himself into their life so terribly. What was he doing? Should she run? Her first impulse was to fly, but a fascination held her. The oaf's face was averted and they were screened from his gaze.

Looked at now, the creature's countenance was less repulsive than she had thought. Emily had only seen it convulsed with murderous passion, and those who had described it to her had beheld it under similar circumstances. Yet at best it was horribly misshapen.

"Is he crying?" asked Walter. Strange to say, the oaf seemed to be shedding tears and the quick sympathy went out from Emily's bosom, in spite of the past.

"Hark!"

Emily pulled Walter back, as he leaned forward too eagerly to catch what he was saying.

The oaf moaned in a guttural tone that swelled to its close, crescendo. Then he threw himself on the mound before which he knelt.

It was a grave. No headstone covered it. The mourners of the dead who house there were either forgetful or poor. But strange little bunches of withered wild flowers were strewn upon it. And a heap of fresher flowers lay at one side. What was the monster doing?

With his fingers he scooped out hollows in the earth, then lifted the cut daisies and buttercups he had brought, with many a late violet and honeysuckle, and laid their stalks one by one in the cavities. Holding them in place, he propped them up with the loosened earth, till all along the narrow mound there was a bloom of red and yellow and blue. Then the oaf rose and looked down upon his work, with a childish pleasure.

"Does he think they will grow that way?" asked Walter, but Emily put her finger on her lips. The oaf began muttering in a low, indistinct murmur, like one soothing a child.

Suddenly he drew his soiled hands across his brow. The streaks of earth added to his hideousness and his expression had changed. Some new current of thought was in his mind. He ground his teeth, as Walter had seen him in Shagarach's office, and roared with fists clenched at some invisible adversary.

"Run, run," called Walter, dragging Emily with him along the little footpath—on, on. They could hear their own footsteps echoed behind, but the roars did not appear to be gaining on them.

"Faster! Faster!" urged Emily, as Walter weakened. The briers scratched her dress, the boughs brushed in her face, but what were these to the monster behind them? She dared not turn, lest his fierce eyes should be glaring into hers and his grimy hands clutch at her flying hair.

"I cannot keep up," cried Walter breathing hard, when they had covered a quarter of a mile.

"Oh, Walter, try!" cried Emily, dragging him in her turn.

"I cannot. I can only walk. He is not behind us," he added. Emily slowed up and peeped around timidly. The expected image did not confront her. The woods had a less lonely look here, but they were perfectly still.

"Have we escaped him?" she said, all flushed and out of breath. Without the wings of fear, she could not have run a third of the distance.

Walter held his breath to listen before he answered. There was not a stir in the woods save the sighing of the leaves.

"Let us walk on fast," he said, and Emily was glad to moderate her pace. But they had not proceeded twenty steps, when again she started off, dragging Walter by the hand. This time the sound was on their right. The oaf had crossed the path and was tearing through the woods. With the advantage of the smooth path they might outstrip him and get to the road, where succor could be had.

"Oh, I cannot go farther," cried Emily, fainting. "Leave me, Walter, and bring help as soon as you can." The elastic sinews of the boy had recovered their strength and he was now the fresher of the two.

"Only a little farther, Miss Barlow. I can see the road through the trees."

The pursuer seemed to have slowed his own pace to a walk. Once they caught a glimpse of his form. He was not aiming at them straight but slantingly toward the road, as if he would head them off. At present he was almost abreast and gaining.

"There is the road and a cottage," said Walter, but the pursuer was ahead of them now, running swiftly. They could see him leap the wall only ten paces off, just as they emerged from the footpath. Bewildered and spent, Emily turned the wrong way and ran straight into the arms of Mr. Arthur Kennedy Foxhall.

"Turnpike toll!" exclaimed the manikin, deliriously prolonging the accidental embrace, while Emily strove to tear herself away in a flurry of amazement, horror and disgust.

"Let her alone!" cried Walter, clutching at Kennedy's neck. But the manikin took no account of the boy, merely cuffing him over the ears, and endeavoring to force a kiss upon Emily.

"Forgive me, Emily—Miss Barlow," he said at last, while she stood flaming like a rose with indignation. "Forgive me if I press my suit too ardently——"

But he was not afforded an opportunity to continue his amorous speech. Walter Riley possessed a spirit which rose against cuffing. Weak and weary as he was, he drew off after a moment's survey, to get the import of the conversation, and sent the manikin spinning with a blow that brought blood drops from his nose. Kennedy felt the trickling organ in momentary confusion, but before his idol he could not show the white feather.

Whack! Whack! He brought his cane—bulldog end for a handle—down on the boy's shoulder, neck and head —bursting the bandages over his still acutely tender burns. Walter clinched, but Kennedy threw him off and continued his caning. Even Emily's intercession only brought her a smart rap over the fingers with which she tried to grasp his weapon.

"You brute!" she exclaimed, and threw herself between Kennedy and the boy. But help from another quarter was at hand. A tall, lithe form vaulted a neighboring wall and the swish of a horsewhip cut the air. It must have cut something else, for Kennedy hopped and turned, and presently was capering with as much agility as if the ground were redhot iron. Emily could hear the repeated swishes and the manikin's supplications, but she did not look up. She was stroking Walter's forehead. The boy had fainted in her arms.

"It's me, Harry. It's Kennedy. Don't you know me?" This cry caused her to turn.

"It's a coward. Run."

Emily had heard the voice only once before, in that eventful ride to Hillsborough; but she would have known Harry Arnold instantly from his photograph. How broad-chested he was! How superb! Yet there was something feverish in his excitement now. He came toward her, raising his hat.

"I have to apologize for a slight acquaintance with that blackguard, which led me to refuse at first to credit his conduct. Otherwise I might have been of assistance earlier."

"Slight acquaintance? You owe me twelve hundred and by George you'll pay it," snarled Kennedy, moving away. Harry never turned.

"The boy has fainted. He must come up to the house."

The "cottage" in view, then, was the Arnold house. A carriage stood in front of the terrace at the head of the gravel drive which led up from the turnpike. Harry had probably just arrived home from an afternoon spin through the suburbs.

"Thank you, Mr. Arnold——" Emily stopped, but the mischief was out. Harry had lifted the unconscious boy tenderly in his strong arms and was carrying him up the drive. He turned and smiled, showing his beautiful teeth, but, seeing Emily's confusion, did not speak the words that were on his lips. Inside the house he called for Indigo.

"Some wine," he ordered.

"And a little sweet oil, if you have it," added Emily; for the neck bandage had been torn away and the vitriol burn was bleeding from one of Kennedy's blows.

"This is Walter Riley," said Emily, at last recovering from her embarrassment, "Mr. Shagarach's clerk, who was assaulted about ten days ago."

She studied Harry's face as she bathed the tender part with the sweet oil and poor, sick-eyed Walter revived under the wine. But there was no expression other than one of surprise crossed with sympathy.

"And yourself, may I ask?"

"I am Miss Barlow."

Harry's astonishment reached a climax at this, but he was too well bred to display it.

"I am delighted to have you for my guest, Miss Barlow. It is unfortunate that my mother is not at home. We have both admired your efforts in behalf of Rob. And Miss March was just speaking of you."

By the time that Walter was ready to go home, Emily had fixed with feminine absoluteness her opinion about Harry's innocence.

But then she was under a heavy debt to Harry. He had rid her once for all of the impertinences of Mr. Arthur Kennedy Foxhall.

CHAPTER XLVII.

THE HEEL OF ACHILLES.

"I shall be compelled to alter my theory at one point," said Shagarach.

"Yet your general conviction remains unchanged?"

"Absolutely. Your cousin is capable of the crime. A powerful motive was present. We have traced him to the door of the room. What factor is wanting?"

"I cannot believe it of Harry," said Robert, shaking his head doubtfully. "But what has occurred to cause you to reconstruct your theory?"

"My interview with Dr. Whipple, his physician."

"Harry was ill at the time, I believe?"

"He is able to prove an alibi."

"A hard obstacle to get over," said Robert.

"But not insurmountable," replied the lawyer. "Dr.

Whipple happens to be the most methodical of men. 'At 3:48 p. m., on Saturday, June 28, I took Mr. Harry Arnold's pulse in his own room at Woodlawn,' said he, consulting his notes. 'It was eighty-three beats to the minute.' "

"Rather high," said Robert.

" 'Abnormal,' Dr. Whipple observed, 'something on his mind, I should say. Overexcitement, worry, the fever of modern life.' His diagnosis was incorrect; but the time is important. The fire was discovered, you remember, at 3:30."

"So Harry couldn't have set it and got to Woodlawn," said Robert, as if sincerely glad.

"Not in his mother's carriage, as I had surmised," said Shagarach. "But an express train leaves the Southern depot at 3:29. It arrives in Woodlawn at 3:45. Harry crossed Broad street from the passageway after setting fire to the study—it is barely a minute's walk—there caught the train and reached Woodlawn at 3:45. His house is close to the station. Dr. Whipple found him feverish and with rapid pulse from the excitement of his crime and the hurried escape."

"His mother stated, however, when she called, earlier in the afternoon, that she had left him at home ill," said Robert, thoughtfully.

"She is solicitous about his delicate health," said Shagarach, with almost imperceptible irony. The delicate health of the powerful canoeist, the victorious steeplechaser, need hardly weigh on the most tender mother's mind. This was their last consultation before the trial, and the lawyer shook Robert's hand with a word of encouragement when he left the young man to his hopes and forebodings.

The lawyer turned into a byway which carried him through the Ghetto.

Solomon and Rachel were sitting on their doorsteps, fanning away the heat of the August afternoon.

"There goes Shagarach," said some one.

"He who fawns on the gentiles," said another, "that he may obtain places from them."

"He is ashamed of his father's blood; he will deny his mother," was the taunt of a third.

"Who is it?" asked the boys, flocking up.

"It is Shagarach, who was called an apostate in the Messenger last week."

Jewish boys nearly all learn enough of Hebrew to read the characters. They understood the answer and passed it along to their comrades.

"Here comes Shagarach, who was printed among the apostates," they cried, edging near the lawyer, while the older folks prudently contented themselves with passing remarks.

Shagarach only turned a deaf ear and a pitying glance upon his misguided people. But as he chanced to look into the window of Silberstein's store, the first page of the Messenger, conspicuously spread out, attracted his attention, and he saw, under a black heading, among a list of "apostates" his own name, with the description "Gentile Judge." The malevolent features of Simon Rabofsky scowled at him from within, but were instantly withdrawn. Shagarach, however, stopped and rung the bell, while the circle around him stared in wonder. Was the pervert going into Nathan Silberstein's house?

There was a long pause before any one answered. The maid who finally came was wiping her hands on her apron.

"Good-evening, Mrs. Silberstein," said the lawyer. "I am Meyer Shagarach, of whom you have doubtless heard. I desire to see Simon Rabofsky, who, I perceive, is within."

A great flurry of moving chairs could be heard, as though the convocation was breaking up.

"Bid him not depart." Shagarach was already in the narrow entry, with the door closed behind him, and the stupefied woman in front. "Simon Rabofsky," he cried, after the form which was disappearing through a rear door. It stopped reluctantly.

"I wish to confer with you and with Moses Cohen. He is there. I saw him through the window. The others may go or stay, as they please."

Cohen and Rabofsky stood before Shagarach in the store.

"Sit down. Draw down the curtain," said the lawyer to Mrs. Silberstein, who with her husband and the others stood on the threshold listening.

"'Vengeance is mine,' saith the Lord. As an interpreter of the scriptures, you have met that text, Simon Rabofsky?"

"It is graven on my heart," said the money-lender, with unction.

"Liar, thief and hypocrite!" cried Shagarach, "you are as vindictive as the viper, who stings the hand of his benefactor. Our conference shall be short. I spare your white hairs before these people who respect you. See to it that I walk through this street unmolested and I may forbear for a time to punish you for the perjury you committed and the receipt of stolen articles."

"I had not known the people of Israel so far forgot their good teachings," said Rabofsky, "as to insult a peaceful passer-by, like the gentile ruffians."

"Go forth without excuses," said Shagarach sternly.

"I will gladly remind them," said the cowed usurer, leaving the room.

"Moses Cohen, you will retract and apologize in your next issue, or I shall prosecute the Messenger for slander."

"I have only told the truth," answered the young editor, doggedly. "You are no longer a Jew."

"I am always a Jew," said Shagarach. "Though I worship not with the ancient rites and forms, adapted for simple minds, my God is the God of my fathers and my heart is with my people. I value them, I love them, better than some who prey on their prejudices and wring ducats by pretended piety."

"But——" urged Cohen, stiff-necked and arrogant.

"I have spoken," said Shagarach. "You have slandered me. Retract."

When he left Silberstein's house the Ghetto was deserted. The people had fled within, and he saw Rabofsky far up the street, warning them with uplifted hands. Only two or three children, with eyes like jewels, played on the curbstone, innocent of the guile that comes with years. Shagarach lifted one of these in his arms and kissed her. "Good-by," lisped the baby, as he continued his walk.

Bitter tears came into the strong man's eyes.

That night he wrote late in his chamber; and though he was usually the earliest of risers, the next morning his mother knocked on his door repeatedly in vain.

"It is the trial day, my son," she said, loudly. Slowly he arose and rubbed his eyes. His clothing was dusty with the bedding lint. And when he came down to the breakfast table his look was mournful and abstracted.

CHAPTER XLVIII.

OYEZ! OYEZ!

"This is the gravest charge known to the law," said the district attorney, "and the man found guilty of it by a jury of his peers is condemned, under the statutes of this commonwealth, to be hanged by the neck until he is dead."

Dead! The solemn word reverberated through every listener's heart. The crowded court-room was hushed. The jurymen had just been contemplating their own portraits in the last newspaper which they would see for many days, and now bent forward in the first flush of eager attention. Court officers were carrying whispered messages to and fro. On the bench sat Chief Justice Playfair, silver-haired and handsome, between two of his judicial brethren. The case was considered of such importance that three judges had been assigned to decide upon the legal questions which might arise.

On the threshold of an ante-room Inspector McCausland was cordially shaking hands with Shagarach. In the front row of the spectators sat Mrs. Arnold, thin-lipped and cold, beside a sad-faced woman in black. She had bowed distantly to the prisoner—no longer fettered, but permitted to occupy a seat in the "cage" in full view—between Dr. Silsby and Emily Barlow, who had bravely elected to join him. Evidently he was not one of those who grow plump on jail regime and batten under the shadow of the scaffold. The young man's dark cheek was lean, his eyes unwontedly bright, but he never flinched from the district attorney's gaze.

"You have learned from the reading of the indictment," thundered the district attorney, stroking his patriarchal beard with one hand and holding his notes in the other, "that the immediate act committed by the accused was not murder but arson. It is true that he did not deliberately procure the deaths of the seven persons who were deprived of their most precious property, of life itself, in that calamity with which our city rung on the evening of June 28. He did not draw their blood personally with the usual weapons of homicide—pistol, dagger, bludgeon or ax. But the evidence will show you that a new weapon, more dangerous, because more deadly, than any of these, was used on this occasion, and that he set on foot forces which did procure the deaths of the victims, and which, but for the vigilance of man and the mercy of Providence, might have doubled or trebled their number—yes, laid the greater part of our fair city in ruins.

"For myself, I might be willing to suppose that the accused did not foresee the consequences which would follow his rash deed; that he trusted to a confined and local destruction, of property merely, following his application of the match to his deceased uncle's study. But the law, justly and wisely, we must admit, presumes foresight, imputes deliberation and malice, when loss of life follows the commission of a felony, and taxes the felon not alone with the initial damage but with all damages that accrue. I leave it to your own good sense, gentlemen, whether the fire-fiend who applies the torch in the heart of a crowded city is not potentially as guilty as the Malay running amuck with brandished dagger or the anarchist hurling his bomb. There can be only one answer to the question. Our own lives, the lives of our wives, sisters, children, are imperiled by any other doctrine than that which the law lays down.

"Therefore, reluctantly, sorrowfully, with misgivings and fear, we have impeached Robert Floyd of the murder of Ellen Greeley, who was burned to death in her chamber; of Rosanna Moxom, Katie Galuby, Mary Lacy and Florence F. Lacy, who died of injuries received while attempting to escape from the Harmon building; of Alexander Whitlove, who was caught between the floors of that building, in a heroic attempt to conduct his elevator to the imprisoned occupants of the upper story; and of Peter Schubert, the fireman who lost his life nobly in the performance of his duty."

This catalogue of the victims moved the spectators, and Emily noticed the woman in black crying softly in her handkerchief.

"I will not attempt to instruct your consciences or call to your minds the responsibility which rests upon your shoulders as well as upon mine. For I am convinced that every man before me approaches this case with the same unwillingness which I myself have felt, but also with the same determination to uphold the law, to do justice and nothing more or less than justice, to all parties, that I myself have formed."

The district attorney spoke this disclaimer of officiousness or persecution with genuine feeling, but it was scarcely necessary for any who knew him. The name of Noah Bigelow, like that of Shagarach, was guaranty in itself that the cause would be tried with courtesy and fairness. Yet something in his bearing might have told the psychologist that the nature of the man, unsuspicious, candid and slow to entertain a conviction of guilt, would be equally slow to part with such a conviction when it had once obtained a lodging.

The outline of the evidence to be presented consumed more than an hour in its delivery; and the reading, in a high drawl, of the minutes of the previous trial, occupied the remaining time until the noon recess tediously. If the jury had not .been provided with a typewritten copy it would have profited little by this latter proceeding.

CHAPTER XLIX.

THE BATTERIES OPEN FIRE.

Assistant District Attorney Badger conducted the examination of the first witness for the government, who gave his name as the Rev. St. George Thornton and wore the manner of an Oxford graduate.

"You knew the uncle of the accused, Prof. Arnold?"

"Excellently. He had been for many years an attendant at my church."

"The Church of the Messiah, of the Episcopal denomination?"

"The Episcopal church, sir; we do not consider it a denomination."

"You officiated at Prof. Arnold's funeral service, I believe?" said Badger, disregarding this nice distinction.

"I did."

"This took place on June 26, I believe?"

"On Thursday, June 26; yes, sir."

"And saw the accused, Robert Floyd?"

"Yes, sir."

"Kindly describe his actions and appearance on that occasion, Dr. Thornton."

"In common with others who knew him, I was greatly struck by the absence of any signs of grief."

"Such as what?"

"Such as tears and—and general signs of dejection."

"As though he were meditating upon something else than the death of his uncle?"

"As though his thoughts were far away."

"That is all," said Badger, and Shagarach, who had apparently expected something more substantial than this, arose.

"You have officiated at hundreds of funerals, I presume, Dr. Thornton?"

"At many hundreds, sir," answered the clergyman, gravely.

"And the ordinary marks of grief, as you say, are tears?"

"It is a rare burial in which tears are not shed."

"So rare that the exceptions impress themselves upon you, like the burial of Prof. Arnold?"

"Yes, sir."

"Would you say that in this class of rare exceptions the absence of tears was always due to callousness in the mourners?"

"Always? No, sir; not always."

"Generally?"

"I should not attempt to say, sir."

"You would scarcely judge the sincerity of a mourner's sorrow by the copiousness of flow from his lachrymal glands?"

"Hardly."

"One moment," said Badger, detaining Dr. Thornton for the redirect. "Did you mean to emphasize the tearlessness of the accused as the principal feature of his bearing which attracted your attention?"

"No, sir; it was the coldness, I may say the general indifference expressed in his countenance, which struck me."

"Will you allow me to see your eyeglasses, Dr. Thornton?" asked Shagarach. "The lenses are concave. You are near-sighted?"

"Yes, sir."

"Badly so, I should say?"

"Yes, sir."

"That will do."

"John Harkins," answered the next witness to Badger's preliminary question.

"Were you ever employed by Prof. Arnold?"

"I was."

"In what capacity?"

"As coachman."

"When?"

"About a year ago, just before Mungovan."

"How long did you remain in his household?"

"About two weeks."

"Did you notice anything unusual in the relations between the accused and his uncle?"

"Well, I heard them quarr'ling two or three times."

"What do you mean by quarreling?"

"Oh, they were talking angrily to each other."

"Did you listen so as to hear the import of any of these conversations?"

"Well, I didn't listen, but I heard what they were saying."

"How often did you hear what they said?"

"I heard the old gentleman say once that he was a young rogue to be herding with the like of them cattle."

"Who?"

"The young fellow—his nephew."

"Called his nephew a rogue to be herding with such cattle?"

"Yes, sir."

"Those were his own words?"

"As near as I can remember."

"What kind of a master was Prof. Arnold?" asked Shagarach.

"He was a pretty good man. I haven't anything against him."

"Particular, wasn't he?"

"Yes, he was particular."

"Why were you discharged at the end of a fortnight?"

"He didn't give any reason; just said I didn't suit, that was all."

"But he paid you in full?"

"Oh, yes."

"And you found him not unreasonably exacting?"

"Well, he used to grumble a good deal."

"At you?"

"At me, yes, and the others, too."

"You never heard the others complaining, however?"

"No, sir."

"What did they say when you told them of his grumbling at you?"

"Oh, they said when you get used to him you won't mind."

"When the two 'quarreled,' as you call it, how many of the voices were raised in what you took to be anger?"

"How many?"

"One or both?"

"Why, it was the professor that was angry."

"Didn't he always talk loudly?"

"Yes, sir."

"When he 'grumbled' at you?"

"Yes, sir."

"When he 'grumbled' at the other servants?"

"Yes, sir."

"But they didn't mind it?"

"No; they said I wouldn't mind it after awhile."

"Did Floyd seem to mind it, when you saw him after these 'quarrels,' as you call them?"

"I didn't notice."

"Will you, upon reflection, swear that these quarrels were anything more than frank, warm discussions, misunderstood by you at the time, but such as any two men of independent mold and opposite views might indulge in?"

The witness was greatly puzzled.

"Well, I can't say. It was pretty loud talking, that was all."

The redirect by Badger brought out nothing new for the government's case. It was felt that their attempt to show strained relations between uncle and nephew was no great success. But the next witness was looked to curiously. He gave his name and position as James L. Carberry, secretary of Bricklayers' council No. 31, C. L. U. He was a powerful man, with a conspicuously well-filled sleeve, suggesting that mighty flexed arm, grasping a mallet, which is the workingman's favorite symbol. But the low brow hinted at a degree of honest dullness. While Carberry was taking the stand Badger asked leave to submit a newspaper clipping to the jury.

"This bears upon the point we shall now endeavor to prove, your honors—namely, the anti-social opinions of the accused."

Against Shagarach's protest and exception, Chief Justice Playfair allowed the jury to read an article from the Beacon, signed "Robert Floyd," in which the following sentence was marked as especially obnoxious:

"When the highest court in the land decides that offensive combination of capitalists in trusts is right, but defensive combination of workingmen in labor unions is wrong, then the time is ripe for revolution."

Shagarach's defense of his client's right to freedom of speech and thought was eloquent. But courts are and no doubt should be the sanctuaries of orthodoxy, and any other conclusion than that which Chief Justice Playfair and his two colleagues reached, in a matter so personal to themselves, could hardly be expected.

"You know the accused?" asked the district attorney of Carberry.

"I have met him," answered the witness.

"State to the jury the occasion upon which you met him."

"It was at a meeting of the union one Sunday afternoon, about six months ago."

"Did you have any conversation with him at that time?"

"Yes, sir."

"On what topic?"

"On strikes and labor questions and anarchy and——"

"Will you state what opinions, if any, the defendant expressed in regard to anarchy?"

"He told me he sympathized with the anarchists."

"Anything further?"

"Yes, sir; he said in his opinion assassination was justifiable."

"Where did this conversation take place?"

"In a little smoking-room off the hall."

"Were you alone?"

"Yes, sir."

"Do you remember the particular occasion which started your discussion of anarchism with the accused?" asked Shagarach, after a consultation with Floyd.

"No, sir."

"Wasn't it the arrest of Dr. Hyndman in London?"

"Oh, yes, I believe it was."

"It was for Dr. Hyndman that Floyd expressed sympathy, was it not?"

"Yes, sir, it was Hyndman."

"Do you happen to know whether Dr. Hyndman is a philosophical anarchist or not?"

"Sir?"

"Do you know what school of anarchism Dr. Hyndman represents?"

"No, sir."

"Do you know whether he advocates bomb-throwing?"

"I suppose so."

"You take it for granted, then, that all anarchists are bomb-throwers?"

"Yes, sir."

"Had Dr. Hyndman thrown a bomb?"

"I don't remember."

"Don't you remember that he merely made an anarchistic speech, in denunciation of society?"

"No, sir."

"You didn't inquire into the matter much?"

"No, sir."

"But Floyd, you say, expressed sympathy with the anarchists?"

"Yes, sir." This was said emphatically.

"Didn't he say that he sympathized with Dr. Hyndman?"

"That's what I told you."

"No, sir, it is not what you told me. Didn't Floyd say he sympathized with Dr. Hyndman as opposed to the bomb-throwing anarchists?"

"I don't remember that he did."

"Didn't he say that he sympathized with Dr. Hyndman's objects, but not his methods?"

"I don't remember anything about that."

"Then you didn't carry away a very clear idea of the conversation, did you?"

"I think I did," the witness replied with positiveness. Then the cross-examiner dismissed him, satisfied to have made it apparent that fine distinctions would pass through Mr. Carberry's mind like beach sand through a sieve. The redirect examination went over the same ground, and Badger placed a Mr. Lovejoy on the stand.

"You are treasurer of the Beacon company, are you not?"

"Yes, sir."

"All checks in payment for services rendered pass through you?"

"Through my subordinates or myself."

"Have you calculated, as requested, the total sums paid to Robert Floyd for special articles during the time of his employment?"

"I have."

"Will you state to the jury the earning capacity of this young man at the time of his uncle's death?"

"The question is prejudicially framed, Brother Badger," said Shagarach. "Please do not incorporate your own inferences when examining a witness."

"How much had Floyd earned while with you?" asked Badger.

"From January to June, inclusive, six monthly checks were made out payable to Robert Floyd, for services, and three smaller checks for expenses incurred. The amount of the former checks was $309."

"During six months?"

"Yes, sir."

"Mr. Hero Leander," said the next witness.

"City editor of the Beacon, I believe?"

"Yes, sir."

"Will you state any conversation you had with Inspector McCausland on Monday morning, June 30?"

"The conversation on my side was conducted in the
deaf-and-dumb alphabet. Mr. McCausland entered our
office and inquired which was Floyd's desk."

"And what did you do?"

"I pointed."

"To Floyd's desk?"

"Yes, sir."

"Mr. McCausland."

A buzz of expectancy went around when the inspector
walked in from the ante-room and mounted the stand.
He wore a rose in his buttonhole, but the smile had left
his countenance. With his testimony, it was felt, the real
case for the prosecution began.

"You arrested the accused, I believe, Mr. McCausland?" asked the district attorney, amid the breathless
attention of the court.

"I had that disagreeable task to perform."

"Where was the arrest made?"

"On the steps of the Putnam hotel."

"What was your first act upon reaching the station?"

"I stripped the accused and confiscated the clothes he
wore."

"These were the clothes he had worn at the time of
the fire, also?"

"He stated so."

"You have preserved those garments?"

"Yes, sir."

"You also confiscated the desk which Floyd had occupied at the Beacon office?"

"The drawers of it, yes, sir."

"Have you preserved the contents of that desk?"

"Yes, sir."

"Will you inform the jury what you found in the drawers of Robert Floyd's desk?"

"Three copies of the anarchist organ, Freiheit. There they are."

"Do these papers preach philosophical anarchy, Mr. McCausland?"

"I should say not. They are in German, but the leading editorial of this one—which was kindly translated for me by a friend—recommends the 'stamping out by fire and sword of John Burns and all such peace-mongering worms.' "

"A forcible expression, surely. It is the Most organ, in short?"

"Yes, sir."

"Will you state the further results of your search in the desk?"

"I found this paper of powder, a part of a fuse, a written formula for manufacturing a bomb, a blotter with part of a note on it, legible by the help of a mirror——"

"That will do for the present, Mr. McCausland. And wil you state what you may have found in the pockets of Floyd's coat?"

"A quantity of powder. There were grains of it also on the knees of his trousers."

"Similar to that found in his desk?"

"Yes, sir."

"What else?"

"A burnt match," said the inspector, just as the clock struck five and the constable's gavel sounded a prelude to adjournment.

CHAPTER L.

THE BOMBARDMENT CONTINUES.

Nearly the same gathering was admitted to the courtroom on the second day as on the first. But, wedged in between Mrs. Arnold and the unknown woman in black, Emily had pointed out to her the famous novelist Ecks, who sat with his head inclined toward the still more famous playwright Wye. Wye was mooting volubly the chain of testimony which had been spun around the accused on the foregoing day, which seemed to possess for him all the circumscribed but inexhaustible interest of the chessboard or a dramatic intrigue. But Ecks was sketching in pencil the principal characters of the trial.

"We shall summon Mr. McCausland again," said the district attorney. "At present we surrender him to the counsel for the accused."

A keen glance shot from lawyer to witness, comparing the two great opponents. Shagarach's face was a mask, stern and impenetrable, but McCausland visibly braced himself for the encounter. Equal they might be in a sense, as Mount Everest is the peer of the Amazon, but as different in their spheres as the river and the mountain. In the detective's subtle eye the keen observer might have discovered a finesse and a suppleness not altogether remote from the corresponding traits in the cracksman whom he had impersonated. But Shagarach could no more have counterfeited Bill Dobbs than McCausland could have acted with success the role of Count L'Alienado.

"Would you hang a kitten on the evidence of a burned match, inspector?" asked the lawyer.

"If he were old enough to scratch it," answered the detective.

"Will you turn out the contents of your upper right vest pocket?"

McCausland's face became rosy with embarrassment, but he obeyed the request. A ripple of laughter went around when among the broken-up fractions of a card of lucifers there appeared one that was blackened at the end. The inspector allowed the merriment to die, then coolly remarked:

"It is the match I found on Floyd."

And it was felt that he had held his own.

"Phineas Fowler," called the district attorney. The old chemist tottered to the stand and held a parchment hand high in air while the clerk administered his oath.

"What is your business, Mr. Fowler?"

The pantaloon trembled visibly and twisted the two horns of his forked beard one after the other with nervous fingers, blinking about all the while like an old Rosicrucian projected into the daylight world.

"A chemist," he piped, in a treble so high that the thoughtless smiled, but so feeble the chief justice bent forward to hear and the stenographer requested him to raise his voice. Ecks began sketching away rapidly at the advent of this character. The very odor of acids seemed to exhale from his shivering person.

"What lines of trade do you supply?"

"Photographers, dyers, armorers——"

"The last class with explosives and fulminating compounds, I presume?"

"Also with oils and varnishes," answered the pantaloon, his voice breaking in the desperate effort he made to be audible.

"Would you call him senile or venerable?" whispered Ecks.

"He must have sold Floyd the powder," answered Wye, intent on the imbroglio.

"Have you ever met the accused?"

"Yes, sir."

"When and where?"

"In my office twice."

"What was the date of the first visit of the accused to your office?"

"June 23."

"And of the second?"

"June 27."

"On what business did the accused call to see you, Mr. Fowler?"

"He was inquiring about bombs," answered the witness, a strong back-country twang coming out as he proceeded and adding to his other peculiarities.

"What did he especially desire to know about bombs?"

"How they were made."

"Were you able to inform him? Have you made a study of this subject?"

"Oh, yes. There's nothing mysterious about it."

"You entered into a minute discussion, then, with Floyd on the subject of bomb-making?"

"Well, no; I answered his questions. Didn't volunteer nothing." Mr. Fowler grew reckless of the niceties of speech as he accelerated his replies. "Don't believe it's a proper matter to be preached from the housetops."

"Your room is tolerably near the top of the house, however?"

"Top story, sir."

"Well, proper or improper, what was the upshot of your conversation?"

"He was coming again and I was to sell him some powder."

"Anything else?"

"Yes, three feet of fuse."

"Will you describe this fuse?"

"Why it's just common fuse, made out of linen cloth, sprinkled with a slow-burning mixture—nitre, sulphur and a little powder—sheathed in rubber and fitted into a metal plug."

"You sold Floyd three feet of this fuse?"

"Yes, sir."

"And how much of the powder?"

"Two pounds."

"Common gunpowder?"

"Yes, sir; American army powder."

"You were to sell him these commodities, you say. Did he actually return and purchase them?"

"Yes, sir; I had them all done up when he called again."

"Called on June 27, as he had promised to?"

"Called on June 27, sir."

"Which was the day before the fire and the day after his uncle's funeral, according to Dr. Thornton's testimony as to the date."

"I dare say you are right, sir," squeaked the pantaloon, who evidently stood in trepidation of his burly examiner.

"For what purpose did you understand that the accused wanted this powder and this fuse?"

"Told me he wanted to make some sort of a bomb."

"Did he ask you for particular directions?"

"Well, yes."

"Did you furnish him the shell or envelope of this projected bomb?"

"Oh, no; he said he had a teakittle to hum," said the pantaloon, whereupon the repressed volcano of merriment exploded once more, to the indignation of John Davidson, who occupied a front seat, listening to the testimony of his townsman. The chief justice looked stern and the district attorney's deep bass rumbled on without a pause.

"A teakettle at home. And how was that to be converted into the covering of a bomb?"

"Why, I told him to put the fuse inside and draw it through the nozzle, so the plug would stop up the spout, then shovel in the powder, tamp her up with nails and pellets, fasten down the lid and you have a bomb ready made. The kettle, I understood, was a frail one, hardly stronger than a canister."

"Not a concussion bomb, Mr. Fowler, I suppose?"

"No, sir. Those are filled with dynamite or giant powder. I don't deal in the high explosives."

"This bomb would have to be fired through the fuse?"

"Yes, sir."

"But it would explode with considerable force."

"Well, I guess it would rip things jest a trifle." Here the pantaloon forced the ghost of a smile himself.

"Kindly bring in the safe."

It came in on the shoulders of two stout porters, all breached and battered and bubbled in places, as if the iron had melted like tar.

"The explosion of this shell, the construction of which

you have just described, would blast away a very considerable obstacle, you say?"

"Lord, yes! Slit a cannon."

"Would it be sufficient—I ask your opinion as one having experience in this line—would it be sufficient to cause the mutilation visible in that safe?"

"All that and a sight more."

"And the accused gave you to understand that he had undertaken the construction of just such a bomb?"

"I took him so."

"Very well. So much for that. Did you examine the piece of fuse which Mr. McCausland found in the desk occupied by Floyd at the Beacon office?"

"I did."

"What kind of fuse was it?"

"Same as I sold him."

At this point a small piece of fuse, some six inches in length, was submitted to the jury for inspection and passed along from hand to hand.

"And the powder found in it?"

"Same powder."

"And the powder in Floyd's coat pockets?"

"Same powder."

"And the grains on the knees of his trousers, where they may have spilled?"

"Same powder."

"That's the black side of the shield," whispered Ecks, as the district attorney sat down.

"Now for the white," answered Wye.

"It is not part of your regular business, I presume," said Shagarach, "to furnish anarchists with bombs?"

"Oh, no, sir," answered the witness, making corkscrew curls of his beard points.

"Or incendiaries with igniting material?"

"No, sir; never did it before in my life, sir."

"Why did Floyd say he wanted this powder and fuse and information as to the construction of bombs?"

"Said he was studying up anarchism."

"For what purpose?"

"Wanted to write an article on it, he said."

"And you seem to have believed him?"

"At the time, or I wouldn't have sold him the goods."

"What made you believe him?"

The witness paused, puzzled and shifted from foot to foot.

"Well, I can't say, sir, as to his credentials."

"Couldn't he have procured these materials in some less public way if secrecy had been an object with him?"

"Plenty of other ways of getting such things, sir."

"Yet he walked in openly to your office?"

"Yes, sir."

"Told you his name?"

"No, sir."

"Gave you his card?"

"Yes, sir; business card; said he was a reporter."

"Where is the card?"

"I don't know, sir."

"Did you notice the name?"

"No, sir; took no particular notice. Thought it was all right at the time."

"But the young man stated that he was studying up anarchism?"

"And wanted to see for himself just how easy it was to make a bomb."

"That will do."

"Rather an eccentric whim," said Wye. "Putting up a clever defense, though."

"Did you notice how the defendant's jaws are set?" answered Ecks.

"Mr. Hero Leander," called Badger, and the city editor again took the stand.

"Did the Beacon ever give Floyd an assignment to write up anarchy?"

The witness shook his head.

"Mr. McCausland once more," said Badger, while the city editor, whose occupation had taught him to reduce laconicism to a science, rushed off to write up his own

somewhat abbreviated testimony for the evening edition
of his paper.

"Did you find any manuscript or notes of an article
on anarchism in the desk occupied by the accused?"

"None, sir."

"Or in the garments he wore at the time of the fire?"

"None."

"You had no opportunity," asked Shagarach, "after
the fire to search Floyd's room at his uncle's house?"

"I wish I had," replied the inspector.

"Then you could not testify that such notes or such
a manuscript were not in existence before the fire?"

"I could offer an opinion."

"Mr. Chandler."

In the interim, during which our old acquaintance, the
patrolman, was hunted up, the jury curiously examined
the powder, which McCausland handed them.

"You recognize this article, Mr. Chandler?" asked
Badger, pointing to the safe.

"I do."

"You removed it or had it removed from the ruins
of the Arnold house after the fire?"

"Acting under Mr. McCausland's instructions, I did
so."

"It presented the same appearance as now?"

"As far as I know."

"The safe will be removed to the jury-room later for
inspection," said Badger.

"What was the date of Prof. Arnold's death, Mr. Chandler?" asked Shagarach.

"He died on a Tuesday. Let me see. The fire was
on the 28th; then it must have been the 24th."

"How is that competent, your honor?" objected
Badger.

"Perhaps Mr. Shagarach can explain its relevancy,"
said Chief Justice Playfair.

"Easily, your honor. Fowler, the chemist, has testified that Floyd's first visit was on the 23d, which was
Monday. His uncle died on Tuesday, suddenly and

unexpectedly. The prosecution asks us to believe that the accused either foresaw in some occult manner his uncle's death or contemplated blowing up the house while his uncle was still alive."

"Admit the testimony," said the judge.

"District Chief Wotherspoon," called the district attorney, relieving his assistant. The witness was rugged and weather-beaten and his uniform was not brushed for inspection. He had just answered an alarm.

"You had charge of the fire forces in the early part of the Arnold fire, did you not?"

"Yes, sir; until Chief McKay arrived I was senior officer."

"Do you recall the explosions which took place?"

"Perfectly."

"How many in number were the explosions?"

"Two."

"Two distinct explosions?"

"Yes, sir."

"Will you state to the best of your knowledge the portion of the burning buildings from which the explosions came?"

"The first one was a single discharge. It came from the second story of the Arnold house."

"Where the study was located?"

"Yes, sir."

"You feel positive?"

"I do. I was climbing a ladder at the time and was thrown off my hold by the shock."

"And the second of the explosions?"

"The second came after an interval and was different in character—more like the setting-off of a bunch of firecrackers, but greatly exaggerated in the volume of sound. There can be no doubt this was the fireworks shop in the adjoining building."

"But the first one positively came from the study?"

"Positively."

"A very loud report?"

"Very loud."

"Such as might have been caused by the explosion of the bomb Mr. Fowler described?"

"I should say so."

"At what time," asked Shagarach, "did the explosion take place? How long after you arrived?"

"I couldn't say exactly; a few minutes."

"One?"

"More than one."

"Two?"

"Yes."

"Three?"

"Possibly."

"And when did you arrive?"

"At 3:32."

"How long had the fire been going when you arrived?"

"As nearly as I could estimate from the headway, about five minutes. Opinions varied a good deal on that point."

"Let us say five and add the three which elapsed before you heard the explosion. Then if there were a bomb in the study or library and its fuse were lighted at the start of the fire that fuse must have burned for eight minutes before it reached the powder."

"He's a genius," exclaimed Wye, but Ecks was sketching Shagarach's forehead and did not answer.

"I suppose so," said the fireman.

"A somewhat incombustible fuse. But if the fuse were not lighted at the start then presumably the fire started at the opposite end of the room and worked its way slowly toward the fuse?"

"Presumably."

"Even so, it seems likely that the fuse must have been boxed up tightly or it would have caught earlier."

"It certainly does to me, sir, though I haven't given the subject any thought."

"It is not a difficult one," said Shagarach. "Wouldn't you say, then, that this fire must have been started by some one who was ignorant that there was a bomb in the room in close proximity to the safe? Otherwise he would have lighted the fuse."

"Perhaps."

"And consequently by some one else than Floyd?"

"I object," said the district attorney. He ought to have objected long before, since Shagarach's previous question was wholly out of order, but his attention had been distracted by McCausland.

"If it had been the incendiary's desire to secure a gradual spread of the flames, so as to permit himself ample time to escape, while at the same time insuring the destruction of the safe, would it not have been prudent for him to apply the match at the other end of the room, as he appears to have done?" asked the district attorney. But Shagarach objected to this in his turn and the two questions were left unanswered, locking horns like tangled stags in the minds of the wondering jurors.

"May I add one further question to my cross-examination of Mr. Fowler?" asked Shagarach, when the fireman was dismissed.

"How long, Mr. Fowler, would it take for that bomb to explode after the tip of the fuse had ignited?"

"About a minute," answered the chemist.

"For the present," said the district attorney, "we are obliged to rest this portion of the case. The fatality which has pursued all the occupants of the Arnold house, even to the discharged coachman, Dennis Mungovan, has deprived us by Miss Lund's death of a witness who would have directly and immediately connected .the bomb which Floyd constructed with the mutilated safe. This afternoon we shall enter upon a different phase of the subject—namely, an earlier attempt on the part of the accused to obtain possession of the will."

CHAPTER LI.

GLORY ALLELUIA.

"Saul Aronson," called the district attorney. Shagarach's assistant had been amazed to find a subpoena thrust into his hands just as he returned to his desk after the noon recess. Of what service could he be to the prosecution? As little as possible, he inwardly determined, while he made his way to the stand.

"Do you know a young lady named Miss Serena Lamb?" asked Badger, in his iciest voice. The cruelty of it was exquisite. If he had discharged a revolver at Aronson point blank the witness could not have looked more terror-stricken. To have the secrets of the affections thus held up to public scorn! To be compelled to wear on his sleeve the heart whose bleeding in his bosom he had with difficulty stanched! His face grew pale—or, rather, a mottled white. But Shagarach rose on purpose and his master's presence acted like a cordial on the fainting witness.

"Yes, sir," he stammered out, marveling what was to come; how long the torture would be prolonged.

"That is all for the present," said Badger.

"Prof. Borrowscales," called the district attorney, and a shadow of disappointment fell on the court-room. There is no testimony less amusing than that of the writing expert and none more inconclusive. At least eleven jurors out of twelve disregard it and form their own opinions by the rule of thumb.

"You are a professor of penmanship?" asked the district attorney.

"An expert in handwriting, yes, sir."

"Of many years' experience?"

"Twenty-nine."

"Have you examined the papers submitted to you by Inspector McCausland?"

"I have microscopically."

"Describe them, please, for the benefit of the jury."

"This one is a page of manuscript purporting to be the work of Robert Floyd and bearing his signature. The other contains a chemical formula."

"The bomb formula, taken from the desk of the accused," explained the district attorney. "Anything else?"

"A number, apparently jotted down on the same sheet."

"Please read out that number."

"No. 1863."

"What do you say as to the identity of the handwritings, professor?"

"I give it as my conviction that they are the same. The capital Q——"

"Never mind the capital Q," interrupted Shagarach. "We admit that the formula was written by the accused."

"Retain the autograph for one moment," said the district attorney. "There was another article submitted to you for comparison. What was that?"

"A blotting-pad," said the professor, holding it up in his fingers and showing a clean side, bearing the reversed impressions of two or three lines of writing.

"Will you kindly hold that up to the mirror you have brought and read what may be read of the writing taken up by the pad?"

"Looks to me as if it came from the back of a postal card. Just fits that size and says:

" 'Dear Aronson: The lock that I told you about still sticks. Please come and open it. I will not trust it to an ordinary locksmith. ROBERT FLOYD.' "

"As to the signature and writing? Are they genuine?"

"Beyond peradventure and on the strength of my twenty-nine years of experience."

"During your twenty-nine years of experience," asked Shagarach, "have you ever failed to arrive at the conclusion your employers expected?"

"I object," said the district attorney, and Shagarach withdrew his question. It was one of those ramrod questions, the office of which is simply to drive the charge home and then be withdrawn.

"Will you kindly write your own name on that?"

He handed up a common paper block and a pen. The expert flushed a little and put the pen in his mouth. This blackened his lips and raised a titter. His tongue rolled in his cheek like a schoolboy's while he wrote. The effort was unconsciously prolonged. Shagarach took the autograph and passed it to the jury. A broad smile spread from face to face like a row of lamps lighted successively by an electric current. Then the half-legible scrawl was passed to the district attorney and Shagarach sat down.

"I do not understand," said the district attorney, "that you profess to be an ornamental writer?"

"It is not necessary, Brother Bigelow," interrupted Shagarach again. "We acknowledge the note on the postal card."

"He has a spark of humor, after all," said Ecks, who was still in his seat.

"What do you suppose Aronson has to do with it?" asked Wye, while the jury studied the blotter, one after another, mirror in hand.

"Pineapple Jupiter!" called Badger. The old negro hobbled to the stand and immediately opened his mouth in a good-natured smile, which set the spectators' lips working responsively.

"This is a murder case, involving life and death," said Chief Justice Playfair, with dignity, and the court officers rapped their staffs and bustled about, commanding silence.

"You know Mr. Aronson, the last witness but one?" asked Badger.

"See him most every day, sah."

"Do you also know a young lady named Miss Serena Lamb?"

"See her most every day, sah."

"Did you ever introduce Mr. Aronson to Miss Lamb?"

"Yes, sah."

"When and where?"

"Well, you see, I fotched him up to her and says I, 'Here's a convert, sister,' says I. 'Hallelujah!' says she, and that's how I done it, sah."

"Where was this?"

"Down on the square, sah—Salem street."

"And when?"

"When?"

"Yes, when did you introduce Mr. Aronson and Miss Lamb?"

The negro scratched his woolly poll.

"Clean forgot de time, sah."

"Was it a year ago?"

"'Bout a year, sah."

"Couldn't you fix the time exactly? It is important."

"Well, you see, sah, it was about de second-last time I got a hair-cut."

This answer provoked a roar, but the district attorney took the witness in hand.

"Can you count?"

"Oh, yes, sah; I can count, sah."

"Up to how far?"

"Up to ten mostly, sah."

"You can't read?"

"Born before Massah Linkun, sah. Chillun can read. Old folks picking cotton; no time for school, sah."

"And you reckon time by the occasions when your hair needs cutting?"

"Yes, sah; wife and I reckons pretty close on that, sah."

"An excellent way for want of a better hour-glass," said the district attorney. "About how often do you get your hair cut from winter to winter?"

"Oh, about six times, sah. My ole wool grows putty stiddy-reg'lar, sah."

"Six times? You have had your hair cut lately?"

"This morning, sah. Wife said I wasn't looking

'spectable enough to come into court before genteel gemlen."

"And you introduced Miss Lamb and Mr. Aronson about the second hair-cut before that?"

"Yes, sah, third-last time. 'Scuse me."

"It must have been four months ago, then. That will do. Mr. Hardwood."

A business-looking old gentleman took the stand.

"You are a member of the firm of Hardwood & Lockwell?" asked Badger.

"Senior member."

"What is your business?"

"Safemakers."

"How long have you been established?"

"Thirty-seven years."

"Do you recollect filling an order for a safe from Prof. Arnold?"

"I do, sir. It is the first order on our books."

"Are those books in existence to-day?"

"They are, sir," said the old business man, with pride.

"Do you happen to know whether that safe ordered by Prof. Arnold was still used by him at the time of the fire which destroyed his home?"

"I have reason to believe so. I remember seeing it and reminding him of the circumstance in his house within a year."

"You regarded it as in a way the foundation stone of your business prosperity?"

"It was our first sale."

"What, if you recollect, was the number of the safe— an old-fashioned article, I presume?"

"Somewhat antiquated in style, sir. I have consulted our books, at the request of the officer—Mr. McCausland, I think. The number of the safe sold to Benjamin Arnold was 1863."

"Were you here," asked Shagarach, "when Prof. Borrowscales read out the number which was jotted down upon a sheet of paper in Floyd's desk?"

"I was. I was struck at the identity."

"You have no means of knowing, however, whether or not that number was a memorandum of the date in the life of Bakunin, the anarchistic writer?"

"I have not."

"Mr. McCausland, again," said the district attorney.

For the third time the inspector came to the box from the ante-room through the door at which he watched and listened.

"You occupied a cell adjoining that of the prisoner in the state prison at one time?"

"Yes, sir."

"Will you state any conversation relevant to this trial which you may have overheard?"

"It was a soliloquy rather than a conversation."

"Describe this soliloquy, then."

"Floyd used to talk at night a good deal. He wasn't sleeping well." The court was hushed at this strange introduction. "There was a communication between our cells and by listening carefully one night I managed to make out what he was saying."

"And what was he saying?" asked the district attorney, while Floyd studied the witness' face with more curiosity than he had yet at any time shown.

" 'Don't tell anybody, Aronson.' "

To the surprise of everybody the accused burst out into a hearty laugh, which rung through the court-room and evidently nettled the whole prosecuting force. Then he bent over to Shagarach and whispered in his ear. Shagarach jumped to his feet, promptly as usual, for the district attorney had finished. His opportunity had come.

"What crime had you committed, Mr. McCausland, that the state should isolate you in one of its prison cells?"

"I was a voluntary prisoner," answered the detective. He had put his neck in the noose and must bear the strangling as cheerfully as possible.

"For what purpose?"

"A professional one."

"You were there to win the confidence of the accused and extort a confession of guilt from him if possible?"

"Yes, sir."

"Did you succeed?"

"Owing to the cleverness of the prisoner and his having been forewarned, I failed."

"Not owing to the fact that he is innocent, you think?"

"I think not."

Shagarach seemed satisfied not to press this further and asked for the blotter, which was in the foreman's hand.

"You were requested to state any conversation relevant to this cause which you had with the accused while in prison. You answered with a few meaningless words pronounced in sleep. I confess the relevance of all this later testimony escapes me," said Shagarach.

"The next witness, Miss Lamb," answered the district attorney, "will make the connection of all these threads of testimony plain."

"Do you know Mr. Aronson, the piano dealer?" asked Shagarach of the witness.

"By sight."

McCausland, though he kept his own identity as hidden as possible, knew the whole city by sight.

"Is it not possible to construe this note on the postal card as referring to the refractory lock of Miss Barlow's piano, which the accused had recently purchased for her as a birthday present?"

"Out of the $309 he earned?" asked McCausland.

"That and the lifelong income he has enjoyed from his mother's property," said Shagarach. Whereupon McCausland, Bigelow and the whole court-room stared, and even Chief Justice Playfair's trained eyebrow was perceptibly lifted.

"Miss Serena Lamb," called the district attorney. How Aronson blushed and fidgeted when his idol, with eyes downcast in virgin shyness, tripped in from the corridor at a constable's beck and mounted the stand!

"Glory alleluia!" she said, with her right hand raised, when the clerk had repeated the formula of the oath.

"You are a member of the salvation army, Miss

Lamb?" asked the district attorney. Her bonnet and garb sufficiently answered the question.

"You are acquainted with a young man named Saul Aronson?" was the first question put to Serena.

"I was made known unto such an one," said the girl, in quasi-scriptural parlance.

"By whom?"

"Pineapple Jupiter."

"How did Aronson first present himself to your attention?"

"As one who had seen the error of unbelief and wished to repent. Alleluia!"

"As a convert, then? Did you ever have any private conference with this convert?"

"I did."

"Will you kindly tell the jury when and where?"

"It was the month of May at my home in the city."

"In the parlor of your house?"

"Even so."

"On what date, if you remember?"

"Early in May, but the day escapes me."

"State the substance of your conversation."

"The youth had been a sinner, but his heart was touched and he unburdened his misdeeds to me, of which this was the gravest:

"While he was still unregenerate a certain youth of his own age"—she looked full at Robert—"had tempted him with a bribe to enter a certain house wrongfully and open a certain safe. For the youth had cunning in that craft. The room he entered was filled with books and a canary bird slept in his cage, for it was evening, and a desk stood before a window in one corner."

"I desire to call the attention of the jury to this description," said the district attorney. "It corresponds strikingly with the description of Prof. Arnold's study in the printed copy of Bertha Lund's testimony at the hearing, which is in their possession. Proceed, Miss Lamb."

"And the name of the tempter was Robert Floyd." The hush deepened perceptibly as Serena paused.

"Upon his knees with many tools," she resumed, "he toiled at the door, but it was firm and resisted his skill. Nevertheless the youth stated that he would have succeeded had not an interruption come and startled the guilty pair."

"Are there any further details you desire to add to this recital?"

"Only that it was done on the Sabbath and surely unblessed labor."

"You have not seen the convert since?"

"Never, but I have heard that the courage of his faith deserted him."

"Is the man here?" asked the district attorney, turning toward Aronson—poor Aronson, who sat open-mouthed, goggle-eyed, with gaze riveted on the pale sweet face in the bonnet. Now a thousand eyes were turned upon him, but still he saw only the rosebud mouth and awaited breathlessly its answer.

"That is the man," answered the witness, pointing. The greater "Ecce homo" of history scarcely drew forth such a murmur from the bystanders. But the gavel of the crier was heard rapping for attention, for the court had risen promptly at the strokes of the clock.

"One moment, your honor," said Shagarach, rising, after a whispered consultation with his assistant, now voluble and stuttering with excitement. "I desire to ask that the court issue a warrant for the arrest of the last witness, Miss Serena Lamb, on the charge of malicious perjury."

CHAPTER LII.

THE ROSEBUD MOUTH.

"What in the world is he smiling for?" asked Emily. Inspector McCausland's smile was a barometer of her own uneasiness, and she could not help remarking his unusual geniality at the opening of the court on Wednesday.

The previous day's work had closed with a sturdy wrangle between Shagarach and the district attorney. Whether it was that Shagarach's charge of perjury was not sufficiently supported (it was merely Aronson's word against Serena's) or that Bigelow's inelastic mind characteristically clung in the face of cogent proof to the convictions it had already formed, he had objected might and main to the proposed issue of a warrant and even gone so far as to protest against his learned brother's effort to intimidate a witness of the weaker sex. Mc-Causland had amicably agreed to secure the attendance of Miss Lamb for cross-examination, and so the confusion subsided. Miss Lamb was there and so was the inspector. But what made him smile?

"Good morning, Miss Barlow," said a familiar voice, close to Emily's ear.

"Bertha Lund!" she exclaimed. There it was, the large, fair Swedish face, with sparkling blue eyes that danced with the pleasure of the surprise. After a moment of silent study Emily gave her a bear-like squeeze and only released her that she might shake hands with Robert.

"It's none of my doing, Mr. Robert," said Bertha. "If I could, I'd have staid home in Upsala, but I gave my word to Mr. McCausland that I'd come back, and here I am to keep it."

"But we thought you were lost. We saw the body and buried it," cried Emily.

"Oh, that was another Bertha Lund. Mr. McCausland thought it was me, too."

"Another one from Upsala?"

"Why, if you took all the Bertha Lunds and Nils Nilssons in Upsala you could fill a big town with them," said the housemaid, laughing.

"And how did you happen to go home to Sweden?" asked Robert.

"Mrs. Arnold wanted another house-girl and I'd told her about my sister Christina, who is old enough now to be handy. She was kind enough to pay my passage over so I could bring her out with me, and let me stay all summer, too. Did you ever see such goodness?"

"She's a very uncommon mistress, certainly," said Emily.

"It was the day after we were talking at Hillsborough that I started," said Bertha. "Do you remember?"

"Yes, indeed," answered Emily, brightening up, "and now let us finish that talk. I have a hundred questions I want to ask you. Shall you testify to-day?"

"No; I've only just got here and the lawyer said he would leave me till the last. The voyage is very tiresome, you know."

"Then come with me," cried Emily, with animation, and drew Bertha after her into the ante-room. Here Robert caught a glimpse of her from time to time questioning, explaining, measuring with her hands, as if she were satisfying herself on doubtful points of her theory. And when she finally came out, in the middle of Miss Lamb's cross-examination, her face wore a smile so auroral that even Chief Justice Playfair's eyes left the witness and wandered over toward the true-hearted girl.

"Mr. Aronson told you that he worked on his knees at this mysterious safe?" was Shagarach's opening question to Miss Lamb.

"On his knees," answered the maiden, still bonneted and fanning herself with Emily's fan, which she had forgotten to return in the excitement of the previous evening.

"Mr. Aronson is not an uncommonly tall man, is he?"

"A trifle taller than you are."

"But yet not above the average," persisted Shagarach.

"Perhaps not."

"The government wishes us to believe that there was a bomb purposely placed under this safe. That would raise it from the floor several inches, would it not?"

"I suppose so. I know nothing about the bomb."

"Will you kindly explain how the locksmith could be kneeling while at work on a safe which, according to the testimony of Miss Lund, at the hearing, was resting on a shelf as high as her waist from the ground?"

The witness fanned herself nervously and once or twice opened her lips to reply, but no sound came forth. A wave of frightened sympathy passed through the spectators in the prolonged interim of silence, like that which seizes an audience when an orator falters and threatens to break down.

"You do not answer, Miss Lamb?"

"I feel faint," said the girl. A chair and a glass of water were hurried to her aid.

"Are you sure this is the man Aronson who visited you?" asked Shagarach when she had recovered.

"Oh, yes."

"Then we have two Aronsons in the case; Mr. Saul Aronson, my assistant, and Mr. Jacob Aronson, the piano dealer, who will testify to having received the postal card copied on the blotting-pad. And this Mr. Aronson who visited you declared that he had been a locksmith, if I understood your story?"

"He said so."

"That is not surprising. Mr. Aronson, my assistant, was formerly a locksmith. What was the date of your interview?"

"The first part of July. I can't remember the exact day," replied the witness, a bit nettled. The rusticity was rubbing on again in her manner, and to Saul Aronson it actually seemed that her cheekbones were becoming prominent, like those of her horrid aunt whom he had met on that fateful evening. But this may have been an optical illusion. The sympathy of the spectators trembled in the balance. She seemed so young and dove-like. But there stood Shagarach confronting her, hostile, skeptical, uncompromising.

"Mr. Aronson had made this alleged attempt to open a safe on Sunday evening, you said?"

"On the evening of the Sabbath."

Here Aronson gesticulated and whispered in Shagarach's ear. The lawyer listened calmly.

"When did you first become acquainted with him?"

"I don't remember exactly. He came to our meetings for a long time before I was introduced to him."

Serena blushed a little and Aronson's cheeks were all abloom.

"He was a convert to your faith?"

"So we thought."

"How long had he been converted?"

"I don't know."

"Pineapple Jupiter says he introduced you to Mr. Aronson about four months ago, if the district attorney reckons rightly from his periodic hair-cuts. Then at the time of the visit to your house in July he must have been a convert nearly two months?"

"Perhaps."

"But the will was only drawn on June 7. And Mr. Aronson, I understand you to testify, yielded to this temptation before he was converted?"

The witness did not answer, but looked around the court-room as if for sympathy.

"Are we to understand that he broke into the safe before the will was placed there?"

The witness fluttered her fan nervously and her lips were quivering. She looked down.

"Sunday evening, you said. You are probably not aware that Prof. Arnold read in his own library every Sunday evening up to the time of his death?"

Serena began to cry. Instantly the tension of the audience was relaxed and comments passed to and fro.

"She belongs to the romantic school of statisticians," whispered Wye. Ecks responded with a cartoon of "Miss Meekness, making a slip of the decimal point."

"Religious mania; hysterical mendacity," a doctor diagnosed it, with a pompous frown.

"Little minx had a craving for notoriety," said a woman, elderly, unmarried and plain.

"I should say it illustrates the pernicious effect of novel reading on a rustic brain," murmured a clerical personage, clearing his throat before he delivered himself.

Suddenly Shagarach's insistence left him. His voice softened. With his very first question, the distressed look, half of reproach, half of sympathy, toward Serena, cleared away from Aronson's face.

"Wasn't Mr. Aronson agitated on that evening, Miss Lamb?"

She blushed amid her tears and her answer was less defiant.

"Extremely agitated."

"Wasn't his story to you somewhat confused in the telling?"

"Very confused, yes, sir."

"And perhaps the outlines blurred still more in your memory by the lapse of time?"

"Perhaps. I meant to speak of that myself," answered Serena, brightening. Whereat the entire court-room brightened. Shagarach's inflections became kind, almost genial now. One would have thought she was his own witness, he stroked her so gently.

"And his accent was somewhat hard to follow?"

"Oh, very."

"He is not perfectly familiar with our language as yet?"

"No, he speaks it poorly."

The court-room was all curiosity.

"Didn't this picture of the study, which you have quoted, come in as part of his description of a law case?"

"Why, yes; he began talking about the Floyd case."

"In which he was deeply interested at that time, as my assistant. That, however, he did not make clear to you?"

"No."

"Can you swear that this whole picture of a Sunday-night entrance and experiment on the safe was not an imaginary one—a piece of fiction, invented and vividly told in the first person to illustrate what Robert Floyd might easily have done if he had desired to destroy the will, but what——"

Shagarach inclined slightly toward the jury, "but what he evidently did not do?"

"**Perhaps. Truly I** couldn't catch half of what he was saying when he began to talk rapidly."

"I myself am a locksmith. He could come and give me money. We go Sunday night. Nobody home. House all still. I get down on my knees. File a little. Drill. Somebody come. I go away. Come again. Try again."

Serena smiled a smile that sent waves of sunshine through the room. Shagarach had not once descended to mimicry of his assistant's dialect. But the broken fragments of speech, the confused arrangement, seemed to call before Serena's eye an amusing picture of her lovelorn swain's incoherence.

"Perhaps I was altogether mistaken," she volunteered.

Shagarach waved her with courtesy to the nonplussed though apparently still obstinate district attorney. A long conference followed among the prosecuting lawyers, while Emily heaved a sigh of relief.

Over in his front seat Ecks was gazing at Shagarach, as if trying to pierce the great brow, not opened showily, but masked, as it were, by the loose-falling hair. The marvelous skill of his tactics—first, the breaking down of Serena's story through its intrinsic discrepancies, then the building up from her own lips of a hypothetical case in the jurors' minds—all without deviating a hair line from true courtesy and delicacy of treatment — sank deeply into the novelist's heart. He did not reply to Wye's comment on the underplot.

"Incarnate self-control!" he muttered to himself.

But alas for poor Saul Aronson! It was bad enough to be compelled to flee from suspicion post haste through the gateway of public ridicule. But to realize at last that Serena was human and no angel—capable of pique, brusqueness and tears—capable even of resisting Shagarach! The scales of illusion fell from his eyes and he hung his head, a chastened youth.

"The redirect is deferred," said Bigelow, and Serena, after returning the fan to Emily, stepped softly out. Her footfalls barely broke the dead silence as she picked her way through the crowd.

Aronson lifted his eyes to her face. What imperfections he noted now! The eyebrows too level, the rosebud mouth too small and the cheekbones unmistakably present, even if barely breaking the curve. It was fated so. Doubtless in time he would follow old Abraham Barentzen's counsel and take some comely daughter of Israel to wife, well-dowered, a good housekeeper, and free from tittle-tattle. But never again would his naive heart palpitate with such virginal ecstasy as when he first gazed through the rose-misted spectacles of love on that sweetly imperfect gentile maiden.

"We shall now offer a mass of evidence," said the district attorney, "tending to prove the crucial point of exclusive opportunity."

Seven witnesses took the box, one after another, and in response to Badger's questions, swore that they were neighbors of the Arnolds, were wide-awake and observant about the time of the fire, but saw no person coming out of the house either in front or rear. The evidence was negative, but cumulatively it produced its effect, leading the minds of the jury away from Serena Lamb and her legend to the real core of the puzzle. By the time the last witness on this point arrived, a cordon of watchers, completely environing the house, had been drawn around it by the government, and it seemed impossible that any one could have slipped through unobserved.

CHAPTER LIII.

A DUMB EYEWITNESS.

"Hodgkins Hodgkins," answered the first witness who testified after the noon recess.

"When did you first learn that Prof. Arnold had made a will?" asked the district attorney.

"On receipt of a letter from my esteemed friend, dated June 15."

"What was the reason of Prof. Arnold's informing you of his action?"

"A long-standing, I may say a life-long friendship, had induced him to select me as his executor."

"When you heard of his death, what action did you take?"

"I was in New York at the time on important business, which I proceeded to expedite as far as its weighty nature would permit. Large bodies travel slowly, you know. Then when the transaction was completed to my satisfaction I repaired to the city and visited the home of my departed friend, the testator."

"Did you let Floyd know of your coming?"

"I apprised him of my intention and instructed him to lock the room in which the document was guarded."

"Did you actually call on the afternoon of the fire?"

"A short delay, occasioned by my failure to find Mr. Hardwood, the locksmith, who was to assist me in opening the safe, retarded my arrival until 3:45. At that time the paper was beyond my reach."

"You could not testify as to the contents of the will?"

"Only in a general way."

"Do you know any reason why, if the accused were expecting you, as he stated that he was when he ordered the housemaid to dust the room, do you know any reason why he should leave the house suddenly, without any instructions as to your reception?"

"That's the best point the prosecution has made!" exclaimed Wye.

Ecks was executing a series of caricatures illustrating the involution of Hodgkins' face back into a crab-apple. "You leave out his cunning," suggested Wye, looking over the heads.

"Not unless he had lighted this fire," said the senior member solemnly. At which answer Shagarach rose with a shade more promptitude than usual.

"Why do you profess to be the executor of Benjamin Arnold's will?"

"I am so styled over his own signature," answered Hodgkins, flourishing the professor's letter.

"Wasn't it proved in the probate proceedings that you were only to carry out certain minor legacies?"

"It is not becoming in me to anticipate the decision of the honorable court in that matter."

"As executor, then, did you try to uphold the will of your friend?"

"In my opinion as a lawyer, it cannot be upheld."

"In my opinion as a lawyer, it can. I ask you a question. Did you make any effort to uphold the will of which you claim to have been nominated executor?"

"I satisfied myself that the task was fruitless."

"You represented a client desirous of breaking the will at the probate proceedings, did you not?"

"The will was already broken, canceled, destroyed."

"Do you or do you not perceive a gross indelicacy in your desperate attempt to break the will of which you say you were appointed executor, in order to retrieve the fallen fortunes of the disinherited heir?"

"I am not here to discuss my conduct with you, sir," answered Hodgkins testily, for the cross-examiner flusters quickly when he becomes the cross-examined.

"When did you arrive in New York?"

"Friday evening."

"When did you call on the Arnolds?"

"On the Arnolds?" repeated Hodgkins, as if he did not understand the question.

"On Harry Arnold, I mean?"

"Oh, Friday evening."

"You went there directly?"

"I did."

"They were your clients?"

"I am Mrs. Arnold's legal adviser."

"You told Harry Arnold of your intention to call at his uncle's on the following day and open the safe?"

"I believe I announced my intention to approach the affair with expedition."

"Did he object or suggest a postponement?"

"I cannot remember that he approved or demurred."

"Do you mean to testify that you informed Floyd by letter the hour at which you would call?"

"I announced my general intention of calling."

"In the same letter in which you requested him to lock the study?"

"There was only one letter. It was dispatched from New York."

"Then how did Floyd learn of your contemplated visit?"

"I have understood that he was informed by Mrs. Arnold that afternoon."

"From whom did you understand this?"

"From Mrs. Arnold herself," said Hodgkins, looking toward that lady.

"You told her the hour?"

"Half-past two."

"And Mrs. Arnold called on Floyd, I believe, at about 2:45?"

"I believe so. I am not informed as to the exact minute."

"Was she there by appointment with you?"

"Not exactly. However, I had informed her of the time."

"As you stated before. Then Floyd only knew of your proposed visit at second hand through Mrs. Arnold?"

"I had not informed him."

"You might have entered and taken the will away without his knowledge, then?"

"It might have been done, though I assure you we had no such intention."

"When did you arrive at the house?"

"At 3:45."

"And Floyd had left a little before 3:30. He had waited for one hour, without the courtesy of an appointment from you. Then because he chose to leave the house, and did not wait upon your pleasure, you infer that he must have committed arson and procured the death of seven of his fellow-creatures. That will do."

"Charles Checkerberry."

A railroad conductor stepped forward to take the oath.

"What names!" said Ecks to Wye. "It's like a census of Bedlam Proper."

But Wye did not answer. He was wondering if he could weave the safe explosion into the plot of his next melodrama.

"You are a conductor on the Southern railroad?" asked the district attorney.

"Yes, sir."

"What time did your train leave the city on the afternoon of Saturday, June 28?"

"The express train left at 3:29."

"Did you see the accused riding on that train?"

"Yes, sir."

"Get a full look at him."

"I am positive that is the man. I remember the fact because he had no ticket and had to pay his fare——"

"To what point?"

"To Woodlawn."

"Go on."

"He paid his fare and declined to take the coupon, which is worth ten cents when presented at the ticket office. Told me to keep it myself."

"This generosity is not common among passengers?"

"No, sir. That is why the incident impressed itself upon my memory."

"Did you notice anything unusual in the appearance of the accused?"

"I noticed he seemed rather excited."

"And got off at Woodlawn?"

"Yes, sir; jumped off at Woodlawn and crossed the fields over toward the woods."

"On the unfrequented side of the station?"

"Yes, sir; toward the cemetery. There is only one house on that side."

"Whose house is that?" asked Shagarach.

"The Arnolds', I believe."

"Do you know Harry Arnold?"

"No, sir."

"He rides in on the Northern line usually, I presume?"

"I believe so; it is more up-town."

"In the city, you mean?"

"Yes, sir; a great deal more convenient to the high-toned section."

"Then if this passenger were Harry Arnold he would have had to pay a cash fare on your railroad, as well as one not used to riding over the road, like Floyd?"

"I suppose so. We don't exchange tickets with the Northern."

"You see a great many hundred faces in the course of a week?"

"Yes, sir."

"How many tall, dark young men, wearing full mustaches and answering to the general description of the accused, should you say you had seen since June 28?"

"Oh, I couldn't say as to that."

"A hundred?"

"More, probably."

"But out of these hundred or more you have a distinct recollection of this one, the accused?"

"Yes, sir."

"And would swear his life away on the strength of your recollection?"

"Well, not exactly——"

"That is all."

"One moment," said the district attorney. "Your occupation and experience give you exceptional training in the study of faces, do they not?"

"Yes, sir."

At this moment Harry Arnold came into the court-room, attended by a great St. Bernard. The young man had hardly stepped inside the bar, when a deep bark was heard and the dog leaped toward the accused, standing on his hind legs and placing his paws on the wall of the cage, while he licked Robert's hands like a spaniel. Emily was deeply affected and tried to distract Sire's attention, but he had eyes only for his master.

"Down, Sire," said Robert.

Shagarach had paused during the interruption.

"Will you kindly shut your eyes, Mr. Checkerberry?" he now said.

The witness did as requested. Then Shagarach stepped up to Harry Arnold and whispered to him. Harry looked at him oddly. But he shook off the momentary confusion, and, scarcely looking at the witness, exclaimed:

"Am I the man you saw?"

"You are," answered the conductor.

"Open your eyes. Which of these two men spoke to you?" asked Shagarach. Robert stood up beside his cousin. The resemblance was indeed striking. Both were about the same height and both strongly marked with the peculiarities of kindred blood. The conductor turned from one to the other.

"Very well," said Shagarach. "It is the face of Jacob, but the voice of Esau. For the present, that will do."

"Miss Senda Wesner."

While the bakeshop girl was pushing her way forward from the back seat which she had occupied, Sire, who was squeezed where he lay, gravely arose, climbed the vacated witness-box and spread his great limbs out, majestically contemplating the spectators.

"This is the one eyewitness of the crime," said the district attorney.

"But unfortunately dumb," added Shagarach. Just then an impulse seized Emily, who had left the cage for a moment—Emily, the most shrinking of girls—and catching a large waste-basket which stood under the lawyers' desks to receive the litter that accumulates in trials, she stood up and shoved it toward the dog.

To everybody's surprise, he scrambled to his feet in alarm, backed hastily away and barked continuously at the harmless object. Then before the whole court, judges, jury and all, Emily clapped her hands and gave a girlish shriek of delight—only to sink in her place afterward, as the spectators smiled, and hide her blushes behind her fan. But it was some little while before Sire would let her pat him.

"You work opposite the Arnold house, Miss Wesner?" asked the district attorney.

"Directly opposite. I can look right over into their windows," said Senda.

"But I hope you don't."

"Well, I try not to, but sometimes, you know, you can't resist the inclination," chattered the bakeshop girl.

"You can always try."

"Oh, I do try, but you know——"

"Yes, I know. We all know. At what hour did you see Floyd coming out of his house on the afternoon of the fire?"

"The fire was going before 3:30, because I saw it. And I'll swear Mr. Floyd left the house at least four minutes, probably five, before."

"Walking to the right or to the left?"

"To my right, his left," answered Senda, glibly.

"And the flames broke out shortly after he went out?"

"Well, of course——" began the witness, all primed with an argument.

"Please answer yes or no."

"No—I mean yes."

"You heard the explosion?"

"Heard it? Why——"

"Where did it appear to come from?"

"It came from Prof. Arnold's study, as plain as your voice comes from you, but I don't see——"

"That will do," said the district attorney, handing the witness over to Shagarach.

"What do you say to my sketch of this Hebe?" asked Ecks.

"The drawing would be creditable in a gingerbread doll," answered Wye.

They were a sorry pair of lookers-on, both of them, appearing to regard the whole panorama of creation as a sort of arsenal of happy suggestions, especially established by Providence for the embellishment of their forthcoming works. But Hans Heiderman in his back seat didn't think she appeared homely at all in her red-checked dress and flaming hair, done up in Circassian coils. Of course he was looking at the soul of the girl, which was better than gold, and which neither Ecks nor Wye, for all their wise smiles, the least bit understood.

"You are rather accurate in your observations of time?" asked Shagarach.

"Oh, yes; I'm noted for that. I haven't looked at the clock for an hour, but I could tell you what time it is now."

"Shut your eyes and tell me."

"It is—about seventeen minutes past 4."

"Seventeen and a half," announced Shagarach, taking out his watch. Every man in the room, except the judges, had done likewise, while the ladies all studied the clock.

"Very good. At what time would you fix the explosion in the study?"

"About 3:34."

"One minute earlier, then, than District Chief Wotherspoon. Now, Miss Wesner, do you recollect anything about a peddler in a green cart that used to come to Prof. Arnold's?"

"Oh, that peddler. Yes, indeed, I——"

"How long had he been vending his goods through Cazenove street?"

"About a month. I know I never——"

"Had you seen him before that?"

"Never saw him before in my life, but——"

"How often did he come by?"

"Two or three times a week."

She had almost given up the attempt to work in her explanations edgewise. The rapid volley of questions prevented all elaboration.

"How often did he stop at Prof. Arnold's?"

"Almost every time."

"Was it Bertha who came to the door?"

"No, sir; it was Ellen generally. She was the cook, you know; got $4 a week, but she wasn't a patch on Bertha just the same."

"When did he stop coming with his—vegetables, was it, he sold?"

"Yes, sir; vegetables, and once potted plants."

"And when did he stop coming?"

"Just before the Arnold fire."

"You never saw him after the fire—as a peddler, I mean?"

Shagarach had not yet received an answer from the superintendent of Woodlawn cemetery, and was still in the dark about his assailant. But from the evidence he had he was satisfied that he could prove a connection with Harry Arnold.

"No, sir; not as a peddler."

CHAPTER LIV.

THE FOOL OF THE FAMILY.

So McCausland was right, after all. The oaf had just been captured by the local police of Woodlawn, and inquiry had vindicated the inspector's surmise.

Far back in our story there was mention of a half-witted brother of the Lacy girls, who jumped from the Harmon building and were killed. Nature had made one of her capriciously unequal divisions of talent in this family, gifting the daughters with all graces and allurements of character, but misshaping their elder brother, Peter, both in body and mind. And Fate, instead of rectifying the hard allotment by the merciful removal of the oaf, had deprived the household instead of its fairer inmates, leaving the monster to flourish on, sleeping, breathing, performing all animal functions healthily, but reflecting only sorrow into the heart of the mother who bore him.

The death of his sisters had converted this harmless driveller into a maniac, nursing one deadly thought. At the Lacy common table the case of Robert Floyd was, of course, followed with keen interest, especially since the shyster, Slack, had persuaded certain advisory relatives, and through them the mother, that some compensation in money for the loss of her girls might result from an appeal to the courts. Shagarach's name, as the defender, the possible savior of Floyd, this wrecker of their household peace, had impressed itself on the addled intelligence of the oaf, and being sufficiently taught to read and endowed with the cunning of his sort, he had begun with the incoherent letters to the lawyer, and ended with three assaults which had so nearly cost him his life. Floyd, behind the prison bars, was beyond his reach; but if the criminal records of the time had included any attempt to force a way into a jail cell it is probable that the maniac would have essayed an imitation of this. For, as McCausland had keenly noted, each of his attacks had been made under suggestion from the daily chronicles.

Since the fire he had wandered away from home—though previously a devoted house-haunter—probably making the rude hut in the forest his abode and indulging his mania amid that forest solitude in long fits of brooding. Just why he chose this habitation the mother could not say, unless it was to be near his sister's grave. From time to time he had returned, always to beg a little money or some articles of necessity, and when questioned on his doings he had manifested a temper which he was rarely known to exhibit before.

The mystery of his identity with the peddler was explained by Mrs. Lacy when Shagarach asked her the whereabouts of her son during June. It seems there was a street vender named Hotaling, who added to his revenue in summer time by hiring young men to exploit the outlying suburbs with spring produce. Strictly speaking, a license would be required, even though their sales were made beyond the city limits. But Hotaling dispensed with this formality, and the teamsters he employed were unsteady fellows, of the least savory appearance, whom he rewarded with a commission, keeping their accounts correct by the terror by which he personally inspired them. Among Hotaling's possessions was a green cart, and the driver selected to occupy its seat had been Peter Lacy, who had wit enough to harness a horse and make change (indeed, he was very shrewd at a bargain), and who accepted a pittance as recompense. The simpleton's district had been Woodlawn. But his road from the city market took him close to Cazenove street.

When, the next morning, the district attorney announced that Harry Arnold and Bertha would testify, closing the case for the prosecution, Shagarach knew that his time was at hand.

"Mr. Hodgkins has attested the existence of a will and the accused himself at the preliminary hearing admitted knowing that he was virtually disinherited. We have, however, thought it well to strengthen this vital point by calling a witness who will testify to the same admission made upon another occasion. Mr. Harry Arnold."

"You are a nephew of the late Prof. Arnold?"

"Yes, sir; his brother's son," answered Harry. He was just the least bit nervous, his glances wandering from Shagarach's face to his mother's and then resting with a brighter expression on that of Rosalie March, who had come into the court-room to-day for the first time. The wild rose in her cheeks was blooming warmly through the gossamer she wore to hide them and her blue eyes were lifted trustfully to her lover's. Once they caught Emily's and she bowed with a smile. Emily returned the bow, but her heart was too full for smiling. She was sorry Rosalie had come that morning, for Shagarach's manner told her that he was condensing his thoughts in the resolve to wring the truth from Harry.

"And a cousin of the accused?"

"Yes, sir."

"Your relations have always been pleasant, I presume?"

"We have never had any permanent falling-out."

"And are so still?"

"Yes, sir, on my part. I hope with all my heart the jury will find him innocent," answered Harry, with every appearance of candor.

"Have you ever had any conversation with him on the subject of your uncle's will?"

"Only once."

"When was that?"

"Within a week after the fire."

"And where?"

"At the county jail."

"It was while the accused was in custody of the sheriff, I believe?"

"Yes, sir."

"How did you happen to visit the accused at that time?"

"I was his only living kinsman. My visit was one of sympathy."

"And what statement did the accused make regarding his knowledge of the will?"

"Why, I believe he owned incidentally that he was disinherited, but everybody knew it then. It was all over the town. So was I, it seems, for that matter," added Harry.

"Everybody's knowledge is nobody's knowledge. We cannot take things for granted because rumor has spread them broadcast. We want your specific testimony that the accused acknowledged having learned from his uncle that he was to receive only an insignificant fraction of the fortune which all his life he had been expecting."

"That is my recollection of it."

"Was there any further conversation on the subject?"

"No, sir; it came up incidentally."

Shagarach paused a moment before beginning the cross-examination. Harry eyed him and during every second of the pause the witness' color mounted. Something in the lawyer's appearance still confused him.

"This was a visit of sympathy?" asked Shagarach.

"Yes, sir."

"Then you have seen the accused frequently since his imprisonment, I presume?"

"Well, no, I have not."

"When did you see him last previous to yesterday?"

"Well, not since the first week."

"Not since this visit of sympathy, do you mean?"

"That was the last time."

"Then all your sympathy expended itself in that single visit?"

"No, not exactly."

"Why didn't you renew it?"

"Rob and I didn't part good friends."

"Indeed? And what was the cause of your disagreement?"

"Some thoughtless words of mine."

"Then you were at fault?"

"Wholly. I have been sorry since."

"But you have kept your repentance to yourself until now, have you not?"

"Well——"

"And volunteered to testify against your cousin?"

"No, sir; I was subpoenaed."

"From what quarter do you suppose these rumors of Floyd's disinheritance arose?"

"I don't know."

"Consider that answer carefully."

"I have done so. I don't know. I read it in the papers."

"You knew Floyd was disinherited before your visit to his cell?"

"No, sir."

"You knew you yourself were disinherited before the fire?"

"No, sir."

"You knew a will had been made?"

"Yes, sir."

"From whom?"

"From my mother."

"Your mother and yourself share most items of family interest between you?"

"Naturally we do. We have no secrets from each other."

"Wasn't it your mother who first informed Mr. Mc-Causland that Robert had been disinherited?"

"I don't know."

"Yet you read the papers, you said."

"I must have skipped that item."

"How did Mrs. Arnold know this fact?"

"I don't know."

"You are very rich, Mr. Arnold?"

"Yes, we are considered wealthy."

"So rich that I presume you were indifferent whether Prof. Arnold added to your fortunes or not by a bequest of his property?"

"He may have thought we didn't need anything more."

"How large a stud of horses do you keep?"

"In all? Only six."

"How many servants?"

"Six."

"For a family of two?"

"My mother and myself. But then, we entertain a good deal."

"You have a summer residence at Hillsborough?"

"Yes, sir."

"And a house at Woodlawn?"

"Yes, sir."

"The supplies for your table are not generally purchased from a common street vender, I presume?"

"I don't know. I don't attend to the commissariat."

"Shouldn't you suppose they would come from market?"

"Game and such things, yes."

"And greens?"

"Yes, I suppose so."

"When did you first hear of the burning of Prof. Arnold's house?"

"That's hard to say at this distance of time."

"I wish you would try to recollect."

"Why, I think the morning afterward—Sunday morning. Yes, it was in the Sunday papers. I remember now."

"You remember distinctly?"

"Yes, sir."

"What paper?"

"The Beacon. We take no other."

The Beacon was the paper upon which Robert was employed, thus forming a curious bond of communication between the two Arnold households.

"You were not in town, then, that afternoon?"

"No, sir."

"Positive of that?"

"Why, yes; I was ill—or, rather, just convalescing from a fever. Dr. Whipple called, I believe, to see me that very Saturday."

"In the forenoon or afternoon?"

"Afternoon."

"About what hour?"

"About 3:45."

"And this fire started at 3:30?"

"I heard a witness say so in the testimony yesterday."

"Of your own knowledge you couldn't say when it started?"

"No, sir."

Harry was red as fire during all these rapid questions, some apparently aimless, some sharply pointed.

"A man could not start that fire in Cazenove street at 3:30 and reach your house in Woodlawn at 3:45, could he?"

"Not very well."

"He might, however, start the fire at 3:28 and reach your house at 3:48?"

"I don't know," said Harry. "Twenty minutes isn't long."

"Isn't there a train which leaves the Southern depot at 3:29?"

"I never use the Southern depot."

"Never?"

"Well, not enough to know the trains."

"I have not said that you did, Mr. Arnold. It happens, however, that there was a train—an express train—which left the Southern depot at 3:29 on June 28, arriving in Woodlawn at 3:45. A person starting from Prof. Arnold's house at 3:28 could have caught that train, could he not?"

"In one minute? Yes, by hurrying."

"And, leaving the train at Woodlawn at 3:45, he could have arrived in your house at 3:48, could he not?"

"Yes, sir, by walking briskly."

"Across the fields?"

"Across the fields."

"Wasn't it 3:48 when Dr. Whipple visited you on that Saturday of the fire?"

"Why, of course I could not swear within a minute or two."

"But a minute or two is momentous at times—when a train is to be taken, for example."

"Oh, yes."

"What were you doing all Saturday afternoon before the doctor arrived?"

"Why"—Harry hesitated—"I was ill in my chamber."

"Reading?"

"Perhaps. Killing time lazily."

"You have frequently to do that, I presume?"

"Sir?"

"You have no orderly programme arranged for every day?"

"Well, it varies."

"But never includes any useful occupation, I believe?"

"Well, I can afford to enjoy life."

"You are rich, you said. How fortunate to be rich! The great problem of life then is solved for you by the drawing of a quarterly check?"

"Well, not exactly."

"If you require money, however, you simply ask for it and it comes forth like the genii of the lamp?"

"I can usually meet what expenses I incur."

"Do you remember a man named Reddy?"

"Reddy?" repeated Harry, coloring a shade more and glancing over at Rosalie.

"Reddy," repeated Shagarach, insistently.

"What is his business?"

"He is dead," said the lawyer, and the witness knew that evasion was futile.

"Oh, yes, I knew that Reddy—slightly."

"Do you remember forfeiting several thousand dollars to him one evening in a certain room?"

"Yes."

Harry was driven to the wall. He set his teeth, and now, finally at bay, his spirit seemed to return.

"Where did that money come from?"

"From my mother."

"And from whom did she get it?"

Harry hesitated.

"From one Simon Rabofsky, a money-lender, was it not?"

"Yes."

"She had sold her family jewels, had she not?"

"Yes."

"She kept you in funds?"

"Yes, but she knew nothing of my habits."

"Then you lied to her to obtain money?"

"Yes."

"And you lied to the court awhile ago when you said that you were rich?"

"No, sir; it was only a temporary embarrassment."

"Have the jewels been redeemed?"

"I believe not."

"Do rich people generally pawn their family heirlooms and permit them to be sold?"

"Well, no."

"Then you were so circumstanced that your disinherit-

ance under your uncle's will might seriously incommode
you?"

"Well, his money might afford us relief."

CHAPTER LV.

WEATHERVANES VEER.

"Do you know Ellen Greeley?"

"I did know her slightly."

"Never corresponded with her?"

"Oh, no."

"You have a key to your own house, I suppose?"

"Certainly."

"And can slip out and in unobserved?"

"If I choose to."

"Which door do you generally use going into your
uncle's house?"

"The front door always."

"And in coming out?"

"The same."

"You knew, however, that there was a side door opening into the passageway?"

"Yes."

"How long are you back from Lenox?"

"Two weeks."

"Do you remember an evening entertainment there at
Mr. March's?"

"The purple tea? Yes, sir."

"Do you remember falling into a species of trance on
that occasion?"

"Perfectly."

"Do you remember what was on your right hand when
you awoke?"

The witness drew a deep breath before he answered.
He no longer had the heart to look toward Rosalie,

though her eyes were turned with stony fixity upon his face and she had even lifted her veil.

Shagarach's manner was now as imperious, as fierce, as on that memorable evening.

"Yes," answered Harry; "it was a lemon-colored glove."

"Whose glove?"

"Mine."

"A lost glove?"

"Yes."

"A right-hand glove?"

"Yes."

"Where had you lost it?"

Harry hesitated.

"Will you look about the room and tell me if you see any person besides your mother whom you saw on that Saturday afternoon of the fire?"

Walter Riley had recovered by this time from Kennedy's caning and occupied a front seat among the spectators. But it was Rosalie's eye that Harry met—met and hastily avoided. Had she seen him after all that afternoon when he crossed Bond street from the burning house? Would this remorseless inquisitor contradict his denial with the affirmation of the woman he loved?

"Wasn't it you instead of Floyd who paid a cash fare to Conductor Checkerberry on the 3:29 train and whose voice he recognized here yesterday?"

"Yes," said Harry, "it was."

"Then you had heard of the fire before Sunday morning?"

"I had."

"And you lied again when you testified to the contrary?"

"I am sick of lying. Let me tell you the truth."

"It is the truth I am searching for."

"You have tripped and tangled me," said Harry, speaking slowly, "so that my actions when I make a clean breast of them may look worse than they were. I wish I had told you the truth from the beginning. I was a fool to hide it at all.

"I did leave Woodlawn that Saturday for my uncle's house on the 3 o'clock train and returned on the 3:29 from the city. I had been wrought up by Mr. Hodgkins' visit of the night before. He was going to open the safe at 2:30 the next day and the will would be read at last. If I were disinherited I should be absolutely penniless, dependent on my mother, and her property, I knew, was encumbered."

"Your mother, then, was your father's sole heir?" asked the district attorney.

"Yes, sir."

"Encumbered largely through your extravagance?" added Shagarach.

"Through my extravagance. I was on pins and needles, too nervous to sleep, to eat—the servants can corroborate that—until this should be settled; too nervous even to await my mother's return."

"She had driven in to meet Mr. Hodgkins?"

"She had. It must have been nearly 3:25 when I arrived and the appointment of Hodgkins was at 2:30."

"You took the Southern line?"

"Yes."

"Why?"

"Because I heard the train coming. I acted on the impulse, flung out of the house and headed it off."

"Go on."

"I walked toward my uncle's up Broad street, entered the passageway, mounted the steps and found the side door open."

"Open?"

"I mean unlocked, not ajar. There was no one stirring in the lower floor. I wondered whether Hodgkins had come and the safe was opened. Then I went upstairs to the study."

"Your glove in your left hand?"

"As I remember it, yes. I forgot to mention the barking of the dog upstairs. When I got to the study door

the barking was louder and the dog seemed to be pawing at the door inside. Smoke was streaming out through
the keyhole and I could hear a loud crackling inside.
I looked at my watch"—here Harry's delivery grew
broken and he stuttered over the words—"I looked at
my watch and saw that I had time to catch the 3:29.
So I ran out the way I had come, slammed the door,
knocked over some boys that were blocking up the alleyway, crossed Broad street and dove into the little passage
called Marketman's row, which opens at the other end
opposite the door of the depot.

"The 3:29 train was just steaming out when I caught
the last car. At Woodlawn I jumped off on the unused
side of the station and crossed the meadows to my house.
Dr. Whipple had just come and had been directed to my
room. I doubt if even the servants knew of my departure
and arrival."

There was a pause when Harry finished. He looked
straight at Shagarach, flush-cheeked and ashamed, but
with all the Arnold boldness.

"You have left out the vital part of your story," said
the lawyer, when it appeared that the witness had nothing
more to add. "Why did you fly from a stream of smoke
issuing through a keyhole?"

"There were two reasons, shameful both of them, but
I ask you to remember that I had recently risen from a
fever and that I was greatly excited at the time. In
the first place, the image of the safe in that study had
haunted me for days."

"Although you have testified that you did not know
you were disinherited. Is that another lie?"

"No, sir; it is the truth. I had absolutely no knowledge of the terms of my uncle's will."

"Then why were you apprehensive? Why did the image of the safe in which it was guarded haunt you?"

"Because—because I feared what actually did happen.
I feared that he had bequeathed my share of his property
elsewhere."

"Go on."

"I knew that the destruction of the safe would set me back to my position as heir, would assure me $5,000,000. It could do me no harm. That idea flashed through me as I stood on the landing, with my hand on the knob. And then my own position! I might be accused of setting the fire for that very purpose. This was the thought that led me to flee. I remember looking at my watch, as I said. The 3:29 train would place me in safety almost before the fire was under way."

"And as a matter of fact, you were back in Woodlawn almost before the first stream of water was played upon the burning building?"

"I reached there at 3:45."

"You didn't stop to liberate the dog?"

"No, sir."

"You didn't think it your duty to save property and life by checking the flames or at least giving the alarm?"

"No, sir."

"You simply wanted your uncle's money."

"I wanted my uncle's money."

The gathering indignation of the audience expressed itself at this avowal by a sharp, spontaneous hiss. But the prisoner only bit his lips. The officers rapped for order and Chief Justice Playfair arose.

"I cannot find it in my heart to rebuke this manifestation, unseemly though it be in a temple of justice. For I knew Benjamin Arnold for many years. His cheek at the age of nearly fourscore had the rosy flush of a boy's and his unimpaired vigor was a living attestation of the pure youth and honorable manhood through which he had passed. He deserved a better return from his brother's son than the avaricious greed for his riches which the witness has confessed."

"Your honor," said Harry, "I have not made myself understood. It is not for me to parry your honor's rebuke. I have richly deserved it. I have been selfish and a seeker of my own pleasure. But it would be unjust to my better self, which is now struggling to the surface, if I did not disown the entertainment of such feelings now. I am on the stand under oath and I told you the simple truth about my motives at that critical moment."

"I find it hard," replied the chief justice, "to understand such a frame of mind. If you were present and consented to the fire, as you admit, by failing to check the flames or give the alarm, then it appears to me that you are morally if not legally a self-confessed accessory after the fact."

"The explanation can only deepen my blame, your honor. I itched for money at that time. Yet all that I received flowed from me faster than it came. I had exhausted my mother's income, trenched upon her credit, borrowed of my friends, and still I craved more. I was a victim of the passion for games of chance."

"Then you were capable of the gravest crimes," said Chief Justice Playfair.

"The fact that the witness took the 3 o'clock train when the will was supposed to have been read at 2:30," said the district attorney, "seems to me evidence that he had not contemplated a crime in coming."

"I do not charge that he contemplated a crime when he started from the house," answered Shagarach, promptly, "but I do charge that, finding an opportunity to hand, Harry Arnold, who by his own confession was present at the door of his uncle's study at the time this fire started, yielded to an evil impulse, ignited the loose papers lying about and fled."

"Harry Arnold has, indeed, been traced to the study door," retorted the district attorney, "but Robert Floyd was inside the room."

"Then we must bring Harry Arnold across the threshold," said Shagarach, resuming the cross-examination.

"Did you not know when you entered the house that the safe was unopened, owing to Hodgkins' detention?"

"No, sir; I knew nothing about that. When I went I expected to meet Hodgkins there."

"Then what good would it do you to see your uncle's study burned if it contained only an empty safe?"

"I didn't know whether the will was in the safe or not."

"And you didn't know whether the will disinherited you or not?"

"No, sir."

"But, acting on the possibility that there might be a will there, which might disinherit you, you ran away and left the house to burn?"

"It was contemptible, I admit."

"Hadn't you met your mother that afternoon?"

"Not after she left Woodlawn."

"What time was that?"

"Before 2 o'clock."

"She left in a carriage?"

"Yes, sir; one of the family carriages."

"And arrived at your uncle's toward three?"

"She has told me so."

"Leaving there a little after three?"

"Yes, sir."

"She might have driven around, then, for fifteen minutes and returned by the Southern depot just in time to meet you?"

"She might have done so."

"And inform you of Hodgkins' detention?"

"She might have done so, but whether you believe me or not, I never saw my mother until she came home that evening."

"Or any messenger from her?"

"Or any messenger."

"Did you set the fire?"

"No, sir."

"Did Floyd set it?"

"I refuse to believe that he did."

"Then who did? It must have been one or the other of you two."

"Or both of them," whispered Inspector M'Causland to John Davidson, but the marshal shook his head.

"It is a mystery I cannot solve," said Harry Arnold.

"Let us help you, then. You testified before that you never corresponded with Ellen Greeley?"

"Why should I correspond with the girl?"

"In order that she might sell you what information she could overhear about your uncle's will."

Shagarach brought his face closer to Harry's and his eyes seemed to blaze like searchlights, illuminating the depths of the young man's soul.

"Will you kindly read that aloud?" The lawyer handed his witness a letter. Harry glanced it over curiously, then read:

" 'The peddler has not come for two days, so I send you this by a trustworthy messenger. As I wrote you in my last, the professor said in the study: "Harry gets his deserts." That was all I could hear. Only he and Mr. Robert talked for a long time afterward. The will is in the safe in the study. If I hear anything more I will let you know, and please send me the money you promised me soon.' "

"Whose handwriting is that?" asked Shagarach.

"I never saw it before."

"It is unsigned, unaddressed and undated, is it not?"

"Yes, sir."

"Presumably, then, a letter in which both sender and receiver desired to conceal their names?"

"Perhaps so. I cannot offer an opinion as to that."

"Don't you know that letter was written by Ellen Greeley to you?"

"No, sir; I never received such a letter."

"I am aware that you never received it. But you received the previous letters referred to in this case, did you not? You received the letter stating that 'Harry gets his deserts,' meaning obviously that he gets nothing, did you not?"

"No, sir; I have never received a shred of communication from Ellen Greeley."

"Do you know the peddler referred to in this letter?"

"No, sir."

At this point Mrs. Arnold, who had sat through each of the three previous days' sessions, arose hurriedly and passed out. Shagarach just caught a glimpse of a lady's back departing, but the vacant seat told its story. He paused in his examination of Harry. It was Mrs. Arnold who had put McCausland on Floyd's track, Mrs. Arnold who had stolen Harry's photographs from Jacob, Mrs. Arnold who had driven up to the house in a carriage, Mrs. Arnold who would naturally deal, through her servants, with a street vender calling at the house.

"A subpoena blank!" he cried suddenly to Aronson. His pen flew over the paper, filling in names and other details.

"Serve that at any cost," he said to his assistant, and Aronson smooched the ink, so eager was he to obey.

"You do not know the peddler?" said Shagarach, taking up the cross-examination.

"No, sir."

"You never saw a peddler in a green cart that used to call at your house in Woodlawn during the month of June?"

"Not to my knowledge. Of course, there are peddlers everywhere and some of them have green carts."

"Wouldn't you regard it as a peculiar circumstance if a particular peddler began calling at your house and your uncle's house about the time your uncle made his will and stopped his visits after the fire?"

"I don't know that I should attach importance to that circumstance. It might be accidental."

"But he might also be a go-between."

"Between whom?"

"Between you and Ellen Greeley."

"I never conducted any intrigue of any kind with Ellen Greeley."

"Did you know the man who was captured here yesterday?"

"No, sir."

"Wasn't he the peddler referred to in Ellen Greeley's letter?"

"The letter you handed me? I do not know."

"Is this one of your lies or the truth?"

"This is the truth."

"How are we to distinguish between your lying and truth-telling?"

Harry was silent.

"The only means of distinction thus far has been our own superior proof of the facts."

"I can only give you my word. If you choose to doubt it I am helpless."

"Will you please explain how your mother, who has left the court-room, I perceive, was able to inform Mr. McCausland that Robert Floyd was disinherited by his uncle and thus guide the finger of suspicion toward an innocent man from you, the incendiary?"

"I had no hand or finger in setting that fire. Circumstances tell against me. I have debased my own word, ruined my credibility, by a series of perjuries, all flowing from one initial folly. I can now understand my cousin's position—the shame of being misunderstood, unjustly suspected, though I am not fortified, as I feel that he is, by a consciousness of stainless honor throughout the affair. If he is guilty, then I am, and I ask—or, rather, I insist—that you shall place me under the same restriction of liberty as my cousin. Let me sleep under the same roof, endure the same privations, until he is acquitted and set free. For if to have had wrong-doing, ever so remotely, in one's heart is guilt, then I am the guiltier of us two."

"The sheriff, I think, will provide you a lodging," said Shagarach, coolly, and after a conference between the chief justice, the district attorney and the lawyer it was announced that a warrant for Harry Arnold's arrest would be granted and that he would spend the night in a cell.

"There are still several points against the prisoner not met," said the district attorney, when Shagarach moved for Robert's discharge.

"It is a new doctrine that a man should be held because there is reasonable doubt of his innocence," said the lawyer. But the district attorney was rigid and the

chief justice thought it best, since there was only one
more witness for the prosecution, to let the jury decide
upon the facts, which were properly their province.

"Forgive me, Rosalie," said Harry, humbly, as he
passed her, going out, and her eyes, though they were
full of mortification, disillusion, rebuke, told that she for-
gave him because she loved him.

"Arnold or Floyd?" was the alternative on the lips of
the multitude surging homeward after that dramatic day,
and Robert for the first time was actually cheered when
he left the courthouse.

"Looks as though we might have two hangings instead
of one," remarked Inspector McCausland to a reporter.

"Did you notice the expression on that woman who
went out?" said Ecks to Wye.

"No."

"Guilt," said Ecks, shuffling his notes into his pocket.
Then Emily saw Rosalie March's beautiful face soiled
with tears and hastened down to comfort her.

"I am sorry," she said. "Don't fear for Harry. Nobody in the world set that fire. It just caught——"

But why importune readers with Emily's theory, when
they have doubtless already guessed it in detail?

CHAPTER LVI.

MARK TIME, MARCH!

Now that Robert's acquittal was almost assured,
Emily's pity began to overflow toward Harry Arnold and
Rosalie, whose position was exactly her own of the day
before. For the vox populi had generally determined on
Harry's guilt, though there were not wanting some who,
like the father in the parable, were disposed to welcome
the brilliant prodigal with lavish entertainment, freely extending the forgiveness he implored, while slighting the
steadfastly loyal son who had never wandered from the

path of virtue. This was poor recompense to Robert for his summer-long immurement, but he was put together of a substance impervious to the acid actions of criticism or neglect—the oaken fiber of the English Arnolds.

In all quarters curiosity was active about the defense. It was said by some that the prosecution had broken down, or might break down at any minute, and even if the last reluctant victim were haled up by Bigelow to the shambles, where Shagarach stood, ax in hand, awaiting her, that it would be hammering on a driven nail to put on the long array of witnesses who had been summoned in behalf of the accused. Nevertheless the newspapers were at pains to worm out the names of these witnesses and to diet the public with prophetic outlines of their testimony.

The gist of it all was that Shagarach meant to clinch his client's defense by building up a case against Harry.

Of course Emily found it hard to communicate her own confidence to Rosalie March, although Bertha was to take the stand the following morning and her theory would then (as she believed) receive a triumphant demonstration. What made Harry's face fall more bitter was that the date of his espousal to the beautiful actress had just been given to the world. From Rosalie's hard glance at Shagarach, Emily knew there was as much blame in her heart for the lawyer as for her lover. And Rosalie was not the only girl who would have ransomed Harry Arnold, perjurer, self-seeker, gambler, as he owned himself to have been, with her life, if such a price should be asked.

"Are they sisters?" asked the thoughtless, misled by their golden hair, when the two beautiful girls went out together, leaving Mme. Violet behind. But a student of faces would never have fallen into such an error. One placid and aloof, even toward the audiences whose favor she courted, the other impulsive and approachable, throwing out tentacles of sympathy toward every human being with whom she came in contact, they supplemented rather than reflected each other; otherwise they would hardly have been drawn together so strongly, and made such a concord of friendliness.

Several surprises awaited Emily when she reached home. The first and pleasantest was an envelope, surcharged in the upper left-hand corner with the name of a certain magazine. This she opened with trembling fingers, for it was not quite three weeks since she mailed to the editor, unsigned, Robert's article on, "Proposals for a Consumers' Trust," that fruit of his prison reflections which Dr. Silsby had found so unpalatable. When an oblong slip of paper, perforated at the margin, slipped out, she knew it was a check; and the editor's letter was very urgent that "so striking a contribution should not be given to the world without its author's signature." Here was the beginning of a career for her sweetheart. She looked forward to the time when his qualities and talents should be recognized, and she herself perhaps be pointed out as the wife of Floyd, the famous writer, or thinker, or worker, or whatsoever other name they chose to give to the best, the truest and the most abused of men. The check, too, was of comforting value, and, since she was a shrewd little housekeeper withal, this discovery did not abate one particle of Emily's joy.

And yet, so little was she a lover of lucre for its own sake, the very first item on which her eye lighted in the evening paper, though it meant a money loss which the whole cash box of the Forum, converted into checks, could not make good, evoked almost a scream of delight from Emily and sent her flying into the kitchen where her mother was steeping the tea. The good lady wiped her honest hands on her apron and with a "Do tell!" fingered the Evening Beacon, which to-day is skimmed and to-morrow cast into the oven, as respectfully as if it had been a fancy valentine; then read, with Jennie, a slip of 14, on tiptoe leaning over her shoulder, that Judge Dunder had finally decided to uphold the late Prof. Arnold's will. Even Shagarach had hardly expected this decision. For Judge Dunder was a confirmed devotee of legal technique and it had been supposed that nothing less than a verbatim copy of a destroyed will would be sustained by him.

But the main clauses of the will had certainly been reproduced, with an abundance of circumstantial detail. The only hiatus was a remote possibility. There may have been some smaller bequests that could not be traced. Apparently Judge Dunder had in this case resolved to wink a little at chicane and decide for justice in the broader sense.

"Harry Arnold may have to do something to justify his existence now," said Mrs. Barlow after supper to Emily. She had a prejudice against wild young men.

"Oh, Rosalie has enough for two," answered Emily, who was standing before the mirror putting her hat on for a visit to Walter Riley.

The first sight that met her eye when she reached the sidewalk was a squad of salvation army soldiers, with Serena Lamb at their head, parading through the street, chanting their invitation to sinners. Serena held her tambourine high in air and her shrill voice dominated the chorus like that of a precentor in the kirk. But the exercise seemed to lack its usual spirit this evening. Was it because nobody took any particular notice of the group? Curiosity about them was wearying itself threadbare, and even the toddling urchins no longer gathered at the drumbeat as they used to. Emily had often admired the devotion of these sisters, but, looking at this unnoticed and discouraged band, she wondered if the antagonism of the multitude were not in truth the very sustenance of their zeal. Might not all their heroic energy exhaust itself, like the nerve of a boxer, compelled to waste his blows in the air, if the atmosphere of opposition should change to one of apathy?

CHAPTER LVII.

A STERN CHASE.

"At any cost!" The last words of his master tingled in Saul Aronson's ears when he left the court-room with the summons in his hand. Ever since the disclosures of Serena Lamb he had been more than usually abashed in his demeanor. For in some measure he felt that it was he who had brought this threatened catastrophe upon their cause. Here was the opportunity to retrieve his misstep. He would prove his fidelity and serve the writ "at any cost."

Mrs. Arnold had secured a few minutes' start, but Aronson did not doubt his ability to overtake her. She would probably call a cab, since she was an all-day attendant at the sittings and it was unlikely her family carriage would be waiting for her. Impatiently he rang the elevator up, and then, deciding just as it arrived that it was quicker to walk down, balked the boy by tacking off toward the staircase and descending it two steps at a time. When he reached the exit, the square was deserted. But just around the corner, like the whisk of a vanishing tail, he caught a glimpse of a rapidly driven cab. After this he sped, down the crowded main thoroughfare, dodging the pedestrians as well as he could, with his eyes on the distant vehicle, and yawing wildly at last into the arms of a man who stood waiting on the curbstone.

"Where in the ——" but the man was a herdic driver and his language may as well be left to the imagination. Aronson saw the badge on his hat; that was enough.

"Catch that carriage," he said, "and I'll give you $2."

"Jump in," cried the driver. The door was locked in a jiffy and presently they were bumping over the cobble-stones.

"Stop there!" shouted the burly policeman who used to escort Emily so gallantly over the street crossing.

"It's a runaway!" cried the herdic driver, giving himself the lie by a savage snap of his whip. The officer was in no trim for a spurt, so he fell behind puffing. Still they bumped on, till Aronson's anxiety mastered him and he rapped at the window for attention. The driver stupidly reined up.

"Go on!" cried the passenger, and the whip-lash circled once more with a crack. They were out on the long bridge to Oxford now, and the fugitive could not be far ahead.

"Hello!" shouted the driver. The jehu in front turned his head.

"Haul up!" he hailed.

The driver in front obeyed and the two herdics were soon abreast, Aronson getting a dusty toss in his impatience to get out. As he picked himself up, a great fat man put his head out of the other herdic window and began to ask the cause of the detention.

"Is Mrs. Arnold in there?" inquired Aronson, putting his head into the herdic, just by the fat passenger's.

"Mrs. Arnold? What Mrs. Arnold? Take your head out, you impudent,—drive away, you——" cried the fat passenger, settling back on the cushions which he almost filled with the breadth of his back. Aronson was left standing alone on the road, puzzling his wits what to do.

"You lost the right carriage," he said.

"I followed the one you pointed out," answered the driver, surlily.

"Well, take me back."

"Where's my $2?" asked No. 99, and Aronson had to pay him this sum, as well as an advance fare for the ride back, before he would turn his horse's head. Going in town, the animal made up for time gained by a heartbreaking leisureliness of pace. No one could blame the poor hack horse. There had been some attempt to make him look respectable by docking his tail, but it was no

more successful than a silk hat on a prize-fighter, designed to foster the same illusion.

It was just 5:40 when Aronson reached the Northern
depot and the train for Hillsborough had left at 5:38. He
had the misery of knowing that Mrs. Arnold was probably well on her way to her summer residence by this time,
and that there was no train earlier than 7 o'clock. In the
interim he bought a ticket, supped, reflected, counted his
money and studied the subpoena.

A village bell was tolling 8 when Aronson stepped from
the passenger car out on the platform of the Hillsborough
station. They had left the sunset behind them in their
eastward ride and the country village was dark.

"I want a carriage to Mrs. Arnold's house," he said to
the station-master.

"Hacks are all in now," answered the official behind
the grating, turning to his books. But he underrated the
persistency of his customer.

"I'll give you $1.50 for a team," said Aronson. The
suggestion worked magically and in less than an hour he
was let down before the veranda of the Arnold mansion.
A ruby porch-light flooded him with a kind of delighted
confusion. How mild and solemn the country is at night!
How suggestive of grassy comforts the humming of the
crickets! All the shepherd that lay deep down in Aronson's nature, as in that of every one of us, even the
plainest, had time to show itself in the interval between
his ring and the servant's answer.

"Mrs. Arnold is in Woodlawn," answered the housemaid. "Can you leave your business?"

"No, I want to see her personally."

Woodlawn! She had escaped him then. The teamster
was waiting and the servant diminishing the aperture of
the door to a suspicious crack, while he collected his
thoughts.

"How long has she been in Woodlawn?" he asked.

"She just moved in yesterday morning," replied the
servant, closing the door with a slam.

"Take me back in time for the next train," said Aronson to the driver.

"Too late for the next train," came the drawling answer. "Next train is at 9:15 and it's most 9 now."

"When is the last train?" asked Aronson, figuring on a midnight visit to Woodlawn.

"That's the last train to-night."

Here was a wild-goose chase indeed, but Aronson had a keen suspicion that it was the goose who was the chaser.

"What is the first train in the morning?"

"At 6:15 a. m.," answered the rustic, who usually knows his local time-table better than his prayers.

"Can I lodge here for the night?"

"Dunno. Sam Cook might put you up. He used to keep an inn. Maybe he can find a spare bed for you under the roof somewheres."

"Drive me to Sam Cook's," said Aronson. All the nocturnal interest of the countryside had vanished from him now, and it was with no kindly feeling toward Hillsborough that he stretched his limbs in the old boniface's spare bed, laying the subpoena under his pillow and muttering a petition to Jehovah that he might not oversleep himself and lose the 6:15 a. m. But the real danger proved to be that he would get no sleep at all. For at midnight he was still tossing.

A cow-bell, furiously jingled, awoke him at sunrise, and he was in the city at 7:15, on schedule time.

"To Woodlawn," a sign on one of the tracks read. But the hands of the mock clock pointed to 7:45 and there was another half-hour of waiting. All the world was out of bed, for the steeple bell had just tolled 8 when he arrived in Woodlawn and inquired his way to the Arnolds'.

"Just moved back!" thought Aronson. "I should say so."

Mats were hanging out of windows, servants were mopping panes, a hostler was hosing a muddy carriage in the stable; everything showed that a general scrubbing process had begun. To his surprise and pleasure, he recognized the housemaid who answered his ring as Bertha Lund. She was dressed in her smartest pink, for this was the day of her testimony.

"I want to see Mrs. Arnold," said Aronson, blurting out his message like a schoolboy.

"Mrs. Arnold? Well, you've come too late," answered Bertha.

"Isn't she here?"

"Here! She's on her way to Europe by this time."

"To Europe!"

Saul Aronson's jaw dropped and the subpoena began to burn a hole in his pocket. Was this a subterfuge? He would be on the alert.

"When did she start?"

"Why, this morning. You must have passed her coming out."

Passed her coming out! It was like chasing his own shadow, this constant missing of the game he hunted.

"But wha—wha—what made her go to Europe?" stammered Aronson. He remembered hearing Shagarach say one day that flight was confession. Was Mrs. Arnold involved in her son's guilt? Then all the more reason for waylaying her before she gave them the slip.

"Can't a lady go abroad if she chooses? Mrs. Arnold goes abroad every summer."

"But Harry——"

"Yes, we're cleaning things up for Harry. They'll live here after they're married, you know, Harry and Miss March."

"But he was arrested!"

"Arrested!"

Bertha had left the court early on the previous day and did not read the papers.

"Didn't his mother know Harry was arrested?"

"Arrested! Harry? What for?"

"For setting his uncle's house on fire," answered Aronson, who as a loyal partisan was one shade more thorough in his conviction of Harry's guilt than Shagarach himself.

"Setting his uncle's house on fire! Nonsense!"

"What boat did she take?" asked Aronson, breaking in upon Bertha's astonishment with a gesture of impatience.

"The Venetia, of the Red Star line."

"And it starts so early in the morning?"

"Yes; somewhere between 8 and 9."

Aronson looked at his watch. It was just 8:15. If he could catch a train back, he might be in town at a little after half-past. And then—a delay! These great steamers are often delayed!

"Toot! Toot! Toot!" came the warning whistle of an engine, and Aronson was dashing down the path, never stopping to pick up his hat that was lifted off by the wind, bent only on beating his steam-propelled rival to the station. It took him the whole journey townward to recover the wind he had lost in that unwonted quarter-mile run. People laughed at his hatless head, but he did not heed them. Besides, if he had been a philosopher, he might have retorted that hats on a dog-day are simply one of the nuisances of civilized conventionality. So he took a wharf car and in less than half an hour was running out to the edge of the great Red Star quay, there to behold the Venetia proudly backing into the channel on the flood of the tide and turning her head oceanward. I regret to say this spectacle filled Aronson with violent wrath, and the wharf loungers must have taken him for a wild man as he smote his fists together and danced about.

"Missed your boat?" inquired casually a sea-beaten man, but Aronson was too irate to appreciate his well-meant sympathy. He only ran to the edge of the wharf and looked off, shading his eyes from the glare of the water.

Presently he found the man at his elbow again.

"I can catch her for you if it's anything important," said the tar.

"I'll give you—I'll give you—" and then he checked himself, appalled at his own rashness. "How much will you charge?" he asked.

"Well, the Venetia's steaming for a record this trip.
"How much?"

"She's got a start of a mile, and going twenty knots."
"How much?"

"There were some picnic folks I expected down here to charter my tug. Don't see them, but they may drop in. I suppose you'll allow something for the disappointment if they come."

"How much?" persisted Aronson, but the Venetia had just disappeared behind an island and the thought of returning empty-handed to Shagarach acted like a rowel in his flank. "I'll give you $50," he cried, suddenly.

"Done," said the Yankee, wringing his hand, and then Aronson knew that he ought to have offered $25. But it was no time for haggling. "At any cost," he repeated to himself. The mariner hurried him in and out among the wharves, till they came upon a battered but resolute-looking tugboat, on which two or three deck-hands were lounging.

"Get steam up, Si," cried the skipper, and after a delay which seemed an hour to Aronson the water began to be churned to foam before her bow and the little craft had started on its long chase.

Past the islands of the harbor, past the slow merchant schooners, past the white-sailed careening pleasure sloops, past the harbor police boat, past the revenue cutter, past the excursion steamers to local beaches, past the crowded Yarmouth, they flew, cheered on by the passengers—for everybody soon saw it was a race.

Aronson was studying the wide beam of the Venetia in front. How slowly they were gaining! They were out beyond the farthest island in the harbor, the lighthouse shoal that is covered at high tide, and still the Red Star liner bore away from them with half a mile of clear water between.

"Cheer up, shipmate," cried Perkins; "she's gettin' bigger and bigger. Heap the coals on down there, Si."

The Venetia must have sighted her pursuer long ago, and indeed the faces of her passengers on the bow were becoming more and more visible every moment. But this was a record trip, and it would be beneath her dignity to slow up for every petty rowboat that hailed her. So her engines continued to pump and she clove the glorious waters swiftly.

"Ahoy!" shouted Capt. Perkins.

"Ahoy yourself!" came the answer. Aronson thought he saw a woman's face that he knew on the deck.

"Heave to! A boarder!"

"Tell him to get out of bed in time," came the ungracious reply. Evidently the Venetia's third mate was under orders not to stop for any belated passenger.

"What's your errand?" asked the skipper, a little puzzled, of Aronson.

"I have a subpoena from the court," cried Aronson, all agog.

"Oh, you're a court officer."

Then he rounded his hands and holloaed up:

"A court officer aboard!"

Court officer! This made an impression. The third mate withdrew from the gunwale and presently reappeared with the captain.

"Lash her to!" cried the captain. The tug-boat hugged her great sister and a ladder was let down, upon which Aronson mounted. With the white paper in his hand he looked decidedly formidable.

"I have a subpoena for Mrs. Alice Arnold, one of your passengers. She is wanted as a witness in a murder trial. There she is," he added, for Mrs. Arnold stood in front of the crowd that had rolled like a barrel of ballast toward the center of interest. The captain was nonplused. He was not familiar enough with law terms to know the limits of a subpoena's authority. But he felt that he was to some extent the protector of his passengers.

"I don't understand this," he said, turning to Mrs. Arnold.

"It is a great annoyance to me if I must go on so trifling a matter," she said. She was pale and her manner was haughty. To Aronson it was something more.

It bore every indication of conscious guilt. He had not foreseen resistance. The document, with Shagarach's name appended, he had thought would open caverns and cause walls to fall.

"There is the lady. She prefers not to go. I presume you will have to compel her. But I don't see that I can permit violence on board my ship."

The passengers seemed to gloat on Saul Aronson's discomfiture, and Shagarach's faithful courier was almost beside himself. In the distance lay the city, crowned with its gold dome, dwindling from sight. The lonely ocean roared around him. Capt. Perkins' tiny tug still hugged the larboard of her giant sister.

"It appears to me that paper's no good," said the second mate suddenly. He happened to be a little of a lawyer. "Let's have a look."

Aronson reluctantly saw the summons leave his hand.

"Suffolk county. This ain't Suffolk county," cried the mate, while the ring of passengers laughed.

"Shinny on your own side, youngster," he added, returning the paper.

"But it's America," cried Aronson.

"Just passed the three-mile limit," said the captain. He was an Englishman, the mate was an Englishman. They had no particular love for anything American, except the output of our national mints.

"I'm afraid the captain's right, young man," said a kind, elderly gentleman, who might be a lawyer recruiting his health by an ocean trip before the fall term opened. "You've got beyond your jurisdiction."

Mrs. Arnold had gone below and the hatless invader reluctantly abandoned his prize. On the homeward voyage he gave way to exhaustion and fell into several naps of forty winks' duration, during the last of which a grotesque dream troubled his peace. He found himself chasing Serena Lamb around an enormous bass drum, as big as the Heidelberg tun, on the stretched skin of which the oaf, the manikin and the pantaloon were dancing a fandango. Still he chased Serena and still she escaped him, the toes of the dancers pounding a heavy tattoo. Faster and faster pursuer and pursued whirled around the side of the drum, till Aronson's head swam like a kitten's in hot pursuit of his own tail. At last in his despair he hurled the subpoena at Serena's head.

The three dancers disappeared with a bursting sound into the hollow of the drum, and he awoke to find the tugboat just bumping its side against the dock. The sea had smoothed down to a lack-luster glaze, but it was less dreary than the heart of the baffled pursuer.

"We may as well cancel that little debit item now," said Skipper Perkins, flinging a coil of rope ashore.

"At any cost," repeated Aronson sorely to himself. He had done his best, but Mrs. Arnold was out of sight of land—a fugitive from justice.

CHAPTER LVIII.

THE MIRACLE.

It was after two o'clock when, breathless, spiritless, and penniless, Saul Aronson arrived at the court-room again. The examination of Bertha was nearly ended.

"Will you take these spectacles, Miss Lund?" said Shagarach, handing Bertha a pair. They looked like the "horns" that used to straddle our grandfathers' noses, being uncommonly large, circular in shape and fitted with curved wires to pass over the ears.

"Do they bear any resemblance to Prof. Arnold's?"

"I thought they were his at first."

"Let us suppose they are. Will you kindly leave the stand and adjust them on this desk near the window exactly as the professor's spectacles lay on his desk that afternoon?"

Bertha took the spectacles without hesitation, walked over to the crier's desk and placed them on its edge, with their wires toward the window. Then she laid a book under the wires. This made the glasses tip a little downward. The sun was shining in fiercely.

"I believe there was a waste basket in the study?" continued Shagarach.

"Yes, sir."

"Like this one?" He held up an uncommonly capacious basket, over two feet high.

"The very same kind."

"And as full as this is?"

"Fuller. It was just bursting with papers."

"What kind of paper?"

"Black wrapping paper that comes off the professor's books."

"Something like this?"

"Just like that."

The paper in Shagarach's wicker basket was not black, exactly, but of a deep shade which could hardly be described by the name of any known color.

"Why are you wearing a white dress, Miss Lund?"

Bertha blushed a little.

"Because light colors are cooler."

"Coolness is a strong recommendation on a day like this. Do you remember whether the Saturday of the fire was as warm?"

"It was very hot, I know."

"The hottest day of a hot June, was it not?"

"Well, I couldn't answer that. The thermometer goes up and down like a jumping-jack here."

"You had pulled up the study curtains so as to let in the sunlight, I believe?"

"Yes, sir. That was for the poor canary. And, besides, the professor used to say the sunlight was good— good for plants and animals and everything that has life in it."

"The sun, then, was shining down on the desk where the spectacles lay?"

"Just as you see it here, sir."

She pointed to the desk, by which she was still standing.

"You know, from your own experience in dresses, that dark colors absorb more heat than light ones?"

"Sir?"

"Light dresses are cooler than dark ones?"

"Yes, sir."

"Brown paper burns more quickly than white?"

"Oh, yes. You can kindle a fire with brown paper better."

"Will you take the waste-basket and place it on the floor just as far from those spectacles as the waste-basket in the study stood, and in the same direction."

Bertha measured off a short distance with her eye, picked up the basket, shifted it once or twice, and finally set it down with a satisfied air.

"There!"

"It stood just behind the desk, then?"

"What is the drift of all this?" interrupted the district attorney, his deep voice falling on a breathless silence. A presentiment had spread from one to another that the solution was at hand.

"We are reproducing the exact condition of the study at the time the fire occurred. These spectacles, containing powerful cataract lenses, are made from the same prescription as Prof. Arnold's, by his optician, Mr. Dean. The large basket, a mild eccentricity of the professor's, and the black paper, are also duplicates."

"What do you hope to prove?" asked Chief Justice Playfair. His answer was a shrill cry, like a bird note, from Emily, who had never withdrawn her eye from the waste basket.

"It's catching!"

Every eye in the court-room turned. Those who sat near enough beheld two tiny holes, like worm holes, suddenly pierced in the black paper, where the rays of light converged through the tilted lenses. Each had a crisp, brown margin around it. Gradually they widened and spread, as though instinct with life, one working faster than the other. Then suddenly a little circle of flame curled out, and before the onlookers realized the miracle in progress, the waste basket was throwing up red tongues of fire and sighing softly. If it were not for Sire's furious barking the railing of the bar might have caught. As it was, its varnish had begun to crackle before the nearest court officer recovered his presence of mind and threw the blazing basket out of the window.

Gazing at Shagarach the spectators waited breathlessly for an elucidation. Before speaking he walked over and shook hands warmly with Emily. When he turned at last, his words came forth like a whirlwind.

"I think nothing more is needed to convince us of the source from which this fire originated. We have reproduced every circumstance of its occurrence in order to provide you with ocular demonstration. The sun supplying extraordinary heat, the burning glass duplicated by an expert and placed in position by a trustworthy witness, the focal distance estimated by her, the highly combustible fuel, identical in color and substance—can you not turn back in imagination and see happening in that deserted study all that has happened here? Can you not follow it on to the destruction of the mantel fringe just above, the awaking of the sleepy dog, the mad leap of the flames from wall to wall, and at last that whole irresistible carnival of the elements? It was no human torch, but the hot gaze of the sun, condensed through these powerful lenses, which lit that funeral pyre and dug graves for seven human beings. Fate, working out its processes in that lonely room, was the mysterious incendiary toward whom we have all been blindly groping."

As Shagarach pointed upward in his awful close, the audience, on the very brink of an outburst, held back their enthusiasm for an instant. But the chief justice was seen to bow his head, and at once the excitement broke all barriers. A loud spontaneous cheer, rendered half articulate by cries of "Shagarach, Shagarach!" scattered to the winds the customary restraints of the surroundings. Women embraced each other; strangers shook hands warmly; Emily Barlow rushed over and hugged Rosalie

March, and drops were glistening on Chief Justice Playfair's eyelashes when he lifted his head. McCausland,
standing agape on the threshold of his ante-room, completed the happy picture.

By a natural reaction the outburst was succeeded by a
spell of tense repression, amid which the district attorney
rose and moved the withdrawal of the case against Robert
Floyd. The foreman of the jury announced that he and
his associates had long been agreed upon the innocence
of the accused, and Chief Justice Playfair, dignified as an
archbishop blessing his flock, expressed in his golden
idiom the common feeling of thankfulness that the trial
had so felicitous a termination.

And so the logic of Richard McCausland and the
psychology of Meyer Shagarach were both overmatched
by the intuitions of a loyal girl—a girl who knew something about lenses because she dealt with cameras, and
who brought to the problem a concentration of thought
as powerful as that of the sunlight on the professor's
spectacles. Both the lawyer and the detective came forward promptly to pay her their homage; and the last
she saw of McCausland he was focusing one of the lenses
on the end of his cigar, readily obtaining the desired red
light.

But Emily was not holding court even for them while
there was still a stroke of work to be done. Her second
thought was of Harry in his cell. With admirable
modesty avoiding Robert's kiss, she took him and Rosalie
by the hand and made them friends at once. Then, leaving Beulah Ware to chat with Brother Tristram, the trio
sped over to the jail. At the court-house door they met
Dr. Silsby, who came flying along, florid and out of
breath, mopping his face with a napkin which he had
probably mistaken in his hurry for a handkerchief.

"Is it over?" he cried.

"Over? We're acquitted," cried Emily, using a reckless plural. "What makes you so late?"

"Stopped to nib a quill after lunch," grumbled the director of the Arnold Academie, as he gave Robert a pump-handle squeeze.

It was a changed Harry that stepped out of the cell in murderers' row. In the confidence of the preceding night the two cousins had grown closer together than ever before. After all, as Harry had said on the stand, they were both Arnolds and the sole survivors of that eccentric blood.

But a stronger bond was soon to rivet them together in the waxing amity of the two girls, one of whom was dearer than kin to each of the cousins. Rosalie's exclusiveness and the wealth she continued to enjoy with an equanimity he could not understand at first prevented Robert from doing full justice to her. But on acquaintance she proved as merry (among her chosen few) as any lassie, and a certain child-like innocence, all the more singular from her association with the stage, made a charming foil to the ripe womanly beauty of her person.

Moreover, as the months roll by, and Robert learns more and more what men and women really are, he lowers his standards gradually as to what may be expected of them. Not that he has given up his ideals. Far from it! He is still a socialist; and, what is better, a sower of good seed in action, placing goodly portions of his income here and there, with something of his uncle's bow-wow manner, to be sure, as though it were no personal pity tugging at his heart-strings, but only an abstract desire to see things ship-shape in the world, an impatience at disorder. But this affected matter-of-factness doesn't suffice to shake off the blessings of his pensioners.

If he chooses to set all orthodoxy by the ears with that series of fire-brand polemics which, as readers remember, succeeded the "Modest Proposal for a Consumers' Trust," so that one old granny among his opponents has already christened him "the Legicide," what do Mrs. Lacy and Mrs. Riley know or care? I fancy most of us, if we were burdened with a maniac son or blessed with the love of a dutiful boy like Walter, would accept assistance for their sakes, and ask no questions of the giver.

Mrs. Arnold is too old now ever to forget that her maiden name was Alice Brewster. It was the fear of staining that name with the published details of a petty intrigue that caused her to sail for Europe so suddenly. For it was she, conscious of her own financial straits, and anxious for Harry if his inheritance should be cut off, who had conducted the correspondence with Ellen Greeley. In this there was nothing criminal; but much to wound her pride. So she had fled from the ordeal of testifying before Shagarach, and the disclosures which she foresaw were inevitable.

Her embarrassments have since been tided over and the family fortune saved, at least from total shipwreck. The match with Rosalie March guarantees to Harry the gratification of all his tastes; and, as the young couple are coming to Woodlawn to live, the sting of separation is softened. Ah, the fond jealous mothers who must forget their own honeymoons to chide the child that only obeys divine injunctions in cleaving to another when the time is ripe!

Of Emily Barlow what more can be said? Praise is superfluous; intrusion on her betrothal joys, soon to merge into marriage happiness, deeper if less unmixed with care, an impertinence.

Of late the whole world seems conspiring to bless her. Only the other day Tristram March won the sculpture prize at the academy with his life-size group "Driftwood Pickers at the Sea Level." The critics have gone mad over the boldness of his conception—one figure erect and peering far off, two stooping and adding to their fagot bundles. The whole ocean is there in that fretted line of surf—a bare suggestion. One interpreter has gone so far as to see in the figures a type of humanity itself, on the margin of some mysterious beneficent element which surrounds it. But the salient fact to Emily is that Tristram won the prize, and is striving might and main for another more precious—the hand of the dark, collected

girl who gave him both subject and inspiration during
their memorable week at Digby.

And Shagarach—the iron will, the giant mind—what
is his destiny? To be always a criminal lawyer, a con-
sorter with publicans and sinners? Always, we may be
sure, to protect the innocent, to whatever sphere the
buoyancy of his genius may lift him; and whether he
wear ultimately the ermine or the laurel wreath he will
never forget one cause, which brought him, with much
added celebrity and some unhappiness, the friendship of
three couples so rare and fine—that great search for the
Incendiary which is registered (not without pique) in
Inspector McCausland's private docket as "The Eye-
Glass Fiasco."

THE END.